THE WOMAN WHO DARED TO DARE

THE WOMAN WHO DARED TO DARE

William Coles

THAMES RIVER PRESS

The Woman Who Dared To Dare

THAMES RIVER PRESS
An imprint of Wimbledon Publishing Company Limited (WPC)
Another imprint of WPC is Anthem Press (www.anthempress.com)
First published in the United Kingdom in 2014 by
THAMES RIVER PRESS
75–76 Blackfriars Road
London SE1 8HA

www.thamesriverpress.com

A CIP record for this book is available from the British Library.

ISBN 978-1-78308-206-3

This title is also available as an eBook.

To Richard Martin, my splendid friend on the
Wilts and Gloucestershire Standard – who egged me on to
ever greater excesses until I'd finally notched up
my first front-page apology.

ACKNOWLEDGEMENTS

Like Kim, I also started my journalistic career as a trainee reporter on the *Wilts and Gloucestershire Standard* in Cirencester; most of the events in this book actually happened.

I would very much like to thank you all those executives and reporters on the *Wilts and Glos* who took me in hand in the late 1980s. They include the various mad-masters who had the hellish task of dealing with not just me but my excruciating copy: my editor Anne Hayes, as well as Bill Charlton, Gerry Stribling, Katie Jarvis, Alison Fawcett, Ros Jess and Mick Gruenbeck. And then there were the reporters, forever spurring me on to some new devilment: Richard Martin, Jo Kearney, Sarah Singleton, Sarah Billington, Yvonne Goide, Yves Wray, Tom Flint and Tom Fremantle – and not forgetting the sports editor who happily scribbled away in the corner, John Renowden.

I should also mention my two friends who are still at the *Wilts and Glos*, Mike Weaver and the absolutely lovely Lyn Gillett. The paper is still hanging on in there in Dyer Street, Cirencester, and I am assured that – thankfully – it has not changed one little bit.

CHAPTER 1

There are two types of swimmer: those who live to follow the black lines in the pool, up and down and they go, length after mind-numbing length; and the wild swimmers who live for the sea and for the rivers, who thrive on the cold and the scrapes and the bruises. And this, also, is how lovers are divided. Are you a creature of comfort who looks for love in the snug of your bedroom, between satin sheets and behind locked doors? Or are you a lover of all things wild and airy, with the stars high overhead as the wind stings at your skin?

I am a wild swimmer. And as for my love-making - well, we will come to that shortly. Though doubtless even now you can hazard what sort of lover it is that I am.

I had learned my swimming stroke in the outdoor pool at Cirencester, but I honed my swimming in the rivers of Gloucestershire, and in one river in particular: the Thames.

In Lechlade, near where the Thames rises, it is nothing but a small country river, but then, it swells and it grows until London where it is this wide, dirty brown streak.

I had swum the Thames many times in and around Gloucestershire – and, almost always, I had swum it with Sasha.

This time, on a whim, as a dare, we were swimming the Thames in London, and that is much, much more dangerous. It is not the distance that is the killer. We could swim 400 yards, easy. But there are tides in the Thames in London, and there are potholes, and around the bridges there are rippling down-surges, which can suck you to your death before you are even aware that they exist.

And there are other ways that the Thames in London can kill you; and those, also, we shall come to.

But the Thames is nevertheless the Thames, the most famous river in the British Isles, and so for all us wild swimmers, it is a challenge that has to be swum.

The gauntlet had only been thrown down that afternoon. It was spring 1990, a Saturday, and Sasha and I had been swimming in Lechlade. In those days, we didn't even bother with wet-suits. I'd been watching her from the bank. In the water, swimming above the reeds, Sasha was like a sea-otter, lithe and supple. Like all the best swimmers, she was very slippery in the water. Some swimmers are thrashers, but Sasha was fluid; she hardly made a splash. Her body seemed to meld itself to the river, her long dark hair flowing free behind her.

"When are we going to swim the Thames properly?" I called down to her. I'd already got out because it was cold.

Sasha looked up out of the water, her wet head bobbing black beneath the bridge. She laughed and she smiled, her teeth this quite brilliant white against her black hair.

"Why not today?" she said. "I dare you."

"Well, if it's a dare."

"It might be."

And that is the beauty of being in your 20s, carefree, commitment-free: you can do just about whatever you want.

She got out of the water. There were some tourists walking over Halfpenny Bridge, cameras bumping on their fat stomachs. They watched her. I watched her. Her hair fell long and sleek down the back of her neck. She patted it with a white towel. She was wearing a black swimsuit, a swimmer's swimsuit. A swimsuit to show off her legs. They were very long, olive-skinned; she was half-British, half-Argentinean.

I had known her for a year. I found her very beautiful.

But I had yet to lay even a finger on her.

She towelled herself down. I admired her legs and her swimmer's shoulders. She pulled on her white towelling robe, and then very discreetly and efficiently pulled on some khaki shorts. She then turned her back to me and pulled on a white T-shirt.

Putting her wet things into a bag, she slipped on some flip-flops - and just like that, we were ready to go.

We decided to catch the train down to London. I drove us straight to Kemble station just outside Cirencester. In those days, I was driving a grey Mercedes. It was an old automatic with peppery white plastic seats.

Sasha sat next to me in the front. She eased her seat back as far as it would go, and then she reclined it even further. She kicked off her flip-flops and rested her bare feet on the glove compartment, so that her toes touched the windscreen.

I looked again at her legs. How could I not look at her legs? They were only a few inches from my face. I have always been the world's most complete sucker for long legs. I would have liked to have kissed her legs. I would have liked to pull over into a layby, snatch a rug from the boot, and then lead her by the hand to the adjacent field, where, initially at least, I would have started to kiss her legs, my tongue trailing down the inside of her thigh and then just lingering behind her knee. That is a much under-rated erogenous zone, but a wonderful one for all that. Most of these hearty lovers, they go straight in for the kill, going, I don't know, for those erogenous zones that we know so well. But if you have the time and the patience, then…

I digress.

For of course I did not kiss Sasha's legs and nor did I even touch her.

That was not part of the plan.

For if you aspire to date a very beautiful woman, then you are going to have to do things very differently from all the other scores of swains who will be yapping at her bedroom door.

So while all the other young Turks were buying her flowers and champagne and whatever else it was that they thought might take her fancy, I was playing a quite different game.

I was in it for the long-haul.

And that meant that I would never - even once - touch her.

Or compliment her.

Or flirt with her.

The plan – and I had stuck to it rigidly – was that I would be the absolute antithesis of every other young buck in Cirencester; and there were quite a few of them, too. Rich young South Americans come over for the summer to play polo in the park; rich peers come to join Prince Charles' various royal parties at nearby Highgrove; and, above all else, the rich young landowners come to Cirencester to learn their trade at Britain's pre-eminent seat of all things agricultural, the Royal Agricultural College, or RAC as it was known.

Over the previous year, I had seen many young men making their plays for Sasha, and, meanwhile, I was like that placid bull in the field. I chewed the cud; I bided my time. I watched and I waited.

I did not know what I was waiting for. But I hoped that when the time came, I would recognise it. And that I would seize it.

As we drove to Kemble station then, I was trying to have a perfectly normal conversation with Sasha, as if she were just a good, wholesome mate with whom I could drink and laugh and swim, and whose looks had not even registered on my mind.

"Can you get your dirty bloody feet off my dashboard?" I said.

"My dirty bloody feet off your dashboard? Well, I might get my dirty bloody feet of the dashboard," she said. "If you ever bothered to clean up your dirty bloody car in the first place."

She opened a can of Coke. She drank and passed me the can and I drank too. I've never much liked the taste, but if you're a wild swimmer then Coke is good for killing the bugs that you've swallowed in the swim.

"Are you saying my car's dirty?" I said. We were on a long stretch of straight road, purring along behind a puttering brown Mini.

"It's not dirty, no," she said. "It is absolutely, disgustingly filthy. Look at this!" She leaned towards me and wiped her finger over my dusty head-rest. Her finger lightly touched the back of my neck. I did not even flinch.

She waved the dusty black finger under my nose. "Look at this!" she said. "And you're complaining about my feet on the dashboard! Have you ever even cleaned this car?"

"It was pretty clean when I bought it," I said. "I think it was."

She laughed triumphantly. "How long ago was that?"

"A year ago," I said. "When I got my job on the paper. I needed a set of wheels. It was really cheap too."

"You amaze me." She chuckled as she spat on her dirty finger. She produced a small packet of tissues from her pocket and wiped her finger on a tissue. She looked at the tissue for a moment, and made to put it into the ash-tray in the side of the door. The ashtray was already overflowing with sweet papers.

"Toss it in the back," I said.

"Are you sure?" she asked. "It just doesn't seem right."

"Go for it." With a flick of her thumb the tissue was tossed onto the back seat, where it joined assorted beer bottles, both empty and full, as well as Coke cans, crisp packets and a huge pile of old newspapers.

For a while we drove on in silence. I crumpled the empty Coke can and that also was tossed into the back. Sasha looked at the Mini ahead of us. I could smell its rich black exhaust.

"Are you going to overtake this car?" she said. Sasha always loved speed - whether it was in cars or the ski-slopes; or on her beloved polo ponies.

"In this heap?" I said. "Do you know about the acceleration in this thing?"

"I know it can go at 120 miles an hour. You showed me."

"It can go at 120mph," I said. "But it takes about ten minutes to get there."

"Pathetic."

"We'll see who's pathetic when we get to London."

We were in luck at Kemble station. The next London train was in a few minutes, so the thrill of the adventure was not dissipated on the station platform.

We found a couple of window seats on the train and I went to the bar and bought four small bottles of red, four small bottles of white, two cans of Coke and ten miniatures of Brandy.

"That is a lot," Sasha said as I got back to the table.

"And we're going to need it," I said. "It's going to be freezing."

We drank the wine and we plotted our plan of action. We would be getting into Paddington at around dusk. From there, we'd take the tube to Tower Hill. I liked the thought of swimming the Thames at Tower Bridge. It had history. Perhaps we might even end up at the Traitors' Gate.

We'd hide our bags underneath some bush or bench on the north side of the river, cross over Tower Bridge to the south side of the Thames, find the nearest ladder down to the river, and then finally we would dive head-first into the hostile element.

That was our plan. It was not that big a deal, but for us country bumpkins it would be a very small adventure; besides, how many other people do you know who have swum the Thames at night in London?

"What about the tides?" Sasha asked.

"I have not got a damn clue," I said. Hah - is it not amazing to think of it now, of this Stone Age era that we used to live in two decades ago, when there were no mobile phones, no internet, no Wi-Fi and no way on earth of learning about the tides of the Thames?

"Can we find out?"

"We'll just chuck in a stick," I said. "Should be a pretty good indicator."

Sasha was not convinced. She was sat in her chair, staring out at the sunset as she stroked the bridge of her nose. She often stroked the bridge of her nose when she was deep in thought; I had come to know this reflex very well. It was an unusual nose for a woman, with a bump in the middle and a tweak to the side. It was the sort of nose that you might have seen on a rugby forward. I loved it. It had character. A vainer woman would have had it straightened out by a plastic surgeon, but not Sasha. It would be some time before I learned how she'd broken it. Her mother had hit her in the face when she was a teenager.

She looked at me. "Anything else we haven't thought of?" she said.

I shrugged. I barely gave it a thought. "Shouldn't think so," I said. Blithely. Airily. Cockily. In the manner of a young swaggerer who was riding for the most spectacular fall. "It'll be fine."

We were delayed at Swindon. It was quite dark by the time we got into Paddington. The wine had all been finished and I had started on the brandy. I was feeling tiggerish and bouncy; Sasha was more circumspect. She definitely wanted to do the swim, but she did not want to do anything reckless. While we were on the Tube, it was me who was doing most of the talking. We were both wearing our towelling robes; we must have looked a strange sight.

I could smell the river. You can't smell the Thames if you live in London. But if you are an outsider, with unclogged nostrils, then you can smell it. It is a mix of light sea-salt and London grime.

The river was in spate. It was roaring and wild, thrashing beneath us like a living animal. There was a hard wind coming in flat from the West. We could see the white waves crashing against the north buttress.

If I'd been by myself, I would not have swum it then. But we had just caught the train to London specifically to swim the river. And I was with Sasha. Not - necessarily - that I wanted to impress her.

But it would have been difficult not to have made that swim.

The tide was going out full and hard. I tossed a white plastic cup off the bridge. In seconds it had been swept far off down the river.

"Do you want to stay while I dump the bags?" I asked.

"I'll come with you."

We might have held hands as we walked along by the side of the Thames, but we did not. We had never held hands and it would have been wrong to have started holding hands now. It was not part of the strategy. The time was not right.

Sasha squirmed into her swimming costume. I hid the bags under a bush and, barefoot, we trotted back to Tower Bridge. I was wearing nothing but a pair of baggy swimming trunks. We had our swimming goggles.

I don't really remember being aware of the traffic or the pedestrians - or anything much at all. I just remember being hell-bent on swimming the Thames. That was what we were going to do; that was what we were there for, and this one thought turned all else to darkness.

A few cars honked us as we went over Tower Bridge. A truck-driver rolled down his window and jeered. I can't speak particularly for myself. But Sasha was a very striking sight, long, loose-limbed, hair flying behind as she loped along in her black swimsuit.

We took a right on the south side of the river and after a while we found a ladder down to the water. The river was high and there was no river-bank to be seen. We just had to climb down a few rungs and then dive into the water.

"So here we are," I said.

Sasha looked at the Thames. Now that we were on the verge of diving in, the river was like a winking black abyss, its white tops flashing and frothing as they were caught by the street-lights. "It's different from Lechlade," she said.

"I've never swum anything like it."

And still we dithered, and the longer we waited, the worse the river looked.

I remembered a story from my last year at school. My housemaster Francis Frederickson had run himself a piping hot bath. The water steamed. Frederickson had dipped his toes into the water and had recoiled. But being ex-army, he had given himself a pep talk. "Come on Frederickson, man or mouse!" he'd said and had jumped into the bath. Shortly afterwards, he was taken to hospital with third degree burns.

I spat into my goggles, and rubbed the inside of the lens. The spit stops the goggles from steaming up.

I put the goggles on.

"Man or mouse!" I said. "See you on the other side!"

I climbed down the ladder and hit the river in a flat racing dive. I stretched my legs down. I did not touch bottom.

I turned to Sasha who was standing on the parapet. I had already been swept far downstream. "Come on in!" I yelled. "The water's warm!"

Though in truth, the river was freezing, that sort of electric cold that stings your skin and wicks the heat from your core.

I started to swim. Over the previous year in Cirencester, I had learned a very simple, economical freestyle technique. It was never

8

meant for quick little sprints. It was a long, lazy, rolling, gliding crawl, and I could keep it going for a long time.

Most people who you see in the pool are nothing but thrashing windmills. They do a length, or perhaps two lengths, and then, utterly shattered, they cling to the side of the pool to get their breath back. These are not swimmers. These are not even sprinters. They are not slippery in the water. Their bodies are angular, like a squat square ship ploughing slowly up the river.

As a swimmer, you want to be long and slippery and splash-free, with your hands and arms slipping into the water so smoothly that they don't even make a ripple; and then your torso, rolling easily from side to side, as it tucks into the space that was made by your arm. But you keep that front arm outstretched, keep it there until your other hand has all but touched it, and once you can do that, you have learned the secret of the glide. After each arm-pull, you glide on your side, easily and efficiently. And as for your legs, well, these naturally want to sink, but they should be counterbalanced by the heaviest part of your body, your head. Your head must be immersed fully and totally into the water. There is a tendency to thrash with your legs, but if you are swimming long distances, your leg muscles will just be burning through huge amounts of oxygen. Instead, you should strive for just a little two-beat kick. For each pull of the arm there is a single kick with the leg. And that is the essence of efficient, smooth swimming; that is all there is to it. Though it is deceptively simple. Much like a happy marriage.

I struck out across the Thames, head deep down in the black water. I could see nothing when my head was in the water, and I could see very little when I came up for air. As you breathe, you only move your head just a little to the side, still streamlined as you suck down the air.

It was a mistake. It was not something I knew about at the time. For although I was a wild swimmer of sorts, I'd never swum in anything as remotely treacherous as the London Thames at night.

But I swam and I kicked, efficient and smooth, and I soon got into my old routine. I was almost underneath Tower Bridge itself when I stopped and looked back for Sasha. She was no longer on the parapet. I spotted her about 50 yards away, her arms smoothly easing into the water.

I continued to swim.

Although my swimming technique was about as smooth and economical as I could make it, it did have a fault. It was not a glaring fault. But it was a weakness - and sometimes, though not often, these weaknesses can find you out.

When I swim, I need a lot of oxygen. I need to breathe much more frequently than most long-distance swimmers. Most swimmers will breathe every three strokes, or perhaps even every five, and this means that they're alternating the sides that they breathe on - first to the left, and then to the right.

I was taking a breath every two strokes, which meant that I was always breathing on the same side, my right side. My other side, the left-hand side, was blind.

That was nothing much in itself. But it was combined with one other weakness in my swimming technique: when you are wild-swimming, you must be much more aware of what is around you. It is quite different from swimming in a pool. When you are following the black lines, you can just get your head down and keep on motoring. But in the wild, particularly a busy waterway like the Thames, you have to keep an eye out for anything that should not be there. In practice, this means that every five or six strokes, you should be lifting your head clear out of the water to have a good look round and to check that everything's clear.

And if you don't keep an eye out…

Well, most of the time, it will make no odds either one way or the other. You will reach the end of your swim and nothing untoward will have happened.

Most of the time.

I must have been about halfway across the river. By now I'd been swept clear under the bridge. I had a very solid rhythm going. The current was much brisker than I'd thought it would be, but that was neither here nor there. It would just mean a slightly longer walk in the cold before we picked up our clothes.

I have my head deep down in the water. It is so deep that not even the slightest portion of my head is above the surface. And then after perhaps ten seconds, I roll slightly to the side, and take my quick snatch of air and see the bright lights of London. And I roll my face back into the water, and the darkness is so complete that I might be staring into a vat of black ink.

I didn't see it.

I felt it.

It was a rippling shockwave that pulsed at me through the water.

I registered it and I knew something was wrong. A moment later I heard it. The noise was coming through the water. It was the low droning pulse of a heavy-duty propeller.

I stopped swimming and looked all about me. My head turning this way and that, trying to see where the danger is coming from. But even though I could now hear the screws turning, I could not see anything. Wherever I looked, there was just nothing but the black river and the black night.

I stared towards where I thought the sound was coming from and suddenly I caught sight of two white bow waves funnelling underneath the bridge. A moment later, I saw the dredger itself, this huge wall of blackness bearing down on me.

I didn't know if Sasha had seen the ship. "Sasha!" I screamed at the top of my voice, and then I was thrashing as hard as I could for the river-bank - no time now for easy gliding, and nonchalant two-stroke kicks, I was swimming for my life. This fizz of adrenalin washed through me, and the cold was forgotten as my arms flailed through the water, as fast as I could, thrashing my way out from underneath the dredger's bow. I was enveloped by this wall of thundering noise. I kicked and I thrashed, and I wasn't thinking about Sasha or what a stupid way to die that would be; all I was thinking of was the next pull and the one after that, and keeping my fingers tight together as I tried to drag every possible inch out of the water.

The dredger shot past. I do not know by how much it missed me, but we're talking nothing more than a few feet. The next moment, even as I was still thrashing through the water, I got hit by this monstrous bow wave. It swept over me, pitching me upside down, tumbling me over and over in the water. I came up for air. I saw the side of the dredger shooting past. It loomed above me like a black canyon. The ship swept imperiously on its way, and a moment later, I am being hammered by the dredger's wake. It was like a white popping field of thunder. I caught a snatch of air and the water throbbed over my head, and then there I was, bobbing in the black Thames, watching the dredger recede into the night.

A short moment of euphoria and then I was anxious for Sasha. She'd been way behind me. I wondered if she'd been right in the path of the dredger. I looked out into the darkness of the river, but I could see nothing, no bobbing head, nor tell-tale arms.

I swam to the north bank. There was no way out of the river. I had to swim some way downstream before I found a ladder. I got out and ran to get our clothes. I put on my towelling robe and, shivering, went over to the embankment to start scouring the river.

I looked upstream and I looked downstream. I was looking for any glimpse of Sasha's arms or legs - but I could see nothing at all, not a thing, just the black Thames glittering in the streetlights.

I was starting to think the unthinkable. She couldn't be dead.

Could she?

I was imagining all manner of nightmares. Had she been hit by the dredger? Concussed and drowned, or swept to her death, and even now she was lying dead on the bottom of the river?

I continued to look upriver. I realised she couldn't be upriver. If she'd been in the Thames this long, then she must have been swept way, way downstream.

I must have been out of the water for fifteen, twenty minutes. I was getting cold and my teeth were chattering. My eyes were smarting from staring out over the river so long.

I didn't know what to do.

Should I call the police? There certainly didn't seem any point in just blindly waiting by the river bank.

But she couldn't be gone - she couldn't be! Not my Sasha, the woman who I had loved from afar for so long, and yet who I'd never once touched.

I'd give it five more minutes. Then I'd call the police. And then I'd get the dressing-down that I so richly deserved.

I heard the patter of foot-steps slapping on the pavement. They were coming from upriver - from towards Tower Bridge.

I looked up - and there she was, running towards me. Her swimming suit was ripped at the neck and there was blood dribbling down her shoulder.

I stared at Sasha in the most complete astonishment. I had no idea where she'd popped up from.

She threw herself into my arms and I gave her a hug to end all hugs.

Now that she was safe, she started to shiver and then she started to cry. And I held her, and I held her, and she buried her face into my shoulder and she wept.

I pulled out her towel and her robe. She had a bad graze and a cut on her shoulder. I pressed my towel hard against the cut and then I helped her put the robe on.

I got out the brandies and offered her one. She took it and drank from it, and let out this monumental sigh of relief. She finished the bottle and tossed it into the river. She put on her flip-flops and, very slowly now, we started shuffling back to Tower Bridge and to the Tube station.

I gave her another brandy bottle. She drank it in one and, again, hurled the empty into the river.

I was carrying both bags. She had her arms crossed in front of her. She was not crying any more.

At length, I said the thing that was uppermost in my mind. "Thank God you made it."

She did not reply. She took another brandy bottle. The brandy poured down her cheeks and throat as she upended the bottle.

"What happened?" I said.

"Bow-wave knocked me into the bridge," she said.

"Jesus."

"Had to swim back," she said. "Ages to find a way out of the river. Ran back over Tower Bridge."

"Wow." It sounded rather lame. "I'm sorry."

"You should be," she said. "Stupid, stupid idea." And then she stopped and she gave me the most resounding slap across my cheek, a real roundhouse blow that rattled my teeth.

I didn't say anything. I didn't move. I looked at her.

She took a fourth brandy bottle from the bag, opened it and drank it. As she drank the brandy, her eyes never once left mine.

I found another miniature, and I also drank the brandy - so there we were: cold and drinking brandy, realising that we had both come within an inch of killing ourselves.

And that, I think, was the moment when I realised that the tide had turned. After a year of quietly and patiently biding my time with this woman, the moment was upon me - and I had to act fast. For we lovers must take the current when it serves, or we shall lose our ventures.

CHAPTER 2

I lived in an extraordinary house in Cirencester - certainly the strangest place that I have ever lived in. And, I'd hazard, not many other people will have lived in a place like it either. They might, perhaps, have spent a night or two in a house like mine. But they won't ever have lived there.

Women either loved it or they hated it.

That was one of its beauties.

For the more fastidious women, the all-round quirkiness of my home was very often not to their tastes. They did not like the cold, or the strange cracking sounds that would periodically detonate throughout the day. They did not like not having a warm, cosy bathroom - or the fact that I had an ice-box rather than a fridge. And there were other things, also, that they did not like about my snug little home - and that was absolutely fine. It was more than fine - it was fantastic! Because, of course, if they did not like my odd little home, then they were not going to be much of a match for me. Our sex-life might be sensational, but if they did not thrill to my home, then we never really going to be compatible. My home was a beautiful crucible in which to test out any new relationship. If a woman did not take to it, then, though it was just a small thing, it would be like the tip of an iceberg, revealing all the other flaws which would finally come to sink us.

I had come across my home in a suitably unusual way.

After some months of learning typing and Teeline shorthand at a secretarial college, I had eventually secured an interview with a weekly paper in Gloucestershire. Although I didn't land that job, soon afterwards I was offered a job as a trainee reporter on a sister paper in the Bailey Newspaper Group - the *Wilts and Gloucestershire Standard*.

I had a very formal signing on. For I was to be not just a trainee, but an indentured trainee - which meant that, for at least the next two years, and until I was qualified, I was going to work for peanuts pay at the *Wilts and Glos Standard*. For the paper's part, they would give me all the training that I needed to become a world-class reporter.

I had not been to Cirencester before. I had not stepped foot in a newsroom before. And like a new boy at school, I approached it all very gingerly. I was not as noisy as I normally am.

For the first two weeks I'd been staying in a B&B, but I was keen to put down roots in Cirencester. The editor gave me a free advert in the paper to look for accommodation.

I was in the newsroom, thwacking away at an ancient typewriter, keys hammering into the green copy-paper. It's how I've learned to type, and even now that I work on a super-sleek laptop, I still pound away at the keys, hammering these little plastic keyboards into submission.

I was writing up a story about - and I still remember it - a frying-pan being stolen from a house in Lechlade. But I had no idea how to construct the story. Should it begin with, "Cheeky thieves stole a frying-pan"? Or perhaps, "A frying-pan was stolen…"?

It all seemed completely impenetrable. I knew, precisely, what I wanted to say - that a frying-pan, a nice new one, had been stolen by some cheeky thief in Lechlade.

I just didn't know how to write it.

I looked round the newsroom, wondering if anyone might give me a steer. In the corner, the news editor George, who'd been a Sergeant-Major in the artillery in the war and who still revelled in local journalism; two reporters, Siobhan another trainee, who was a Goth with platinum white hair and who always wore jet black. And there was Phoebe, much more experienced, much more twitchy. I liked them.

One other trainee reporter, Rudi, sleek and bespectacled, the mischief-maker-in-chief; and then the sports editor, the diligent Leonard, who'd used to work in the printing hall in Dursley, but was trying his hand on the editorial side.

The reporters were sat at this island of four desks in the middle of the newsroom. The walls had once been creamy, but the tops of them had turned brown from the millions of cigarettes that had been smoked over the decades. Above all else, I remember the place being awash with paper - green copy paper, old newspapers, cuttings and "blacks", which was the carbon paper that we used to make copies of the stories. And to think that it was only 25 years ago! Difficult to imagine, I know.

Rudi came over and stood behind me. He was drinking coffee as he read over my shoulder. "Try this," he said. "Police are searching for a thief who stole a frying-pan from a house in Lechlade last week."

"Thanks," I said.

"Any time."

George beckoned me over to his desk. Unlike every other desk in the room, George's was immaculate. Type-writer in the middle, cup of coffee on a beer-mat to the side, and then three neat piles of papers that he was working through, one with press releases, one with council bumf and a smaller pile of readers' letters. "Cadet-Kim," he barked. "I have fresh orders for you."

"Yes, Sir!" I said, standing at rigid attention with my notebook in hand.

"You are both requested and required to interview a Cirencester lady who is rebuilding the privy at the bottom of her garden."

"Sir?" I scribbled in my notebook.

"Lady Claire Roberts-Tait, widow of the late Sir Anthony Roberts-Tait, who used to be the Ambassador to India."

"I'll get stuck straight in."

"It's not any old privy," he said. "It's a three-seater! Can you imagine them - all sitting in line abreast."

"Just like your days in the army!"

He sent me on my way with his trademark phrase. I've never heard it since, but for me, it is still a magnificent call to arms: "Be brave! Be fearless! Imitate the actions of a tiger!"

I skipped out of the newsroom, down the stairs and past the office of Hugh, my surly editor, who'd once dreamed of working on Fleet

Street and who was now stuck in this Cotswolds backwater; he never much took to me.

I walked down Dyer Street, past the Church of St John the Baptist, and off to Cirencester Park. Cirencester is - or at least used to be - as charming a market town as you will find in England. It is the retirement capital of England, home of creamy cottages and trickling rivers and quaint country pubs.

Lady Claire had a beautiful Georgian house next to the park. I stood outside the front door, and then, like male reporters the world over, I checked that my tie was straight and that my fly-buttons were done up. I rang the bell, and from inside I could hear the click of a walking-stick on floorboards.

The door was opened and this woman looked at me. She was tall and imperious and I had the sense that in her day, she'd been an absolute knock-out.

"Can I help you?" she said. A woman, also, who did not suffer fools gladly.

"I'm so sorry to bother you," I said. "I'm from the local paper, the *Wilts and Glos*. I understand that you have rather a fine privy."

"*Rather a fine privy?*" she said. "*Rather a fine privy?*" She looked me up and down. I thanked my stars that I had polished my shoes that morning. "It is only the finest privy in the whole of England."

"Precisely what I've been told," I said. "I've come to the right place!"

"From the *Standard* are you?" she said. "You're not quite what I'd expected."

"I am an acquired taste," I said.

"I'm sure you are," she said. Her hand strayed to her pearl necklace. "What is your name?"

I remembered a tip that Rudi had given me a few days earlier. In journalism, it helps ease the social wheels if you can get people to use your first name. "Kim," I said simply.

"Kim?" she said, toying with the word. "You better come in then, Kim. Close the door behind you."

We sat in her formal drawing room, with oak panels and leather-bound books. There was a picture of Sir Anthony above the fireplace. He had a moustache and a cravat, but most splendid of all, he had a glass of red wine in his hand and was roaring with laughter; that is how I, also, would like to be remembered.

The spring sunlight streamed through the windows, making rainbows on the yellow carpet. Outside I could see the garden. It looked enormous.

It was barely gone 11am, but she brought out an unopened bottle of very dry, very cold Tio Pepe sherry.

"I do like sherry in the morning," she said. And as she poured the sherry into two exquisite cut-crystal glasses, I remembered how, on my first day in the office, George had explained to me the first two rules of interviewing. "Rule number one!" he said. "Accept any drink that they offer you, whether it is instant coffee or Crème de Menthe! Do not forget that, Cadet Kim! Rule number two! Before you even think of asking any questions about your stupid, stinking story, you have to be fully and completely connected with the interviewee! Do you understand that? Before anything else, an interviewee must be charmed by you. They must like you - difficult though that may be! Only when they have been fully charmed can you start ticking off your long and dubious list of questions. Have you got that?"

I had most certainly got it.

So when Lady Claire offered me sherry, I drank with a will; and when she wanted to talk I listened, and I did my best to charm.

"How long have you been here, on this paper of yours?" she asked me. We were sat at a gorgeous antique card table, our glasses nestling on the green baize.

"I have been in Cirencester for two weeks," I said. I took another sip of the Tio Pepe. It is the driest sherry that I know, almost bitter. I did not like it, but I drank it all the same.

"Cirencester?" she said. "Don't you mean Sisseter?"

I looked at her and I laughed. The twee middle-classes used to call Cirencester "Sisseter", but the name is now nothing but a relic.

"I prefer the name Corinium," which was the Roman name for the town.

"Very good," she said. "You don't happen to play bridge as well?"

"Badly," I said. "My father taught me."

"That will be just perfect. I must have you over."

"You'll fleece me alive," I said.

She chuckled to herself as she topped up my glass. "I do hope so," she said. "Have you found anywhere to live yet?"

"Not yet, no," I said. "I've just put an advert in the paper."

"We shall have to find you something," she said.

Lady Claire told me a little of her life. She said that she'd almost been on the shelf when she'd married at thirty. She had gone to America in the war, and from there had travelled with her husband to some of the world's most exotic embassies in Argentina and France and India. The couple had never had children.

We had drunk almost the full bottle of sherry before we went out to the garden to see the privy. It was as old as the house with roof and walls of Cotswold stone. There was a rickety door, black and rotten at the bottom, and two high square windows. Inside it was musky with a tiled floor. The lavatory comprised a thick wooden plank, just over two metres long, with three dinner-plate sized holes for the family ablutions.

Lady Claire was waiting outside for me. "It's all fully functional, you know," she asked. "I am having a new beam made. It will be made of oak. I shall have my initials etched into the corner."

"So that we can think of you as we go about our business?" I said.

"Is it something for your paper?"

"They'll love it," I said. "As, I'm sure, will Big Toilet Monthly."

"Is that a joke?"

"Yes it is."

"My husband was a joker," she said. "I see that I have attracted another one into my life."

We walked about the garden. It was slow going. Lady Claire had a bad hip. But I was in no hurry. The garden was at least four or five acres. It had probably once been part of the park and there was still a connecting gate - step through it, and in two steps you were in that wild land of lovers, where every glade and every bower is a bed to make love on.

We arrived at the herbaceous border, a work of pastels, light blues and greens and muted browns. The border was thick with shrubs and perennials and plants which I did not know; my step-mother Edie would have loved it.

I met Frank the gardener. He was in his forties or fifties, with thick fair hair down to his shoulders and a ruddy face that spoke of being out in all weathers. He was sipping from a hip flask and admiring his handiwork. He'd been trimming the edges of the border.

He saw us and wiped his lips, tucking his hip-flask into his jerkin.

"Good morning, Frank," Lady Claire said.

"Mornin' Mum," he said. He spoke with a broad West Country brogue; it has always been one of my favourites.

"This is Kim," Lady Claire said. "He's come here from the local paper to do a story on our privy."

We shook hands. I could feel the callouses and the thick, scarred skin. "Hi Frank," I said. "How's it going?"

"How do?" he said.

"What a lovely garden," I said.

"Right."

The interview was over. He nodded to Lady Claire and turned back to his border.

Around the house was a formal lawn with a yew hedge, but beyond the hedge, all was wild and verdant with an orchard and chestnuts; and four elms which had been uprooted in the 1987 hurricane, and which had been left to lie where they fell; and a tinkling spring with a beautiful girl in white marble for ever pouring water into the pool of granite below; and there was even a maze with a high holly hedge and its very own folly in the middle. And that maze also has its own story, and we shall come to it, but really: is it any wonder that now that I am middle-aged, and my love-making is confined to the boredom of the bedroom, I yearn for the thrill of love in the outdoors.

Then: standing aloof and alone near the far wall by the park was a Cedar of Lebanon. It was the undisputed king of the garden, with huge branches in layered clouds of green.

The cedar had a tree-house.

I have always loved treehouses. Throughout my childhood they were my little safe-haven away from the hubbub.

But this treehouse was majestic, a palace compared to the scrubby little shanties of my youth. For a start, it had a proper oak staircase, supported by telegraph poles, that snaked around the tree, until, five or six metres up, it led onto a balcony. From there, a beautiful house had been built around the trunk of the tree, with thick wooden walls and a shingle tile roof. The house was supported by two of the cedar's thickest branches.

I gazed at the treehouse.

I was besotted.

"Ah yes," Lady Claire said. "My husband's treehouse. Every man must have his den, and that was Sir Anthony's. He used to write up there - and if he was in the doghouse, he would sleep up there too. It doesn't get much use any more, I'm afraid."

"It looks amazing," I said.

"Why don't you have a look round?"

"I'd love to" I said - and I did.

The staircase was narrow, barely three feet, and was a little slippery. I held on tight to the thick oak banister, round and round the tree, my fingers trailing on the bark. I walked onto the balcony. I was now in the very heart of the tree, foliage thick all about me. The balcony stretched all around the treehouse. I walked the balcony, marvelling at the views of the garden and the park. It was only just about the most romantic place that I had ever laid eyes on.

Over to the south-west, the balcony had been expanded to accommodate an oak dining table, with six oak chairs. It was in the perfect position to catch the sun at noon and the dusk at sunset. It had a grand view out over the park. I stroked the grey oak and imagined the dinners that had once been eaten there.

On one branch there was a small walkway with a rope handrail. The walkway was made of planks of oak which had been tied to the branch, and at the end of it, perhaps seven yards out, was a tiny platform with just enough room for a deckchair and a small side table. I imagined Sir Anthony dozing there in the afternoon, at one with his Cedar as the tree creaked beneath him.

I looked out over the maze and its folly in the middle. I wondered if I would ever walk it. The maze abutted the wall that led into the park, and beyond the wall I could see one of the broad avenues that had been carved out of the forest. There was a horsewoman cantering up the alley with two polo ponies beside her. She was a fine rider, guiding her polo pony with just her thighs, while in her gloved hands she held the reins of the two other ponies. She was a woman who was in her element, entirely absorbed by her horses. I do not know for sure, but I like to think that that was the first time that I saw Sasha.

The treehouse itself was an elongated hexagon, with handsome wooden windows on each of its six walls. As I walked around the balcony, I had tantalising glimpses of what lay inside.

There were two doors to the treehouse, one by the staircase, and another opposite leading onto the main balcony. Outside the staircase door was a heavy-duty doormat. I wiped my feet on the doormat and tried the brass door handle. There was no lock on the door. Why ever would you need to lock up a treehouse? But I do wonder about that door handle and that lack of a lock; such a small thing. My life would have been very different if there had been a lock on that door.

The handle was well oiled and as I pushed the door with my finger, it soundlessly opened. I stepped into the treehouse.

Until that moment, I do not think that I had ever truly experienced envy.

I wanted it.

I wanted it so much.

It was perfect - just perfect, a room to work in, to live in, to sleep in. A room to make love in from dusk until the ecstasy on your lover's face was lit by the dawn's first rays.

The floor was of polished oak, with two lush Indian carpets at either end. There were a couple of damp patches where the rain had seeped through.

I walked into the middle of the room and closed my eyes. The smell of cedar sap enveloped me, and from deep within me, a chord seemed to reverberate, chiming with my soul.

Oh - for a sanctuary like that. I would have given everything I owned for a treehouse like that.

Slowly, very slowly, I made my inspection, savouring every nook and every detail.

Over by one window, a small Pembroke table which could be expanded. On the table was a fine pewter candelabra, and beside it, two wooden chairs, snagged and stained, and each with its own patchwork pillow.

At the rear of the treehouse, overlooking the main balcony, was a brown sofa with a small barrel beside it. On top of the barrel was a second candelabra. I looked at the sofa more closely. It was a sofa-bed, with a firm, plump mattress.

Underneath a window on one of the long sides of the room was a small wooden cupboard. I pulled out a couple of the slim drawers. They were empty. I was already taking ownership of my tree-top lair.

An old metal icebox in the corner, for Sir Anthony to chill his wine and his beer. A cupboard which contained a frying pan, a casserole pot, a kettle and some crockery and cutlery. And over by the rear door was a corner cupboard, antique walnut, with a beautiful patina the colour of dark honey. Through the corner-cupboard's glass door I could see some cut-crystal rummers, some matches and three boxes of candles.

I have been saving the best for last. I had never seen one of these in a treehouse before. Slightly set off from the middle of the room was a Jøtul, a Norwegian wood-burning stove, substantial, with a black metal chimney that went up through the wooden rafters. Beside the Jøtul was a basket full of dry wood, tongs, and a shovel and two wingback armchairs. The chairs were well-worn and comfortable, the sort of the thing that the London clubs provide for their members to ease into after a heavy luncheon. Between the two armchairs was a cube-shaped bookcase, with another pewter candelabra on top. The bookcase had shelves on all four sides, but no books. As I touched it, the bookcase revolved.

I sat in one of the armchairs and tried to take it all in, my eyes staring up at the cobwebs in amongst the rafters. I smiled at some little piece of age-old carving in the tree trunk, each letter about five inches high. The bark was at least three inches thick, and the letters had been carved deep with a chisel. ART ♥ Lady C. I smiled at the thought of them making love in this room.

It was the house of my dreams and I think it still might be. But our old homes are always suffused with memories, so that when I think of the treehouse, I don't just remember the candles, and the bed, and the ice-cold mornings when my breath turned to frost as soon as it left my lips. For as I remember that treehouse now, I also remember Sasha, lying there on the rug by the fire, her head nestled between my knees as I brushed her long hair.

It was my absolute paradise, with nothing but the absolute basics. No junk, no electricity, and no modern bits of frippery. Though, rather charmingly, it did have just those few odd little luxuries like the cut-crystal rummers and the ice-box. And that, I know, is what I hanker for in life. I do not yearn for luxury. I like things to be Spartan. But if I had a choice, I would like a small handful of luxury items. A pair of nice drinking glasses; one small but exquisite painting; a first edition; a duck-down pillow; and, for choice, a Laguiole corkscrew, complete with a fly on its back.

It is the contrasts that make life sweet.

I wanted it. I had to live there. I would have taken that treehouse over a flat in Mayfair; over Cirencester's grand Apsley House; over a castle in Scotland. And even two decades later, I probably still would. I would that I were back there, back in my Cedar of Lebanon, with the wind howling through the leaves and with the tree itself grinding in melodious harmony to my love-making under the stars.

By the time I got down, Lady Claire had gone inside.

I found her in the drawing room. She was doing the Telegraph crossword.

She looked up at me from over her reading glasses. "I take it you liked it," she said.

"It's breath-taking," I said.

"Yes," she said. "Sir Anthony loved it too." She continued to inspect me, before looking at Sir Anthony's picture over the fireplace. "I think he'd be rather pleased to think of you living there. You would like to live there?"

"Live there?" I blurted. "I would love to live there! It's the most wonderful house I've ever seen."

"How did I know you'd like it?"

And so, over a lunch of tinned chicken soup and a bottle of Sancerre, the deal was done. With immediate effect, I was to become Lady Claire's tenant. The payments would be in kind - for I would not just be her tenant but also her champion and her bag-carrier, and also, I like to think, a warm and spriggish tonic on a cold spring morning. I would do her shopping and any other such chores as she saw fit, and I would also be expected to pop in periodically for games of bridge and bottles of sherry and wine.

And in return, I would have the run of the garden, and specifically, full and complete ownership of the treehouse. I would have a key to the back gate, which led out onto the park, and I would also have a key to the front passage, which ran by the side of her house. If she had any notes or requests for me, these would be left in the mailbox by the front gate.

There were only two minor details to be sorted out: the matter of my washing and of my general ablutions.

"I can't be having you in the house before breakfast," she said. "That would not be seemly."

There was no difficulty, of course, as to my toilet. I would have the triple-seater privy all to myself. And when it came to my washing, Lady Claire suggested that I use the granite bath in the garden that was for ever being topped up with spring-water from my girl in white marble.

I sloped back into the office, past the reception, and was just going up the stairs to the newsroom, when I heard a great bellow from behind me. It was Hugh, the editor.

"Where the hell have you been?" he yelled.

I turned and ambled back to his office. The door was open and Hugh was sat behind a desk in the middle of the room, a small ball of prickliness. He was short and compact, with a thick thatch of spiky grey hair and a weird Fu Manchu moustache that always seemed oddly out of place in the Cotswolds. He was wearing a three-piece tweed suit in green, with the waistcoat just that little bit too snug.

His office was as neat and clean as can be, and I mean *really* clean. The sort of cleanliness that can only occur in the home of a Obsessive Compulsive which was what Hugh was - though the term had not really been coined in 1989. First thing when he got in in the morning, he would disinfect his phone, his desk and his typewriter; he also carried round a small bottle of disinfectant in his waistcoat pocket in case he ever had to shake anyone by the hand. On his desk was his typewriter as well as a picture of his homely wife; and a cup of black instant coffee on a leather table-mat; and, directly behind the type-writer, a Mansize box of Kleenex tissues. There was a desk by the wall with three trays - In, Out and Pending; and on the walls were a few of his certificates, including not just his English degree but his Journalistic qualifications; there was also a photo of him handing over a cup to some gardener at the local show. By the window were four spotless potted plants, very lush green, and it had taken me some time to work out that they were all made of plastic - very bad Feng Shui. Plastic plants kill a room's energy.

In front of Hugh's desk were three wooden chairs, and there was an orange armchair in the corner with a reading light. I don't know what sort of image the editor was trying to convey with his office, but it was not a good one.

"Hi, Hugh," I said. "How's it going?"

"How's it going?" he said. "What do you mean, 'How's it going'? What have you been doing?"

"I've been with Lady Claire Roberts-Tait," I said. "She's got a great story! She's doing up this three-seater privy in her garden."

"But you've been out nearly the whole day." Just at the mere thought of coming into contact with me, he had squeezed out some disinfectant gel and was dry-washing his hands. "You've been there the whole day!"

"She waylaid me," I said.

"What does that mean?"

"She insisted I stay for lunch."

"You should have called George," he said. "He has to know where you are." When I did not instantly reply, Hugh repeated himself, "He *has* to know where you are."

"She's going to be my new landlady," I said.

"You're moving in with her?"

"No - I'm moving into her treehouse."

"Don't be so ridiculous!" Hugh said. "Get back to the newsroom. Get back to the newsroom! There are all the planning applications to type up!"

Three days later, I tried my new shower-bath for the first time. It was 7am and I had just got up. I had the muzz of a hangover. In those days in Cirencester, there was hardly a single morning when I did not wake up with the wispy tendrils of a hangover.

I tramped through the dewy grass in my Wellington boots and my dressing-gown, with a towel slung round my neck and some shampoo in my pocket. I imagined the girl in white marble washing away my shampoo as the water poured from her ewer over my head.

She was grey in the early morning light, and I heard her long before I saw her. Her pond was about the size of a large double-bed. The water was clear and about a foot deep.

I kicked off my boots and let my gown fall to the ground. Like the girl, I was naked. I looked at her and wondered who she was and what we would have made of each other.

I took the shampoo bottle and gingerly stepped into the water. It was like ice-water, tapped neat from the bottom of a glacier.

I stepped back again, dickered, and then belly-flopped into the water.

I had not had quite so unpleasant experience in a long time. I did not stay in the pond long enough for the girl to wash my hair.

But as it is… well I thank my stars for my primitive bathing facilities. For oddly enough, it was on account of that cold, cold plunge-bath that I was able to court my Sasha.

CHAPTER 3

I spent some time pondering about where else I could get a shower in the morning. Lady Claire's house was out of the question, for as she had explicitly stated, it would not have been "seemly" for me to have been trotting through her house before breakfast.

If I'd known the other reporters better, then I might have been able to cadge the occasional shower with them, but that was never going to be a long-term solution.

And then the answer came to me. There could only be one possible answer, because there was only one possible public facility in Cirencester which had hot showers: the swimming pool.

The pool was quite close by to my treehouse, and in those days it opened at 7am, every day of the year except Christmas Day. I would be able to kill two birds with one stone. I could get a hot shower - bliss! - and I could have exercised before breakfast; I would be rolling into work with a virtuous glow of good health.

I decided to start my swimming and showering sessions on the Monday morning. I had set my alarm for 6.45am. I pulled on swimming shorts and tracksuit bottoms and slipped on my dressing-gown. I wore old Timberland boots, laces undone. I had my towel and my red bathing cap and my goggles. I must have been a strange sight as I let myself out of the garden gate and into the park.

I liked walking alone through the park. There was frost on the ground, and with each step I would make a little gliding slide. I looked back at my meandering tracks in the frost.

The swimming pool was just behind what used to be the Castle Barracks. It is one of Britain's oldest open-air public pools, built in 1869; they put in heating in 1931. I walked down the riverside pathway and over the bridge. The attendant had a coffee in front of her and was reading a copy of The Mirror.

"Good morning!" I said breezily. "I am hoping to be one of your 7am regulars."

"Are you?" she said. Her name was Sue, I later found out. She was perhaps in her sixties, very spry. "Want to buy an annual pass?"

"First I'll have to see your showers."

"The showers are wonderful," she said. "I clean them myself."

"Excellent!" I said.

"You really going to be here every morning?"

"I will be," I said. "For some time to come."

"Have this one on me, then."

"Thank you."

I walked past the pool to the men's locker-room at the far end. It was clean and basic and it had three showers, with not just shower gel dispensers but also shampoo.

I dumped my clothes in a locker. The pool was 25 metres long and half of it had been laned off. It was giving off this light mist in the cold air. That was a good sign; it meant the water was warm.

I had the pool to myself. No health and safety in those days, so no life-guards to pace about the pool-side. I love having pools to myself. It's the same with big art galleries. I like to have rooms to myself, pictures to myself.

I did a racing dive and swam the length of the pool underwater. When I am in a pool, that is how I like to start all of my swims.

My strongest stroke, in those days, was the breaststroke. I could do the crawl, but my technique never held up and after just a couple of lengths, I always blew up.

I swam a couple of lengths of breaststroke, long, easy glides, exhaling in the water. Then just for the hell of it, I did a length of crawl. I tumble-turned, and it was while I was swimming back that I noticed another swimmer walking out to the pool.

I paused at the end of the lap to get my breath back. I felt like I'd been sprinting.

I looked over at the other swimmer. It was a woman, I saw, in a business-like black all-in-one costume and matching black swim-hat. She was just putting on her goggles. Very long legs, I noticed those too. She glanced at me, though my goggles had tinted lenses and she could not see that I was looking at her.

Interesting, I thought to myself. Very interesting. I pushed off from the wall, and started to do length after length of breaststroke.

She took the lane next to me. She had a very slick stroke, just as you'd expect of somebody who was in the pool at 7am on a Monday. She did two very fast lengths of crawl, legs powering, water spraying up behind her. She stopped and readjusted her goggles, and then started off doing a much slower, easier crawl - gliding, effortless. It looked so easy. I had never seen anything like it. And no splash - no splash when her hand entered the word, and hardly a splash from her feet. Straight off, she swam ten lengths of crawl, bottom and legs neatly tucking in as she did smooth, elegant tumble-turns.

What a stroke. What an unbelievably beautiful stroke. She hardly seemed to be kicking at all. I counted the number of strokes that she took to complete a full 25 metre length. She took just nine strokes! Nine strokes! Terribly slow, and languid, with her head fully immersed in the water, and this beautiful rolling glide. She was very slippery in the water. It was extraordinary to watch.

I did not try to race her. I was just the guy in the next lane who was enjoying himself, and who was swimming length after leisurely length of my beautiful breaststroke.

After about fifteen minutes, I'd stopped for a breather. I'd pulled up my goggles and was just lying against the end of the pool, both arms resting easily out of the water. The view was spectacular. There was a brown wooden fence around the pool to hide us away from peeping Toms. Through all the mist of the pool you could make out the trees and the sky; not quite wild swimming, but certainly an improvement on swimming indoors.

By chance, the woman had stopped at the same end. She had taken off her goggles and she was also looking at the view. We happened to catch each other's eye. But that was all we were going to do. I had worked it all out beforehand. I was not going to engage.

I gave her a smile and a pleasant nod. Then I pulled down my goggles and swam another sixteen lengths of breaststroke, and when I was done with that, I climbed out of the pool, and without a backward glance, I went to the showers.

The showers were everything I could have hoped for - well, after my freezing plunge-bath in Lady Claire's garden, absolutely anything would have been an improvement. The water gushed hot and plentiful. I revelled in being able to properly wash my hair for the first time in over a week - and proper lather, too, from the soap so that I could have a proper wash. By the time I left the swimming-pool, I gleamed.

So, having found my showers and having discovered how this tall beauty liked to start the day, I signed up for a year's membership of the pool. "You liked it then, did you?" said Sue when I gave her a cheque the next morning.

"Very much," I said.

"And you're a morning-bird are you?"

"Yes."

"It's usually just you and Sasha," she said. My ears pricked up. Sasha. So that was her name. I latched onto it, savoured it. Sasha. I liked it. It was exotic. Sasha. I wondered where she was from. She certainly did not look like she was from Cirencester.

"And I'll be seeing a lot of you too," I said.

"You will - Kim."

For the next month then, regular as clockwork, I would turn up at the pool at about 7.10 in the morning, and would dive in and do a few lengths, and at about 7.20, Sasha would come to the pool. She had two swimming costumes I saw, one in black and one in navy. I came to know these swimming costumes quite well. They were not for parading in - they were for swimming. So at the legs, there was no high cut to reveal a few extra inches of thigh; at her front, the clinging fabric stretched all the way up to her collar-bone. And from behind, there was not a single centimetre of exposed buttock.

But her back was exposed, with just a criss-cross in the middle from the tie that stretched from her shoulders to her hips.

She was far, far sexier than any woman that I have seen in a bikini. It was first that she seemed so unaffected by her looks; they were neither here nor there. Sasha was just the woman who came to swim, and the swimming costume was what she needed to put on in order to enter the pool. But because the costume revealed so little, all I could actually see of her was a fresh face, and taut toned arms and those long legs, and lean hidden curves - and as for the rest, that had to be filled in by my imagination.

I do not know if my imagination is a blessing, or perhaps a curse. But it is what it is, and it is most vivid, and so in my mind's eye, Sasha only had the best body of any woman in history, and there she would be, stripping out of her wet swimming costume, and I would be kissing her, and kissing that cute kinked nose of hers, and…

Isn't it amazing how a person's blemishes can be the making of them? And how we can love their seeming faults, like their wonky front tooth, or their scarred arm, or their lumpy bunioned feet almost more than any other part of them.

Though perhaps it is just me. I am aware that I have esoteric tastes. But anyway - I began to adore that nose even more than I did her legs.

And we still did not speak.

I had never known such self-discipline.

But right from the outset when I'd seen her come to the pool on that first Monday, I had pledged to myself that, come what may, it would never be me who made the first move. No - I would be the guy who did things differently. I would be the one guy on earth who was completely oblivious to her.

Which meant: that for the space of four weeks, we never spoke.

I did not swim quite so early at the weekends, but on the weekdays, for twenty days on the trot, there I would be swimming my breaststroke, and there would be Sasha in the lane next to me, swimming her beautiful crawl. And we never once said a word. We would occasionally catch each other's eye, and I might smile and give her a little nod; and after a couple of weeks, she had also thawed enough to smile at me.

But we never spoke. Not one single word.

It was almost laughable. Can you conceive of any other situation where, day in, day out, you are regularly coming into contact with another human being, and yet never once speaking to them? It was nothing, of course, to do with shyness. I can talk and banter with any stranger on earth. And I think she knew that.

I wonder what she made of this new guy in town who every day was swimming his breaststroke and his bad attempt at front crawl - and who, unlike any other guy on earth, never said a word to her. I did not chat, I did not flirt, I did not leer at her. I just swam my lengths, and if we caught each other's eye, then I would smile. But never anything more. I wanted nothing of her.

After four weeks, it had actually turned into a joke. We knew each other's morning routines so well, but we never once spoke to each other. I knew that by 7.20 she would be in the pool, and that she would do two fast lengths. She would then re-adjust her goggles to see that they were tight. She would then do ten easy lengths, and have a breather, followed by ten lengths on one side, ten lengths on the other, ten lengths on her back, and to finish, ten more lengths of that beautiful, gliding nine-stroke crawl, with one arm always outstretched in front of her.

And as for me, I suppose she knew that I was the guy who swam quite an efficient breaststroke, and who after his shower trotted off to some random place in the park.

I wonder if she was intrigued. Certainly I don't think there would have been that many in Cirencester who would never have said a word to her.

On Friday mornings, we would be joined by two elderly gents, Bob and Graham. They both knew Sasha and would bawl out good morning to her, and very soon they were saying hello to me as well. Out they would come to the pool at about 7.30, and they would wave to me and to Sasha, and Sasha and I would both individually say hello to these affable old men - but still we never said a word to each other.

Which was fine by me. Because I had a plan, and I was not going to crack. If she didn't want to say a word to me till Christmas, then… we would not be saying a word till Christmas.

★

And then my girlfriend came up to visit.

Perhaps I should have mentioned her earlier. Her name was Belinda, though she was universally known as Mousie. I never found out why.

Mousie asked where I was living.

"You'll love it!" I babbled. "It is only the most fantastic house that you have ever seen!"

"Really?" she'd queried.

"It's different," I said. "You've never been in a place like it."

"Oh, God," she said.

Yes, indeed. As with so many things in my life, there were some people who adored my treehouse; and there were some people who hated it. You were either in one camp or the other, and there was no middle ground betwixt them.

And as for Mousie - well you shall soon see how she took to my treehouse.

We had met at, of all places, a secretarial college. Five months earlier, I had left my previous job, as a hotel waiter; though perhaps "left" is not quite the right word for it. More correctly, I think, I had been asked to leave the Knoll House, an old-style family hotel in Studland, in Dorset.

After quitting the hotel, I had set my heart on becoming a journalist, though it took me several months to find a job. In the meantime, and in order to get out of my parents' hair in London, I had gone down to stay with my country bumpkin uncle and aunt who lived on a farm near Winchester. For over two months I lived in a small caravan, occasionally being allowed into the farmhouse to have a meal and a wash. On weekdays, I would cycle the ten miles into Winchester, where I had enrolled myself into Miss

Sprule's Secretarial College. I was learning to type and I was learning shorthand - Teeline shorthand. Teeline is much easier to learn than the phonetic-based Pitman, but it is not nearly as fast.

I must have been the biggest pain in the neck that Miss Sprule's had ever seen. I was the only guy in the place, and it must have seemed to my worthy teachers, in their long tweedy skirts and their well-ironed tops, that I spent my entire time playing the goat. Not a joke nor a quip would be left unspoken as I idled away my hours in the classroom.

As for my fellow students, who had largely set their hearts on being secretaries or PAs, they treated me like some freakish alien.

But my teachers faced one completely insurmountable problem: despite my perpetual sky-larking, I just kept getting better and better. After three weeks, I had far outstripped my fellow students in both my typing and my shorthand. It was inexplicable.

The reason was simple enough. My uncle and aunt liked to be tucked up by 8.30pm at the latest, though occasionally they would push out the boat on a Friday night and go to bed at 10 o'clock. I'd often have dinner with them and my pretty cousin Tabby, but come 8.30, I'd be stumbling back to my caravan. Sometimes at the weekends, I might mooch off to the local pub, The Ship, but most nights, there I'd be in my caravan, four hours at a time, going through my typing drills and listening to my shorthand tapes of Miss Charlotte McMicking droning on at eighty words per minute.

What a sad little life, but it has stood me in good stead. I am one of the fastest typists in this business; most journalists are only able to type with two or four fingers. They tap away at the keyboards like demented pecking chickens.

Anyway - my furious night-time practice sessions in the caravan continued for about six weeks, until one evening Miss Sprule's students went out for a drink. I sat myself down next to Mousie, who was the prettiest student in the class; she was also rather prim. I don't really do prim; I prefer women to be earthy, and jokey, and matching me for verve and adventure. But as it happened that night, well one thing led to another. I don't know how one thing led to another, but what I do remember was Mousie saying, "God, I so didn't want to do this -" and the next moment we were snogging in the back alley, as she fended off my lustful pawings.

We started dating - which in those days meant that if I wished to proceed any further with the physical side of things, then I would have to commit myself exclusively to Mousie, and take her out for dinners and such like.

It was very hard going. I'm sure the feelings were mutual. A lot of the time I was bored. But nevertheless, she was extremely beautiful - though I realise that a woman's beauty is all so utterly immaterial. I have done my best, of late, to curb my natural appetites. Not that it has done me much good.

Eventually, after about four weeks of the most ardent courtship, Mousie had fallen under my spell. Her parents had been off to a wedding, and we had made love one Saturday afternoon on her small single bed with its teddies and its pink cover-slip. Though the radiators were full on, Mousie had insisted on drawing the curtains, and turning off the lights. We had then both had to get under the covers. I don't really remember much about it; in fact my abiding memory was of the critical moment, with Mousie holding me so tight that my face was ground into the mouth of a gaping Teddy Bear. It only had one eye, and even at the time, I could sense its displeasure at the manner in which I was despoiling his mistress.

Then, having made love, we were now obviously an item, which meant that soon after I'd started my apprenticeship in Cirencester, she came up on the train to pay me a visit.

It was a Friday night in April and absolutely pouring with rain. I had gone to Kemble station to pick Mousie up in my old Merc. The damp had been getting into the alternator and the car had been sputtering all the way there. I wondered if we'd make it back. But even if we didn't… well we could just bed down for the night in the car, drink some of the beer, and as it was the car had still yet to be properly christened…

In my dreams.

Picking up your lover at the station, and with that promise of all that is to come in the night.

I remember that.

It doesn't happen like that when you're married - not even when you've been away on quite a long trip. Well maybe it does, but it just seems that with kids and the general passage of time, even the most beautiful partner turns into nothing but wallpaper. You can be all too aware of their beauty, but your heart no longer races and fizzes like it once used to do.

So, as I waited for Mousie at the station in the pouring rain, I had all but forgotten the dullness and the tedium - and what I was primarily thinking about was lying naked with Mousie on the rug, her long light hair in a halo about her head, as we made long and languorous love in the candlelight by the fire.

I had, as best I could, turned my treehouse into a snug love-nest. I had bought white wine and cheap Champagne which had been left to cool in the ice-box; had emptied four tins of Waitrose chicken stew into the casserole pot which even now was simmering on the Jøtul; had purchased a new Arctic-tog duvet, plus sheets, pillows and plain white duvet cover for the bed; and had chopped up enough wood from one of the fallen elm trees that we would be able to keep the stove well-stocked for the entire weekend without even once having to set foot on the ground.

I had also attempted to repair some of the wooden shingle tiles which had slipped off the roof. While Frank had held onto the ladder, I had tried to knock the tiles back into place; I thought they might hold for a little while, but in these sort of practical matters, I am a bit of a bodger. Of more concern than the roof tiles was the canvas sheeting which had been tacked into the tree trunk. The canvas was torn, and in several places I could see that there was nothing to stop the rain rolling down the trunk and into the treehouse. But there was nothing I could do about it at the time; besides, with the Jøtul going full blast, any moisture would soon be dried off.

The train pulled in. Mousie was the only passenger to step out, and as she came towards me, with the rain flickering through the yellowy lights, she looked absolutely stunning. She was wearing a long black coat that stretched almost to her ankles. As a token of my ardour, I had even borrowed one of Lady Claire's old umbrellas.

Mousie had a small cotton bag slung over her shoulder. I held my arms wide and gave her a huge hug. Her kiss was dry and perfunctory, like pressing my lips to a piece of old leather. She did not hug me but patted my arm with her free hand.

"Mousie!" I said. "It is so good to see you!" I tried to kiss her again, but this time she ducked it completely. I ended up kissing the hair by her ear.

"Just wait!" she said.

Just wait, indeed! Was she not aware that I had been fantasizing about this moment for nigh on the past month? That if she'd been up for it, I would have happily whisked her off to the Merc to immediate and frenetic love on the back-seat, amidst the detritus and the empty beer bottles?

But no - seemingly not. Already, after only two months together, we were some middle-aged married couple who must observe all the proprieties before they are allowed to have sex: drinks must be drunk, questions must be both asked and answered, and conversations must be engaged in, and only once you are fully connected on an emotional level can you connect on a physical level. For guys, of course, it is the other way round. Only after they have connected physically can they connect emotionally.

But really, why ever can't we connect, both physically and emotionally, at the same time? Is it so revelatory to have a conversation as you make love - or must it always be done with sighs and heartfelt stares into each other's eyes?

I took Mousie's bag and, while holding the umbrella over her head, I guided her to the car. I had not brought a torch and she stepped straight into a puddle. "My tights!" she said.

"Don't worry," I said. "We'll have them off you in a jiffy and drying in front of the fire."

"I bought them this morning."

I opened the car door for her, holding the umbrella overhead as she stepped inside. I opened the back door and tossed in her bag.

Mousie looked over her shoulder. "You might have cleaned the car," she said.

"Been too busy preparing our love-nest," I said cheerily, as I got in beside her.

"Sex, sex, sex – is that all you think about?" she said, arms crossed tight in front of her.

"Only with you, Mousie," I said.

"Can't we just calm down?" She stared out of the window. The rain poured. "I've only just got here."

"Sorry," I said. We bumped out of the station car park. "I'd thought that you'd be as pleased to see me as I am to see you."

"It's not…" she said. "I just don't feel the urge to strip off all my clothes the moment I see you."

I had an inkling of what was ahead of us that weekend when I took her through the garden. She'd said already that she needed to go to the toilet.

At first, as we'd pulled up outside Lady Claire's house, Mousie had been delighted. "You live here?" she said, clearly astonished.

"Sort of."

We'd walked down the passageway past the house and into the garden, and immediately Mousie was plying me with questions. "Why are we out in the garden?" she said. "Are you living in the gatehouse?"

"There is no gatehouse," I said. I led the way to the privy, and gestured for Mousie to go inside. "Your toilet," I said.

"This is a toilet?" she said. She looked at the privy fearfully. "This is your toilet?"

"It is. It's a privy. A three-seater privy, no less. I'll go inside and get the torch."

I left her with the umbrella and got the torch. I clicked it on. Mousie did not look happy. Without a word, she took the torch and went into the privy. Five seconds later, she came out again.

"I can't go in there," she said.

"Okay," I said. The torch was pointing up to the umbrella and I stared up at the rain. "Perhaps I could ask Lady Claire. Or we could go to a pub?"

"It's fine," Mousie said - though everything was so not fine.

I led the way through the garden. Mousie refused to take my hand, and was stumping along beside me. We walked through to the orchard, and already I could see the treehouse, windows aglow in the night and little puffs of smoke coming up through the chimney. It looked, or so I thought, like the most charming sylvan scene imaginable.

"What's that?" Mousie said.

"That's my home," I said.

"What?" she said. "You're living in a treehouse?"

"Not just any old treehouse."

Mousie humped and complained that her feet were getting wet in the long grass. We made it to the treehouse and I led the way up.

I remember Mousie's reaction when she walked into the treehouse for the first time. I closed the door behind us, and went over to the Jøtul to open the stove doors. I had left a couple of candles burning by the window. Without saying a word, I went round lighting the rest of the candles. With the fire and the candles, and the smell of the stew, and the rain hammering at the windows, I thought it quite magical.

And then I looked over at Mousie, who was still standing by the front door, arms crossed, and looking as if she'd been asked to spend the night in the lions' den.

"Let me take your coat!" I said. Grudgingly, she took off her coat. I hung it on an old wooden peg that had been hammered into the tree trunk. I opened the bottle of Champagne. It was Champagne, but certainly not the expensive stuff; I had neither the money nor the inclination to start splashing out on Bollinger or Taittinger or Krug. But still, Champagne is Champagne. It is fizzy and it is cold, and when you are busily trying to re-connect with your lover, then it does not much matter what it tastes like.

"Moet?" she said, as I filled one of the cut-crystal rummers.

I raised my glass and looked her in the eye. "Here's to you," I said.

Mousie took a very dainty sip. She did not actually grimace, but she did not smile either. "I think I prefer Bollinger," she said.

I still find it amazing to think of the cartwheels that I used to perform for a woman in order to get her into bed. A lot of the time, I felt like I was only going along in second-gear - and with the hand-brake on. And what women like Mousie saw of me was only a very vague shadow of what I was really like, as if everything I did and uttered had to be edited to check that I might not offend.

So, instead of telling Mousie where to get off, I merely accepted her rebuke. "Bollinger?" I said. "I better remember that."

At length, eventually, and after a bottle of Champagne and a bottle of Sancerre, Mousie had begun to thaw. We'd had a candlelit dinner at the Pembroke table by the window, stew mopped up with fresh white bread, and them some Stilton and Cox's apples to follow. She didn't want the cheese.

She went outside for a quick pee. "I did it underneath the tree," she said, as she came back in, barefoot and smiling. "Do you think Lady Claire will mind?"

"She couldn't care a hoot," I said.

And then, after approximately three hours with Mousie, it came to the moment that I had long been dreaming of. And it will be a long time before I forget it either.

I was sitting on one of the armchairs and Mousie was sitting on my lap - not straddling me, but side-saddle. She had her arms around my neck and we were kissing. Try as I might, the kisses all seemed rather mechanical. Every minute or so, she would break off, give me a hug and sigh out loud; I was finding it difficult to get any sort of momentum.

Ever so slowly, I was undoing the front buttons of her shirt. She was wearing a white bra. I slipped my hand under her bra.

She broke off, wriggling away from me. "Not here," she said. "Let's go to the bed."

"Why not here?" I said. "I'd love to see you naked in front of the fire?"

Mousie wrinkled her nose with distaste at the very thought of stripping in front of me. "No, let's go to bed," she said.

"Okay," I said. Bed certainly seemed better than nothing at all.

I was allowed to take along one single candle, and by the time I arrived at the side of the sofa-bed, Mousie was already under the covers. Her knickers and bra were lying on top of her skirt on the floor.

"It's cold," she said, curled up on her side, with the duvet tight about her. "Get in quick." It's probably down to me, but I don't know how much she ever enjoyed making love.

Still - we swains do what we must when we are in the heat, and here, now, in my bed was a woman who wanted to make love with me, and though it might not be everything that I wanted, I was certainly not going to spurn it. Young men in love are like dogs who lie beneath the kitchen table, for they are grateful for any scrap or morsel that happens to fall to the floor.

I put the candle by the bedside and sat on the bed and unlaced my boots. I hurled them across the room and then peeled off my jeans and shirt, and those were tossed against the window. As I pulled off my boxers, Mousie demurely looked away.

She squealed as I ripped back the duvet and dived into the bed beside her.

"You're so cold!" she said. "Get your feet away from me!"

"Maybe I should wear socks," I said. "That's a very sexy look."

"I wish you had a bath here," she said. "I'd love a hot bath."

"Is there any other way that I might be able to warm you up?" I said, and I trailed off as I started to kiss Mousie on the lips. We were side on to each other now, kissing and kissing, and gradually I started to work my lips down to her chin, and her throat, and then of course to her breasts and her belly, and…

"Not there," she said. "I'm just about to start my –"

"That's okay," I said.

With her hands she guided me away again. "I said not there."

"Okay," I said, and then, sensuously, or at least as sensuously as I knew how, I let my tongue glide down the inside of her thighs, dabbing at the back of her knees. Mousie giggled and twisted to the side. "That's ticklish!" she said. "Don't do that!"

I tried again. I tried to kiss her feet and her toes, but she was having none of it. Now that she was in bed with me, she did not seem to want to spin the act out any longer than necessary - though I am aware that this may well have been because of own ineptitude.

For a while we kissed.

I have never been very good at asking for what I want.

But if you don't ask, you don't get.

So I move obliquely. Tangentially. "What are the chances of returning the favour?" I asked.

Mousie looked at me askance. "Let's have sex," she said.

Hmmm. Oral sex is an interesting one. Some lovers they like it and some they do not. And for those that do not like it... well of course each to his or her own. But as for me, a disinclination for oral sex would be an indication that... a lover might not have a sufficient degree of raunch for a long-term relationship. Let me be blunt: lovers who do not want oral sex are unlikely to be searching for sex outdoors, or on desk-tops, or kitchen tables, or in the rain, or the sands, or the sea. Not that I have ever looked for depravity in my lovers, but if oral sex is off the menu - so to speak - then it usually means that many other items will be off the menu also. This may not be a killer in the short-term. In the short-term, particularly if you're only seeing your lover every fortnight, then you'll be just thrilled to be having sex, even if it's just the missionary position that's on offer. But if two lovers are endeavouring to stay faithful, then in the long-term - perhaps, just possibly - they might have more chance of staying together if there is more variety to their sex lives.

By now, Mousie was on top of me. I was lying back, and though there was just the one candle and it was on the barrel, I could see enough of her. She saw that I was watching her and for once she revelled in the look of lust upon my face, and she was unabashed by her beauty. She smiled at me, leaning back, breasts jutting forward, her fingers linked behind her head.

We were not quite making love - not quite yet. But I was in no rush. If Mousie wanted to spin it out till dawn, then I would not be pressing to hurry her.

I stretched up to stroke her breasts. I almost couldn't believe that I was being allowed to watch as I stroked her. "You look sensational," I said. "I wish you'd let me see you naked more often."

She giggled and drew a lock of hair across her mouth. "You really think so?"

"I really know so."

Mousie giggled and she writhed, and for once she was enjoying being in control, and entire mistress of the situation. She was not even draping herself in the duvet any more. She was naked and was sitting astride me, and though things might yet have got better, I have to say that it was all looking pretty damn good.

Mousie let out a delicious giggle.

I watched her as she leaned right back, eyes shut.

And then: the most piercing scream. Mousie leapt off me as if she had been bitten by an adder. She scuttled off the bed, clutching the duvet in front of her. She looked absolutely terrified. She whimpered and pointed at the ceiling.

I looked up at the rafters. At first I couldn't even see it, but in the end I did. There was a large spider there, mildly going about his business as he spun his web. The spider was hanging now from a single strand of thread.

Mousie had moved away from the bed, with just her head peeping round the trunk of the tree. "Do something," she squeaked. "Get it away."

I stood on the bed and swatted at the spider with a pillow. I might have hit it and I might not, but anyway I wiped the remains of the web off the pillow and tossed it to the floor.

Mousie looked at me. "Has it gone?" she said. "Did you kill it?"

"Dead as dead can be," I said. "I'm sure there'll only be another hundred to get rid of."

It took some time to coax her back into bed, and suffice to say that the moment was well and truly over. It was a long time before Mousie got to sleep that night.

The next day it was still raining. I made coffee and grilled toast in front of the fire. I could see that she was eager to get out of the tree-house. "Where can I wash?" she said. "I feel so grubby."

When I mentioned the swimming pool, Mousie demurred.

Things got worse when Mousie got her coat. It was a very fine full-length black coat with a beautiful red silk lining. I had left it hanging on a peg on the trunk of the tree - and when she retrieved the coat in the morning, she let out another great howl. The rain had got in through the torn roof canvas and had trickled down the tree trunk. The lining of her coat was sodden and stained with green lichen.

She borrowed my coat to go on a bracing walk through the park. She was not at all happy. How it makes me laugh to remember all those lust-fuelled fantasies that I'd had of what I would be doing with Mousie on our first weekend together in the treehouse: sex in the evening, sex in the morning, and then breakfast, and more sex, and then perhaps a pint or two over lunch in the pub, and more sex, and tea, and more sex and dinner, and then perhaps one last session before bed. Not so possible now, of course, while I am pushing fifty, but for a young swain in his early 20s: eminently doable.

And as it was - not only were we not having sex, but I was bored witless. Maybe I should have tried harder to entertain. Maybe Mousie was still smarting from the spider incident.

When we were out walking in the park, I tried to quiz her about what she wanted to do, and where she wanted to go. She just said she was very happy working as a secretary for the BBC.

Anyway - the point was that by Saturday evening, I needed reinforcements. We were going for dinner at one of Cirencester's pubs, The Slug and Lettuce, and before we went in, I told Mousie that I had to make a phone call. She stood outside as I went into the call-box. How quaint it all now seems - actually making a phone call from a phone-box, and putting 10 pence pieces into the slot.

Fortunately, he was in.

"Rudi!" I said. "I need you!"

"Hi, Kim," he said. "Just got a friend here. We're, er, having a drink."

"Fine – well have your, er, drink, and when you're finished, can you kindly bring her over to the Slug and Lettuce?"

"What's up?"

"Look just come to the pub – I'll buy you both dinner." It seemed a small price to pay.

"Okay," he said. "We'll come after we've finished our drink."

I went with Mousie into the Slug and Lettuce. I hear that, recently, the pub has reverted back to its original name, The Crown. But 25 years back, the pub's name had been changed to the achingly trendy Slug and Lettuce. It was a rustic pub, quite large, with a number of little annexes for quiet conversations and stolen kisses. It was a favourite of the young-bloods at the agricultural college. There were long tables and long pews, and a flagstone floor around a huge fire that put my little Jøtul to shame. The walls were yellow and the beams were black and in the middle there was a handsome L-shaped bar. Turn your eyes to little slits and you could all but imagine the farmers who'd used to drink there over a century ago.

Mousie wanted Gin and Tonic. I had a pint. By chance, my favourite table in the pub had just been vacated. It was by the fire, round and substantial. In the corner, with her back to the wall, Mousie had the best view in the pub, looking out over the bar and the tables. My view was a little limited. I could see the tables but not the bar itself. We watched as drinks were bought and drinks were drunk. There was a stack of logs by the grate. I tossed more wood onto the fire until the flames were licking up the chimney.

Rudi came in with Ruth. They went well together. She was one of the women from the paper's advertising department. I remember she had short black hair and a stupendous laugh; she was fun.

The women talked with each other and I talked with Rudi. "So what's up?" he said.

I clapped him on the knee. "Thanks for coming!"

"Any particular reason?"

"I'll tell you on Monday."

And then I noticed the three women at a nearby table. It was a table that was made from a very old butcher's block, warped with age and slashed with the cuts of a thousand knives.

One of the women was Sasha. I looked but I did not stare. I noticed her long legs stretched out to the side of the table; jeans and dirty riding boots. Beside her was an older woman in her late forties, blonde hair, and she would have been beautiful except she was drunk. She was twisting a lock of her hair and was laughing very loudly. Her laugh seemed a bit forced.

Sasha was toying with a glass of white wine. She was talking to a young blonde woman, about her own age.

Discreetly, I watched what they were doing. I did not want Sasha to catch me staring.

A young man, heavyset but well-dressed, came up to the ladies' table. He had two bottles of Champagne - the sort of expensive Champagne that Mousie would have liked - and he proffered the bottles to the women. The older woman was delighted. She seemed much more interested than the other two. The man pulled up a seat to sit between her and Sasha.

Over the next twenty minutes, I would periodically look over at them. Eventually the young man left. He patted Sasha on the shoulder. She gave him a brief smile and continued to talk to her friend. For all of ten minutes, the three women remained undisturbed.

And then: well this may all be fairly standard fare if you are a beautiful woman, but I had not seen it before. Earlier in the evening, I had noticed an older man in the pub. He was in his thirties, blue blazer, altogether smoother and richer than the rest of us. He looked like one of the Argentinean polo-players that came over for the season. Like me, he had been watching Sasha for some little time.

The man had gone off somewhere and now he had returned to the pub with a huge bouquet of red roses. Heaven knows where he had got them from. He went straight to their table, got down on one knee and presented the flowers to Sasha.

On my table, we all of us stopped talking to watch him. He was smiling super-white teeth.

Sasha just smiled and said thank you - but really no thank you. She sent him on his way. He couldn't be stopped though. By now he'd stood up. He continued to smile and to laugh and Sasha smiled too. But she was holding firm. She did not want the flowers.

More banter, more pleading from the man. Sasha shrugged and shook her head. She wasn't budging. In the end, the charmer realised she would not succumb. He laughed and pulled out a rose and gave it to Sasha. She broke off the stem and tucked the rose behind her ear. The man tossed the rest of the roses onto the table and left.

Sasha ignored the flowers, giving a little shrug to her friend.

And that was that.

I now knew for a certainty what, hitherto, I'd only surmised. As with all beautiful women, there were going to be many men who were paying court to Sasha. I also knew that she would be very difficult to impress.

So - from a purely hypothetical point of view - if an average guy was going to woo this woman, then he would have to do something very different. He most certainly could not be showering her with gifts, or roses or bottles of Bollinger. Though he might, perhaps, win her over with his words.

If he were a wordsmith.

In the short-term, at least, the best strategy would be to continue to ignore her. To be the very last person on earth who could fall under her thrall.

Later, though, the general plan would be to be the master of the pithy quip; to be exuberant and entertaining and yet also utterly disinterested in this woman or her beauty. Always to leave her wanting more. Above all, if you wanted to court this woman, you'd have to be playing a very long game. You could not hope for quick results. But, given perhaps a year or so, a cool, dispassionate man might have some small chance of winning her heart.

I went to the bar to get more drinks. I remember them distinctly. I bought a pint of Pedigree, a gin and tonic, a large glass of claret and a large glass of Chardonnay. The pub was quite busy by now. The barman gave me a tray for the drinks.

I was easing my way back to the table when a woman shouldered her way past me. She was laughing hard and looking behind her. She knocked into the tray. It tipped up and the drinks cascaded over my chest before all four glasses shattered on the flagstones.

People jumped away from me. For a moment, I gaped and then I just started laughing. It was so out of the blue and so completely ridiculous. The woman who'd caused the mishap had already disappeared. I recognised her as being the older woman who'd been at the table with Sasha and her friend.

I didn't even bother to wipe the beer and wine off my shirt. I was still smiling. I winked as I caught the eye of one of the young barmen. I was just turning to go back to the bar for a dustpan and brush, when someone touched me on the elbow.

I turned. It was Sasha.

"I am so sorry about that. My mother..." She tailed off as she recognised me. "Can I pay for your drinks?"

I looked at her. I am quite tall, and she was a match for me. For a while, we just looked at each other. A memory of dark, dark eyes, almost black; astonishingly beautiful. And of a nose that had a cute little kink. And this mane of long hair. And that single red rose that was tucked behind her ear.

Her friend was by her side. I saw that they had left the rest of the roses on the table.

"That's all right." I smiled. For some reason, I was very relaxed. I am not normally so relaxed in the company of extreme beauty.

"No honestly," she said. "Let me pay for your drinks."

"It's fine - really."

"Really?" she said. "Your shirt's soaked."

"It was funny. My friends are still laughing." And I laughed too. "I think it must be the first time I've seen you with your clothes on." A beat. "Sasha."

And then – because I had already decided how best to woo this woman – I smiled at her. I gave her a little nod. And I turned and melded into the crowd to go back to the bar.

The next day, I had had my swim, and Sasha had swum beside me. We looked at each other, quite serene, but as ever, we did not say a word.

The previous night was forgotten.

I had showered and washed my hair, and then towelled it, and since I didn't have a brush, my hair was standing up on end, as wild as StruwwelPeter.

I'd just left the men's changing rooms when, at the same time, Sasha left the ladies' changing rooms. This had never happened before. She was patting her hair. For a moment we stopped and looked at each other. She was wearing jeans and black riding boots and a thick white cable-knit jumper; and as for me, well I've probably looked better. I was wearing my blue tracksuit bottoms, and a vivid red dressing gown.

And we smiled, both aware, perhaps, of the slight jockeying for position that had been occurring over the previous four weeks.

"Good morning," she said. And still we stood there by the pool without moving.

"Good morning," I said. "How was your evening?"

"It ended better than it started."

We walked by the pool towards the kiosk. I opened the gate and held it for her. She walked through.

And again we lingered with each other, just standing there on the bridge outside the pool complex.

"Well – shall we have another swim tomorrow?" I said.

"We might even say good morning to each other." A beat. "Kim."

And maybe it's just my middle-aged memories, but I fancy that at that moment there was a genuine spark between us. I did not know that she even knew my first name.

"Let's give it a try," I said.

Then, remembering that we must always leave our ladies wanting more, I gave her a little wave and without a backward glance, I tramped off on the riverside path to my treetop eyrie.

From that moment, one chapter in our lives had ended and another had begun: we were talking to each other.

The next day, as usual I was first into the pool. I was doing my lengths when I became aware that Sasha was in the lane next to me. But this time, as we paused for a rest at the end of the pool, I took off my goggles. I looked at her, and I positively beamed. "Good morning!" I boomed, hitting the last syllable hard.

She laughed, which was a good thing, and then she tucked a lock of her hair by her ear and underneath her swim-cap. "And good morning to you too." She took off her goggles.

"It's a nice morning isn't it, Sasha?" I said. If you can use it judiciously, there is a lot of power to be had from calling a woman by her name. I leaned back. It was pouring with rain.

"I love swimming in the rain."

"You and me both then," I said, and, because our time was up, I pushed off and I swam.

After that, the ice was now properly broken, and each day without fail we would always say our good mornings. I would then confine myself to two quips, or at the most three, and then off I would swim. That is the beauty of Grand Strategy - there's no need to get bogged down with the minutiae of tactics. The plan was just to leave Sasha curious and wanting to know more.

And I was happy with that. I was not going to force the pace. Slowly, slowly, catchee-monkey, as my grandmother used to say. And on this particular stalk, I felt like I had all the time in the world.

CHAPTER 4

I'd better introduce you to Paris.

Paris was a student at the Royal Agricultural College, with good looks and a wealth of charm, but always with that sad hollow air that comes from having a rich father who showers you with gifts but not an ounce of love.

There were rich students aplenty at the RAC, with their sports cars and their battered Land Rovers; they used to say that the entry requirements to the RAC were either five O Levels or 5,000 acres. But even amongst these rich young Turks, Paris's fortune was legendary. His surname alone was something to be conjured with; I cannot give it to you, as Paris is still very much alive. But anyway, his great-grandfather had been an oil baron and the money had continued to cascade down through the generations.

I first came across him in the newsroom. George the news editor had called me over to his desk. "Cadet Kim!" he'd said. "There is a young lad who has recently started at the RAC. His name is Paris and his father is one of the richest men in England; you may have heard of him."

I had indeed heard of him.

"Get yourself up to the RAC. Interview Paris and come back with a good story. Be brave! Be Fearless! Imitate -"

"The actions of a tiger!"

I did not go anywhere near the RAC. I instead imitated the actions of a fat gun-dog and went off to the pub.

Perhaps I was a little more squeamish in those days, but I did not much fancy going cap-in-hand up to the college, and asking for permission to interview this braying twenty-year-old Hooray Henry. Of course

I had no idea what Paris was like, but if his dad was loaded, then it was odds-on that he was going to be a repellent, spoiled brat.

Two hours later, with beer on my breath, I reported back to George that I had not been successful in my mission, but that I had left a note for Paris to give me a call.

I forgot all about this multi-millionaire heir. But I did not forget his name. You were not going to forget a name like "Paris" in a hurry. In mythology, Paris was the handsome buck who won the heart of Helen of Troy, the world's most beautiful woman; as a result, the city of Troy was razed to the ground. Was Helen worth it?

You don't even have to ask the question.

Of course she was.

One Saturday evening, early May, I had walked through Cirencester Park to the nearby village of Coates. I like walking by myself. I like going to pubs by myself; there is more chance of an adventure. If you are with somebody else and you're in a pub or a restaurant, then their feelings have to be taken into consideration; your wings are slightly clipped. You can't really go for it in the same manner that you could if you were solo. Perhaps it's just me, but a lot of the time when I am in company I find myself reining back. I appease. The handbrake is on. I am not as noisy or as vituperative. But when I am solo, then I can do as I please. I can get rollickingly drunk or I can leave on the instant.

So although I like going to pubs with friends, I also enjoy being a stranger in a strange land.

On a whim, then, I had walked to the Tunnel House at Coates - and maybe I'd find someone to give me a lift back, and maybe I wouldn't. I did not know what would happen, but it would be different.

The Tunnel House is right by the entrance to the two-mile Sapperton Tunnel, which in its time was the longest canal tunnel in Britain. It is a classic rural pub, tucked away down a half-mile dirt track. The RAC students loved it there and love it still; it is their palace and their fiefdom.

I'd cut through Cirencester Park and was walking along the track to the pub. It was quite dark with the trees thick on either side.

I was about halfway down the track when a red pick-up thundered past. I would say that it was travelling at 70mph. I jumped into the ditch. The pick-up sped past in this sudden blaze of noise and light, bouncing and skittering over the pot-holes. I had already heard about this particular student dare. On the stretch to the pub, the students would try to reach 100mph. The road was winding and narrow and there were pot-holes and tree roots, and even if you did reach 100mph you still had to slam on the brakes in order to make the turn at the end. It was highly hazardous.

I laughed as I climbed out of the ditch. If the jokers wanted to risk their necks in order to join the ton-up club, then good luck to them.

The Tunnel House was originally used as a hostelry for the tunnellers to eat and to rest, though the pub had burnt down in 1952 and was rebuilt a few years later.

The students loved stealing the pub's bric-a-brac. They'd steal the signs and the pictures and the enamelled adverts. They'd steal absolutely anything they could lay their hands on, and unless an ornament was screwed tight to the wall or the mantelpiece, then it wouldn't last a week.

But there were two things that the students never quite managed to steal. The first was a parrot which used to hop around on its perch opposite the bar. The parrot was green and squawky and it had the run of the pub.

In stunning contrast to this free spirit was the second thing that the students had never managed to steal. I inspected it as I waited at the bar. It was quietly dozing in a glass pen beside by the bar; it was one of the biggest snakes I'd ever seen, a reticulated python that was at least thirteen feet long. The glass pen was quite large, at least seven feet long, but not nearly big enough for the snake. The snake had to spend its days coiled up, biding its time; I felt for the snake. I was rooting for him. He was like the lover who aspires to woo a very beautiful woman. He was waiting for his moment to strike.

I shall tell you how it turned out for him.

The snake was largely fed on dead chickens, and in the mornings, before the pub opened, he was allowed out of his pen. The publican would slide up the glass door and, like a convict being given his daily hour of exercise, the snake would uncoil itself and slide out into the bar-room. Sometimes it would glide past the log basket, forked tongue sipping at the air as it searched for a way out; sometimes it would hide beneath the benches; and sometimes, it would just eat its chicken and lie there, coiled by the bar, seemingly asleep.

The parrot enjoyed baiting the snake. When the python was in its pen, the parrot would often fly down and peck at the glass, trying to attract its attention. The python never moved. It just continued to doze. Was it even aware of the parrot's existence?

One morning, the python's door had been opened up, but the snake had hardly moved. It just lay there asleep in its pen, this world-weary animal which, till the end of his days, was confined to life in this glass hell-hole.

As usual, the parrot flew down to investigate. It started pecking its beak against the glass, tap-tap-tap, doing what it could to try and wake the giant.

The coiled snake continued to sleep. Tap-tap-tap went the parrot, as it fluttered and squawked about the pen - and then, quite suddenly, the parrot realised that there was no glass and nothing at all between it and the python, and that this sleeping monster was not asleep at all but was wide, wide awake, eyes bright and teeth shining. And in that instant, the snake knew that the moment was upon him. And he seized it.

It happened so quick, so fast, that the parrot was swallowed whole before it was able to shrill so much as a single squawk.

That was the end of the parrot - and, I am happy to say, it was the end of the snake too. He had bided his time, quietly, ever so patiently, and after he'd made his move, he received his due reward. A few days later he was transferred to the comparative luxury of Bristol zoo.

So that was how it turned out for the python - and as for that other snake in the grass who was so quietly biding his time by the bar: well you will soon see how it turned out for me.

A group of students was standing by the bar, drinking pints. You could always tell the RAC students - they were well-built and confident, and they liked to wear check shirts and thick cable-knit jumpers.

After eyeing up the snake, I sidled in beside them and asked for a pint. There was one student in particular who stood out. He was wearing red trousers and was about the size of a small steer with huge dinner-plate hands. He was standing at the bar, and lined in front of him were ten shot glasses. Each glass was filled with whisky. He picked up the first glass, downed it in two seconds, and moved onto the next one and then the next one; in his fat sausage fingers, each glass was the size of a thimble. He finished the lot in under a minute, and then picked up two pint glasses, one in each hand.

I happened to catch his eye. I smiled at him as I waited for my drink. "Did you get your ton up on the way down?" I said.

"No," he said. He tipped his pint to me and then downed it in one. I have not seen this done often. He seemed to open his gullet and pour in the beer as easily as if he were pouring it down the sink; it took no more than four seconds.

I left the students and went over to a long table by the fire. I took off my coat and my scarf and set myself up in the corner, back to the wall.

I had brought along some newspapers; tabloid newspapers. Even though I had only been a journalist for just a few weeks, the tabloids were already beginning to weave their spell on me. They were punchy mischief-makers; they seemed like a fun place to work. The style of writing seemed deceptively simple and I was trying to crack the code, reading and re-reading the stories over and over again. And I was not wrong about that style of story-writing; it would take me another six years before I eventually cracked it.

But with my snug seat by the fire I was enjoying myself, and I was enjoying the general hubbub as the pub filled up. I bought myself another pint and settled in for the evening.

"Excuse me." I looked up. It was a young man, charming, I could tell that from just the first two words that he had spoken. He was a student, though much more clean-cut than the others; there was a touch of the USA about him. He had a very square chin with a Kirk

Douglas dimple in the middle. He was a very attractive guy; I could see that the women would have flocked to him. But he did not seem to be aware of this power; or if he was aware of it, he did not much care to use it. "May we invade your table?"

"Be my guest," I said, gesturing to the table, and I smiled at him and the charmer obviously liked what he saw because when he sat down he sat down next to me.

The rest of the students came over in dribs and drabs until there were about a dozen of them in all, and there was this unspoken acknowledgement that I was now a part of the students' team.

I put my papers away and for a while I was happy just to listen. They were talking about the RAC's May Ball that was going to be happening in a few days. It seemed that women, or at least local women, were in short supply.

One student was dominating the table. This was the student with the red trousers and the meaty hands. His name was "Dangerous". And let me tell you something. If a man - or a woman - is called "Dangerous", then they are, literally, Dangerous. You would be well-advised to give them a wide berth.

I had just caught the tail-end of Dangerous's conversation. "Who'll have me?" he bellowed. He was sitting in the dead centre of the table, a Pashah holding court. "Who's got the bottle?"

"What's he on about?" I said to the charmer.

"He wants to play the wad game," the charmer said. "You bring out your wallet. The person who's got the biggest wad of money wins."

"And what do you win?" I asked.

"You win the other person's wad."

"Great game," I said. Yes indeed - it was unusual, but the Wad game was quite popular in the brash Loadsamoney era of the late Eighties.

Dangerous had the floor. "Who wants my wad?" he said. By now the colour of his cheeks was a match for his red trousers. He had another two pints of beer in front of him.

The rest of the table ignored him. A couple of the girls tittered. They were not local and they were not from the College. They looked like they'd come up from London for the weekend.

I coughed very softly. "May I play?" I said.

Dangerous looked at me, sizing me up. He picked up his pint, continuing to look at me as he drained it. "You want to play the wad game?"

"My wad against your wad. Winner takes all."

The other conversations at the table dried up. "Let's play," he said.

"Though I should warn you," I said. "I did have a win at the point-to-point today."

"I hope it was a big one."

"It was," I said. "Substantial."

The Charmer gave me a nudge with his knee. "Don't do it," he said softly.

I winked at him. I burst out laughing for sheer devilment.

I made to haul my wallet out of my hip-pocket but then I stopped. "Can we have a little rider on this?" I said. "It doesn't seem quite fair me taking all this money off a young student like you without the rest of the table benefiting. What about if… whoever wins has to stand a round for the rest of the table?"

Dangerous looked at me, weighing me up. "Who are you?" he said.

"I'm just the guy who wins at the races," I said. "I'd feel bad about taking all this money off you. It would be nice to treat your friends."

"Okay," Dangerous said. "Drinks for the table."

"Sod that," I said. "Drinks until last orders."

Dangerous looked at me - and shrugged. "Until last orders."

"You've got a bet," I said. I leant over and we shook hands. His fingers engulfed mine, a tiny child's hand in the paw of a bear. "I'll show you mine if you show me yours."

Dangerous was looking pretty cocky. He leaned back in his chair and, without taking his eyes off mine, stretched back into his Barbour. He pulled out a brown pigskin wallet and tossed it onto the table. It bulged.

I pulled my black leather Filofax out from my coat. It was nearly two inches thick, with a zip round the outside. I carefully put the Filofax on the table in front of me.

The all stared at my Filofax. It was difficult to tell what it contained. "After you," I said.

"All right."

He pulled out the most enormous wad of fifty pound notes.

I took a long and leisurely sip of my pint. I could feel the Charmer's legs tremoring with excitement next to me, heels pumping up and down off the ground. "That's a lot of money," I said. "Do you normally go around with that sort of wad - or did you get it specially for me?"

"Eight grand," he said. It was more or less exactly two years' salary for me - my entire earnings for my apprenticeship on the Standard. Dangerous threw the wad on the table. The fifty pound notes splayed out between the beer mugs. "Count it if you like."

"I'll take your word." I looked about the table. There was a great sense of anticipation. From my general demeanour, it didn't look like I was losing my wad any time soon.

"Come on then," Dangerous said. "What have you got?" He made to stretch for my Filofax.

"Ah-ah-ah!" I wagged my index finger. "Well Dangerous, I did try to warn you. I did try to tell you that I'd had a big win at the races. But you didn't listen - and now you're going to have to pay the price."

I eased open the zip of the Filofax. The Charmer had this glassy look on his face. "How we doing there?" I asked chirpily.

My bulging Filofax was finally unzipped. Dangerous didn't take his eyes off it.

"Open it," Dangerous said.

"Anyone want a side-bet?" I asked the table. "Anyone else want a slice of the action?"

There were no takers.

"So - my winnings off the horses?" I said. "Let's see how much we've got."

I flipped open my Filofax, and from in amongst all the receipts and the address cards, I pulled out a rumpled five-pound note. I slid the fiver over the table to Dangerous.

"Oh dear," I said. "It looks like you've won."

For one second, there was this quite beautiful silence before the table erupted with laughter. The Charmer was hammering me on the back, and the girls screeched; Dangerous was actually the last person at the table to cotton on.

I raised my glass to Dangerous. I turned the glass upside down. It was empty.

"Shit," he said, but the others howled him down, and a minute later he was humping off to the bar for the first of the many rounds that he'd be buying that evening.

Dangerous was still at the bar when there was a gust from the door and, of all people, in walked Sasha. She looked around the pub, caught sight of our table and walked over to us. She made directly for Paris, who was getting to his feet. I watched as she bent down. She kissed him on the cheek. As she kissed him, she was looking at me.

The charmer had stood up by now. "Sasha," he said. "How nice to see you."

"Hello," she said.

"Do you know…" Paris gestured to me. "Do you know my new friend?"

"Hi Sasha," I said. "How are we doing?"

The charmer looked at the pair of us. "So you know each other?" he blurted.

"Sort of," I said, and we sat down at the table.

Sasha was sat between me and Paris, where she nursed a small glass of white wine. She was wearing jeans and a red shirt - not that it made much odds. It would not have mattered what Sasha wore, she was always going to look just delectable.

I couldn't work out what Sasha's relationship was with Paris. I didn't think they were dating, otherwise they'd have kissed each other on the lips. But Paris certainly seemed keen. As for Sasha, she was no Ice Queen, but she was perhaps a little aloof. I was aware of the flicker of interest that she had sparked around the table.

She talked with Paris for a couple of minutes before turning to me.

"What are you doing here?" she said.

"Just came out for an evening stroll."

"Not here in the Tunnel House," she said. "I've been wondering what you're doing in Cirencester."

Her face was about a foot away from mine, knees turned in towards me, though we did not touch. By God she was beautiful; if I'd followed my natural inclination, then and there I'd have kissed her on the mouth.

"Why don't you guess," I said. "Much more interesting than me just telling you, so that I can tidily be tucked away into my pigeon-hole."

Sasha sipped from her white wine. She held the glass by the stem. She left a light trace of dark lipstick on the rim of the glass. "I can tell you what you're not."

"Well I am not what I am."

"You're not a student," she said.

"But I'm sitting here with these students."

"Yes, but you're not a student. You're definitely not in the polo scene –"

"But you most definitely are –"

"You've been doing your homework."

"Just a happy shot in the dark."

"But we were talking about you. And you're not a land agent. And you're not an estate agent. But you're not a local either –"

"It must be all so thoroughly discombobulating."

"Discombobulating? Now that's a word I haven't heard in a while. Is that a clue?"

"It might be."

The charmer had been hanging on her every word. She turned to him, a smirk on her face. "Is Kim always so perplexing?"

"I only met him tonight," the charmer said. "I think he's tricky."

"Tricky?" Sasha said.

"Not tricky – just complex," I said.

Sasha looked at her watch. "I must go," she said.

"You won't stay for another?" said the charmer.

"I'd love to – but no," she said. "I was only popping in." The three of us stood up, and the charmer kissed her on the cheek. I smiled and nodded to her. We did not touch.

"Till tomorrow," I said.

"Till tomorrow."

She left, and if I'd followed my natural inclination I would have watched her leave, but I did not. I looked at my pint and drank my beer, and it was the charmer who waved at her effusively as she turned at the door.

"Nice girlfriend," I said.

"She's not my girlfriend," he said.

"Oh well."

"I'd like her to be."

"Tricky one is she?"

He laughed at that. "Not tricky. She's complex."

We drank like navvies and by last orders, we must each of us have had at least a gallon of Dangerous' beer.

It was the end to an ecstatic evening.

But I did something very stupid when I left the pub.

I got into the back of Dangerous' red pick-up. There were about seven students in the cab, while another six of us were sat on straw-bales at the back. I sat next to the charmer by the tail-gate.

At a very minimum, Dangerous must have drunk a dozen pints of beer.

I was befuddled, but it's no excuse. I suppose I'd thought that because Dangerous was drunk, he'd take it easy.

Not a bit of it.

We screeched off down the track, headlights weaving and within ten seconds, he must have hit sixty.

The charmer and I were holding on for dear life. The car was bumping and banging all over the track, and I remember laughing hysterically as the trees and the shadows flashed by in this blur.

Dangerous hammered the brakes, and we clipped a gate-post as we slewed round off the track.

I thought it was bad.

We hadn't even started.

We were driving back to Cirencester, still at a good clip, when I saw gun-fire from one of the windows, and quite accurate too. One of Dangerous' passengers was blasting the street-signs with buck-shot. By the time we'd raced into Cirencester, he had notched up six signs and a street-light.

I wondered what on earth would happen next. Were we going on a shooting spree through the middle of Cirencester?

I heard the wail of a police siren, and a moment later a police car was coming straight at us. The police car blocked the road, but Dangerous just bounced up onto the kerb and drove along the pavement.

The police car followed. I was hunkered down low in the back. I didn't know what was going to happen, but I had a feeling that it wasn't going to end well.

We came to a roundabout and went round the wrong way. A minute or so later, we were going up another dirt track. I realised Dangerous was taking us into the park. Way behind us, I could see the police car's headlights.

"I'm bailing!" I yelled.

"I'm coming with you!"

We waited until Dangerous had come to a bend. He slowed imperceptibly and we jumped off the side. We landed feet first in some bushes, no bones broken. We crawled into the darkness.

The police car screeched past, lights winking and klaxon roaring. I saw two tense police officers in the front.

I rolled onto my back and looked up at the stars. The charmer did the same.

"What an adventure!" I laughed.

"Perhaps we should be introduced," the charmer said.

I lolled over onto my side and we shook hands. "Kim," I said.

"Hi Kim - I'm Paris," he said.

I would not for the world have guessed that this young man was one of the richest men in the RAC. Though I could have guessed that he'd set his heart on Sasha.

She was that sort of woman.

★

One day, about a month later, Rudi asked me to a party. It was a polo party. Rudi was never a polo-player, but he was seeing one of the stable-girls who lurked on the periphery of the polo-set.

The polo crowd in Cirencester was interesting. There'd been a polo park in Cirencester for well over a century and Prince Charles, amongst others, used to play there. The polo rule-makers had constructed the most brilliant set of rules for the game, which meant that even the lousiest polo-player ever to sit astride a horse could still become a champion. It was ingenious. Each polo-player had an individual rating ranging from minus two to ten. The top professionals would each be worth about eight or nine points, and meanwhile the journeyman hackers would be ranked with just one or two points. So far so simple. Now for the clever bit. Each team comprised four players and in the top games, the high-goal games, the maximum number of points allowed in any one team was just thirty. This meant that if you happened to be a multi-millionaire who didn't know one end of a polo-stick from the other, then you could still be a winner. You'd just have to hire three ten-point players from Argentina, and then together with your own zero-point score, your squad would have tallied up its full thirty points.

It happened a lot. Almost every time I went up to the polo fields, you could see some fat, sweating middle-aged Brit who was hacking away at the ball - and meanwhile all about him would be these superbly toned, bronzed South Americans, who were being paid an absolute fortune to spend their summers in the Cotswolds.

The millionaire hackers always seemed a bit of a joke, but still these were the guys who had the money, and who at the end of it all would get the cup and the kiss on the cheek from the trophy-girls.

The millionaires' high-goal polo was the one to watch in Cirencester. Each team had quite an entourage. Stable-girls and stable-boys to look after the sixteen-or-so polo ponies that were needed for each squad. An in-house vet and trainer to make sure that at the start of every match, the ponies were in peak condition. And also a team manager, whose general job, or so it always seemed, was to be the team concierge, arranging the fixtures and generally keeping the talent happy.

This, then, was the Cirencester polo pool in which I was about to immerse myself. I knew of them. I knew that they were these exotic birds who earned more in a day than I made in a month. And I also knew that, as regards courting a woman, it would be difficult for me to compete with them…

And since I could not compete, well then, I would do something completely different.

Rudi had popped over to the treehouse for supper and then we had walked through the park to the party. It was in an old stable-block that had been converted for the summer into a club. Rudi mentioned his name to the bouncers and we were tagged as we went in. At one end of the stables was a huge bar with bartenders serving just about whatever you wanted; the Champagne and wine were flowing like water. At the other end of the stables was the dance floor, flashing lights, booming music. And in between were the old horse's stalls which had been turned into drinking booths, with tables and plump velvet banquettes.

I did not know a soul.

But that was fine. I am the cat that walks by himself; I am never happier than when I am flying solo.

Rudi introduced me to Jo who was pretty and vivacious and keen and who was therefore destined not to last longer than a week with Rudi. I listened attentively and I asked questions and, at the right moments, I laughed.

I had long realised that in Cirencester, being a trainee hack on the local paper was never going to cut much ice. So if people asked me what I did, I would tell them and make a joke, and we would move onto more pleasant matters and they could talk about that which they most liked to talk about: they could talk about themselves. I had soon become a master at deflecting questions with other questions.

I was listening with half an ear to a young stable-boy when Rudi nudged me. "I am in love," he said.

Discreetly, I looked over to where he was staring. He was staring at Sasha. She was dressed not just to kill, but to crush your heart and break it in two. I had never seen her before in make-up and clothes to match.

She was wearing a black dress that did not reveal too much. The dress was so much sexier than a dress that hides too little. For what a dress hides, the rest will be filled in by your imagination - which will invariably be more beautiful than the reality. Or perhaps not invariably. Sometimes, though not very often, reality can indeed live up to the most fantastical expectations.

I looked at Sasha, but I did not stare at her. That was not part of the plan; the plan, as you already know, was to be the only man in the entire world who was thoroughly indifferent to her charms.

I was sipping a beer when I had that sixth sense prickling that tells you that you are being watched. I do not know how this intuition works, but nor do I need to: all I know is that I have it.

I turned my head. Sasha was the distance of three stalls away, about seven or eight yards. She was holding a Champagne flute by the stem and she was being feted by at least two or three men.

She was looking at me.

I smiled at her. She'd been watching me and I had caught her; and then, because I like doing it, and because it is a devilish thing to do, I winked at her.

And I turned back to my new friend the stable-boy.

I threw myself into the party. Aware that I was now on show, I laughed uproariously. I listened enthralled; I endeavoured to fascinate.

For although wallflowers can have their attractions, more often than not we are drawn to ebullience and to confidence.

It took her thirty minutes.

I felt a presence by my side.

It was Sasha, and now that she was up close to me, she looked absolutely breath-taking.

"Hi," she said.

"Hi," I replied. And we look and we smile and we appraise each other. She had heels on, so she was a little taller than me.

My inclination was to kiss her on the cheek. That is what I would normally do at a party if a woman had come up to me; if I knew her, even if I only knew her vaguely, I would welcome her fulsomely.

But I did not. That would have meant warmth and touching, and doing all the other things that all the other young men did with her; and I had to be different.

Rudi was lurking, stoat-like, by my side.

"Sasha - may I introduce Rudi?"

"Hi Rudi," she said and they shook hands. Rudi clasped her hand in both of his, trying to captivate with his eyes, but she looked at me.

"You never did tell me what you were doing here,"

"You never guessed." I drank, and by chance the ring on my left hand happened to catch her eye. It was a silver ring, thick and chunky. It was the only jewellery that I ever wore.

"You still won't tell me?" she said. "Okay - tell me about that ring."

"Is this twenty questions?"

"The ring?"

"It's a Claddagh ring."

"And the story?"

"It'll have to be a story for a story. You will also have to tell me a story." I laughed, and then when she was still waiting for an answer, I told her. "They're friendship rings - from Galway. Have a look."

I took off the ring and gave it to her. She held it up to her eye.

"It's a heart with a crown on top," she said. "And it's held between two hands." She put it on and then admired it on her ring finger. "It's very pretty." Normally I would have given it to her. If friends like anything that I own, then I give it them. But this was Sasha and so giving her the ring was the last thing I was going to do.

"They say that an Irishman Richard Joyce was captured by pirates and forced to be an Algerian slave. He became a goldsmith and started knocking out these rings to remind himself of his sweetheart back home -"

"Sweetheart! I love that word -"

"Eventually, Richard became so popular that he was offered his master's daughter in marriage. But he still remembers his… *sweetheart* back in Galway, and he goes back to her in Ireland, and there she is still waiting for him, and he gives her the ring."

"Though I'll bet he'd made another ring for his master's daughter, just in case things didn't work out back in Ireland –"

"What a wicked mind you have."

"The heart is for love," Sasha said, still admiring the ring on her finger. "And the hands are for friendship. And the crown?"

"For loyalty and fidelity," I said. "But you're not quite wearing it right."

"No?"

"When the heart faces out, it means that your heart has yet to be won. It only faces in when you're spoken for."

"Ahh." She took off the ring and gave it back to me, dropping it into the palm of my hand. "An important thing to know. Can we continue with the twenty questions?"

"We can."

"Where do you live?" she said. She watched as I slipped the ring back onto my finger. I waved it in front of her face – heart out. "I see you walking through the park, but I have no idea where you go. Do you live in a tent?"

"Or perhaps a gypsy caravan?"

"Or perhaps you have a bothy in the trees."

"Sort of," I said. "I live in a treehouse."

She turned to Rudi. "Does he really live in a treehouse?"

Rudi nodded. "He lives in a treehouse."

Sasha clapped her hands in delight. "A treehouse!" she said. It was the first time that I had ever seen her enthused. "What's it like?"

I shrugged. "It's okay," I said.

"You're not pulling my leg?" she said.

"Come over," I said. "Come over for dinner. Rudi – you'll come too?"

Rudi was not going to be missing that dinner any time soon.

"Excellent," I said. "We can all get lost in the maze afterwards."

Sasha laughed out loud. "And a maze as well –"

She broke off. A small round man in a white suit had come up beside her. His extreme wealth was as evident as the fat jowls on his chin. He was sweating and he had a bottle of pink Champagne in his hand. I knew immediately who he was. He was the *Patron;* it is pronounced as in the French.

He touched Sasha's arm. "Sasha – come here, there's somebody I want you to meet."

"Of course," she said before turning to me and Rudi. "Excuse me."

"That's quite all right."

The man in the white suit had barely bothered to look at me. Rudi and I were so insignificant we didn't even register on his social scale. But I do not mind that; I do not mind in the slightest if a stranger cannot be bothered to give me the time of day.

The man had Sasha by the hand and was dragging her into the thick of her party.

"I never found out what you did," she said.

"And I never got that story from you."

"Another time."

I talked with Rudi and Jo and I looked at the people on the dance-floor. There was a woman who was going completely crazy, her arms and head were flailing to the music. She was dancing by herself, colliding into the other dancers. She was either drunk or on drugs.

The woman staggered into a table, and didn't notice when a glass smashed on the ground. She was a little older than most of the people, long blonde hair, and at first I couldn't quite place her, but then I remembered. She was Sasha's mother.

CHAPTER 5

I spent some time pondering who else to invite over for the dinner-party in the treehouse.

In particular, I wondered whether to ask Mousie. There's nothing – or so it's said – that adds to a man's allure quite so much as having a girlfriend. It's like the classic gag: the best way to get yourself a girlfriend is, obviously, to already have a girlfriend. Intuitively I feel that it was right. A man does become more attractive if he already has a lover; and if he hasn't got a lover, then that rather begs the question… what's wrong with him?

So Mousie might have been an asset during the evening, but I did not want her to be a part of this new life that I was carving out for myself in Cirencester. We were now seeing each other about once every fortnight. She was sharing a little flat in Winchester with a girlfriend, and I would usually drive over to see her every fortnight; the tree-house experience had not been repeated.

I would usually be welcomed with white wine and a roast chicken, and we would eat it, decorously and soberly, and then after we had eaten – and only after we had eaten – we would go upstairs to the candlelit bedroom to make love.

Long-distance relationships last far beyond what ought to be their allotted life-span. The sex – and the sex alone – can keep you on your toes for a couple of days, and then you're away again, and so long as you don't spend too much time in each other's company then you can easily be notching up the anniversary of your first kiss. So my relationship with Mousie bumbled on; she was not the love of my life, but going out with her seemed preferable to not going out with her. It's certainly not the best reason to continue a relationship, but… this story is not about reasons, or even best reasons. It is how it is.

But if not Mousie, who else then to invite along for dinner?

★

The only fortunate thing was that I'd cooked the stew beforehand. Otherwise it would all have got rather fraught.

On the Saturday morning, I'd had some breakfast at a local café and had then mooched off to the Waitrose opposite the Standard's offices. I was going to cook about the only thing that you could reasonably cook on the Jøtul, a stew. I already had a large casserole dish. I bought three pounds of stewing steak and carrots and new potatoes and onions and shallots and leeks and parsnips and parsley. Then bread, biscuits, Roquefort and Cox's apples for pudding. A few bags of ice for the ice-box. And for the six of us to drink: a case of claret, six bottles of Chablis, two bottles of Prosecco, a bottle of Armagnac and a bottle of Bailey's which is still as sick and sweetly as it ever was, but which I still love. Perhaps it's because, even now, a full twenty years on, when I drink Bailey's, I always think of Sasha.

And one last thing, mustn't forget those: some batteries for the radio that I had filched from the office.

I lugged all the food and the drink back to my treehouse, and started to cook. Since I was going to be cooking over such a low heat, I didn't need to be doing with all that brazing and the rest. I peeled and diced the vegetables, dipped the meat in flour and salt, poured in water and a bottle of red and set the stew on the stove to merrily come to the boil. I didn't know how it would work out, but it was bound to be fine: dinner parties are very rarely about the food. They are about the company and the wine; the food is pertinent, but it is very low on the list of priorities.

I had the afternoon all planned. I would chop some wood; a quick clear-up of the treehouse. I might even set the table. Then a swim in the pool, a shower and a shave, and by 7pm, I would be opening the first bottles of wine, and I'd be as ready as I ever could be for my guests - and for Sasha.

I wondered how I'd play it. I'd be warm. I'd be funny. But I would not flirt. Would never flirt. And, though the opportunity might arise, I would not kiss her. It was way, way too soon to kiss her.

I promised myself that, no matter how much I'd had to drink, no matter how much the stars twinkled, or how much fairy-dust was shimmering in the air, that - come what may - I would not kiss her. Not a kiss, nor a finger; not even if she were on her knees and begging me. Well, let's not get too carried away. Because I was, after all, a human being…

But the plan, anyway, was that I would be doing my level best to be lively and fun and entertaining, but - unlike any other guy she'd ever met - I would not be making a move on her.

I went to chop the wood. I usually chopped the wood at the weekends, so that there was always a good pile of it by my front door. After a few months, I became quite a decent axe man. After I'd moved into the treehouse, Frank the gardener had loaned me his chainsaw and I'd spent an afternoon chopping up the three fallen threes in the garden. I'd diced them like long carrots. But the roundels were still too big to go onto the fire, so these had to be split. Frank had a special splitting axe. It is different from a felling axe, with a much fatter wedge-shaped head. You look for any splits or nicks in the wood and then you drive in the axe, and you nibble away at that weak spot, that flaw, until with a great rending crack the wood splits in two. I like it when the wood finally splits in two. It is a very satisfying sound. But actually, do you know what I prefer? I prefer the process of splitting - of targeting my spot, and seeing if, with my full weight behind it, I can land a bull's eye. Very often, I prefer the journey to the destination. The destination may well be fine enough, but I think that ultimately I am one of life's travellers.

It was hot work cutting the wood. I was stripped to the waist - just jeans and work-boots. I glistened with sweat. I was hacking away at a very tough log. It had seemed, at first, to have no weak spots. I'd chipped away and chipped away, and nothing was giving. I'd flipped the log over, and there, just towards the edge, was the tiniest of cracks; it was not much, but it was enough.

I looped the axe high over my shoulders and drove it down into the wood; if you're cutting wood for a long time, you don't need to use much effort. Just get the axe up high and then let its weight do the rest.

The crack started to open up. I levered the axe head from side to side.

"You in training for a Coke advert?"

I looked up. It was Phil, one of the Standard's photographers. He was small and compact. Women loved him.

I left the axe in the wood. "Hi Phil," I said. "How can I help you?"

"Been a pile-up on the dual carriageway," he said. "Wish you'd get yourself a phone. It would save me having to be the errand boy."

"Shit," I said.

It was a feeling that I would come to know very, very well over the next decade. It is Kim's First Law of Journalism - and it states that the bigger the date, the more important the event, the more expensive the tickets, then the greater the chances are that you won't be turning up. Instead, there will be this curt little call on the phone, and the next moment you're careering off to cover whatever story it is that happens to have tickled the mad-masters' fancies.

If you've just bought a couple of tickets to the cinema, or you've arranged to see a mate in the pub, then you will most indubitably make that date. But if you've got tickets to the ballet or you're entertaining somebody like Sasha, then it's odds-on that your mad-masters will have you haring off on some crazy new mission.

This was the first time it had ever happened to me.

I did not take it well.

"But I've got five people coming over for dinner!"

Phil laughed. "Ohhh," he said in mock sympathy. "That sounds really bad."

"We're only a bloody weekly paper!" I moaned. "We can pick it all up from the Swindon Evening Advertiser on Monday."

"Editor's request," Phil said. He picked up the axe and took a half-hearted swing at the log. The blade glanced off the wood and sank into the turf. "He wants you to be blooded. It's quite a big accident. Both lanes blocked. You might even get your first front-page by-line."

"Okay, okay," I said. "Just give me five minutes."

I had a quick wash in the fountain and went back to change in the tree-house. Phil was already there, poking round the stove. "Nice place," he said. He lifted the lid off the casserole dish and inhaled. "Not bad."

I towelled myself down and put on shirt, jacket and tie. Reporters, even country bumpkin reporters on weekly papers, have to look smart, with ties and jackets; it would have been quite wrong to have turned up to an accident spot wearing just jeans and a T-shirt.

I turned the bed into a sofa, put more wood onto the fire and left glasses and wine on the table. I wrote a brief note telling my guests to make themselves at home.

I'd put up a small mirror on the trunk of the tree. I sleeked down my hair and grabbed my notepad and a couple of pens.

I wondered how long it would be before I'd get back. It would be slightly embarrassing if I didn't make it back before midnight. Though as I thought about it, I cheered up. As regards Sasha, it would be the perfect first date: I'd be standing her up. It could only add to my allure.

I had seen dead people before, on the burning ghats in Varanasi in India, where throughout the day, scores of bodies are cremated by the side of the Ganges.

But I had never seen the body of somebody who'd just been killed. The accident had happened just underneath a pedestrian bridge, so Phil and I had a bird's-eye view of the wreckage. The firemen were already there. Some five vehicles were involved - a lorry and a white van and three cars. It was difficult to tell what had happened. The lorry was slewed across the road on its side, and one of the cars, a Renault, had been flattened. Although the accident had only occurred on one side of the road, some of the wreckage had spilled onto the other carriageway. The entire dual carriageway was closed and the queue of traffic stretched back as far as the eye could see.

The firemen had cut off the top of the Renault. It was a red Renault and it looked as if it had been smashed to the ground with a giant fist. It was on the hard shoulder and I could see directly into the car. They had the arc lights out. There was a lot of blood. Behind the wheel was the remains of the driver. I remember that I did not feel anything much. Not shock, nor horror, nor even fascination; I was just the observer, looking down into the car, and watching as two firemen put what was left of the driver onto a stretcher.

I've often thought about it since. Is that how you would want to go? One moment driving along on a Saturday evening, just leaving home in Cirencester and going off to the pub; or to see your lover; or to get back home after the football. You are just bumbling along on the dual-carriageway, humming along to the radio, dreaming of all that is yet to come - and the next moment, Bang, you're dead, killed as cleanly and efficiently as a fly swatted out of the air. No pain, no terror, just nothing at all; one moment you exist, and the next you are done.

I went over to have a word with the senior police officer, but of course he knew nothing about what had actually happened. The firemen and the ambulance men also didn't have anything to say. I returned to the bridge. Phil was still happily snapping away - though none of the shots were usable. Local papers are not in the business of carrying grisly photos of dead bodies.

The carriageway was going to be closed for some hours. A mile off, I could see the police were going through the laborious business of backing the traffic up so that they could get off at the nearest slip-road.

I looked at the cars underneath the bridge and swore softly to myself. I had just realised the completely blindingly obvious: right directly beneath me were scores of eye-witnesses who must have seen the whole accident from start to finish. And for at least the next hour they'd still be the stuck in their cars.

"Phil!" I said. "Stop wasting your time there - come with me!"

I did not ask for permission to go down onto the road. That would have been a mistake. Kim's Second Rule of Journalism states that if you have a good idea, then you should act on it immediately - because it is much easier to apologise than to ask for permission. Meaning, of course, that if I asked the police for permission to go onto the dual carriageway, then they'd refuse me point blank; but if I just went down and started interviewing the drivers, well… you shall see what happened.

It was past dusk. I decided to start on the drivers just a few cars back from the accident.

I went into reporter-mode. You are suddenly sheathed in Teflon; you are impermeable, resilient to any insult and any threat. You will do what you can to get that exclusive.

I tried the first car, an estate. There was a family inside, mum and dad in the front, two kids fighting in the back. I knocked on the driver's window. He wound it down.

"Sorry to bother you," I said, repeating a reporter's opening mantra. "I'm Kim - from the local paper. Just wondered if you saw what happened."

The children stopped fighting and looked at me with terrified eyes. The driver and his wife hadn't seen much. They'd heard a bang and a lot of smoke and had drifted to a stop.

I diligently took their names and moved onto the next car. Knock on the window, wait for it to be wound down and then, in my most charming manner, ask what they'd seen. Most were only too happy to talk. If you're the first reporter on the scene, then eye-witnesses want to talk about what it is that they've seen; it can be cathartic, particularly if they've seen something gruesome.

I hit pay-dirt with a little Mini. It was right up close to the accident spot.

I knocked on the window. A middle-aged woman slowly wound the window down. Next to her was an older woman who looked completely traumatised. Her skin was quite white in the arc lights.

"Sorry to bother you," I said. "From the local paper - just wondered if you'd seen what happened."

"It could have been us," she said. "Another second and it would have been us." She held onto her passenger's hand. She was in shock as the whole arbitrariness of it all began to sink in: if she'd left home ten seconds earlier, it might have been her car that had been crushed by the lorry.

I squatted down by the side of the window, so that I was lower than her, and with my notebook on my knee, I very slowly coaxed the story out of her. They were mother and daughter – and they'd seen it all. The little red Renault had been stationary on the hard-shoulder. The lorry-driver had drifted off his line. The lorry crashed into the Renault then jack-knifed onto its side and the three cars following had slammed into the wreckage.

I took it all down, word for word in my trusty Teeline shorthand. Behind me, I could hear the soft click of Phil's camera.

Now that I'd found my prime witness, I hunkered down and I listened, and after I'd listened I got all her details, those lovely little details which are so crucial for a newspaper story – name, age, address, marital status, number of children and job as well as telephone numbers for both work and home.

I wondered if I'd missed anything. I had – I hadn't found out why she was on the road in the first place.

"And where were you travelling to?" I asked.

"We were off to my sister's in Swindon –"

She broke off. I sensed someone behind me.

"What are you doing?"

I looked up. A traffic policeman in peaked cap and fluorescent jacket was standing over me.

"Excuse me," I said to the woman. I stood up. "From the local paper, the Wilts and Glos," I said to the policeman. He was bristling. "Just having a word with some of the drivers."

"This is an accident scene!" he raged. "You're interviewing witnesses even before they've spoken to the police."

Quite so. And I now uttered the immortal line that is the perfect fail-safe for every reporter in the land and all other such scamps who have gone ahead and done something without permission.

"I'm sorry," I said. "I just didn't know."

The police officer glared at me. "You're right in the middle of an accident scene!" he said again. "Can't you see the firemen cutting out that body?"

I took a deep breath. "I'm so sorry," I said. "I had no idea."

"Get away," he said. "Get away from here now!"

The policeman raged and I pocketed my notebook, but really there was nothing he could do - and at that moment I saw the light: never ever ask permission to do anything. Particularly not in this Health and Safety era, where there are rules and regulations to cover even a leaf's fall from a tree. And then when some authority figure comes up huffing and puffing to tick you off, just give them your sweetest smile, and say, "I'm so sorry."

The policeman scowled. I thanked the driver for her help. She waved to me as I wandered off the carriageway and back up to Phil's car by the footbridge.

He was already in the car. It was one of the office's little red Fiestas. The engine was running.

He stretched over and shook my hand.

"Brilliant!" he said. "Bloody brilliant!"

"You got the pictures?" I sat down beside him. The car was warm.

"Just taken the film out - stuffed it in my boot," he said happily. "Thought he might try and impound the camera."

"And no sign of any other papers," I said. "It looks like we've got ourselves a little exclusive."

"Particularly now that you've queered the pitch for everyone else."

"Excellent!" I said - for even on the little local papers, there is nothing finer than the knowledge that you have landed the opposition in the mire.

CHAPTER 6

The supper was in full swing when I got back home. Even as I entered Lady Claire's garden, I could hear the sound of merriment and laughter. My treehouse looked preposterously idyllic, the windows ablaze with candlelight and pom-poms of smoke puffing up from the chimney.

I went up the stairs. The seventh stair up creaked. It always creaked. I paused for a moment on the balcony. I could hear Rudi's voice. Siobhan was laughing. They'd got the office radio going and were playing my one tape. During my entire time in the treehouse, I only ever had that one tape; bizarre but true. It was Mozart. On the one side of the tape were the highlights of the Marriage of Figaro, and on the other was The Magic Flute. It was the Magic Flute that was playing now, the overture. I loved the overture; I still do.

I knocked on the door and went in. It looked... well I wish I could have captured that moment, because it will always be my favourite home. They had lit every candle that they could find and the Jøtul doors were open and the fire was roaring and there were empty wine bottles by the window. They'd drawn the Pembroke table out into the middle of the room, and though they had drunk a lot of wine, they had yet to touch the stew.

I took it all in. It was an amazing feeling to come from the car-crash and to immerse myself into a supper party - my supper party. Rudi was square in the middle of the table, with Lady Claire next to him, with a yellow shawl about her shoulders; and then Siobhan, hair whiter than white, and completing the Gothic look with a tight black corset; and next to her was Paris, in a white open-necked shirt, starry-eyed and in love. And, of course, there between Paris and Rudi was Sasha. She had a top of grey silk. It shimmered in the candlelight. She looked pleased to see me. They all looked pleased to see me.

"The hero returns!" said Rudi, and he poured me a glass of red, and I sat down between Siobhan and Lady Claire and for a while I just beamed. Sasha was sat diagonally opposite me on the other side of the table.

After you've been on a news story, it takes some time to decompress. There you are, in the thick of the action, asking people about the harrowing scenes that they have just seen - and the next moment, you're with friends and colleagues, and yet your brain is still whirring with the story. I did what reporters do all over the world. I drank red wine and I told my tale, and because it was so fresh and so raw, they listened and they were enthralled.

When somebody has the floor and has a good story to tell, it is most important not to side-track them with footling irrelevant questions. It stops the flow and the pace. So I talked, and because they were my friends, they listened until finally I was done.

"What did the police officer say?" Rudi said.

I'd already told them, but he wanted to hear it again.

"He told me that I was on an official accident scene," I said.

"And then you just apologised and he told you to sling your hook?"

I laughed and shrugged, and the plates were brought out and the stew was served. Perhaps it was just the wine, or the euphoria of the story and having Sasha in my very own tree-house, but the stew seemed like the best that I had ever tasted. The wine and the stock had boiled down to a thick, glutinous gravy and with the bread it was delicious. I was ravenous. I realised that I hadn't eaten since breakfast.

And as I sat and ate, I slowly emerged into the real world and into real conversations, and I started to register what was happening around the dinner table. Lady Claire, though she did not say much, was quite content to listen to the chatter; she even seemed to enjoy my stew. Rudi, as ever, was dominating the conversation, telling tales of derring-do from his time on the Standard. Paris was utterly smitten. He could not take his eyes off Sasha. The pair of them were talking about horses. Occasionally her eyes would slide away from Paris to look at me. And I would look at her, and our eyes would linger - though we had not yet said a word to each other.

For a first outing, I would have not have had it any other way. Sasha was in my home and with my friends - and yet we were not alone, and we could not speak.

We almost finished the stew between us and when that was done, we started on the cheese and the apples, and with the Jøtul and the candles and the tree trunk right in the middle of the room, there was some ethereal magic in the air. We drank and we drank, and I don't know what time it was, but Lady Claire eventually took her leave. I held onto her arm as she went down the stairs, and escorted her back to her house.

"I wonder what your strategy is?" she said. She had now taken my arm. She had her stick in her other hand. "Or even Grand Strategy?"

"I'm sorry?"

"Tactics wins you battles, as Sir Anthony used to say. Strategy wins you wars. And Grand Strategy is what you're going to do after the war is won."

"I don't know."

"But I know who you're fighting for -"

"Sasha."

"She's blossomed. And I can also see your tactics -"

"I didn't know they were that obvious."

"Once you have Grand Strategy, then everything else falls into place."

"Grand Strategy..." The words spun slowly in my head. It sounded large and all-encompassing. Grand Strategy! Broad and over-arching all; it soared!

"You might take her to the maze," she said. "It's left-right, left-right, all the way into the centre. You can't go wrong. But very difficult if you don't know the way. Particularly in the dark."

"Thank you," I said.

"The folly should be open," she said. "I used to go there with Sir Anthony when we wanted to be alone…" She trailed off, musing over her memories. "You might like it there."

"We'll give it a try." I opened the door for her and kissed her on the cheek.

"Thank you for a lovely evening, dear," she said. "Got a little bit of competition with Paris and Rudi, haven't you?"

She waved and as I mooched back to the treehouse I mused over Grand Strategy. It was gone midnight.

I was about to go back inside the cabin, when I saw that somebody was standing quite motionless on the balcony, hands leaning on the balustrade. I could see her in silhouette. She was staring out over the park. It was Sasha.

I stood next to her. For a while we just stood in silence, staring at the dark park and listening to Rudi's chatter.

"I know where you sleep," she said. "And where you eat, and where you pee. But where do you wash?"

"I shower at the swimming pool," I said.

"Is that why you started swimming?" she said. "So you could use the showers?"

"That's right," I said. "There is a little fountain here, but it was freezing. The pool was the only place I could think of that had a hot shower."

Sasha burst into this peel of laughter. She laughed and she laughed, holding her sides she thought it all so funny. "I couldn't understand what you were doing there!"

"It certainly wasn't for the swimming."

She was still laughing. Unwittingly, I had said the funniest thing she'd ever heard. She was leaning over the balustrade - and just continued to laugh. I watched her. A laugh must be one of the sexiest things a woman can do with her clothes on; and probably with her clothes off, too.

Her hair was falling about her face, and all I could hear was the sound of her snickering laughter. I hadn't seen a woman laugh this hard in a long time. She was beautiful.

"You come for the showers!" she said, and that set her off again. I lolled on the balustrade and watched her. I could have watched her all night.

At length, she was spent. "Thank you," she said. "Thank you for that."

"A pleasure."

"You and your breaststroke!"

"It's a very good breaststroke."

"It is a good breaststroke," she said. "But I will teach you freestyle."

"Thank you," I said.

"And I will laugh every time I think of you in the showers," she said, and that set her off again. "And you're a reporter?"

"I'm afraid I am," I said. "You've found out my dirty little secret."

"It sounds fun."

"Covering the big marrow contests and the parish council meetings?" I said. "It's ever so glamorous."

And I turned. And I looked at her. And for the first time on the balcony she now turned to look at me. And if ever there had been a moment for me to follow my natural instincts, then I would have taken a step towards her, would have taken her in my arms, and would have kissed her.

But I did not. I continued to study her face, which was half in light and half in darkness, and there, then, she seemed almost beyond beautiful; beyond human. Her lips, her skin, her hair: they took my breath away.

The laughter was still curling at the edges of her lips; quite intoxicatingly sexy.

"I think you owe me a story," I said. "I told you the tale of the Claddagh ring. I've told you about being a reporter. Now it's your turn."

"I'm not very good at stories."

"Then this is what we'll do," I said. "I shall make up a story for you - and you will have to guess what it is."

"You'll make it up for me?"

"Just ask questions - and I will answer them Yes or No."

This was partially true - though I had not made up a story for Sasha. She would in fact be making up her own story. If she asked me a question that ended in a vowel, I would say 'Yes'; questions that ended in a consonant, would get the reply 'No', and questions that ended in the letters 'X' or 'Y' would get a 'Maybe'.

"Very well," she said. She leaned out over the balcony and turned to me. "Is it about me?"

"Yes."

"Is it about you?"

"Yes."

"Are we in Cirencester?"

"No."

"Are we in England?"

"No."

"Does it involve a maze?"

"Yes."

"A very big maze?"

"Yes."

"Wow - we're in a labyrinth!" she said. "What a funny way your mind works."

"The story has been specially tailor-made for you, Sasha."

"Are we wearing any clothes?"

"No."

"No clothes!" she snorted. "And when we're in this maze, can we see the stars?"

"No."

"Is there anyone else in the maze?"

"Yes."

"Is it a human?"

"Ummm… No."

"We're being chased by some monster aren't we?"

"Yes!"

She laughed out loud. "This doesn't sound like a story - it sounds like a nightmare! Are we being chased by the minotaur?"

"No."

"By a dalek?"

"No."

"By a snake?"

"Yes!"

"How did you know I hated snakes?"

"Lucky guess," I laughed.

"And do you get to fight the snake?"

"Yes."

"And what am I doing?"

"I can only answer 'Yes' or 'No'.

"Am I dancing?"

"No."

"Screaming?"

"No."

"Am I helping you fight the snake?"

"Yes."

"Do we have weapons?"

"No.

"Do we strangle it?"

"No."

"Do we kill it?"

"No." I could not have been more thrilled at how the story was turning out.

"What the hell do we do with this thing then?" She tugged at her lip as she stared out over the park, before looking at me slyly. "Do I kiss the snake?"

"Yes."

"I kiss the snake?" She laughed. "And then he turns into our pet and follows us through the maze?"

"Yes!"

"You are one sick bastard! How did you dream this up?"

I shrugged.

"Does anything else attack us?"

"No."

"So we all make it into the middle of the maze?"

"Yes."

"Do we get drunk?"

"No."

"But we do do something, okay?"

"Maybe."

"And with the snake?"

"Yes."

"I hope it's not revolting."

"No."

"Thank God for that. Do we sit down and have dinner?"

"No."

"Does the snake lick our feet?"

"No."

"Or shed its skin?"

"No."

"Do we eat the snake?"

"Yes!"

She screeched with laughter. "We eat our pet snake? You are totally sick!"

I laughed at her. "It's a story just for you."

"Do we do something after we've eaten the snake?"

"Yes."

"Or is that the end of the story?"

"Maybe."

"Maybe!"

She was still laughing as Rudi staggered out of the treehouse. "Sounds like you're having a lot of fun," he said. "Dying for a leak. Okay to do it up here?"

"Be my guest," I said, and Sasha and I smiled a secret smile as we still stared at each other and listened to the sound of Rudi tinkling over the balustrade.

"Eating our pet snake!" she hissed at me.

"It was the best I could come up with."

Rudi wiped his hands on the back of his jeans and we all went inside. I remember Paris's eyes darting from Sasha to me and back again; he'd got it bad.

We drank Armagnac, and after we had all but finished the bottle, we went out to explore the maze. I don't know quite how it ended up, but I took the bottle of Bailey's while Rudi took a bottle of red wine. I took a glass too, just the one; it was one of Sir Anthony's finest cut-crystal sherry glasses.

I led the way to the maze. It was over in a corner of the garden, with a holly hedge. I'd never been in it. I'd never had anyone to share it with. Mazes are only fun if you're racing each other into the middle.

I have not been in that maze for over twenty years, but as I remember it was big - one of the biggest and oldest private mazes in Britain. I think it was nearly an acre - one hundred yards by forty yards; bigger, even, than the maze at Hampton Court.

The hedge was a good eight feet high, and thick and impenetrable; there was no chance at all of hacking your way through the holly.

It was decided that the ladies should go first, so Siobhan and Sasha set off into the maze, and I waited with Rudi and Paris at the entrance. I drank Bailey's while the other two drank red wine from the bottle. It was quite a mellow evening for May, and the bristling holly hedge gleamed in the light of the full moon. I had this delicious sense of anticipation. I didn't know what would happen. But I knew that something would happen.

Paris was in a fever to get going. He plunged into the maze - took a right turn, I saw, haring off into the wrong direction.

Rudi had kept the wine bottle. He took a swig. "You're a very dark horse."

"It's the only colour to be."

"And you've known her for weeks at your swimming pool? You kept that under your hat."

"I've been keeping her for myself."

I let Rudi head off first, and after a few seconds I went after him, taking careful heed of Lady Claire's directions - first left, then right, then left, then right.

I realised immediately that without the key, it would be a very difficult maze to broach at midnight. In the moonlight, every stretch of hedge looked identical, and apart from the stars, you had nothing to get your bearings on. And if you were drunk… you might even get your bearings, but you'd still just be blundering from one dead-end to the next.

I was not drunk. I was tiddly.

But I did not want to mess up, so I was calling the turns out loud. "Left," I'd say out loud, and would trudge along to the next turn, where I would say "Right".

There was a slight trace of dew on the ground and I could see that one person had already been down this path before me. I wondered who it was.

Sasha blundered into me at the next corner. I was ambling along, and she just came straight into me. I caught her in my arms, and for a moment she, also, had her hands about my waist, and our lips were just a few inches away from each other, but I did not let my hands linger. I laughed and stepped to the side. "Fancy meeting you," I said.

She looked at me. She seemed very happy. And then the penny dropped.

"You know where you're going, don't you?" she said.

"I do, as it happens," I said. "Like to come with me?"

"I think I would. Though would it be all right to keep my clothes on?"

"This time? Yes."

Sasha tagged along beside me. There was just enough space in the maze for us to walk side by side without touching each other. And we did not touch each other. I had the Bailey's and the glass in my left hand, and my other hand was in my pocket. Sasha was on my right hand side, and I tell you that if it had been any other woman but her, I'd have been holding her hand. Somehow, in the maze, in the moonlight, it would have been the most natural thing in the world to have been holding hands. But I did not, and she did not take my arm, and that was fine, because actually I did not want to touch her. Generally, when I am alone with a woman who I desire, I am for ever wanting to kiss her, and before I know it, I have done just that, and have dived head-long again into the hostile element. But with

Sasha, since I'd decided that I would do nothing, nothing at all, for a long time yet, then I was just contentedly ambling along through the maze with her next to me. It was all very cat and mouse. I wonder what she made of it. Well of that… I will eventually tell you. But one thing I know for sure is that there would have not been many single red-blooded men who would have been in the maze with Sasha that night and who would not have tried to kiss her.

"And left," I said, as we walked along another identical straight stretch. "And right."

"So that's the key?" she said. "Left-right, left-right."

"Simple as that," I said.

"Deceptively simple," she said. "And to think - not only have you got your own treehouse, but you've got your own private maze -"

"Which I've never actually visited before until now."

"And your own private three-seater privy."

"Have you tried it?" I asked.

"I have," she said. "Just before you got back."

"Maybe we should give it a go together," I said. "It must have been some years before three people used it at the same time."

"Why not?" she said.

My antennae started to jangle. There are not many women I know who would accede to sharing a toilet with a relative stranger. It betokened a certain wholesomeness, a thrill for the wild and for the earthy outdoors. I liked it. I liked it a lot.

"Maybe when we get out," I said. "I'll turn the torch off to spare your blushes."

"Speak for yourself, sailor," she said, and at the same time, we glanced at each other, and I think it was then that we realised we might have met our match. Not that it would necessarily end in the bedroom. But it would end somewhere. And it would end very differently from the rest of the flotsam jetsam relationships that we might have had before.

And that was also true.

It took us another five minutes to get to the heart of the maze. We were in no hurry at all, just ambling along through this never-ending hedge, happy in each other's company, Sasha inhaling the cool air deep into her lungs.

"And here we are," I said.

Sasha walked up the slight grassy hillock and placed her hand on the stone. "You've got a folly!" she exclaimed.

I had seen it, of course, from my treehouse, but now that I was right next to it, I realised that it was much higher than I'd appreciated. It was a tower, a round tower of creamy Cotswold stone, with crenellations at the top. I unlatched the wooden door and went inside. Sasha followed behind me. It was quite dry inside, and there was a rug underfoot. The room was about eight feet in diameter and eight feet high with two small arrow-slit windows. I could just make out a neat little fireplace. There was a box of matches on the mantelpiece. I lit the single candlestick in the window and the room sputtered to life. It was not what I'd expected. There were two rattan Butaca chairs, Indian style, low slung with arm rests that swivel out and magically turn into foot-rests. They're also known as West Indian Planter's Chairs, very relaxing; you don't so much sit in them as lounge. There was a thick rug on the floor, and by the stove was a Hookah, a hubble-bubble. Under the stairs was a small cupboard. Sasha watched as I took a peek inside. There was some coal and some candles, and tucked away in a little drawer at the top was a plum-sized piece of hash. I passed the hash over to Sasha and she smelled and she giggled.

We continued to explore, walking up the wooden staircase that went up by the side of the wall. Sasha and I had not said a word. It was all quite thrilling.

I had the candle in front of me. I held it high overhead as Sasha crept up behind me. I started to laugh. Even given Sir Anthony's esoteric tastes, this was something that I would never have guessed: between the two arrow-slit windows, and tucked up against the wall, was a full-size bar billiards table. Sasha picked up the black mushroom in the middle of the table.

"Ever played it?" I asked.

"No - never," she said.

"It's a great game," I said. I touched some of the holes at the end of the table. The baize was quite clean. "You get points for every ball that you pot. But if you knock over one of the white mushrooms, you lose your break."

There was another fireplace, a match for the one downstairs, and on the wall above the pool table were two shelves, one loaded with bottles of liqueur and whisky, and the other with tumblers and shot-glasses and lead-crystal Victorian wine-glasses. Sasha sat on the bar stool by the bar billiards table. I placed the candle of the corner of the table, and put the red and white balls on their two spots. The two white mushrooms and the black mushroom also went onto their spots. I took a cue off the wall-rack, chalked the tip, and eased myself down over the table to play a shot.

"Are you any good?" Sasha asked.

"Once," I said. "A misspent childhood, as they say." I looked at her. She was smiling at me. She seemed so happy.

I was a little rusty. But I had already decided that if I potted the red, then, one day, I would get to sleep with Sasha; and if I did not, then I would not.

There were easier shots to take, but I felt lucky. I was trying to double the red into the middle hole, the trickiest hole on the table. It is usually the last shot that you play in the game.

I hit the red at perfect strength. The ball bounced off the cushion and was trickling towards the middle hole. It would have gone straight in, but it was nudged off its course by a piece of chalk. The red clattered into the black mushroom. The ball dropped into the hole and as it dropped, the mushroom wobbled and fell over.

"What does that mean?" Sasha asked. "What happens when you knock over the black mushroom?"

"That's bad." I laughed, returning the cue to the rack. "When you knock over the black, you lose everything."

"Just like me then."

"That's not very forgiving." I started up the stairs.

"It's how I am," she said. "Those are the rules. One strike, you're out."

"Remind me never to play baseball with you."

Sasha followed me up the stairs. She had the bottle of Bailey's and our one glass and she was swaying slightly as she held onto the bar-billiards table.

There was a trap-door, a thick water-tight trap-door in the ceiling. I gave Sasha the candle and pushed with my fingers. The trap eased open till it was just past the vertical. It was on a chain, to stop it going all the way back. I walked upstairs. I was standing on top of the tower.

Sasha followed - and in any other circumstances, this would have been the perfect place and the perfect moment to have taken her in my arms and kissed her. But I did not. I stepped aside for Sasha to climb the stairs and watched, amused, as her hands flew to her mouth. It was a delight. "It's incredible," she said. We were on top of the tower, and the maze lay all before us, the holly hedge rising like black waves out of this glittering moonlit sea.

There was a garden swing on the roof, fully seven feet across. I put the candle on the crenellations by the chimney and pulled the canvas cover off the swing. The cushions were dusty but quite dry. We thumped them and, satisfied, we sat on the swing, swinging back and forth and staring up at the stars; like the sea, the stars are a sight that I will never tire of.

We were both slouched on the swing, perhaps a couple of feet apart, heels on the ground as we rocked back and forth. Sasha let out this delicious sigh as she stretched back her head.

"At least I know what I want now," she said.

"What do you want?" I filled the glass with Bailey's and gave it to her.

"I want…" She trailed off and she sipped the Bailey's. "I never knew until tonight. I want a treehouse. I want a maze."

"With a folly in the middle?"

"It wouldn't be the same without the folly." She laughed and she turned to me. "I had no idea. When I came… I never expected anything like this."

I leaned against the edge of the swing, so that I could look at her straight. "So that's what you want?" I said. "Is that the Grand Strategy?"

She looked at me quizzically, appraisingly. "Grand strategy?" she said.

"Grand strategy," I echoed.

"I last heard that phrase from my grandfather," she said. She finished off the Bailey's and passed me the glass. Our fingers touched. Her fingers were warm.

"So what is the grand strategy?"

"Up until tonight, I wanted to be a mother. I wanted to have children. I think I'd be a really good mother. And there were going to be other things, like my riding, but all I ever wanted was to be a mum."

"And you'll be a great mum." I poured myself a Bailey's and drank it. I loved it then, and I love it even more now for knowing that it was the first drink that I ever truly shared with Sasha. I held the cut-crystal up to the moon and it transformed into an opaque rainbow.

"But having seen all this, I can see that my Grand Strategy will also have to encompass a treehouse. Maybe a maze. Definitely the treehouse."

"Here's to dreams." I filled up the glass and gave it to her, and there was silence, and we were each alone with our thoughts. I felt that I had reached this state of complete Zen: for the first time I was sitting next to a beautiful woman and I did not want to kiss her nor declare my love. I was happy to look at her and to look at the sky. I was content.

She sipped the Bailey's. She was rocking the swing very gently now, with the glass resting on her belly.

"And your grand strategy?" she said.

"I'm still working it out," I said - which I was. My tactics were clear: to be utterly indifferent to Sasha's beauty. My strategy was also plain: I wanted her to be my girlfriend. But as for grand strategy. What did that entail? What did I plan to do when the war was won?

"What's sex like?" she said.

"I'm sorry?" I said.

She giggled. I think she'd realised how much she'd been drinking. "What's it like to make love?"

"Don't you know?" I said.

"I don't." She looked at me.

"Ahhh," I said. I looked at her anew.

So my Sasha was a virgin. This I would not have guessed.

"It's difficult to say," I said. "But assuming that women are as turned on by it as men, then when it's good it's great. Not, of course, that I'm any sort of an expert. But what I do know is that sex without love is as meaningless as…" I looked at her.

Sasha - a virgin. The thought of it was extraordinary.

"As meaningless as?" she said.

"As meaningless as love without sex."

"You have a way of with words."

"Why are you still a virgin?" I asked. "Are you a Catholic?"

"Church of England," she said. "It's a little to do with that, and a lot to do with my mother. Your parents swing one way - and you swing the other. Do you know my mother?"

"I don't."

"There have been a lot of men in her life. And from the moment that I realised what she was doing with these men, I vowed to myself that I wouldn't be like that. And so there it is - I'm waiting for the man I marry."

"Good for you," I said. "And what do your boyfriends make of that."

"They can think what they like," she said. "But there are other things you can do apart from making love."

"Oh are there really?" I said. "Like what?"

She leaned over and cuffed me on the shoulder. "Cheeky!" She was about to say more, she might even have been about to kiss me, when there was a cry from out in the middle of the maze. It was Paris.

"Help!" he called. "We're lost!"

Sasha and I went over to the wall. In the middle of the maze, about thirty yards away from us, we could just make out Paris's head. He appeared to be perched on Rudi's shoulders.

I waved at him. "That's why we go into mazes - to get lost!"

"How do we get out of here?"

"Aren't you having a nice time?" I called.

"We've drunk all the wine," he said.

"That's a disaster!"

"Get us out of here!"

"I don't know where you are!" I looked at Sasha. She was laughing.

"Is Sasha there with you?" he said.

"She is," I said. "We're having a lovely time."

"You bastards!"

We watched from the battlements as they floundered around the maze, and after about ten minutes, they'd reached a particular dog-leg that I recognised, and I was able to guide them in. I could hear them cooing as they came up the stairs.

We all sat on the swing, me at the end with Sasha next to me and Paris in the middle. It was a snug fit, a tight fit. It was a delightful fit. I was on the end, hip to hip with Sasha, our arms and our shoulders pressed tight together. And our thighs. I remember the heat from Sasha's thigh which was squeezed, firmly, solidly, next to mine, and the bottle of Bailey's being passed back and forth, while I shared my cut-crystal glass with the girls.

Paris went off downstairs to fetch a bottle of whisky, so there was suddenly space for Sasha to move. But she did not move. She stayed just where she was, shoulder to shoulder, her thigh still dead-set against mine; I found it incredibly erotic, much more so than playing footsy under the table. When you're playing footsy, when you've slipped off your shoes and are rubbing your foot against their ankle, there is a declaration of intent. Without words, you are saying, "Shall we kiss, and, if it goes well, perhaps do something more."

But when you're involuntarily squeezed together on, say, a garden swing, then everything is still hanging in the air. You do happen to be pressing your hot thighs next to each other, and you happen to be remarkably close to their erogenous zones - but nevertheless, it is just happenstance. There has been no declaration of intent. You might be getting quite turned on by just sitting next to this person, but still…

you don't know, quite, if the other person is as turned on as you; is up for it; or whether they're just thinking it's pleasant enough, but are still way, way off wanting to kiss you. And - to my mind - that is what makes it all the more exciting. Along with the body-heat and the carnal desire, there is this great unspoken tension in the air.

And just what, precisely, had Sasha been alluding to when she said that there were other things that she liked to do with her boyfriends apart from make love?

I wish I had a photo of the five of us on that garden swing, a moment in time when at least three of us were on the very point of falling hopelessly, deliriously in love. But I do not have that photo, and instead all I have are my memories - my memories of the warmth of Sasha's leg, and of the taste of the Bailey's as I sipped from her glass, and the look of sheer, naked enjoyment on her face as she looked at me, her face not nine inches from my own.

It was all but dawn when, laughing, we went off to visit the three-seater privy. The girls went in first, without a torch. We could hear them giggling inside.

We'd finished the Bailey's and Paris was drinking neat whisky from the bottle.

"I'm crazy about her," Paris said.

"Well good luck," I said.

"She prefers you," he said.

"Me?" I said. "That's only because I'm not interested."

"No - you're fun. She likes you." He was scanning my face. Though he had drunk a lot, I sensed nerves.

"I've already got a girlfriend," I said.

"You've got a girlfriend?" He broke into this beaming smile.

"Her name's Mousie," I said. "She lives in Winchester. I'll be seeing her next weekend."

"You sly dog!" Paris said. He grabbed me in a head-lock. He was ridiculously pleased.

"You should go for it," I said, in my Machiavellian way. "You'll make a lovely couple."

"Thanks," he said. "Thanks a lot!"

Paris was, or so I thought, playing completely into my hands. He'd be blundering straight in, just like all the others, and meanwhile, I would be patiently biding my time, sticking to the strategy, until, one day, eventually, I would make my move.

But, looking back, I think it was a mistake. No – I *know* it was a mistake. Far from Paris playing into my hands, I think I'd just played into his.

CHAPTER 7

I try to see the best in people.

I try to ignore the parts of people's personalities that grate; I like to think that I seek out their good points, and once I have found those good points, then those are the parts that I try to cultivate.

But there's no real way of getting round it.

Sasha's mother was a nightmare.

Or to be fair: Penny was always a pretty good nightmare to *me*.

Of course she must have had her good points - Sasha, for a start. Penny must have done a reasonably good job in bringing her up, though the fact was that she'd had - or as far as I could tell - very little to do with Sasha's upbringing. They'd lived out in Argentina, where Sasha's father had an estate with cattle and horses, and sunshine, and the freedom of the pampas.

But Penny had found herself a lover, a younger man, who might have been richer and who might not, and they'd run off together to America - leaving a three-year-old Sasha to be brought up by her father. Sasha would see her mother once or twice a year, and by the time Penny had split with her American, Sasha was sixteen and full-fledged, and though Penny did her best to make amends, the relationship never seemed to have a heart. Penny strove to do the things that a mother should do with her daughter, but it was all much too late.

Sasha had been brought up with horses since before she could walk. She'd been a useful polo player, but had known from quite a young age that she never wanted to be a professional. But she liked the horses, and she liked the polo world, and when you add into the mix that her grandfather - Penny's father John - lived in Cirencester, then it was quite natural for her to move to the Cotswolds when she wanted to get her first leg up in the polo world. She had looks and diplomacy, and she knew as much about polo-ponies as the actual professionals. Her father died and soon afterwards she was managing a polo team. I'd already seen the *Patron*. He was the fat man in the white suit who'd whisked her away at the party in the stable-block.

When Sasha had come to Cirencester three years earlier, it had been natural for her mother to come too. Penny was between boyfriends at the time, and if she moved to Cirencester, she could live with her father and help look after him. She did her best, I think, to try and forge some sort of relationship with Sasha, but it never really worked; Sasha was the woman who did not forgive. But though she never forgave her mother, Sasha could also never get her mother out of her life. Cirencester is a small town where everyone knows everyone, and so though Sasha might try to lead her own life, her mother would always be lingering somewhere in the background.

It was a problem.

It was a problem for Sasha.

And it was also a big problem for me.

The first time I really met Penny was on a picnic in Cirencester Park. Sasha's team - Jokers Wild - was playing that day and Sasha had laid on a lavish lunch for the players and for the fat *Patron*. It was called a picnic - but it was nothing like any picnic that I had ever been on before. Sasha had driven up to the Park in the team Land Rover, towing behind it not a horse-truck, but a trailer, which was filled up with chairs and rugs, and enough food and drink to have fed a platoon. A small marquee had already been set up nearby to the polo-ground, where Paris and I had shared a bottle of Taittinger before the first chukka.

The polo itself was interesting enough, though I can take it or leave it. The Jokers Wild team comprised three South American players who were all brilliant and the fat sweating *Patron* who was pathetic. Their two styles of play were a study. On the one hand, I watched the Jokers Wild striker catch the ball with his stick, and then, while riding at a full gallop, he was bouncing the ball up and down on his polo-stick. The ball never once touched the ground. He gave the ball one last nonchalant flick into the air and then hammered it over the goal-line. "Why didn't he dribble the ball on the ground like everyone else?" I asked Paris.

"No," Paris replied. "The ground's bumpy. You've got much more control if you can keep it up with your stick."

"But it's also for swank."

"Everything in polo is for swank."

So that was the professionals, with their snazzy Mercedes sports cars, and their endless queue of swooning women. And then there was the team *Patron*, red-faced, aimlessly careering round the polo field and for ever screaming at his teammates to give him the ball. Occasionally, to keep him happy, the professionals would flick him the ball. The striker teed it up really nicely for him. The ball was right in front of the opponents' goal. It was not moving.

The fat *Patron* canters up. He takes a thundering swipe at the ball - the *motionless* ball - and completely misses it.

Such is polo.

After the second chukka, Paris and I joined all the other spectators on the polo pitch, where it was seen as good form to help stamp down all the divots. Hands deep in our pockets, we stepped over the green planks at the touchline and kicked over a few divots before we got bored and went off to the Jokers Wild marquee.

Paris's friend Dangerous was already there, drinking beer. He was talking to a woman, though I couldn't see her face. He'd said something funny, and she'd touched his arm and left her hand there.

We got some Champagne and I went over to join Dangerous.

The woman's eyes lighted on me. She was smoking a cigarette. She blew the cigarette smoke out of the side of her mouth. It was a smoker's mouth. All around her lips were thin vertical lines; as for the skin on her face, it looked thin and shiny, liked a piece of stretched parchment. She had long blonde hair, from the bottle, I presume, which fell about the fur trim of her black leather coat; and very long teeth too, I also remember those. Though we were at a polo match, she was wearing high heels; she was taller than me.

She appraised me, taking me in from head to toe, and back again to my face; it may just be my fancy, but her eyes lingered at my crotch.

"And who are you?" she said, with this husky smoker's voice that might once have been alluring, but now just sound gravelly. By now, she had one hand on her hip. She cocked an eyebrow at me.

I looked at her, very level. "I'm Kim," I smiled.

"Penny," she said, and we shook hands. "Sasha's mother."

"How are you?" I said. I was slightly surprised. During three, four months of swimming with Sasha, and during all the other times that we had seen each other, Sasha had talked about her grandfather John, and her polo, and her swimming. But she had never once mentioned her mother.

"And where have you sprung from?" she said, and as she spoke, she gave my bicep a squeeze.

"I live just by the park," I said. "I live in a treehouse."

"You're living in Cla's treehouse!" she said. "I've seen the smoke coming out of the chimney. I didn't realise anyone was actually living there."

"I'm the woodlander," I said.

"I've often wondered what it's like in that treehouse," she said, and rather than answering her, I let the question hang in the air. I looked at Dangerous and Dangerous looked at me, and at about the same moment, we both of us realised that Penny would have happily slept with either or both of us, and she did not particularly mind which.

Sasha came in later, though she did not have much time for us loafers as she was fussing around her principals. She did not drink. She never drank when she was on the job, but she came over briefly to say hello.

"I've just met your mother," I said. I kept my voice completely neutral. "She seemed very nice."

"Yes," Sasha said, her eyes ranging over my face for any trace of nuance. "Yes."

Paris came over. He kissed the Sasha on the cheek and proprietarily wrapped his arm around her waist. I had not realised that his courtship was going so well. It had been two months since the supper in the tree-house, and unless I was very much mistaken, it looked like they were now dating.

Though Sasha was not nearly ready for any Public Displays of Affection, or PDAs as they were called. She extricated herself from his arm. "Not here," she said, and then when he made to hold her hand, she dropped that too.

I don't know whether this unreciprocated affection was for the polo-players' benefit. Thought it might, perhaps, have been for mine. She may have been talking to Paris. But her eyes did not leave mine.

"See you later," she said, and I turned away, and I saw that Penny was looking at me, sizing me up, like a cat inspecting a caged canary.

After that, there were odd little skirmishes with Penny, which did not perhaps mean anything in themselves; but combined, they had the distinct whiff of enemy action.

I'd seen her at a Christmas party in Cirencester. Penny had got hold of some mistletoe and was demanding kisses from every man in the room. "A Christmas kiss?" she asked me as she held the mistletoe above her head. She was wearing a short red dress and a Santa hat. "Of course," I'd said, and bent to kiss her on the cheek. She moved her head so that we were lip to lip. Her lips were cold and wet and her mouth was partially open; it was like kissing a damp sponge.

Maybe she did that with every guy in the room.

Maybe.

But the first time that I realised that, actually, it was personal was one night when I was alone in the treehouse. I was doing what I generally did in my tree-house when there was nothing going on: I was reading by the fire. How I miss the simplicity of that life. There was no television, no telephone, no post; it seems like it was from another era.

Since cooking was not an easy thing to do in the treehouse, I would generally make up a stew at the weekend. I'd throw in meat and vegetables and a bottle of wine, and would just leave it gently simmering on the stove. I'd occasionally top it up with anything that

I'd happen to chance upon in Waitrose. At night I'd have a plate of the stew and a haunch of bread; it seemed to taste best at midnight after an evening in the pub.

It was about 10 o'clock. I had a bottle of red wine open and I was drinking from one of Sir Anthony's special glasses; even when I am drinking alone, I still love cut crystal.

I heard a creak from the stairs. It was the seventh step up. I wondered who could be coming to visit me at this time; I thought it might be Paris.

I got up and as I got up, there was a knock at the door. I couldn't see who was standing outside. I opened the door.

Penny was on the doorstep. "Hello," I said.

She looked like she'd been crying. Her mascara was streaked down her cheeks and her hair was a mess.

Without a word, she came to me, threw her arms around me, and burst into tears.

I did what any other guy would have done. I held her close. I didn't know what had happened to her, but obviously it had been bad; if she needed a hug, then that was fine by me.

The crying got worse. It had started quite softly, but very soon it had turned into these great racking sobs. She was clinging to me. Her whole body was quivering. I could smell her hair. It smelled of cigarette smoke.

I stroked her back, trying to calm her down, and after a while she did calm down, and the crying stopped. I continued to soothe her, one arm around her waist and the other stroking her back. I could feel her bra-strap through her jumper.

I didn't know what to do.

Should I disengage and offer her some tea or some wine?

Or should I just continue to hold her until she was done with holding me. I didn't know.

It wasn't awkward or uncomfortable. But I was just wondering what was the best thing to do.

She started to kiss me. I didn't realise what she was doing at first. I thought it was just her wet cheek, but after two, three kisses, on my neck, I realised that it was not her cheek but her mouth. She was kissing up my neck and her lips were close to my ear when I let go of her. She was still holding onto me, still trying to kiss me. I gently extricated myself from her arms and took a step backwards.

"Would you like a cup of tea?" I asked.

"I'd rather have whisky," she said.

"I've only got wine," I said.

"Wine'll be fine."

We sat on the two chairs in front of the fire and I stupidly gave her one of the cut-crystal glasses. You should never give decent glasses to people who are drunk.

She was leaning towards the fire, elbows on knees, the glass of wine clasped in front of her. We'd still hardly said a word. I was waiting to hear what she had to say.

For a while she'd been staring at the fire, but then she turned to me and she smiled, and I suppose she was trying to look nice and pleasant, but in that moment, in the flickering firelight, she looked quite mad. She smoothed back her hair, but so vigorously that it looked as if her head was being tugged from behind.

"What do you think of me?" she said.

I looked at her over the rim of my wine-glass. "I think you're very unhappy."

She wiped her nose with the back of her hand. "What do you think of my looks?"

Now that was a more difficult question. I was aware that Penny would not need much encouragement to start trying to kiss me again. How could I diplomatically answer the question?

I didn't even try. Sometimes, often-times, it's best not even to answer a question. There's no law saying that you have to answer every question that's put to you. The politicians know that, but the general public do not.

"What are you doing here?" I said. "Why did you come here?"

"Because I like you," she said. "I like you a lot."

I groaned. I put my wine-glass on the table and massaged my forehead with my finger-tips.

What the hell was I going to say now? Should I ask her to leave? Tell her that her feelings were not in any way reciprocated?

"I don't know what you want. But whatever it is, I'm not going to be able to help."

"Once, when I was beautiful, you'd have been all over me," she said. She looked into her wine-glass. "I've had so many men tell me they love me. And now -" She looked up at me through the fringe of her blonde hair, sort of coy. "And now nobody says they love me."

This was way, way too deep for me. I'd met this woman a few times, but we had never done anything more than exchange pleasantries. I'd tried to be agreeable; she was Sasha's mother.

I didn't particularly like her; I didn't particularly *dislike* her. I wondered where this was all heading.

I remembered the way she'd been kissing my neck.

Would she do something else like that? Should I ask her to leave now? But that would not have been a kind thing to do. And what difference did it make that I hardly knew her. Didn't I owe it to Penny, just as another human being on this lonely little planet of ours, to offer what solace I could? Only a churl would ask her to leave. Besides - I was bigger than her, stronger than her; it wasn't as if I wasn't fully capable of looking after myself.

"I think you should talk to Sasha," I said.

"Sasha!" she shrieked. "She can't stand me!"

Penny drained her wine-glass and grabbed the bottle from the table and filled the glass. Her hand was shaking. The wine slopped onto the carpet.

"She's pretty isn't she?" Penny said. She put the wine-glass to her lips and the glass rattled against her teeth. "I was like that once - prettier even. I was a natural blonde. Not that you'd know that now, though."

She did that thing again with her hair, stroking it back and then holding onto it. It looked like somebody had grabbed hold of her hair and given it a sharp jerk backwards.

"Why did you come here?" I said. "I can't help you. I can't do anything for you."

"I don't want you to help me," she said. "But we can talk - can't we?"

And when Penny put it like that, it all sounded so reasonable. Of course we could talk; with someone who was so deeply unhappy, it seemed like my moral duty to talk to her.

"Let's talk," I said.

"If you were going to kill yourself, how would you do it?"

I remember scratching the back of my head. I grimaced. Although I'd said that I was happy to talk, I did not want to listen to this. I was desperate for her to leave.

"Doesn't riding make you happy?" I said.

"Do you know how I'd do it?" she said. "I used to think that I'd do it with pills, so that my beautiful face would still be beautiful. Not much point in trying to save my looks now is there?" She laughed and started coughing. "For a time, I thought I'd get a car, a Ferrari, or perhaps a motorbike, and then straight off the cliff into the Clifton Gorge. Can you imagine those six seconds of flying through the air - the freedom? But now - do you know what I'd do? I'd -"

"Penny - listen to me," I said. I was horrified at what she was telling me. "You really, really need to call the Samaritans."

"I don't need the Samaritans," she said. The glass slipped out of her hand and smashed on the floor. It was dead, but the glass still sparkled in the firelight. What a waste.

Penny didn't even realise that she'd dropped the glass. She was on her knees now and was coming towards me. "I fancy you, Kim," she said, and she was smiling at me, and perhaps she thought that she looked coquettish and alluring, but it left me cold. "And I think you fancy me too."

She was kneeling now in front of me. She rested her head on my crotch and her arms stretched up around my waist. "Don't you?" she said.

"No - I do not," I said, my voice absolute ice. "I'm sorry that you think I do, but no. I do not."

Penny was moving her head back and forth, rubbing her cheek against the crotch of my jeans. For a moment, I watched.

She looked up at me and licked her lips. She placed a hand on my fly-buttons. "I know what you want," she said.

I stood up. She was clinging to my legs. "No you don't," I said. I took a step backwards so that she was no longer touching me. She was still on her knees. She looked pitiful. "Come on. We're getting you home now."

She didn't want to go, but eventually I got her out of the tree-house. She was holding my arm as I led her out of the garden, giggling to herself. She made to fall onto the grass and I think she was trying to drag me down on top of her, but I held her up. I got her out onto the street and over to the cab rank by the church. I put her in the back and sat in the front with the driver, and when we got to her home, I let her in.

I wondered whether to go in with her, but I did not want to. She kept on cooing at me to join her for a night-cap, but I just waved and said goodnight. I walked back home. I could not get to sleep for some time. Was there anything else that I could have done? Perhaps *should* have done? I didn't know. I'd done the best I could.

Should *I* have called the police or the Samaritans? Or was I merely starting at shadows?

I told Sasha about it the next day after we'd had our showers at the pool. I told her about it - though I did not tell her all about it. I said that her mother had come round and that she'd talked about suicide. But I did not mention that her mother had been hitting on me. I don't know why. I think I found the whole episode so unbelievably tawdry that I just didn't even want to think about it; besides, what girl wants to hear that her mother has been behaving like a drunken slut?

So I did not mention it.

And it might have been a mistake.

After I'd said my piece, Sasha was strangely silent. What do you do if your mother's been talking about suicide?

She sat down on one of the chairs by the reception desk.

"I'm sorry," I said.

She sat with her arms plunged down between her thighs. At first I thought she was just staring at the floor, but she was crying.

I sat next to her and gave her my handkerchief. She mopped her cheeks, and entwined the handkerchief through her fingers. "I don't know what to do," she said.

"Call up the Samaritans?" I said.

"Yes," she said. She blew her nose. "I might do that."

She did call the Samaritans. They did what they could.

CHAPTER 8

Sasha taught me to swim. After our night in the maze, she took me in hand the next Monday when I was at the pool.

"You're going to learn to swim properly," she said. "You're going to swim the crawl."

"My breathing sucks," I said. "My legs always start sinking."

"So what's your point?" she said. She was standing next to me in the pool: those shoulders, those long legs, that black costume that showed off her wonderful swimmer's curves. Over the weeks, her looks had just seemed to get better and better.

"I'm going to teach you about your inner buoy," she said.

"My inner boy?" I said.

"No - not that sort of buoy," she said, flicking water at me. "Your buoyancy. Try this."

She pushed off from the bottom of the pool, arms outstretched, head down, legs straight behind her. She was a long slim torpedo, her whole body submerged. Her legs - her fabulous legs - didn't sink. I was amazed. My legs always started to sink unless they were thrashing through the water.

Sasha repeated the manoeuvre, pushing off from the bottom and then gliding with her hands outstretched. I could not help but look at her legs and her back and, well, just about everything, packaged in this sensuous skin-tight suit, and with the water rippling over her brown skin; she was stupendous.

"Now you try," she said. "Your head is fully immersed. It's the heaviest part of your body so it's going to help counter-balance your feet. You have to adjust your torso until you can float without moving."

I gave it a go, pushing off hard, head down, arms outstretched, and while I was moving my feet stayed up, but as soon as I stopped, my feet sank.

Sasha wrinkled her nose. "And again," she said. "You're looking to stay buoyant."

"My inner buoy."

"Your inner boy," she said. "It's difficult to explain, but it's there. You push down with your lungs and tilt up your bum."

She did the move again and though I should have been studying her technique, I found that I was marvelling at her body.

I tried it again, tweaking and twisting my torso, until suddenly I had it – I was floating, properly floating. When I was not moving, my legs did not sink.

"You've got it!" she said, delighted, and after that I was on my way, and in under six weeks she had taught me to swim, really swim, head deep and hands gliding easily, effortlessly, through the water, and eventually after a while, you know you've got it, because when you swim, you leave no wake – you have become slippery in the water, like a shark, and your hands cleave into the water without a single splash and your feet beat to the rhythm of your arms, fluttering behind you, but never once leaving the water. And then, when you can start to swim a long way, swimming becomes this beautiful meditation, as you focus not on the swimming itself, but on the line beneath your eyes, and although you are aware of all the movements that you should be doing, and that your hands should be entering the water like a knife, and that your feet should never break the surface, and that your arms should carve underneath in a perfect S shape, these habits have become so grooved that you no longer need even to think of them. You have become one with the water; you are a swimmer.

Sasha was as pleased by my swimming progress as by anything else I'd ever seen.

A few months later, we were over at dinner with Paris. Although he was the richest man by far in Cirencester, Paris lived in a relatively modest little Georgian townhouse in the middle of the town.

He lived with Dangerous. Sasha never much liked Dangerous. I did not mind him as he was always a magnet for the weird and the extraordinary - and I like that. I like that a lot. Even though people like Dangerous behave like shysters, I find that I am drawn to the madness. I enjoy seeing people doing things that they're not supposed to do.

It was the first time that I'd ever seen Sasha lose her temper.
Paris and Sasha had been cooking together in the kitchen. They were cooking meat balls in a tomato sauce, and Paris had just put some pasta onto the boil. Sasha was wearing black jeans and a sloppy loose jumper; just her usual terrific self.

The kitchen was much cleaner than your usual student kitchen; I think that Paris had a cleaner around five days a week. Everything was spotless, with pans and knives glittering on the rack above the sink.

It was interesting to see them as a couple. At least I think that Paris and Sasha were a couple, though I'm not quite sure. They certainly didn't behave like a couple.

There was none of that easy lightness that comes when a relationship is going well. She also did not like to be touched by him. At first I thought it might have been just her general attitude: that she did not like these damnable Public Displays of Affection. But after a while, I thought that, possibly, it was down to me.

"So how's it going with you and Mousie?" Paris asked.

"Mousie?" Sasha said. "Who's Mousie?"

"Mousie's his girlfriend."

"You kept her quiet, didn't you?" Sasha said. "The heart on your friendship ring has always been open." And she cocked her head and there was this sense that she was looking at me through different eyes; do we see people differently if we think they're single or spoken for?

"You never asked," I said.

"So how is Mousie?" Paris asked again.

"Mousie's fine."

"What's she like?" Sasha asked me. I smiled and I was not going to answer and in the end Paris spoke up.

"She's very nice," he said diplomatically.

"That's the problem," I said. "I'm not really interested in nice anymore."

"So why do you still date her?" Sasha said.

"Now that," I said. "That is the question to which I do not have an answer."

"Sounds like a pretty crap reason for dating someone."

"You'd be surprised," I said. "Some people are still asking themselves that after fifty years of marriage."

I told them about the golden wedding couples who I'd interviewed. In that year in Cirencester, there were a whole host of golden wedding couples who had got married at the start of World War II. I had interviewed a number of them and, as the photographer waited patiently, would be told a little of their lives. When they were done, I would always ask them to tell me "the secret of their success" - as if there were some magic ingredient which bound couples together for fifty years.

That week, I had asked a couple for "the secret" - and there had been this long drawn-out pause, as these two pensioners had weighed up their lifetime together. I had kept quiet, pen poised over my notebook as I waited for the answer. "I don't know," the woman said, as she remembered years of not necessarily misery, but just numbing stultification. "I don't know why we stayed together." And the man, sitting there in his armchair with his stick by his side: he looks glassily out of the window and he wishes that he were anywhere else on earth but here in this room with this woman.

And I don't know either. Not that I'm even close to notching up fifty years with Elise, but after interviewing score upon score of Golden Wedding couples over the years, I have realised that the happiest couples had one thing in common: they had a laugh. They did not take themselves seriously; they did not take anything too seriously. They had this easy-going intimacy, so that even when there was a reverse, they would still find some small thing to laugh about.

Dangerous loafed into the kitchen. He greeted me in his usual way with a punch to the gut. I'd expected it and I had already braced myself. He went over to the meat-balls. He put his head down and inhaled, then scooping up a meatball with the wooden spoon, and putting the spoon complete into his mouth. He ate the meatball and returned the spoon to the pan. There was sauce all round his mouth. "It needs something," he said. He pulled a bottle of vodka from the freezer. "Some oregano?"

I happened to be watching Dangerous. I saw this look pass between Dangerous and Paris; I did not know what it meant. Paris just shrugged, like the easy-going guy that he was, and Dangerous reached for the jar of dried oregano. He took out a large handful and sprinkled it onto the meatballs.

It was not oregano.

We started the meal with roll mop herring and shots of vodka. Vodka shots are a useful accelerant. Rather than just getting steadily more tipsy, as you do with red wine, you go from sober to sloshed in about ten minutes flat.

Sasha had just a single shot. I had three shots, as did Paris. Dangerous had five.

We moved onto the meatballs.

After the pungent taste of the herring, it took me some while to place the taste.

We were sat at the table in the TV room next to the kitchen. Candles and wine and Dangerous holding court as he told us about his new way of tackling the roundabout just outside the college. It was a large hummocky roundabout, with little hillocks in the middle; Dangerous had started going straight over the middle of the roundabout. It was a funny story – and we thought it hilarious. We laughed, and we continued to laugh, and we were still laughing five minutes later, and that was when I realised what was really in the oregano.

"Where do you get this dope from?" I asked.

"I grow it," Dangerous said. He was sucking up a strand of *tagliatelle*. The sauce splattered over his face. He did not notice. He had the most disgusting table manners of anyone I've ever met. "I grow it on the roof."

Sasha had not been paying much attention. She suddenly zeroed in on the conversation.

"You've put dope in this?" she said. The smile fell from her face. It was amazing how quickly she turned.

The others just laughed their reply.

"You put dope in this without telling me?" By now she was absolutely furious. She turned on Paris. "You knew!" she said. "You knew!"

"No!" Paris said, and burst into a fit of the giggles. He tried to cuddle her, but she was having none of it. She was working herself up into a good old-fashioned Latino rage. I said nothing and I did nothing. I was dispassionately watching her like the reporter that I am. Her mouth was snapping up and down. Her rage was directed not at Dangerous, but at Paris.

"You knew!" she said. "You knew - I saw it."

"Sasha," Paris pleaded. "What does it matter? It's fine."

Dangerous was a picture in himself. He wasn't even remotely bothered by the row that he had helped to engineer. He'd already cleaned his plate and while Sasha was engrossed with Paris, he stretched over, took her plate, and stolidly started to plough his way through her meatballs.

"Get off me!" she said, batting away Paris's hands. "You know I hate drugs. I've had enough of it with my parents."

"I'm sorry."

"You're sorry?" she said. "You just don't get it!" It might have been the booze, and it might have been the hash, but she was working herself up into the most towering rage - I could see it growing and growing, like a small wisp of smoke that transforms into a forest inferno.

Sasha stood up. Dangerous looked up briefly at her and continued to eat. Paris was plucking at her arm. I could have told him that he was wasting his time.

She picked up the pan, and for a moment I thought that she was going to pour the contents over Paris's head, but she did not.

Paris had stood up by now. "I'm sorry," he said, but there was nothing that he could say that would soften the situation.

The pan was put down. She went to the door and Paris followed. "I'm done," she said - and just like that, she left. And Dangerous laughed and I drank red wine, because I do not actually like to get stoned, and Paris eventually returned and got steadily pissed - and I suppose I just assumed that it was a mere lover's tiff, and that soon enough they'd be back together again.

But they did not get back together again.

It may have been just the last straw but anyway, for whatever reason, she called time on the relationship. Paris moped around for a while, but he'd have done better to have stayed low for a while; when you've dumped a lover, they always become more alluring if they've gone to ground.

But I could not *not* mention it to Sasha. I saw her a couple of days later at the swimming pool.

"I was sorry to hear about you and Paris," I said. I'd been waiting for her after her shower. She checked when she saw me; she'd not expected to see me.

"It's okay," she said simply.

"Paris is a great guy," I said. We walked out of the reception.

I remember her reply. "I'll be fine." And without a wave or a glance, she was gone.

CHAPTER 9

My editor was another person who took against me during my time in Cirencester. I suppose it was my fault. Not that I'd change any of it though for, above all else, I am a romantic.

I'd been sent off to Cirencester Magistrates Court. It was about the third or fourth time that I'd been there and, compared to the council meetings, this was high drama.

The bigger cases were, of course, sent up to the Crown Court in Gloucester, but every so often there might be something juicy - drunk-drivers and shoplifters and the occasional burglar. Up they would come, some sheepish, some brazen, and there I would be over on the press-bench at the side, scribbling and scribbling into my notebook. The court as I remember was white, very high-ceilinged, no windows and perhaps a few dull skylights. I remember the smell. The courtroom had this stale muzziness, masked by a heavy layer of disinfectant; it needed fresh air, all the windows and doors to be left open for a week to get rid of the terminal fustiness. There were a few benches for the lawyers and the relatives and, at the front, three comfortable red-leather chairs for the magistrates.

I was the only reporter in the room. For some reason, there was nobody there from the Echo or the Evening Advertiser. Not that they were missing very much. It was just the usual ho-hum stuff of people on remand and people on bail and a few brawlers and a few drunkards. We were about halfway through the morning session when there was a sense of a ripple going through the court-room. I couldn't place it, didn't know what had happened; but something *had* definitely happened.

A woman came into the dock. She was expensively but soberly dressed. I remember blonde hair and make-up and eyes that smouldered; she looked good. She could have been anything from twenty-five to thirty-five. I looked up her details on the court-list. She was forty-three She lived in a Manor House in one of the villages outside Cirencester; obviously quite well-heeled.

She came in, looked around the courtroom, and then very deliberately she looked over at me; with my notepad and pen and the court list in front of me, it was quite clear that I was a journalist.

There wasn't much to get excited about. The woman, Anne Jardine, had pleaded guilty to careless driving. According to the prosecutor, she'd been driving along at night and had tried to overtake another vehicle; the car coming in the other direction, a police car, had had to take evasive action. Anne's sporty little TVR had ended up in a field, and her male passenger had had slight whiplash.

Anne's solicitor laid out the mitigating circumstances. Her client was profusely apologetic; total aberration; most uncharacteristic display of carelessness; clean licence; won't ever happen again.

I have heard the same arguments trotted out a hundred times over; I could spout them in my sleep.

Anne was given a fine and sent on her way, though as she left the dock she looked at me again. And that should have been that. It wasn't much of a story – might have made ten paragraphs at the bottom of page five. Not that I cared much either way; my job was to write up every case that came up in court that morning.

The court was adjourned for lunchtime. Before I left, I went over to the clerk who was sifting through her files. "Who was that woman who was done for careless driving?" I said. "Was she a somebody?"

The clerk looked up, smiled at me. "She's married to a somebody," she said. "Her husband is very rich. He's big with one of the hunts."

"Thank you," I said. An interesting little nugget to include in my story.

I thought I'd pop over to the Slug and Lettuce for lunch; there's only so many Waitrose sandwiches you can eat in a week.

As I left the court, I had this prickling sense that I was being watched. I don't need to look for reasons. I always listen to my intuition. I stopped and looked around. There were a few cars parked up in the car park, but nothing that stuck out. I looked and looked again and then went on my way. The pub was comfortably full. I ordered a pie and a pint, and found a corner table to read the day's papers.

I had six papers, five tabloids and a broadsheet. I scanned the front pages and I sipped my first sip, and felt this warm, luxurious glow of a pint well earned.

I realised that there was someone standing by the table. It was Anne - the woman from the courtroom. I placed my pint on the table and looked at her.

"Excuse me," she said. She looked edgy. "May I talk to you?"

"Be my guest," I said. I folded up the papers and put them onto the floor. "Can I get you a drink?"

"No, thank you."

"Let me get you something. What can I get you?"

"A… A small glass of white wine."

As I stood at the bar waiting for the wine, I wondered what she was doing in the pub. Coincidence? No - she'd followed me there.

So why did she want to talk to me? Some story to tell me, or… something else?

I took the Chardonnay back to the table and sat down. She had her hands in her lap and she was studying the rings on her fingers. They were costly rings, a diamond on one hand and a cherry-sized ruby on the other. It was not a position I'd been in before. I took another sip of beer and waited for her to speak.

She looked up at me. She was very tense. I could see the tendons in her neck. "You're on the Wilts and Glos Standard aren't you?" she said.

"I am." I returned my pint to the table.

"You saw me in court today."

"I did."

"It wasn't a very big story was it?"

"No - it wasn't."

She played with her wine glass, drank some wine, and then started fiddling again with the rings on her fingers. She was twirling the gems round and round on her fingers. I didn't move, didn't stretch for my pint; I was quite calm.

"I wondered…" she said. "I wondered if… you might find it in your heart not to file the story."

"I…" I trailed off. This was one of many things that trainee reporters are coached over. The pat response is to say that these editorial decisions are solely a matter for the editor. But I did not duck her question. "Why not?" I asked.

She paused again and had another sip of her wine. "Do you know who my husband is?"

"I hear he's big with the hunt."

"That's right. Vale of the White Horse. And…" She looked at me now. I saw that she had the most amazing grey eyes. "And he doesn't know about it."

"Right," I said. "And that's the way you'd like it to stay."

"Yes," she said. She spoke almost in a whisper. "Please."

I played for time. I reached for my pint, drank, and then set the glass back on its beer mat.

"He'd be humiliated," she said. Those beautiful grey eyes looking at me. "He gets so angry."

I tick-tocked it over in my mind. I couldn't make it out. The picture was still muzzy at the edges; there was something that didn't quite fit. Not that I minded playing the Patsy. More than anything else, I was intrigued.

"Okay," I said. "I won't file the story."

She looked at me, relief gushing through her face. "Oh, thank you."

"Just tell me one thing." I reached inside my jacket pocket and pulled out my note-pad. "What aren't you telling me?"

"What do you mean - what am I not telling you?"

"Just that." I tapped the edge of my note-pad with my fingertips. "What aren't you telling me?"

"I… I've told you everything. It would make things… very awkward with my husband."

A waitress brought over my pie. I made space on the table and said thank you, but I did not touch the pie. I just continued to look at Anne, the notepad loose in my hands. It is a very powerful thing to look somebody in the eye and to not say a word.

"I like my husband," she said, at length. "I don't want to hurt him. And I don't want a divorce."

And she sighed, and she finished the last of her wine, and she took the plunge. "But he can't give me everything that I need, so I also have a lover." She smiled, pleased, perhaps, that it was now out in the open. "He's a bit older than you. He's a painter. I love him. And on the day that I had that crash… I was supposed to be up in the Lake District with my sister. We were just driving back to Henry's studio - you know how it is. And then… I'm stuck in the field and Henry's got whiplash, and I'm wondering how on earth I'm going to explain it all to my husband. And, until today, I thought I was doing a pretty good job… And then you came along and blew the whole thing wide open."

"Sorry about that."

She smiled at that. "So there you have it - and now that really is a good story for you, Society Lady Caught With Toy Boy Lover -"

"More one for the Daily Mail."

"You'd make a lot of money."

I smiled at that and opened my note-book. I riffled through the pages of the spiral-bound book, found the pages that concerned Anne. I ripped them out and gave them to her.

"Thank you," said. She pocketed them and stood up. "You are very kind."

"Don't mention it," I said, standing up with her. "Well… good luck with Henry and good luck with your husband too."

She laughed. "What's your name?"

"I'm Kim," I said.

"Anne," she said and we shook hands and as she left the pub, I watched her all the way out.

And that should have been that - just another one of the hundreds of stories that occur every week that never quite make it into the paper. I did not care in the slightest that I had robbed the Standard of a story; I liked the woman and I wished her well. If I could help her out by not running her court story, then I wouldn't breathe a word of it.

Later that afternoon, I mooched back to the office. "Anything good?" George asked.

"Just the usual stuff."

I started to write up the dozen or so stories that I'd gleaned from the magistrates court. These stories are fairly formulaic and after a while you can really rattle through them.

The editor happened to wander in to the newsroom. It was early on in the week, so there was nothing much going on. He was wearing another of his tweedy three-piece suits. He was poking here, nosing there. Most of the reporters just carried on with what they were doing, but I looked up from my typewriter. "Hi Hugh - how's it going?" I said.

"All right," he said and he came to stand by my desk. He picked up the court-list and started flicking through it. I kept up an attitude of the most studious indifference - though I cannot act. I may have given off a tingle of wariness.

"What happened with this story?" Hugh said. "Anne Jardine - careless driving?"

I looked up from my typewriter, looked at the court-sheet. "Don't know," I said. "Didn't come up."

I thought that I had safely dead-balled the court case.

"Keep an eye out for it when it happens," Hugh said, dropping the court list on my desk and reaching into his waistcoat for his bottle of disinfectant. "She's a big wheel."

"Cool," I said, and returned to my story writing.

A few weeks afterwards, there was a small party in the Standard offices to celebrate the opening of our new newsroom. It was much lighter, much airier than our smoky old newsroom that looked out onto Dyer Street. And we were also introduced for the first time to this new high-tech gadget: a computer. You may have heard of it. In a stroke, all our typewriters, our blacks and our reams of green paper were consigned to the rubbish skip.

Heaven knows why, but the great and the good of Cirencester were invited along to the party - Mayors and vicars and council chairman and other such movers and shakers as occasionally appeared in the pages of the Wilts and Glos. There was a lot of wine, and the reporters drifted round the new newsroom, mingling with plates of cocktail sausages - and there, of course, was Anne Jardine.

"Hello Anne," I said, and she looked at me and she smiled and kissed me on the cheek.

"I hoped I'd see you here," she said.

"Have a sausage?"

"No, thank you." She smiled again - those beautiful grey eyes hit me square in the face. How is it that a person's eyes can do that? I have no idea, but I know they can.

"So… How's life?" I asked. "How's the husband, how's…"

"The husband who's standing just behind you," she said. "Thanks to you, they are all very well. Thank you for asking." She smiled, rather demurely for her.

I happened to look up and I caught the eye of the editor, and that in itself was not fatal, but what it did was jog his memory - so that the next day when he came into the newsroom, he started badgering George about Anne Jardine's court case.

George knew nothing about it, but rather than letting the thing go, he dutifully called up the magistrates office, who told him that the court case had already happened four weeks earlier. Hugh went into George's office. My ears were flapping like mad as I tried to earwig the conversation.

Then and there I should have left the office.

But I did not.

Hugh sidled up to my desk. "Kim," he said. "I didn't know that you know Anne Jardine."

"I met her at a party."

"And know her quite well too, I see. You're on kissing terms."

"I like to be on kissing terms with most of the women I know."

"Be that as it may." He'd stuck his thumbs into his waistcoat pockets, standing with his legs planted square in front of me like some country squire. "A while back, I asked you if her case had come up in court -"

"I remember," I said. Though wave after wave of alarm was flushing up the back of my neck, I was trying to stay resolutely indifferent.

"And now I find that not only has the case already occurred, but it occurred on the day that you were in court."

"Has it?" I tried to sound concerned. "On the day I was in court?"

"Yes - on the day you were in court…"

He stood there giving me the silent treatment.

"Oh?" I said. "I don't remember it."

"She was up on the day you were representing this paper at the Cirencester Magistrates Court."

"Ahh." I scratched at my cheek, wondering what to say. "I remember I was very sick that day. So if it happened… it must have happened while I was in the toilets -"

"You expect me to believe that?"

I shrugged and looked him in the eye. "Well that's what happened," I said. "I was in the toilets."

"Poppycock!" he said.

"I'm sorry I missed it," I said. "Can't we write it up now?"

"No we cannot - as you very well know," he said. "Court stories have to be contemporaneous."

"Oh. Well I'm sorry."

He sniffed and stalked out of the newsroom and Rudi rolled his eyes at me. I'd acquitted myself as well as I could, but on a small paper like the Wilts and Glos, making an enemy of the editor was always going to be a bad move.

★

After six months in Cirencester, I had my first lucky break with Sasha: for two months, I was sent away to journalism college in Harlow.

I did not have any inkling at the time, but for the first time I was allowed to play to my strengths. That is what Grand Strategy is about: identify your strengths and then play to them.

My paper was sending me to Harlow Tertiary College, where I joined twenty other graduate trainees from local papers all over

England. We learned about councils and courts and libel; and we learned how to interview; and we learned a little of how to write features and news stories; above all else, we brushed up our shorthand. At the time, my shorthand was at eighty words per minute, and I had to get it up to one hundred wpm to become a qualified journalist.

I failed the shorthand exam over and over again. Although I could easily write at a hundred and ten wpm, under stress, my fingers would start to shake and my hand would wander over the page.

It's amazing how your body reacts when under pressure.

I was on my second day in the concrete city that is Harlow New Town when I decided to send Sasha a postcard. I didn't know her address, so I sent it care of the swimming pool. "Hope you're not missing me too much," I wrote. "You will be delighted to hear that, despite the hot showers that are available in Nanny Rafferty's bed and breakfast, I am still addicted to my 7am swims."

I didn't necessarily expect her to reply, but I did scrawl Nanny Rafferty's address at the top of the card - and, not two days later, I got a letter in return.

I studied the writing before I opened the envelope. Quite a big round hand, I saw, in blue-black ink; well-educated, I'd guess; an unusual, interesting hand. There was no name on the reverse, but I knew that it had to be her. Nobody else - and certainly not Mousie - had my address.

"Dear Kim," she wrote. "I do not miss you in the slightest - because as of three days ago, I now have the entire pool to myself. It is bliss. I do my lengths and dream that I am a millionairess with my own private pool. There is no-one slapping the water in the lane next to me. And there is no-one here to remind me that he lives in a tree-house with his own private maze - and that helps, a little, because otherwise I would spend my days seething with envy."

Now, know this: I have a number of limitations. When I was up against those wealthy boys from Cirencester, I had often felt a little out of my depth. They all seemed to be wilder than me and richer than me - and, without doubt, better looking than me.

But I did have one small trump card up my sleeve - and with Sasha, I was now going to start playing this same card over and over again: I would woo her with my words. I would write and I would write, and although we were not dating, it would make no odds, for with my stories and with my jokes and my wry observations, I would ensnare her.

I think I'd realised that from the very moment I sent that first card to her.

And once she had replied to me, I knew that I had a chance; and if my letters failed to delight, which was of course more than possible, well I would at least have given it my best shot.

So, by return, I sent her a jolly letter that was lively and upbeat and funny and sensitive, along with all those other things that we find so intoxicating in a potential partner. But the one thing that I was not was flirtatious. I never alluded to sex in any manner whatsoever. When it came to signing my letters, I would always end them with just my name and a single kiss.

That first letter that I wrote was - though I say it myself - quite funny. I had called up Lady Claire and had got her permission, and had then set about drawing up Sasha a mock certificate which allowed her full use of my treehouse, its bed, and its environs. I bought some red sealing wax and stuck some black ribbon to the bottom of the certificate; my seal was my thumb-print.

She needed some slight cajoling on my part, but in the end she did start to go to my tree-house. She told no-one about it, and would slip in quietly through the back gates. She liked it best, she said, to sit in the chair that was perched far out on the branch on Sir Anthony's meditation platform. "I wrap myself in a rug, and sit quietly on the chair and no-one can see me as I watch the world," she wrote. "One evening I even fell asleep on the chair, and woke up when it was quite dark. I nearly spent the night in your bed, but that felt wrong."

I was writing at least three letters a week to Sasha. You do not need to talk about love or sex in order to woo a woman with your words; of course you *can* do that, but we wordsmiths have many other weapons in our arsenal. We are light and frothy and dancing on this teetering tight-rope as we juggle this barrage of balls in the air, the one moment ribaldly cheeky, and then chafing, and then mock serious, and then, perhaps, wholly serious. We are versatile, the one moment the sledgehammer and the next the sprite; we are this moving target, this blizzard of words, which, over time, can dazzle and intrigue.

And if you're not used to it - if you've never received letters before - then, or so I understand, it can be deliriously intoxicating. They charm; they amuse; they can even inspire. And the beauty of a letter is that it *lasts*. But as for all else - conversations, sweet words and sweet acts of love - they are gone. The beautiful dinners, the long walks though the bluebell woods; even the beautiful kisses. By day's end, they are all, all of them gone. They may live a little in the memory, but even that starts to fade into just this Pleydell-Peaches haze. But a letter - a love-letter, written with an ink pen on fine white hammered paper - that can be read; and re-read; and re-read again. You might read it five times, at least, on the day that it is opened; and on the days after, the letter can still be pored over, again and again, and the jokes, those scurrilous words that have been handcrafted just for you, will be just as funny as on the day that you first read them, and they may yet be amusing your great-grandchildren long after you are dead. Think of that: being able to conjure so well with your words that, generations on, they can still move people to tears.

And as for those swains who believe that they can woo a woman with emails and texts and tweets... well of course it happens. It happens all the time. But if you have anything worth saying, then it is worth writing it by hand upon a fine white page. These are the things that will be read, over and over again, so that even years afterwards, your words will still chime and still resonate.

So hear me now: love-letters are power. That is not to say that when you are courting a woman, she does not appreciate dinners and flowers and all the other trinkets. But - at least as regards my own esoteric tastes - the women who are the keepers are the ones who like the letters best.

I courted Sasha assiduously. And when she wrote back to me, I would reply by return - and though I know that the letters seemed bouncy and fun, they took some time in the writing. Each letter would have at least three, four drafts, as gags were honed and lyrical adjectives were strung together in the most ludicrous flights of fancy.

I did not know, of course, how my letters were being received - but the very fact that Sasha was writing back to me indicated that she was beginning to fall under my spell. How very Machiavellian it all must sound. Perhaps it was. But all I remember of it now is that I was endeavouring to court one of the most beautiful woman who I had ever laid eyes on; and finally, after six months, I had found this unique weapon to separate me from the rest of the pack.

Besides, I liked writing those love-letters. I liked the thought that the next day, Sasha would be holding this letter in her hands - and would, if the words had fallen right, be chuckling at all the right places.

And as for Sasha's letters back to me - well I still have them, every one, tied up now with a white ribbon, tucked away in my old school ottoman. Sometimes, on a wet Sunday afternoon, I might tramp up to the attic and leaf through a few of them - and suddenly, there I am, back in my B&B in Harlow, and rocking with laughter as I read Sasha's words. When I read the letters, I can even hear her voice, though usually these days, it all ends the same way, as I start to cry and dwell on that most pitiful of fantasies: what might have been.

So there you have it.

For all my charms and blandishments, and for all my good deeds in the swimming pool, not to mention my tree-house and my maze, I am quite sure that the first reason that Sasha fell in love with me was because of the letters that I wrote to her. I charmed her with my words. She told me so herself.

CHAPTER 10

And what, meanwhile, of Mousie?

Mousie was certainly not a thorn in my side. But we were in one of those grinding relationships where it is sex and sex alone that is the mortar that binds the bricks. We could rub along well enough together, particularly as we were only seeing each other once a fortnight - and over a dinner and a lunch, I was more than capable of generally behaving myself and being as entertaining as I knew how. I think she quite liked it when I was just a little bit shocking. Nothing that would scare the horses, of course, but she liked the occasional whiff of outrageousness. She would have hated someone like Dangerous, but someone like me, with my multiple gears; I think she found it quite refreshing.

I never found out what her dream was - whether she hoped that one day we might get married. Though perhaps I do her an injustice, it always seemed as if it was my role to entertain and amuse (though never overstepping the mark), and if I was entertaining enough and amusing enough, then I would be rewarded with sex.

She never seemed to much like sex for its own sake.

That was always going to be a problem with someone like me.

In the early summer, I was introduced to one of the few genuine perks that can come the way of a local newspaper journalist: the freebie holiday. Some local tour firm had bought a number of chalets and had offered the Standard's "Travel editor" a week's holiday there in the autumn. In their turn, the tour firm hoped to get a publicity puff in the paper.

"Anyone fancy a holiday in the Dardanelles?" George sauntered into the newsroom.

"Where's the Dardanelles?" asked Rudi.

"Turkey."

"Turkey?" Rudi said. "I hate doner kebabs."

"Good a reason as any for not going. Anyone else?" George held the card invitation above his head.

"I'd love to," I said. It was a part of the world that I had never been to before - and therefore, by definition, I had to go there.

I read the blurb and it sounded just idyllic. Or let's rephrase that. It sounded like it had the potential to be idyllic - if you were on holiday with the right person.

It was a beautiful bungalow high up in the hills with its own pool and its own rock garden. There was, apparently, lots of good walking, as well as a cheap restaurant in the nearest village five miles away. And if you drove for twenty minutes, you could get to Gallipoli, that World War I battlefield where the Brits and the Anzacs were slaughtered in their tens of thousands.

We'd booked to go in October, halfway through my time at Harlow. We were getting a charter flight out of Gatwick.

Going on holiday with a lover is a beautiful test for a relationship. Because on holiday, particularly when you're flying out together, there will always be tensions and niggling little problems - and the question that you need to know is how well your partner deals with all these stresses. And if they do get fretful and snappish, then... well I hope that that lover is seriously delivering in other parts of the relationship, because these tensions are only ever going to get worse.

It started off in the coffee shop. A kid, a teenager, had bought an orange juice, and as he'd turned from the till, the whole glass had been knocked over Mousie. She did not like it. She got very angry, and she got even angrier when I said that it was no big deal.

On the flight. A screaming baby in the row behind us. I don't actually mind babies that scream, particularly not now that I myself am a dad. No, these days when I hear a baby screaming, I just thank my stars that it is not me who has to calm him down.

Mousie tried to change our seats; she did not succeed.

There were other things that annoyed her. On the flight, I bought a bottle of Champagne (as expensive as they had); it was tepid.

Some mild niggle over the rental car; can't even remember what it was.

My general irrepressible cheeriness which, while she was vexed, Mousie found enormously grating.

And then, last but not least, when we finally bumped into our new holiday home, there'd been a mix-up with the keys and it took us an hour to get inside.

No matter - there was nothing that could not be cured by a decent, torrid sex session by the pool, or in the pool, or even underneath the pool showers: whatever Mousie fancied, I was up for it.

I, of course, was up for it the very moment that we'd walked through the door. Mousie was not. "You're like a dog on heat!" she snapped. "We've only just got in through the door, and you're already thinking about sex!"

"I've been thinking sex from the first moment I saw you at Gatwick this morning," I said.

"Haven't you heard of foreplay?" She'd gone through to the bedroom. It had white walls and a double bed and not much else. It smelt of blocked drains.

"Foreplay?" I said. The more she pouted, the more I wanted to lark around. "What's foreplay?"

I dropped the bags on the floor and we explored our home for the next week. It was cosy as can be, with a large kitchen-cum-lounge that looked out onto the patio and the pool and the hills of Gallipoli in the distance.

Mousie walked round and then stood tapping her feet in the kitchen. "The smell is just vile," she said. "Do we have to stay here?"

"No," I said. "I suppose we could go trawling through the local towns. We might find something quite nice. Or we could get a boat to one of the ports. I'm easy."

Mousie did not like to hear this. Ideally, I should have thrown money at the problem; been the resourceful man who has a guidebook to hand and who, at the first phone call, books up a charming boutique hotel. But although she did not much fancy staying in our stinking bedroom, she also did not much like the thought of traipsing through rural Turkey looking for a *pension* to spend the night.

So we spent the night. We had dinner, and it was over dinner that the tremors that I had over our flat-line relationship turned into dark rumblings: I was bored. Perhaps Mousie had a scent of the vibe, because she was crotchety.

If the sex had been sensational, the relationship might have bumbled on for a little longer, but it was not - and this was particularly so because almost all of our love-making was confined to our bedroom with its smell of blocked drains. It is a very particular smell - fetid, dark and rotting, and occasionally I still comes across it: and then there I am, back in the Turkish bedroom with Mousie, with the white-washed walls and the light on the floor, so that I would not embarrass her.

I had suggested, once, making love on the sun-lounger. There seemed something utterly splendid at the prospect of making love with, all around us, this wide, wild panorama of sun-bleached fields and dusty green trees; I might as well have suggested making love in the middle of the concourse at Waterloo Station. Mousie was horrified.

Alcohol helped. I would start drinking beer in the morning and would have wine for lunch, and would continue to tipple my way through the day. And, as they always say: *in vino veritas.*

I'd been inside, drinking on the sofa and reading a book, and Mousie had been out by the pool, topping up her tan on the sun-lounger. We'd hardly spoken since lunchtime. I took a bottle of white wine, two glasses and an ice-bucket out to her. She woke up when I sat on the end of the sun-lounger. I poured out the wine and passed her a glass, and for a while we sat there, just looking at the view. Normally I'd have been touching her. I'd have let my hand stray to her leg, and I'd have started stroking her, and if this warmth had been reciprocated in any way, then I would have kissed her and taken it as a prelude to making love.

But this time, I didn't touch her, and so there we sat, admiring the view, and as the sun set, the herring-bone clouds changed from white to crimson.

Neither of us had spoken for thirty minutes and then at the exact same moment we both began to speak. "I was thinking –" I'd said, while Mousie's first words were, "I don't think –"

We both stopped talking. "After you," I said.

"No after you," she said.

"Ladies first," I said.

"No, please, Kim," she said. "Say what you want to say."

"I was thinking that… we might be thinking the same thing. Is that possible?"

"I think I might be thinking what you're thinking," she said.

"And what do you think I'm thinking?"

"Pour me some more wine," she said, and I topped her up. "I think you know what I think."

"Give me a clue," I said. "Might you be thinking about me and about us?"

"What's to be done?" she laughed. She was wearing an orange bikini and her breasts jiggled. Now that we were on the verge of splitting up, I thought she looked sensational.

"What maybe we should have done a month ago?"

"Or two months ago?" she said. "But you'd booked the holiday and I'd have felt bad about… blowing you out."

"You can blow me out any time you like," I said, and I nodded at her and she laughed again.

"And that too," she said. She was twinkling. "That was never really for me. Sorry about that. Your treehouse wasn't really for me either."

I raised my glass to her. "So – here's to the end of us," I said, and we chinked and we smiled, and because she was now looking more beautiful than I'd ever seen her, I leaned over and kissed her. She kissed me back. "Any lessons that we've learned?"

"I think – I think that if it's not right after the first month, then it's not going to get right," she said.

"We've had some good times," I said.

"It's like I fancy you," she said. "But I don't think we were ever going to work as a couple."

"We gave it a good try."

She leaned forward so that she was sitting next to me, and there we sat, shoulder to shoulder as we soaked up the last rays of the sun.

It was the best break-up I've ever had. Usually there are tears and recriminations, and it's followed by this extended period of mourning, but there was none of that with Mousie. We'd never reached the peaks and so, accordingly, there were none of the corresponding troughs.

I kissed her shoulder blade, with affection rather than lust, and for the first time in our relationship, her hand strayed to my swimming shorts.

"Is your hand where I think it is?" I said, watching her fingers worm their way next to my skin. "You've never once done that in six months of dating."

"I'd never realised splitting up could be so liberating," she said. "I feel quite… randy."

"Now you tell me!"

"And here we are on a sun-lounger," she said. Mousie started to tug at my shorts.

"And now you're pulling at my shorts," I said. "We're not really going to have sex on the sun-lounger?" She was kissing my shoulder-blade, her tongue flickering out, tasting the salt sweat on my skin. "Are we?"

Mousie smiled up at me. "And there might be something else that I want to try for the first time too -"

"Mousie, darling," I said, watching with wide eyes as she licked my arm. "Why didn't we split up months ago?"

"This can only ever happen the once, you know," she said.

"That's as may be," I said. "But this once is happening right now, and I'm in the middle of it!"

"Hush now," she said, and at length and in time, we duly did make love on the sun-lounger, in the dark, with the candles flickering by the pool.

I have one other memory of our last holiday together. I'd seen it as we'd driven back to the airport – seen it, looked at it and longed for it. It still has an allure and a history all of its own: the Hellespont.

★

"The Hellespont?" she said. "What's the Hellespont?"

"A waterway," I said. "A very big waterway that is steeped in history."

"Okay. Tell me."

"Some more tea?"

She moved her cup over the table and I poured from the pot. She watched me pour, my Claddagh ring winking at her, heart out, trumpeting to the world that I was available and open for offers.

We were in one of Cirencester's little cafes; on Sunday mornings, after our swims, we had taken to having breakfast with each other. The cafe was small, clean and cosy, with square tables with Formica tops, and the windows steamed, and the frying-pans fizzed in the kitchen. We'd drink tea and have toast, and sometimes, like the devil I am, I might even ask for a poached egg.

"The Hellespont?" Sasha said. She was wearing a grey cashmere beanie, hair all about her shoulders; it was winter and it was raining, and her hair was still wet from the rain, and she looked incredibly beautiful. Not, of course, that I was ever once going to allude to Sasha's hair, or her looks or her beauty.

I wonder what she made of me. I don't know what she made of me. But what I do know without doubt is that I was the first guy on earth who had known her for over eight months, and who had never once made a pass at her. And I guess, also, that I was the guy who wrote the letters.

"The Hellespont," I said. "Lord George Byron swam it – first of the real open-water swimmers. He swam the Tagus at Lisbon; he swam the Grand Canal in Venice. And he also swam the Hellespont and after he swam it, he said it was the best thing he'd ever done."

"Tell me more," Sasha said. She held her cup in both hands, black eyes staring.

"And Leander swam it too. He swam it every night to be with Hero his lover. She was a priestess. She'd wait for him at the top of her tower, and would have a candle at the window to guide him in. And then they'd make love -"

"Sweet love," Sasha prompted.

"Thank you," I said. "Not, though, that you'd know anything about making sweet love, Sasha, but anyway -" I paused and we looked at each other. There was no hint of flirtation in the air; I think we were just really enjoying ourselves. "In the mornings, Leander would swim back home again to do whatever he did in the day-time, and then at dusk, he'd be swimming back to his Hero - because once he'd had a taste of making sweet, sweet love, he was completely addicted."

"Was he now?" Sasha said. "And how did it all end?"

"Badly," I said promptly, "Just as all great love affairs must end."

"Do they have to end like that?"

"I'm afraid so," I said. Sasha was leaning forward towards me, and I was mirroring her, hands on the table, and was leaning in towards her. I'd have only needed to have leaned forward just a few inches and I could have kissed her. But there was no need for kisses; we were both quite happy just shooting the breeze.

"Not always?" she said.

"Yes always."

"So what happened with Leander?"

"It's a hell of a swim," I said. "Two miles of wild water that separates Europe from Asia, with a very strong current sweeping you down to the Aegean. Hero had put out her candle -"

"And then one night -" Sasha smiled and stroked her nose.

"And then one night," I continued. "The candle was blown out by the wind, and Leander didn't know where he was heading anymore and he drowned."

"And what did Hero do?"

"Threw herself off the top of the tower and that was the end of them."

"But it's not the end of them," she said. "They're now immortals. We're still talking about them."

"Yeah all right, you bloody pedant," I said. "And if they'd just got married and lived happily ever after and died of old age, then there'd be no story and we'd have forgotten all about them. So yes, Sasha, you're right – if your love affair comes to a suitably spectacular end, then you will become an immortal. So do you want to swim it?"

"In memory of Hero and Lysander?"

"And George Byron and his club foot."

"Well if it's a dare –"

"Of course it's a bloody dare."

"Yes!"

We shook hands over the table, and I would have liked to have held her hand for longer, but, very business-like, I let go of her hand and drank tea.

"When are we going to swim it?" she said.

"A year from now?" I said. "I think there might be a race in August. I'll find out."

"We shall see then," she said, and we sized each other up, and I think we both realised that we were making quite a commitment to each other: that for at least the next year, we would be swimming with each other, training with each other; and seeing each other at our best – and at our worst. It would be way, way bigger and broader and more challenging than an actual relationship.

"I was sorry to hear about you and Mousie," Sasha said.

"Ah well," I said and shrugged, because what else does one say when a woman like Sasha commiserates with you about an old love?

"Was the ending spectacular?"

"Not enough to make us immortals, no," I said. "Not nearly as spectacular as you and Paris."

"Ahh," she said. "Paris." And I could not tell whether her voice was tinged with regret or whether she missed him – or if, like with Mousie, the relationship was dead and buried.

But if things for you are only ever black or white, then there is no grey. And if there is no grey, then you're always having to make these cut-and-dried decisions, and for months and even years afterwards, you will be wondering to yourself if you made the right call, or if you'd have been better, for once, to have gone for the grey option.

"If we're going to swim the Hellespont, then we better get in some open-water swimming," Sasha said.

"The Thames?"

"At Lechlade?" she said. "And if you like loony swims, what about the Corryvreckan?"

The Corryvreckan. And let me tell that *that* really is a dangerous swim. It is a whirlpool, the biggest whirlpool in Britain, and that Corryvreckan trip damn nearly did for both of us - though not, perhaps, in quite the way that you might imagine.

CHAPTER 11

We were fully clothed, anoraks and all, but it was still bitterly cold as we walked through Lechlade. We had parked up in the Market Square and were walking to the river. Normally you wouldn't have got me within a mile of that stretch of the Thames but when I saw that Sasha was equally cold, it pumped fire into my veins. When I am courting a woman, then I am capable of almost any sort of foolhardiness – and as for tossing myself into a river in mid-winter: a complete snap.

Our plan was to leave our clothes and our thick coats by that beautifully arched stone bridge, Halfpenny Bridge, before walking a mile or so upriver. There, we'd dive into the Thames and then, if the shock didn't kill us, we planned to swim back to the bridge.

I did not much fancy it. The river was choppy and brown and it looked blisteringly cold. It was far and away the most unappetising swim that I'd ever seen. We stood at the apex of Halfpenny Bridge, looking straight down into the river five or six metres beneath us.

"Ever been to the Caribbean?" I asked.

"I have not," she said.

"Me neither," I said. "I guess it's a lot like this."

"Ever played Pooh sticks?"

"I am the king of Pooh sticks."

"Well the King is just about to get his butt kicked."

There was a stick lying in the gutter. I picked it up, snapped it in two, and gave one to Sasha. Sticks in hand, we leaned out over the bridge.

"Are you ready?" I said.

"Yes."

"Steady?"

"And I'm steady too."

"And go!"

We tossed our sticks into the river, and trotted over the road to the other side of the road.

"You cheated," she said.

"I so did not cheat."

"You went early, and you didn't just drop your stick into the river, you hurled it in."

"You getting your excuses in early?"

"You're a bloody cheat."

"I don't know about that," I said. The first of the sticks eddied out from under the bridge. It was my stick. "What I do know is that I'm a bloody winner."

"You're a cheat," she said. "Right. Re-match. Only this time - my choice of stick. I'm going to show you something you've never seen before."

"I doubt it!"

She'd gone back to the other side of the bridge again and beckoned to me. "Come over."

"Sure."

There was something in her eye. I couldn't tell what she was about, but I had a sense that something was up.

"Are you ready?"

"Don't we need to get a couple of sticks?"

"No, we don't." She pushed up with her hands so that she was sitting on the parapet. "Steady?"

"So what are we using?"

"Human Pooh sticks!" she laughed. "And go!" Without even a glance beneath her, Sasha had suddenly twisted her legs over the side of the parapet and had jumped into the river.

I was just at the parapet as she splashed into the water. She came up, treading water beneath the bridge.

I gaped as I looked down at her.

"Now that *is* something I've never seen before," I said. "Is it normal to play this game with all your clothes on?"

She was smiling up at me, quite delighted at how she had managed to shock me. "How else would you play it?"

"You're batty!"

"I may be batty," she called up. "But I'm in the water and you're not! Are you coming in?"

"Of course I'm coming in!" I said, zipping my wallet and my car keys into the coat of my anorak. "Get out of the way - give me some room."

I pushed up on the stonework until I was kneeling on the parapet and then, very slowly, I got to my feet. Sasha had swum off to the side.

I wondered how deep the water was. It seemed a little reckless to be actually intent on diving into the water. But with Sasha already in the river waiting for me, what else could I do? I had to up the stakes.

"Got your camera ready?" I called.

"Are you going to try a reverse tuck?"

"No, just the swan." I said, and with that I outstretched my arms and pushed off from the parapet. Once, when I was at school, I'd been not a bad diver, but all those skills were long gone. I went over too far, and by the time I hit the river, I was practically flat on my back.

"Nice dive!" Sasha called.

"Not a belly-flop, but a back-flop."

"Are you racing me through this bridge or what?"

"I am the human Pooh stick!"

We set off swimming under the bridge. What a bizarre sight we must have made on that freezing dreek morning; what a memory I have of it all, thrashing through the water, as my coat tugged tight at my arms and my feet flailed.

Sasha beat me easily. She was laughing at me as I emerged from underneath the bridge.

"Was that a first for you?"

"It was," I said. "It feels like most things I do with you are a first."

"Oi!" We looked up. A policeman was standing on Halfpenny Bridge looking down at us. "What are you doing?"

"We're playing human Pooh sticks," I called back. "What does it look like?"

"Human Pooh sticks?"

"It's like Pooh sticks - but with humans."

The copper continued to stare at us. "Have you got your clothes on?"

"We have," I said. "The water looked really cold."

"I hope the fire brigade don't have to rescue you."

"She swims like a fish," I said.

Sasha was on her back, lazily scudding downriver.

"I hope your mothers give you a damn good hiding when you get back home!"

I waved at him. "You hear that Sasha?" I called. "He says you deserve a good spanking."

She laughed. "The only person who needs to be spanked round here is you."

We swam back up to Halfpenny Bridge, and then underneath it and over to the bank. I'd never been for a swim before with all my clothes on. I'd not realised how difficult it was to pull myself out of the water. I grabbed hold of some reeds and heaved myself out. Sasha was still floundering at the edge. I took her forearm in my hands and dragged her out. It was spitting with rain. My foot slipped on the wet grass and I fell flat on my back, but Sasha was out of the water by now. She lay there on the grass, head cradled in her arms, giggling to herself.

We were wet and bedraggled and now quite shivering with the cold. As we walked back to the car, I happened to glance into one of the pub windows. I caught a glimpse of a fire.

"Let's get a drink," I said.

We went into The Crown, wet feet slapping on the old floorboards. I remember low beams and two fires, one at each end of the pub, both of them steeped in a heap of glowing house coal. At the far end, a couple of regulars were nursing pints by the fire.

The publican did a double take as we walked up to the bar.

"Gone into the river," I said. "Is it all right to warm ourselves up here?"

"Be my guest," he said. "What can I get you?"

"Two Whisky Macs, please," I said. "Large ones."

We hauled off our coats and sat on two wooden stools by the fire. I took off my jumper and my shirt until I was down to just jeans and a white T-shirt. Sasha stripped to her blouse. The water started to steam off our jeans as we sat in front of the fire. The publican brought over our Whisky Macs, whisky and Stone's ginger, and without a word, we chinked, and we looked at each other, and we sipped and we smiled.

We were so happy, slowly coming back to life in front of the fire, gradually becoming aware of our surroundings, of the boar's head on the wall, and the antelope's head above the fire, and some old black bicycle that hung from the ceiling. Somehow we both knew that even a single word would break that magical moment.

The radio was on, I remember. It was Radio Four, and after a while, I realised that we were listening to Desert Island discs.

Sasha's ears had pricked up. Desert Island Discs was one of her favourite programmes. So, as the coals crackled and our trousers toasted, we were both in the most exquisite harmony as we listened to her show.

It was then, over the next half-hour, that we were introduced to the most powerful catalyst for love that there has ever been – or ever will be. It can be summed up in one single exotic word, and this one thing trumps all else. It beats the fantastic allure that can be commanded by beauty and power; it beats charm and conversation; and as for gifts and money, this one word beats them out of sight.

The word is propinquity – and it was not a word or a concept that I had ever come across before. But as soon as I heard it, I knew it to be true.

The Desert Island Discs presenter Sue Lawley was interviewing a Grand Dame who had once been the Queen of Hollywood. She had moved over to the States from England when she was nineteen, and because she was pretty and talented, she had soon become a star. She'd married when she was young and rather surprisingly had stayed married - and faithful - for the next fifty years. The couple were soon to celebrate their Golden Wedding Anniversary.

"How did you meet Barry?" Lawley said.

"I met him on the set of my first big film," said the Grand Dame. "He was the gaffer in charge of the lights."

"And you just clicked?" said Lawley.

"It's called propinquity, darling," she said - and even as she said it, I remember that Sasha and I both looked at each other; we'd never heard of the word before. "Falling in love is about frequency and narrative - something with which suppers and moonlit walks just cannot compete."

"So given enough time, you can fall in love with anyone?" said Lawley.

"It's like dear old Professor Higgins in My Fair Lady," said the Diva. "He falls in love with Eliza because he has become accustomed to her face."

"Is that romance?" said Lawley.

"Of a sort. Given enough time and enough narrative, then anyone can fall in love with anyone," said my old sage the Diva. "Princess Grace can fall in love with her gardeners -"

Sasha and I gaped at each other. What? At that time, while Princess Grace of Monaco was still alive, it was not widely known that she was carrying on with the Palace gardeners.

The Grand Dame continued - "and Beauty can fall in love with her beast. Isn't that romantic?"

The diva chose her book - Walter Scott's Ivanhoe - and her luxury item, a flute of solid gold, and when we'd heard out the herring gulls and the last note of "*The Sleepy Lagoon*" theme tune, Sasha stretched in front of the fire, and then yawned, and for a while there was silence.

We were both thinking the same thing.

"Propinquity," Sasha said.

"Prop. Pin. Quit. Tea," I said.

"Frequency. I get that - that's just spending time with each other. But what did she mean by narrative?"

I took a moment to think. It was driving with rain by now, and the pub windows were quivering in the storm; how delightful it was to be by the fire-side. "Narrative would be all the experiences that you've shared," I said. "Good experiences, bad experiences. Terrifying experiences. The more traumatic the experience, the more likely it is that you'll fall in love."

"I wonder," Sasha said as she stared into the rain.

"I'll tell you a story about narrative."

"Is it your narrative?" Sasha said.

"It's about a woman that I once knew. Her name was Karen."

"Tell me about Karen."

"I will," I said - and now that I had the floor, I took my time and had a sip of my whisky Mac. "Once, in another world and in another life-time, I worked on a collective farm in Israel -"

"A kibbutz."

"That's right - a kibbutz. The kibbutzim were initially set up on the borders of Israel as a buffer zone against Syria and Jordan and any other potential invaders, but after a while they became very popular. The kibbutzim were also very popular with the volunteers, who were usually young travellers from around the world. The volunteers would work for a month or two, and would get their board and lodging as well as a bit of beer money.

"Now generally, the volunteers only dated the other volunteers; the kibbutzniks did not think very much of volunteers dating kibbutzniks. They could just about handle female volunteers dating male kibbutzniks. But they certainly didn't like it when swarthy, lusty male volunteers started going out with female kibbutzniks. Getting the picture?"

"I am. Kibbutz women were off limits to the likes of you."

"Very much so. Although we occasionally got to work with these Kibbutnik women in the apple orchards, we never really got to know them. Now amongst these women was a woman called Karen who was about my age, and sometimes we used to exchange the odd word with each other. We had to be up quite early in the morning, at about 4.30, and then we'd all get into the truck so that we'd be in the orchards at sun up. No-one much felt like talking then, but I'd still say good morning to Karen and to the rest of the apple team. I quite liked her - and she may have liked me and she may not have liked me. It was difficult to tell just from saying good morning to each other. After three hours in the orchards, we'd break off for breakfast, and the van would take us up to the dining room. It was a huge hall, self-service and the food was always excellent, and we were always starving. They were the best breakfasts I'd ever eaten."

I paused and had another sip of the whisky Mac. Sasha was engrossed in the story, leaning in towards me. She was interested, eyes quite set on mine.

"But although Karen and I had a lot of frequency, because we were seeing each other every morning amongst the apple-pickers, there was no narrative. We didn't have any thread to bind us, apart from all the apples that we'd picked.

"Then one day, we've been out in the orchards and we've come back for breakfast. We've watched the sun come up and we're all a bit dirty, a bit sweaty. I'm queuing up to get my breakfast and by chance Karen is behind me. I haven't said anything to her because she is a kibbutznik and because I am wondering what to have for my breakfast - and suddenly there is a sound from outside, and to me it sounds like a car back-firing. Except that the car seems to be getting closer and closer, and then the windows start exploding and bullets are crashing into the dining hall. Bullets and glass everywhere, and the most terrifying noise - boom-boom-boom.

"People are ducking for cover. I'm about to run for it when Karen grabs me by the shoulder and yanks me to the floor. From the corner of my eye, I see that three gunmen have come into the dining hall; I learned later that they were terrorists who'd come over from the Syrian border. They were shooting indiscriminately at everything that moved, machine-guns at the hips. The noise was terrific - a wall of noise. Everywhere there is bodies and blood, and this smell of cordite, and one of the gunmen has already started kicking the bodies to check no-one's shamming.

"Karen beckons to me and I follow her. We crawl on our stomachs underneath a hatch in the self-service counter, and she is slithering like a commando and I am right behind her. We crawl through to the kitchens which are now deserted, as the cooks have run away. We stay on our stomachs and slip-slide over the kitchen tiles and then we get out of the kitchen door, and as just as we're going out, we hear gunfire quite close, and we realise that one of the terrorists is in the kitchen.

"But there's no cover outside the kitchens, it's just this flat stretch of scrub-grass and the nearest trees are over 200 yards away, and although we could try to sprint it, we don't know how many gunmen are waiting outside. We don't know what to do, but then Karen soundlessly tugs at my wrist. We run around the corner of the hall where there is a ladder set into the wall that leads onto the roof of the dining hall. But it's one of those security ladders which needs a ladder to get up to it - the ladder starts about ten feet off the ground.

"I quickly give Karen a bunk up. She scrabbles onto my shoulders, and then she's up the ladder. It's more tricky for me. I run at the wall, kick off it, and then stretch up for the ladder. I miss it, but in the same moment Karen has caught me by the wrist, and somehow she holds on just long enough for me to grab the lowest rung of the ladder."

I took Sasha's hand in my own.

"That's all I needed," I said. "I follow her up the ladder and in a few seconds we are onto the roof. It's a flat roof and we could just lie there, but it seems more sensible to hide. We crawl over to the far side of the roof, and as we crawl we can see bullet-holes punctured into the lead roofing strips. We can still hear short, staccato bursts of machine-gun fire from the dining room.

"We hide behind some steam vents which are like breeze-block chimneys, and we sit there in the morning sun, holding each other tight, and wondering if at any second we're going to be shot dead. Gradually the gun-fire becomes more intermittent, and then we hear the sound of helicopters, and then there's no shooting at all, and it's just us alone on the rooftop, sitting in the sun, and we look at each other, and suddenly realise what's happened to us, and then, because there is nothing whatsoever to be said, we just kissed each other."

I was completely engrossed with my tale, could remember it all - could hear the gunfire, and could even smell the rich chicken stew that had been cooking for our lunch in the kitchens, and because I was so in that moment, and because this was how it had happened, I just leant forward and kissed Sasha's mouth. My lips brushed her lips. She looked at me, not quite certain if the kiss was part of the story, or whether the kiss was for her.

"So the sun got hotter, and then we heard sirens coming up to the kibbutz. I peeped over the edge of the roof and I could see police cars and army Jeeps swarming up the main drive. We were safe. But we didn't get down immediately. We just stayed there, lying in each other's arms in the sun. And what we realised was that not only had we survived, but also that we had experienced something rather special, something unique.

"And that, Sasha, is the end of my tale, and that, for your information, is narrative. It's getting through something pretty shitty together, and the more shitty it is, the stronger the bond that you will have."

I'd let go of her hand. Sasha stared at me, and then she stared out of the window and so I did the same. I did not know what she was thinking. She might have been thinking about that stolen kiss and she might not. But I knew better than to intrude into her thoughts. Just the sound of the rain, and the fire in the grate and the gentle tick of the clock.

"What a story," she said.

"Thank you."

"I liked your letters."

"Yours were very funny."

"They still make me laugh." She wiped a speck from her eye.

"I should bloody well hope so," I said. "I spent hours on them!" I was secretly thrilled. Even though I was seeing Sasha nearly every day, I resolved to continue to write to her.

"Did you?"

"What do you think?"

"I think…" and she tailed off, and she looked at me. "Propinquity."

"Propinquity," I repeated.

"It's our word of the week."

And for a while the silence drifted, but there is something else that we reporters also know and that is when to start talking.

"Hey - Sasha," I said, cuffing her on the arm. "I know what you're about, so don't for one moment think you're going to get out of buying your round just because you've been getting all maudlin after your desert island discs."

"Me - maudlin?" she said, and she cuffed me right back. "For the last ten minutes I've had to sit here listening to you witter on about this love of your life -"

"I never said Karen was the love of my life -"

"This sex-bomb -"

"She was certainly that -"

"While I've been dying for a Bloody Mary -"

"And you never once started piping your eye -" I said, and she punched me again on the shoulder and I could have kissed her then, but I did not, and she laughed as she went by me to the bar, her leg brushing against my shoulder, and I watched her as she walked. The back of her blouse and the back of her jeans were still wet, and they clung to her like the most beautiful second skin.

★

I would not want you to think that it was all sunshine with Sasha in that year that I courted her. For the most part, she was easy-come, easy-go, but on certain matters, she was absolutely black and white; if you crossed that line, there was absolutely no going back.

Though, perhaps surprisingly, she was no firecracker. I'd known South American women before, and I'd expected her to have the most scalding temper. But Sasha was the opposite. When she was vexed, she just shut down. It was a slow ice-burn, and when she was giving you the frost, there was nothing to be done but to bide your time.

But if there is one beauty of being a friend rather than a lover, it is that friends need much greater care. With a lover, you can lose your rag, say anything you want, and in fact behave like the most foul-mouthed swine, and yet so long as you're prepared to say sorry and to kiss and make-up - and that is *properly* kiss and make-up with ardour and with passion - then you can lose your temper just as often as you please. But it is different with a friend. Friends are much more delicate flowers, and because there can never be any of the kissing and the making-up - which is the only bit worth having - then if you lose your temper too often, then the friendship can quickly start to wither.

So, while we were friends, Sasha did keep her cold-burn temper in check.

It was a Monday morning in the office, spring 1990; Mousie was ancient history and I was a single man with a swing in my stride. I had, after three failed attempts, passed my shorthand exam and, though my story-writing skills were still negligible, I was learning a little of this arcane craft of news-gathering.

George, the news editor, liked everything to be quiet and peaceful in the morning, so the reporters were quietly going about their business. Siobhan was reading the papers while Rudi was busily doing his expenses.

My phone went - and, at least in those early years as a journalist, I thrilled to its sound. It might be a story!

"Reporters," I said.

"Is that Kim?" It was a woman. I slightly recognised her voice.

"Himself."

"It's Anne here," she said. "Anne Jardine. I shouldn't really be calling you. But I've always felt that one good turn deserves another."

"Absolutely."

"Though this story never came from me."

"Sorry - who am I speaking to?"

She laughed. "Very good," she said, and she went on to tell me about a hunt party over the weekend where everything had - surprise,

surprise – "got a little out of control". In particular, some star polo-player, Ernesto, had opened all the gates, and horses and cattle had been allowed to wander out onto the roads. It had taken half of Sunday to round all the animals up again.

It had the makings of quite a good story. And that is the way of modern journalism. We spike one story for a friend, and they come back later and give us another one.

"Thanks so much for calling."

"I thought you'd like it."

"Anything else you're not telling me, by the way?"

"Whatever do you mean?"

"Any special reason why you want to land this polo-player in it?"

"Kim!" she squawked. "You are incorrigible!"

"Thank you, Anne," I said and I smiled to myself, wondering just what this handsome polo-player had done to so annoy her. "How's Henry getting on by the way?" I asked, impishly asking after her lover.

"I hoped you'd forgotten all about him."

"How could I ever forget Henry?" I said. "He's a lucky guy."

"Kim." She laughed. "If only I'd met you twenty years ago –"

"You'd have broken my heart like everyone else's."

"Probably – though I'm sure you'd have given as good as you got."

"No – never," I said. "In matters of the heart, I always come off worst."

She laughed and perhaps it's my fanciful imagination but as she replaced the handset, I think that I might have heard a sigh.

I made some calls. In the matter of chasing up these nebulous leads, we are like detectives following up a clue. We shake one tree and nothing happens, and then we methodically go on to shake the next tree, and if you shake enough trees then some fruit may eventually fall.

After about two hours of fruit-free phone calls, I realised that I did know somebody who might actually have been at the party: Sasha.

I called her at her office by Cirencester Park. The polo season hadn't yet started, but the ponies still needed to be exercised, matches needed to be teed up, and the fat red-faced owner of Jokers Wild still needed to be kept sweet.

"Sasha," I purred over the phone. "My name is Kim, journalist of considerable influence at the Wilts and Gloucestershire Standard, and I gather that you may have a story for me."

"Not today," she said. "Go tout your tat somewhere else."

"Charming," I said. "Were you at this hunt party on Saturday?"

"I was," she laughed. "A very rich, very middle-aged landowner asked me to marry him."

"Congratulations. I hope you'll be very happy together."

"I'd never met him before and he did seem quite drunk. Do you think he was serious?"

"Have you got an engagement ring?"

"I have not," she laughed. "Though he did buy me £500 worth of raffle tickets. I won a helicopter ride. He wanted to kiss me."

"The least you could do for your new fiancé," I said. I remember that about Sasha. I always loved bantering with her. Now that I am married, I do not banter so much with my wife Elise; no, now our conversation tends to be confined to who will be picking up the girls and what we will be doing at the weekend and what should be watched on the television. "So did you tell the old goat to join the back of the queue?"

"I certainly did not," she said, and I could almost picture her there in her office, smiling down the phone at me as she stroked that beautiful kink in her nose. "That would have been impolite. I do not get that many proposals of marriage –"

"At least not more than once a week –"

"If that –"

"So in between fending off this sugar-daddy, did you see this joker Ernesto opening all the gates?"

"I did," Sasha said – and she told me all about it. She gave me the name of Ernesto's team as well as all his contact details.

Sasha then said that thing that, as a journalist, I have heard so often over the years. "But you can't quote me," she said. "And please don't contact him."

"I won't quote you by name," I said. "I'll just put you down as an anonymous party guest. But I'll definitely call this guy up. He sounds like a jerk."

"Oh please don't do that," she said. "I'd never have told you if I thought you were going to use any of it."

"But I'm a reporter!" I said. "This is what I do!"

"Please don't," she said. "He might get into trouble!"

"That's his bloody look-out!" I said. "What did he think was going to happen when he let all the animals out?"

"Please don't," she said.

"But the story's going to get out anyway."

"I'd rather it didn't come from me."

"I'll see what he says," I said.

At the end of the call, Sasha did not sound happy, but filled with journalistic zeal - "the public has the right to know!" - I called up the hapless polo-player, and because he had never spoken to a journalist before, and because he did not know any better, he made his contrite confession, and three days later it was all over the front page of the paper. "Well done," said George, and that was that. The story made it into a few of the national papers at the weekend - not that I made a penny from it. That rankled, slightly.

Now, if I could have a quiet word with my younger self, I would have grabbed him by the scruff of the neck and slammed his head into the wall; it might, just, have knocked some sense into me. For after twenty years in journalism, I know that stories are ten a penny, and that even a world exclusive isn't worth ruffling your friends' feathers. By the next day, your world exclusive will be - as they say - nothing but fish and chip paper, and meanwhile, months afterwards, your friends will still be smarting. So these days, I am much more circumspect about stories that I've gleaned from my friends. If they do not want their tales to appear in my paper, *The Sun*, then I will not be writing them up.

But in my greenhorn days on the Wilts and Glos days, I truly believed that stories took precedence over all else. Even someone like Sasha.

The day after the story came out, I saw Sasha as usual at the swimming pool. I'd done a few lengths and I'd been waiting for her at the end of the pool. "Good morning," I'd said.

She looked at me, though she did not take off her goggles. "I don't really want to talk to you at the moment," she'd said, and nor did she - and she did not want to speak to me the next day, or the next day either. After cooling my heels over the weekend, I'd realised that, perhaps, I had made a very large mistake. Sasha was still fuming while as for my little exclusive, that was just so much ancient history.

On the Monday, I left a fresh croissant on a plate at her lane by the pool. She looked at the croissant and ignored it.

"A peace offering," I said. "I'm sorry. I shouldn't have done it.",

Sasha looked at me and without a word swam off, but later, when I came out of the showers, she was waiting for me. "Have you got time for a coffee?" she'd asked.

"For you?" I said. "Yes." And so we had that coffee and so the matter was dropped. Since we were just friends, we were of course unable to reconnect in the bedroom, but after I'd paid for her coffee and her toast, and as we left the café, she slipped her hand companionably through my arm and I realised that although I might not have been forgiven, we had moved on.

And had I learned my lesson? Well... sort of.

CHAPTER 12

Slowly, ineluctably, and with all the inevitability of a glacier grinding down a mountain, I was falling in love. First and foremost, however, Sasha was a friend. She was a mate. We swam with each other in Cirencester's pool and we swam in the wild, and we joshed and we teased, and we did all those things that a wise lover would do before he plants the first kiss.

And as week followed week, and month followed month, I realised that although it was her beauty that had first attracted me to Sasha, what I loved was her spirit, her fire, her enthusiasm; her sense of humour. She loved to laugh. We loved to laugh, and we would laugh together at the most outlandish things imaginable.

What better reason to fall in love than that you adore a person's sense of humour?

And, over time, I became quite a reasonably accomplished wild swimmer. I got used to the cold and to the rain, and to hauling myself out of the Thames, and to having my skin stung by those grey spring gales. It may seem grim, but with Sasha for my partner, it became an absolute pleasure. If she had suggested it, I would have followed her to the North Pole to go swimming under the Ice Cap.

It was far and away the longest courtship that I have ever had. There were times, plenty of times, when I thought about making that move, and declaring myself with a kiss.

But I did not. Always, always, the timing was never quite right. And, as I had already determined, I was only going to reveal my hand when I didn't just *think* the moment was right. I had to *know* it was right.

And then we had had that wild swim by Tower Bridge in the Thames in London, and we had both been nearly drowned by the dredger.

There we'd stood on the Embankment, Sasha shivering with the cold.

And she'd slapped me in the face.

It was the hardest hit I'd ever had from a woman. She was tall and she was powerful, and she'd put every ounce of muscle into the blow. My head snapped back. It sounded like a pistol crack. My ears rang.

And at long last, I realised that our stars were aligned; that our narrative was in place; and that, propinquity being what it is, my moment was all but upon me.

I lightly fingered my cheek as I looked at her.

"I deserved it," I said, and I turned and we walked on to Tower Hill tube station. We walked side by side, though with several feet between us. We did not say a word - not on the pavement as we walked by the river, nor as we travelled on the Tube back to Paddington, and nor as we waited for the train to take us back to Kemble. Shock does that to you. It often happens after a near-death experience. Over and over again, your brain is trying to come to terms with your own mortality, and how, if things had turned out just a little differently, there you'd be lying dead on the slab.

While we waited at Paddington, I went off and bought a bottle of wine and a bottle of Remy Martin, as well as two cans of Coke for the bugs from the Thames, and when we got on the train, I opened the bottles. We had the carriage to ourselves. We drank out of white plastic cups. We drank the Coke and then I drank wine while Sasha was on the brandy; we drank stolidly and steadily and in silence.

We'd been on the train for about an hour and it was quite late. We were sitting opposite each other, with a small side table by the window. Sasha had been nursing her plastic cup, but she put it onto the table and then she just looked at me. She had her hands lightly cupped in the lap of her white bath-robe.

I'd been looking out of the window, watching the street-lights flicker past the train. I'd been mulling over how the dredger had just missed me. Another second - another half-second - and it would have hit me, no question.

I realised that Sasha was looking at me and I put my cup on the table and I looked at her. I saw that long mane of hair coiled about her neck, and those full lips that were not quite pink but slightly mauve, and that rich olive skin, and that skew nose that just clamoured to be kissed; and full thick eyebrows; and jet black eyes that never for a moment left mine. The more I looked into her eyes, the more intense the connection that I felt with her, as all these wires fizzed and fused between our brains, and though for the last year I had been biding my time, and keeping my own counsel, I now knew for a certainty that my time had come. Be brave. Be fearless. Imitate the actions of a tiger.

"I love you," I said, very softly, nothing more than a murmur.

Sasha's eyes narrowed slightly. "What did you say?"

"I said I love you," I said, louder, more confidently.

"How do you love me?" she said. "Like a friend?" Without taking her eyes off me, she stretched for her cup.

"You are my friend," I said. "But I love you like a lover."

She drank her brandy. We'd pulled into a station. Doors were slamming and we continued to look at each other. It seemed like a long time before she finally spoke.

"That is as well," she said. "I love you." At that moment, a million steam whistles seemed to blast in my head, loud and long and strident. I was Archimedes as he gets into the bath and screams "Eureka!"; I was Edmund Hillary planting the flag into Everest's peak; I was Winston Churchill as he realised that the war was won.

Had she… had Sasha just said that she loved me?

"How do you love me?" I said. "Like a friend?"

"I've never felt like this about anyone before."

My heart bubbled, that first fizz as the cork is eased off the Champagne bottle. "And to think - I've declared my love - and I haven't even kissed you," I said.

"You haven't?" she said.

"Have I?"

"Yes you have, as you very well know, Kim – when you told me that story about Karen in the kibbutz, and how you kissed her for the first time. And then you kissed me for the first time."

"Two kisses for the price of one," I said. "I wondered if you'd remember that."

"I do remember that kiss," she said. "But nevertheless… This has been a very old-fashioned courtship." And for the first time on the train, Sasha smiled. I think – no, I know – that she was as happy as I was.

"Straight out of a Jane Austen," I said.

"When did you fall in love with me?" Sasha asked.

"Over time." With my eyes still on hers, I filled my cup with wine, I took it, and I drank. "It's about frequency, Sasha. And it's about narrative. It's a thing called propinquity. You may have heard of it."

Sasha raised her eyebrows and nodded at me, as if to acknowledge the hit. "I might have," she said.

"Good for you," I said. "Not many people have."

"You've shown a lot of self-restraint over the last year, haven't you?" Sasha said.

"As have you."

"I've wanted to kiss you a number of times," she said. "That first time I came to your treehouse; and in the folly; and most times when we have breakfast in the cafe." She stroked her nose. "And in the Thames at Lechlade, when you helped me out of the water. And then after you did kiss me in the pub in Lechlade, when I wasn't quite sure if it was really for me."

"Ditto," I said. "Ditto, ditto and ditto."

"It's not propinquity – it's synchronicity."

"And now, of course," I said. "I'd like to kiss you now."

"That is synchronicity, then," she said, and my legs are shaking for very nerves at the sheer anticipation of all that is to come. It was as if I had been sitting quietly in a room that was lit by a single candle, vaguely able to discern all the things that were upon the table – and suddenly, in a single second, the lights were on, and I had my first proper look of the lush banquet that had been laid before me.

"Right now?" I said.

"Right now," Sasha said. She finished her brandy and returned the cup to the table; I did the same with my wine, and there we sat, gazing at each other, revelling in our love, glorying in how our game of cat and mouse had come to this absurdly simple end. I savoured the moment a little while longer.

Sasha leaned towards me, and I thought at first she was going to kiss me, but she did not. She brought her index finger to her lips, kissed it, and then stretched over to place her finger upon my lips. I kissed her finger back and, ever so slowly, she took it back to her mouth and kissed it again, a kiss to her lips by proxy.

It was now my turn. I kissed my finger and stretched over and placed it upon her lips, and I thought that she would merely kiss my finger back, but she opened her lips and the tip of my finger slipped inside her mouth, her eyes never once leaving mine, and I felt her teeth as her tongue rolled round the tip of my finger.

"That is an absurdly erotic sight," I said.

She took my hand in both of hers and started to kiss the tips of each of my fingers. "Is it?" she said in mock wonderment.

"As is that," I said.

"I love your hands," she said, and she held my hand palm up and studied my lines of love and marriage and destiny. She squeezed at the base of my thumb. "And I like your Mons Venus too."

"What is my Mons Venus when she's at home?"

"She is your little mount of love," she said, giving the base of my thumb another squeeze. "Apparently she says what sort of lover you are."

"I thought you were a virgin and proud of it," I said. I slipped out of my chair and sat next to her, thigh firmly next to thigh.

"I don't know if I'm proud of it," she said.

"And what else do my palms tell you?" I asked.

"They tell me everything." She scrutinised my right hand. "At least two marriages, you'll have. A number of children. A longish life. And some lovers."

"And are you in my hand?" I said.

"I am - in the palm of it," she said and she giggled as she studied my hands again. "A writer's hands," she said. "With polished nails and not a callous to be seen."

"I moisturize daily."

"I've never had so much fun before a kiss," she said - and she was right. There was this delicious easiness between us. Normally, before a first kiss, there is this static tension, like a thunder-cloud that crackles with its own pulsing electrical charge. But with the banter, the tension had eased.

"Wait and see what I'm like when I take you to bed for the first time."

"That's very forward of you, Kim," she said, and, still looking me in the eye, she kissed each of my palms and then turned my hands over and kissed my knuckles.

"Is there something else that you would like me to kiss?" she said, and she raised a sphinx-like, minx-like eyebrow.

I nodded at her, cool as you please. "I'd like you to kiss my lips," I said, and then, since two could play at her game, I added, "For the moment."

"That would be perfect," she said. "For the moment."

And there we sat on that rattling train, hand in hand, our faces just a few inches apart as we gazed at each other, and I think that we both realised that we were done with talking. Very slowly now, I lean towards her, she leans towards me, and for the first time, properly, and with love aforethought, we kiss, lip to lip; it is a long kiss, and demure, with lips only a little parted, and just the slightest hint of all that is yet to come. I close my eyes and, in perfect unison, we break off and we enfold our arms around each other, holding so tight that I can feel her ribs through her bathrobe. Her head is pressed next to mine, our lips to each other's ears, so that she only has to whisper and I can hear her.

"Now that you've kissed me, does that mean you're my boyfriend?" she said.

"Without doubt," I whispered. I turned slightly and kissed her ear. I was still in that state of white heat bewilderment where I couldn't believe that this woman, Sasha, was in my arms; that, as of ten minutes ago, this ear that nestled so delicately in front of me was now mine to be kissed. And because I could, and because it was now allowed, I kissed her ear and I held her even tighter. "You are my girlfriend, and as of this moment, all other women are officially off limits. How's that sound? See this ring?"

I took off my silver Claddagh ring, turned it, and replaced it back on my finger. The cupped heart was now pointing inwards.

She giggled as she broke off from me, hands now loose about my waist. "I'm your girlfriend?" she said, weighing each word. "I like the sound of that. Hi, I'm Sasha, I'm Kim's girlfriend."

"And I love you for it," I said.

And we kissed again, more fiercely now, lips to moist lips, and mouths gradually, imperceptibly, opening, and, at length, tentatively touching tongues, and what I realise now is that we were beautifully synchronised in all that we did, mirroring each other's thoughts and actions without a word being said.

I loosened the cord around Sasha's bathrobe and opened it up. She was still wearing her swimming costume, torn at the top from where she'd been hammered into Tower Bridge by the dredger.

"Your shoulder," I said. The raw graze was bruised and bloody and I kissed my finger and placed the kiss upon the bruise.

I touched her collar-bone with my finger and traced a line down over her breast and to her hip.

"And back again," she said, straining a little towards me. "I like watching you do that," and my finger traces up again over her breast, and lingers there and I cup it, and we both look, and we both of us can hardly believe how in the space of a single train journey, our relationship has changed irrevocably. And for me… well don't forget that for an entire year, I had been keeping my urges so heavily in check that I had hardly even touched Sasha's hand; the very act of touching her still seemed barely conscionable. I'd been like a piece of railway rolling-stock, poised at the top of the hill, the brakes fully engaged, though my every instinct had been urging me to hurtle down the track. And now, quite suddenly, the brakes have been released, and I am rolling down the hill and accelerating with every second that I'm with her, so that there I am, her breast in my palm, and I move my other hand up, and she pushes towards me and, very gently, I am cupping both her breasts, and as we kiss, her hand skips into my bath-gown, skin to skin, and…

I realise that the train has stopped. I look up and see that we are at a station.

"We're at Kemble!" I said, and we both jumped up, electric, like kids caught kissing in an empty classroom. The train had those old-style doors, and even as the train started to move, I opened the door and jumped onto the platform.

It was close on midnight. We sauntered along the platform, arms easily about each other's waists, and I would occasionally turn to look at Sasha, just to check that it really was her, now, in my arms.

"We left the brandy and the wine," I said.

"Is it always going to end like this when we start kissing?" she said.

"I do hope so," I said. We were in the ticket hall, and we had been walking for about a minute, but it already felt like I'd been starved of her kisses, and as one we stopped, we turned to each other, and directly started to kiss, hands slipping underneath our bathrobes, so that we could feel the other's body heat.

It took us twenty minutes to get back to the car. Do you remember that day of the first kiss, when you can't get enough of each other, and when every minute has to be affirmed with another kiss and another kiss and another declaration of love?

I unlocked the passenger door, and held the door open and with another kiss, Sasha got inside, and when I got in behind the wheel, we tore at each other till we were panting with desire.

And break off.

And rest.

The back of Sasha's chair was slightly lower than mine, and she was lying there, bathrobe open, arms about her head, legs outstretched, in a position of the most wanton abandon; she stretched a finger to my lips and I kissed her finger, and she kissed it back, and then I did the same. I leaned over and gave her my finger to kiss, and then, soft as a feather, I let my finger glide down her chin, and her neck, and between her breasts, and over her stomach, and still further down until my finger slipped between her long legs, and I gave her the most intimate, the most delicate of caresses, but only for a moment, before withdrawing my hand.

"I didn't expect that when we left for London."

I kissed her. "And I had no idea that I'd finally be declaring my love to you."

"Hold me again," she said, and I stretched over and she clung to me. "I've loved tonight," she whispered. "At least the latter part of it," and we laughed; and then because I am aware that even with the most passionate girlfriends - no, *particularly* with the most passionate girlfriends - it is always best to leave them wanting more, I started up the car and we drove back to Cirencester.

I dropped her off at her house. It was on one of Cirencester's genteel mews which she shared with Susanna, the girlfriend I'd first seen her with in the Slug and Lettuce. We hugged on the porch and gave each other a resounding kiss.

"Would you like to come in for a coffee?" she said.

"I'm going to quit while I'm ahead," I said.

"Sensible," she said, as her hand idly strayed to the tops of my shorts. "I want time to get better acquainted with you."

"There's no rush, is there?" I said.

"None whatsoever," she said with a kiss and a tease. Already I had half a mind to take her up on that offer of coffee.

"Would you like to go on a date with me?" I said.

"A date?" she said. "A date with my boyfriend?"

"A first date too -"

"We have so got this back to front," she said. "I've kissed you and I've said I loved you, and you haven't even taken me out for dinner -"

"I never mentioned dinner," I said. "I just asked you out for a date."

"Kim, even if your date does not include dinner, I would still love to go out with you."

"Very good," I said, in the manner of an army officer whose orders have been carried out to the last letter, and we kissed, and we said goodbye, and I lingered on the doorstep, and then the door banged open again, and out she flew, and into my arms for one last kiss, and when I look back at it now, I would that I was still with her, but as it is, all I have for solace are my memories and my lovelorn dreams.

★

Before my first date with Sasha, I had to go through the painful process of nearly getting sacked.

I had intended to take Sasha out for our date a couple of days later on the Tuesday, but instead, I'd been ordered to spend the night dossing down with Cirencester's vagrants.

George had come over to my desk, which did not bode well. For the usual run-of-the-mill stories, I would normally be called into his office. But he was now stood over me holding a press release.

"Cadet Kim," George said. "You are required to write a feature. Editor's request."

"Fantastic!" I said. Life did not get any better than it was that morning. Twice I had seen Sasha at the swimming pool, and each time we had kissed and professed our love - and, well, really, what more could a man ask for than the love of a good woman and the glorious anticipation of how that love might yet be consummated?

"I'm sure you'll enjoy it," he said, tossing the press release onto my desk. "It is National Homelessness week, and in order to raise awareness of Gloucestershire's homeless -"

"Are there many homeless people in Cirencester?"

"That's for you to find out," George said. "And once you have found out, Cadet Kim, you are to spend the night with them - the better to report first-hand on what it is like to be homeless."

I said the only thing that a reporter can ever say when they have been asked to do a story. Even though you may think that a story is going to end in disaster, there is only one way to handle the mad-masters. "That's great!" I said. "Looking forward to it!"

"Be brave! Be fearless!"

"Imitate the actions of a vagrant!"

Rudi looked at me askance and Siobhan sniggered. We hacks are often called upon to do the most unusual jobs in the name of duty, and some of these jobs are more unpleasant than others; let us just say that I was not licking my lips at the prospect of dossing down on the street for the night.

I went out and found a tramp who showed me a place near the church where the homeless often spent the night. I interviewed him at length about life on the road.

I then made a mistake.

I had no intention whatsoever of spending a night out with Cirencester's homeless. Instead I was just going to make it all up off the top of my head; perhaps you find that shocking. Perhaps it is, I don't know. But, personally speaking, there are sometimes occasions when you've got to be there on the front-line, living it, witnessing it all first-hand; and there are other occasions when it is not quite so necessary. And as for spending a night out on the streets in Cirencester, well I was quite happy to let my imagination run riot. It was easy: you wouldn't have anywhere to pee or brush your teeth; and you wouldn't be able to get a glass of water in the middle of the night; and it would probably be cold and wet, and there might well be bugs and insects crawling over you in the night…

The next morning I posed under a blanket for a few pictures and then wrote the story up in my most purple prose. By the end of the feature, you would have thought that I'd spent the night alone in the Amazon jungle.

The story made a whole page in the paper; George seemed happy enough, and that would normally have been the end of it, just another piece of newspaper for tomorrow's fish and chips.

Except…

My mistake was not that I'd fabricated the entire story - well not as such. My mistake was that I'd told Rudi. On the night in question, we'd sat in the Slug and Lettuce drinking pint after pint as we concocted ever more fantastical details for the feature. It is always the little details that bring a story to life. And it is always your fellow journalists who are going to blab. We are storytellers, both by inclination and by trade - and where's the fun in having a secret unless it can be shared?

Rudi told Siobhan, and then Siobhan told Phoebe, and soon enough the story had gone right round the advertising department, and from there it was but a short step to the editor's ear.

Hugh called me into his office. His office was as spit-polished as ever, and the plastic plants gleamed by the window. It was the end of the week - the day of days, the day of my first date with Sasha. I was as frisky as a puppy.

Hugh was wearing his brown three-piece suit. I wondered why I'd been called into his office - and then I saw my feature in front of him on his desk. This prickle of danger flickering up the back of my neck.

"Close the door," he said and I shut it. He was stroking the ends of his Fu Manchu moustache with the tips of his fingers.

"I hear you made up that homeless feature," he said. "You made up that homeless feature."

"I certainly did not," I retorted. It was the only thing I could say; if a greenhorn reporter were to admit to making up stories, they'd be fired on the spot.

"I'm told you just spent the night in the pub and then went back to your treehouse," Hugh said. He pulled his bottle of disinfectant gel from his waistcoat pocket and started to clean his hands. He had a very particular way of cleaning his hands, like a surgeon scrubbing up before an operation. "You went back to your treehouse."

"That is outrageous," I said. "I was certainly drinking that night - as does every other homeless person before they go to sleep. But I slept rough and bloody cold it was too."

"Where did you sleep?"

"Close by to the church," I said. "It's all in the story."

"Did anyone see you there?"

"I very much doubt it," I said. "I didn't want anyone near me. I might have been mugged, beaten up, who knows."

Hugh drummed his fingers on the desk as he appraised me. "So you spent the night on the streets?"

"Absolutely," I said.

"Why's this story going round that you made the whole thing up?"

"I have no idea," I said, as I mentally cursed Rudi, who could have been the only source for the story. "Malicious gossip."

He gave me the silent treatment. I've had it from the mad-masters many times since. They say nothing and they say nothing, and if you don't know any better, you crack and you start babbling.

I did not say anything. I looked out of the window.

At length, Hugh spoke again. "Fabricating stories is a very serious crime for a journalist," he said. "It'll be the end of not just your apprenticeship but your whole career."

I walked out of the office. It was a big life-lesson: if you have a secret that must be kept, then you cannot afford to tell a single soul. And as for secret lovers, well they are always the most impossible hostages to fortune, for there is no controlling them, and there is no telling just when or how they will explode.

CHAPTER 13

I'd spent some time considering where to take Sasha on our first date. It had to be different, something memorable, and that pretty much ruled out taking her for dinner anywhere in Cirencester.

I'd thought about just cooking her some supper in the tree-house - and how much of it were we actually going to eat anyway before the dinner table was abandoned for the bedroom? - but then I happened to spot something on the way back home from the office, and what started as a small worm of a thought had soon transformed itself into a beautiful butterfly. I didn't know whether she'd like it. But what I did know was that she'd never have been in the place before - would never have dreamed of setting foot in the place. That had to be a good thing.

"Where are we going tonight?" she'd asked on the phone.

"We are going somewhere extremely smart," I said.

"So it's not Cirencester then."

"It is, as it happens," I said. "Can you kindly dress appropriately."

"You want me to dress up too?"

"Of course," I said. I was doodling love hearts onto my notepad. I was so utterly smitten. "Unless you want to stick out like a -"

"Are you dressing up too?"

"Yes, I will be looking as smart as you've ever seen me."

There was a pause. "So where are we going?"

"Well I don't know for certain, but I would hazard that it is probably the smartest place you've ever visited."

"Or you're just setting me up."

"*Moi?*" I said. "This is our first date, Sasha. I want it to be just as romantic as can be."

"Exactly - you're up to something."

"And don't be late!"

We arranged to meet at the Woolpack, which was one of Cirencester's slightly smarter pubs. For our first date, I did not want to be heckled by friends or colleagues.

I wore a grey suit. It had belonged to my father, when he'd been a spry subaltern in the army and it fitted me quite well. Black shoes, white shirt, top two buttons undone. I showered and shaved at the pool – and, not that I was necessarily expecting Sasha to spend the night, but just on the very off chance, I changed the sheets on my sofa-bed.

I arrived twenty minutes early at the Woolpack. The pub was dark, dingy, solemn, a place where for centuries farmers had drunk beer and discussed sheep prices, a much more serious pub than the Slug and Lettuce. I bought a pint of beer and read the papers; a guy I knew, Mike Hamill, had *The Sun's* front page story. It was a story about a married Colonel sleeping with a married Sergeant; I did not know at the time, but *The Sun* has a limitless capacity for sex stories in the military. I wondered if I'd ever make it onto Fleet Street.

I did that thing that guys do when they are waiting for a date. I would read two sentences and would look up at the door to see if Sasha had come in, and then would return to my newspaper – to read the exact same two sentences again. Even when we young swains have declared our love, it still does not do to have our girlfriends think that we are hanging on their footfall, like some family spaniel hanging around the front-door as it waits for its master return.

And then, of course, at 6pm exactly, I feel the urgent need for a pee, and so off I scurry to the toilets, washing and thoroughly drying my hands – wet hands out of the toilet are a passion-killer – and by the time I emerged, Sasha was standing at the bar ordering herself a glass of white wine.

She only looked: sensational. She was wearing a simple dress, very dark green, tight at the waist with a black belt. Her hair cascaded down her back.

I went up beside her, slipped my arm around her waist and as she turned her head I kissed her on the cheek. I could smell her hair. It was appley, beautiful. "How are you?" I said.

"Very well," she said, and she took a step back to appraise me. "And wearing a suit?"

"It's going to be a lovely surprise," I said, leading the way back to my table. "You're going to think you've died and gone to heaven."

She laughed as we sat down. "I don't know why, Kim, but this whole evening whiffs of cheese. What's that all about?"

"I just can't tell you, Sasha," I said.

"I've been doing my research," she said. "There are no smart places in Cirencester."

"Maybe we're going to Cheltenham," I said. "Maybe the cab's booked and it's waiting outside."

Sasha took a sip of her wine and leaned back in her chair. She linked her fingers behind her head, quite the power pose.

"I have a very good nose for these things -"

"I love your nose, by the way."

"That is as well," she said. "My nose tells me that you are lying."

"Tut," I said. "That's not a very good start for a relationship, is it? Sasha, darling, it's our first date. I've waited over a year for this moment. I just want it to be as romantic as can be."

"Exactly," she said. "You're lying through your teeth."

"How it grieves me so to hear those words."

We laughed; even though it was our first date, there was a wonderful easiness and an intimacy about the evening. That's what comes of having paid your dues. That's what comes of having spent over a year in each other's company and not snatched a single kiss. That is propinquity.

I checked my watch. "Come on." I downed my pint and she finished her wine, and I liked that; I like it when a woman does not let alcohol go to waste.

As soon as we were out on the street, we held hands. It felt quite natural - and so wholly unnatural. On the one part, it felt right, and in the correct order of things, to be holding Sasha's hand - and on the other, well I just couldn't believe that I was walking down the street with this beautiful woman. And she was my girlfriend! My girlfriend! It would take me some time to get used to those two words.

We were walking close by to The Standard's offices and by chance, Hugh the Editor was walking on the other side of the street. He saw me and did a double-take. I gave him a wave, as if it were perfectly normal for me to be wearing a suit and walking down the street on the arm of a beautiful woman; he gawked.

"Who's that?" Sasha said.

"My boss – Hugh."

"Do you get on with him?"

"Not overly," I said. "Probably even less so now that he's seen me with you."

"He doesn't love my lying bastard of a boyfriend as much as I do?"

"Lying bastard?"

Sasha brought my hand to her lips and kissed my knuckles. "As far as I know, dear lying bastard, there is not a single place this end of town where we could be going to. What do you say to that?"

"You're wrong. You are so, so wrong. And by the way, it pains me greatly to be called a lying bastard."

"Well I'm right."

"You haven't got a clue!"

We walked past the Standard's offices and started off down Lewis Lane.

"We're going to the cinema?" she said.

"We certainly are not," I said contemptuously, wheeling her sharp to the left. "We're going to the bingo."

"Bingo?" she said, flummoxed. "The bingo hall?"

"Ever been before?"

"I have not."

"That'll make two of us."

I'd signed up with the bingo hall a couple of days earlier, and the more I'd thought about it, the more it seemed like the most perfect venue for a first date with Sasha. Firstly, of course, no-one else in Cirencester would have been insane enough to have taken someone like Sasha off for a date to the bingo. And secondly, just as with my eccentric little home, it would be a small test. Either Sasha would think our bingo date was charming and funny and just the most perfect way to spend our first proper evening together - or she would think it weird and unpleasant, and probably best all round to call a quick halt to things rather than continue going any further down this rather eccentric avenue. I know for a certainty that if I'd given Mousie the bingo test, we wouldn't have lasted one week; she'd have *hated* the place!

And as for my Sasha...

"Wow," she said, as we queued up in the brilliantly-lit foyer to buy our tickets. We were possibly a little over-dressed. "I knew it was going to be smart," she said. "I just didn't know it was going to be *this* smart."

"I did try to warn you," I said. The other people in the queue turned and stared, though for Sasha, that was not so unusual; wherever she went, people stared at her.

I bought our strips of tickets and two fat blue marker pens, dobbers, and we went through to the main auditorium. The bingo-hall doesn't exist anymore, flattened now along with the cinema for some new housing development, but in my mind's eye, it was far larger than I'd expected, with tiers of tables stretching down to the stage far beneath us. As it was a Friday night, the place was heaving. I think we took the average age down to about fifty-five.

People had started to twitch and look. Sasha stood comfortably beside me, little clutch handbag in hand. It was one of the many things I loved about her. She could not be embarrassed. "And what do we do now, Mr Smartypants?" she said.

"We ask one of these ladies what it is that we are supposed to do," I said.

"You've really never been here before?" she said.

"Never," I said. "Exciting, isn't it?"

"It is," she said and she leaned over and kissed my cheek.

"If I didn't know you any better, I'd think you were getting quite turned on."

We were taken to a table by one of the assistants, Jayne, and she explained the rules of the game; as I'm sure you know, it's all pretty simple. Mark off each number as it's called, and there was a prize for the first line, another for the first two lines, and then a bigger prize for a full house. "You've got to call out quick," Jayne said. "If they've called the next number, you've missed it." She was about to leave, but thought better of it. "Don't see many people like you here," she said.

"We thought it'd be fun," I said.

"You've come to the right place," Jayne said - and she was right.

I went to buy some wine, but the wine looked rough, so I bought a selection of spirits and took them to our table on a tray.

Sasha raised her eyebrows when I returned to the table. She had been quietly surveying the hall; she seemed very happy. She looked at the eight glasses. "You don't need to get me drunk, you know," she said.

"Don't ask," I said. "It was the best I could do."

I slipped in at the table. We were quite close together now. Our knees touched, pressed, and a moment later I had her leg squeezed between my knees.

Sasha could tell each of the spirits just by the smell. She took a gin and tonic and I had a whisky, and then it was eyes down, and the caller was giving us Maggie's Den, Number Ten, and Kelly's Eye, Number One, and though the game is easy to understand, you still have to concentrate or before you know it you're three numbers behind and desperately playing catch up.

And Sasha: hair falling down in front of her face, dobbing away with her marker pen, and occasionally smiling with this most wicked glint in her eye. "I'm going to get you for this," she said, and I had to restrain myself from then and there stretching over the table to kiss her.

Now, not that I know very much at all about dating, but this is one thing that is true: if you have won yourself a date with a beautiful woman, then you will not do much better than a bingo hall. There is drama and excitement, and laughs; and new things to talk about and new sights to be seen; and a wealth of material for jokes and quips; and also, unbelievably, this slow steady build-up of tension as you realise that you are two numbers away - one number away! - from a full house, and though you know full well that it's all a lot of hot froth, you can be so utterly in the moment that you start to sizzle as you yearn for your number to be called.

"I am so close," Sasha said. We were over an hour into it now, just past the half-time break. We had drunk all our shorts, as whisky was mixed with brandy and vodka. She looked at me, smiling, lips just a few inches from mine. I blew her a kiss.

"Who'd have guessed that it was going to be this much of a turn-on," I said.

"You!"

Another number, and another dot of her marker pen. "Come on!" she said. "Come on!"

Her legs jiggled up and down beside me, like a punter watching her horse cruising into the final furlong.

"God I'm loving this," she said.

The next number came - "Six and seven, sixty seven." You hear the number and initially you're hoping that it's your number, but when it's not your number, you're praying that you don't hear the shriek. The shriek comes within a second of a number being called. It means the game's over.

Sasha looked at me, teeth snapping together in mock frustration.

"Eighty and four, eighty four," came the next number, and by now there must have been fifty or sixty people in the hall who were just a single number from a full house; but still no shriek.

"This is it," Sasha said. "It's coming now - I can feel it." Her marker pen was poised over a single number on her bingo card.

"On its own, number four."

Sasha punched her hand in the air. "House!" A sigh goes round the hall as everyone else's dreams crumble to dust, but Sasha is sitting there waving her card above her head, saying, "I don't believe it! I never win anything. I never win a thing!"

Jayne came over and checked the numbers, and a few minutes later Sasha was given an envelope with three ten pound notes inside. She was quite absurdly thrilled. She pushed the money towards me.

"We're going shares," she said.

"Don't be ridiculous," I said. "It's yours."

"How did you fix that?"

"I bribed the caller," I said. "I wanted a date you'd never forget."

"Oh it is that," she said. "And it's not even 9 o'clock."

"And I haven't even kissed you yet."

"It's about time you did."

The next game had started, and the numbers were being called, and the lights were flashing up on the screens, but we paid them no heed, leaning towards each over the table with hungry lips, and we kissed; our marker pens clattered to the table. Not a long kiss, but soft and perfect.

"What's next for me?" she said.

"Me," I said.

"You?" she said. She placed the money and her marker pen into her bag. "Let's not waste any more time then." She stood up and I followed her lead; I kept my dobber as a memento.

We sashayed down to the exit, and even though it was midway through the next game, half the hall was watching us. I gave Jayne a five pound tip, Sasha gave a little wave, and a minute later we were out on the street. It was cold and I gave Sasha my jacket; I was pleased that I did that. Even weeks afterwards, I could still smell her perfume on the collar; to wear it was to feel her kiss.

"And where now?" Sasha said, holding onto my arm with both hands. "It better be your treehouse."

"But I was going to take you to Tatyan's. Don't you like Chinese?"

We walked in sync, shoulder to shoulder, hip to hip.

"Don't you have any food at home?"

"Not much - not much at all." I broke off from her hands, and slipped my arm around her waist. "Just a bit of stuff from Waitrose - a roast chicken and some salad; and a loaf of fresh white bread; and some ice for the icebox." I scratched my head in thought. "Ohh - and four bottles of Chablis in the ice-box, just in case you got thirsty…"

"Is that it?"

"No - some apples too, quite a lot of apples, as well as a bar of chocolate. That's in the ice-box, because I didn't want it to melt –"

"So you've got a fire too?"

"That fire will be roaring –"

"Are you trying to seduce me?"

Without missing a beat, I leaned over and kissed her. "Are you sure you're a virgin?"

She slipped her hand underneath my shirt and stroked my back. "This is going to be some test."

And to be fair to her, the treehouse that night must have been some considerable test of her virtue. I knew beforehand that she loved my home, so when I had left it that afternoon, the place was as perfect as I could make it, new candles in the candlesticks and a large log left slow burning in the Jøtul.

But I did not attempt to seduce Sasha that night, nor for many nights after it. It would have been a mistake. We might have made the most ecstatic love, but by sun-up, I knew that she'd have regretted it. No – when we made love, we would make love at a time of Sasha's own choosing.

There was one other reason why we did not make love that night – as I shall soon come to.

But aside from love-making, there are – or so I understand it – other ways in which we can satisfy our lovers; more sinuous, delicate methods in which their desires can be sated. Imagine building up a fire on a bed of last night's hot cinders. You put in fire-lighters, paper and twigs and some coal on top – and for a long time, nothing happens; there is smoke and a small amount of heat, but as yet there is no fire. And this can go on for a long time. The paper may char to cinders, the twigs may crisp and the coals may turn hot, and yet to the naked eye, nothing is happening. I like what happens next: all it needs is one single spark – not even a flame – and the fire is instantaneous, as if all along the twigs and the coal have been hungering for nothing but that single spark.

We went into the treehouse. It was dark inside, with the tree creaking all around us. I threw open the doors of the Jøtul and as Sasha warmed herself by the fire, I lit some candles. I could feel Sasha watching me as I put the candles in the windows and on the tables.

She was sitting on the rug by the fire, feet tucked demurely beneath her. I put on my only tape - The Magic Flute - and opened a bottle of Chablis and poured two glasses.

I gave her a glass and as she took it, lips glistening, neck outstretched, I leaned down and kissed her. We drank and we looked at each other, and still we had not said a word since stepping foot into the tree-house, for fear of breaking the spell.

I had planned on having supper at the table, by the window, but it seemed better by far by the fire. I carved the chicken and dressed the salad with virgin olive oil and served it on two plates. We loll on our sides on the rug, like Roman noblemen, the fire at our bare feet and the food set on the plates between us. Little by little we peck at the chicken, but with Sasha lying next to me like this, I have no appetite for food. We sip our wine and we look into each other's eyes and we dream of all the things that we would do to each other.

Sasha has eaten some of the chicken, but little else, and I pick up the plates and push them under the armchairs. Now there is nothing between us but our wine. I lean over, I caress her cheek and I stroke her hair, from the roots to the tips, and almost instantly she closes her eyes and groans; and when a woman does that, a man would be wise to continue. I stroke her hair again, finger-tips to her scalp, and her hair feels like silk as it runs through my fingers. "Yes," she says, and that is the first word that either of us have said since we've stepped foot into the treehouse.

"What would you have me do to you?"

"Do that," she says, and now we are sitting side by side, Sasha with her face to the fire and I'm stroking her hair, and after a while I have reached this Zen state where although I desire her, I am sated, and all that I am and all that I am about is this beautiful black mane in front of me. I bring her hair to my nose and I inhale, and the smell of apples has never been the same since.

I kiss Sasha on the neck. "I am going to take your dress off now," I whisper. "If that is what you would like."

"Yes."

"I should warn you though," I said. "We're not going to make love tonight."

"What are we going to do?"

"You're going to think you've died and gone to heaven," I say. "Just like at the bingo-hall," and at that, she quite giggles with delight. Her dress has a black zipper at the back. I lift up her hair, and with the other I unzip all the way to the small of her back, and the dress is peeled off and cast onto one of the chairs. Sasha basks in the firelight. It flickers over her skin turning it to molten gold.

"Red?" I said. "I like it."

"I bought them for you."

"You better keep them on for a little longer then." I sipped some wine. Her hand was on her knee and she was holding her wine; she glows with desire. I let my eyes slowly rake over her body, taking it all in. I notice her manicured toe-nails.

"And toe-nails to match?"

"You're spending a lot of time looking at my legs," she said. "Do you want to kiss them?"

"I've wanted to kiss your legs for a very long time." She leant back against the armchair and raised her foot to my cheek. I took it in both hands and kissed it. "How you used to tempt me, when we were driving along, and when you used to put your feet up on the dashboard?"

"What did you dream of?"

"I fantasized about pulling over and whisking you off into some friendly field, and then doing just this -" I dabbed with my tongue and kissed above her ankle. "And I wondered what it would be like to kiss the backs of your knees."

"No-one has ever kissed the backs of my knees," she said.

"Well tonight, Sasha, is the night -"

"Don't tell me - I'm going to think I've died and gone to heaven."

"A much under-rated erogenous zone." I lifted her leg up and very gently kissed the back of her knee. "How was that?"

"I'm not sure," she said. "Do it again." And I did it again.

"It's a slow build-up of tension," I said. "Much like with the bingo. One kiss isn't going to do it. Turn over - please. I need time in order to practise my craft."

"Your craft -"

"My art, if you like."

She lay face down on the rug, side on to the fire, and with her red knickers at a rakishly jaunty angle about her hips. I trailed my tongue from her heels to her hips and then back again; the first time I kissed the back of her knees, she squealed and her foot flew up, but the second time, there was no reaction, and after the third kiss, there came a sigh.

I took off my shirt and, as is my wont, hurled it across the room. She turned to watch me, face on her forearms, as I unbuckled my belt and took off my trousers. "I should be doing that," she said.

"All in due course. For the moment, we are on Project Back of the Knee -"

"Project Back of the Knee?" She chuckled.

"Followed shortly thereafter by Project Elbow and Project Ear -"

"And what about Project Boxers Off?"

"That comes after Project Bra Off -

"Kiss me," she said and, on all fours now, I leaned down and kissed her. Her hands strayed to my boxers. I broke off.

"Despite these lovely kissing interludes, we are still continuing with Project Back of the Knee -"

"You really know how to turn a girl on -"

"Turn you on?" I reached for the virgin olive oil with which I had dressed the salad. "I haven't even started."

I drizzled a little of the oil over her feet and legs and worked it into her heels and between her toes. I knelt between her legs. I marvelled at her calves, her thighs; at this long body that was lying in front of me. I'd catch myself looking at her, admiring her - and then would suddenly realise that this was Sasha. And she was my girlfriend.

"I feel so relaxed," she said. "Considering it's out first time like this."

"It's propinquity," I said. "We've been friends a long time."

"Nothing at all to do with all that drink you've been plying me with."

Softly, with just the tips of my fingers, I brushed the backs of her knees. I did it again more firmly, stroking rhythmically with my fingers. I was staring at her knickers. I would have liked to have bent down and pulled her knickers aside with my teeth, and then to have kissed her.

"I thought it was going to be like a massage," she said. "It's quite turning me on."

"That's good," I said, as I continued to lick and to stroke, and occasionally my tongue would glide a little up the inside of her thigh, and of her own volition, her legs parted further and further to the side, and though it may have been my imagination, it seemed that her hips were pushing back, and that her red silk knickers were then tight-stretched across her buttocks.

I stopped and drank wine and the fire crackled in the Jøtul, and I had half a mind to… to do all manner of things to this beauty, but instead I returned to her knees, with my tongue now cold from the wine, and she groaned again, and she was happy and I was happy, and it might have continued much longer, but Sasha turned over.

"Lovely though that all is, I want my hands on you," she said. "Will you surrender?"

"I'm running up the white flag as we speak -"

"Or perhaps the white boxers," and she leaned forward, both hands at my hips, and my boxers were being pulled down my thighs to my knees. "The backs of your knees will have to wait for another time. I have my heart set on another erogenous zone entirely."

"Which one?" I leaned over and unhitch her bra and, elegant as a burlesque dancer, she slipped out of it, and the bra fell to the floor. "I have many."

"I wonder," she said. "Let's see if you can guess." I looked at her breasts, the first time that I was allowed to see them, and I watched her lips as they kissed about my hips, my thighs, and my stomach, her tongue fluttering over my skin. I kneeled in front of her and she looked up at me and it only seemed like the most erotic sight that I have ever seen in my life.

"May I?" she said, fingers stroking me into a frenzy.

"Oh that erogenous zone?" I said, but before I could say any more, she had moved with her mouth, and for a while even I was silenced; it is one thing to dream about these things that we would do with our loves, but to have it happen is quite another.

She broke off and she smiled at me. "You were using olive oil, weren't you?" she said. "Another thing I haven't tried." She took the bottle, poured oil into the cup of her hand, rubbing it into her fingers before smoothing it onto me. She licked where the oil has been, and I was transfixed by the sight of her tongue, flickering in the firelight, teasing me till I was all but groaning at this hollow pit of hunger that seemed to lie deep in my belly.

And she broke off, leaning back lazily against the armchair, well satisfied with herself. She looked quite brazen, her breasts, her lips and her chin gleam with olive oil.

"Salad dressing will never be the same again," she said.

"Imagine what we'll be doing in a month."

"I wonder," she said, and without any more prompting, she lifted up, and her knickers are pulled down, and I ease them off her legs. She was naked, sitting in front of me, quite casual, her legs arranged just so, and after all our months of swimming together, I have seen her body many times, and I have come to love its every curve, its every indent - and yet though I know it well, without clothes, she seemed to have become exponentially more beautiful. She stretched out and we held hands and she pulled me over towards her, and there we sat, naked in front of the fire, our hands free to roam about each other's bodies - and, later on, much would come of it. I could hear the music, and a log shifted in the fire, collapsing in upon itself into a bed of red ash; and Sasha sighed as we kiss and as my hand trickled tricksy-like up between her legs and she watched, fascinated, as I tasted my fingers. There was a light wind, and the tree itself seemed to be letting out this residual moan, and I could hear a branch dapping at one of the windows... And I heard something else, something that is not right. It was that sly, subtle creak of the seventh step, and it meant that somebody is coming up the stairs.

What to do? Sasha is kissing me, kissing my neck, my shoulders, quite oblivious to that tell-tale squeak on the stairs and what it might indicate. Should I tell her? Warn her? Should perhaps we move to the bedroom, where we can snuggle under the duvet in the darkness? Or should I do nothing at all, pretend that I've heard nothing, seen nothing?

I did not do the right thing, I know that now.

Better by far to have pulled on my boxers and gone to the door, and opened it wide and said what needed to be said, because although it would have definitely killed the moment - oh yes, make no mistake of that - it would have brought things to a very swift head, and all else that was to follow from it would have been neatly nipped in the bud.

But I did not. I ignored that creak on the stairs and I continued to kiss Sasha and through soft-shut eyes, I looked at the door, and though I did not see anything for a while, I eventually saw her standing outside on the balcony. She watched us for a moment and then she was gone; with her white face and her straggly blonde hair she was like some night phantom come to haunt us.

CHAPTER 14

If you have a grand strategy, then with luck your big plan will keep you going till the end of your days. But if all that you have is merely strategy, then one day, eventually, the war will be won, and you will have to find some other fresh windmill to tilt at.

With Sasha, my strategy had been first and foremost to be as aloof and indifferent as I knew how, so that one day she might come to love me. And, thanks to propinquity, the Beauty had indeed come to love her Beast; my strategy, both in whole and in part, had been a resounding success.

Some people, many people, often feel quite deflated when their quest has come to an end. There they are, running at full tilt on this treadmill that they have set for themselves, and suddenly, without really knowing it, they have succeeded beyond their wildest expectations - and the treadmill judders to this abrupt stop, and there they sit in a heap of tears upon the floor as they wonder just what else to do with their lives.

Well I was not like that - not at all. I revelled in having Sasha as my girlfriend; there was not one single thing about her that did not delight me.

In my idle moments, I would occasionally wonder about what it was that I wanted to do next. I stared into the mist and tried to discern anything that had the makings of a Grand Strategy. But for many weeks, my life was led by short-term tactics, and those were chiefly to spend as much time with Sasha as possible; and to delight and amuse and charm her in any and every way that I could conceive; and to have her stripped in my tree-house, or her bedroom, or in fact any leafy bower that happened to come to hand, just about as often as I could lure her there. And, beautifully, pleasingly, she shared my desires, and we took great delight in stripping each other naked and slaking our love.

It might perhaps surprise you to learn that seducing Sasha, making love to her, was not a part of my agenda. It would happen eventually, in the fullness of time, of that I was quite sure. But I was in no hurry to force the pace; gradually and at the most leisurely pace, we were getting to know each other's tastes and bedroom peccadilloes. Besides, there are other ways in which we can satisfy our loves, and oral sex has its own quite different charms, as it comes with its own unusual intimacy; quite a contrast, I can tell you – Mousie who would only make love in a well-made bed, and who had no taste for oral sex; and then, Sasha, my olive-oil streaked Sasha, for whom oral sex was the very bedrock of our love-life, and who adored being pressed into action in even the most eye-popping situations, and yet who always demurred about taking that final step. I never pressed her on the point. She'd be ready when she was ready, and when that time came, I did not doubt that I would be the first to know.

As you would expect, some people they were happy for me that Sasha was my girlfriend – and some they were not.

Most of the office seemed pleased and only slightly flabbergasted. Most, though not all.

George had been leafing through a number of magazines looking for stories, and in the middle of *Tatler* he'd come across a couple of pictures of Sasha. Her polo team, Jokers Wild, had won some competition, and she'd posed with the team, the fat red *Patron* with his arm around her waist as he cradled the cup.

George tossed the magazine down in front of me. "You're moving in very select circles, Cadet Kim," he said.

I picked up the magazine. Sasha looked stunning – much more beautiful, even, than the professional models draped in their jewels and their *haute couture*.

"I do what I can," I said.

The magazine was passed round the newsroom and the other reporters cackled, and I laughed with them, because having your girlfriend appear in *Tatler* is certainly not something to be proud of. Some young thrusters adore appearing in *Tatler*; perhaps they are unaware of how ludicrous they seem.

And that would have been the end of it, except Hugh the editor came into the room, and having those acute little antennae that come to all of the mad-masters, he went straight over to Rudi and looked at the magazine.

"That's your girlfriend?" Hugh said.

"It was quite a surprise to me too," I said. I broke off from my keyboard to look at him.

"That is your girlfriend?" he said again as he read the caption. "Sasha, the manager of Jokers Wild?"

"That'd be the one," I said.

"You been dating a while?" He gave the magazine back to Rudi, and then started patting his pockets for his infernal bottle of antiseptic gel.

"A little while."

"About bloody time you started getting us some stories from Cirencester Park, isn't it then - or is that all a little beneath you now?"

I looked at him, very quiet; the whole newsroom was quite silent.

"I'll see what I can do," I said.

"Do so - if it wouldn't be too much trouble," he said and he stalked out of the room - and we let out a collective sigh, because as it was, local weekly papers are not generally in the business of hunting down exclusives; they are the papers of record. That sordid business of hunting for world exclusives is best left to those driven beasts of burden who ply their trade on the Red Tops.

I was smarting at Hugh's words, but I did ponder them, and in time they would bear fruit - though just not in quite the way that Hugh had expected it.

★

There was one other person who, of course, was not going to be happy that Sasha and I had become an item.

I had not been looking forward to telling Paris the news, and so in the usual spineless way I had not told him. Though in fairness, I had not been on the usual RAC circuit. When Sasha was around we were like every other young couple on earth who have declared their love and who are done with game-playing: we only wanted to be with each other. We did not tend to go to the pub as, even though she might be sitting with me, she was always having to fend off the advances of brooding polo-players and drunken students. We preferred to sit on the balcony of the treehouse and drink chilled rosé, mentally undressing each other before with a nod and a touch we started doing it for real.

But it was late spring and the polo season was in full swing, which meant that Sasha was spending a lot of her weekends nurse-maiding the *Patron* and stars of Jokers Wild. In her role as manager, she not only had to ensure that the twenty-odd polo ponies were all in absolute peak condition, but also had to act as a Concierge for her players, sorting out not just their mounts but their accommodation and even their frenetic love lives. The South American players were absolute catnip to the women of Cirencester. They merely had to enter a room and women turned to pools of rose-scented slush. I wonder what it would be like to have that sort of magic, to have women jump at the very click of your fingers. I can only dream.

My evenings apart from Sasha were spent either getting drunk with my fellow hacks or attending the local council meetings. Each of the market towns around Cirencester had their own town council, or sometimes parish council, and every week or so, the Standard hacks would trek out to the provinces to cover these interminable meetings. What hell! What unbelievable torpor! Sitting with your back to the wall, scribbling inanities into your notepad, and meanwhile it's not even dusk, and through the windows comes the sound of laughter from the nearby pub garden.

I was at Fairford Town Council and I had gone into this sort of catatonic stupor. My eyes were open, and my notepad was on my knee, and for the previous hour this wash of conversation had cascaded over my head and not a word of it had gone in.

I was dreaming, as ever, of Sasha. She'd gone off with the polo-team to Cowdray Park and she was due back that evening. Seeing her polo team get under way was quite a sight. Just transporting all the polo ponies needed two immense pantechnicons, though the ponies were easier by far to handle than Sasha's flighty stars.

Would she pop round for a visit later? It was only one of my favourite things on earth to be asleep in my tree and to hear the rustle of Sasha slipping into the bed beside me.

And I remembered what we had done three days previously, and how, after some considerable time, I had reduced her to juddering speechlessness; and I thought of some of the places in Cirencester Park that we had yet to christen; and, I suppose, I fantasized a little of what it might be like when the day came when we made love. In my mind, there was no "if" about it; it was always a matter of "when".

There was a shriek from the cricket pitch and I jolted back into the present and into the council meeting, and I looked at my watch, and realised that though I had been there for a night and a day, the meeting itself had only been going on for an hour - and would continue till long after nightfall.

I did something that I had never done before. I got up and, after a polite nod to the perplexed chairman, I left the meeting and I left the councillors to carry on spiralling into whatever Black Hole would have them: for that week, the exploits of the Fairford Town Councillors would go unreported in the local paper.

With one bound, Kim was free! In over a year with the Wilts and Glos, I had never conceived of walking out of a meeting just because I was bored - for after all, if I were to make a habit of it, then there wouldn't be a council in Gloucestershire that could hold me for more than five minutes. But I had done it, I had made my break for freedom, and as I walked out into the balmy summer's evening, I felt not just liberated but utterly euphoric. I still do it occasionally, skive away from some dull meeting that has been tasked out for me by the mad-masters; I could not recommend it more. Through your own endeavours, you have liberated two precious hours of this little life that we have, and these hours are all the sweeter for knowing that you alone have wrested them.

I mooched through the St Mary's graveyard. The choir was having a practice session, and the stained glass windows were lit from the inside-out. The windows are Medieval, some of the finest and oldest stained glass in Britain. My favourite part is in the corner of the West Window where, sitting alone, there is a jolly red demon with yellow eyes and white jagged teeth. He is quietly observing all the orderly church mumblings and yet he is not a part of it; I've always thought of him as one of the world's early-day reporters.

I needed alcohol. I popped over the market square to The Bull. There were two motorbikes outside, new and gleaming black; they were big boys' bikes, Harley Davidsons.

The two bikers were standing at the bar with their backs to the door. I saw that one of the bikers had a pint of beer in each hand and I knew of only one person who drank two pints of beer at a time and that was Dangerous.

Dangerous was the first to spot me. "Look what the cat brought in!" he said, punching me in the stomach.

Paris clapped me over the shoulder. "Kim!" he said. "What can I get you?"

I asked for a pint, and we surveyed each other. I was in my reporting gear, jacket and tie, while Paris and Dangerous wore black leather jackets and robust biker boots. Paris had a black scarf tied pirate-like around his head.

"Nice bikes," I said.

"You like them?" Paris said.

"Aren't you two lads a bit young to be having a midlife crisis?"

Paris chuckled into his beer. "Where have you been? I haven't seen you in ages."

"Skulking." I sipped my pint. I wondered if I should mention Sasha. "Skulking and diligently going about my business as a trainee reporter on Her Majesty's Wilts and Gloucestershire Standard. What have you been doing?"

"We've been up to Bristol for the day," Paris said. "Do you like biking? Want a spin? Dangerous has a spare helmet."

"Thanks - but no thanks," I said, looking at Dangerous. He was stolidly drinking his second pint.

"You'd love it," Paris said. "Speed on the open road."

Dangerous belched. "Got a ton up through Bibury."

"Impressive," I said. "Has the Standard already prepared your obituary?"

"They're safe as anything. Honestly." Paris said. "Certainly safer than that old Merc of yours. They've got enough power to get you out of trouble."

I laughed in his face. "Maybe I'm just squeamish about getting my face wiped on the tarmac."

"Who's sounding middle-aged now?"

Dangerous gestured to the barman. He didn't say anything - he never said anything much, least of all anything worth hearing - but just held up four fingers. The barman started pulling four fresh pints.

"We've got the May Ball," Paris said. "Would you like to come?"

"That's very kind of you," I temporised.

"Bring a date if you want - the girls love it. It goes on till dawn, and then we all head off to The Tunnel for breakfast."

"Thank you," I said. "I'll see -"

There must have been a tang to the way my words came out, because Paris instantly smelt something in the wind. "You're seeing someone!" he said. "Who is the lucky girl?"

"She…" I paused and my mouth formed to shape the words, but nothing came out.

"She?"

"She is Sasha," I said, and though they had split from each other six, seven months previously, his face sagged, as bad as if I'd told him of a bereavement.

"Oh," Paris said. Dangerous paused from drinking, his pint halfway to his lips.

I said the only thing that I could think to say. "I'm sorry."

"No, no, it's... it's fine," Paris said, as this mask snapped shut over his face. "How long... how long have you been seeing each other?"

"Just a few weeks. It's very early days."

"You and Sasha?" He started picking at his ear. "How is she?"

"In the throes of the polo season. You know how it goes." And though we are mouthing words, and saying pleasantries, I can feel all these undercurrents that swirl and tug beneath the surface.

"Anyway," said Paris. "Must be off now. Let me know about the ball. It would be lovely to see you... to see you both."

And we left and I went back to the car and, really, was it such a surprise that Paris was so devastated? His Sasha was with someone else, and he was still as smitten as ever.

I thought of Paris as I drove back home. He was my friend and I felt for him; but it could not be helped. As far as Sasha was concerned, she was always going to be the woman who broke men's hearts.

It was all but dusk when I got back. I went out and sat in the deck-chair on the little platform that was set off from the main treehouse. It was where Sir Anthony used to meditate in the morning. The platform, no bigger than a single bed, was out on a limb on one of the main branches, and you reached it via a precarious roped walkway.

I liked it out there on that limb. On the platform, you seemed to be much more fused with the tree than ever you were in the treehouse. I had a glass and a bottle of wine with me, and through the branches I could just make out the darkening park. I was quite camouflaged; I could see, but could not be seen. That is how we reporters like it.

I saw somebody walking across the park and then open the gate to Lady Claire's garden, and a moment later they were coming up the stairs. It was Sasha, and I watched through the windows as she knocked on the door and then walked into my treehouse. I enjoyed watching her in secret. She hung her coat on the peg on the tree-trunk and then strolled through to the bedroom. She sat on the bed and lit a candle, and was just taking off her boots when I called to her.

"Sasha!" I said. "I'm out here!"

She stood up and I saw her smile, and then she came out onto the rear balcony. "I wondered why this door was open."

"Come and join me."

With her hand on the rope rail, she sauntered over the walkway. She never once looked down, and when she was on the platform, she kissed me and then knelt at my feet. "You don't want to sit here?" I said. "Room for two."

She slipped her arms around my calves and rested her chin upon my knee. "I'm happy looking at you from down here," she said. "How was the council meeting?"

"I very daringly walked out," I said - before adding, almost as an afterthought. "I saw Paris in the pub. He's bought a new motorbike." I stroked her cheek, curling her hair about her ear.

"A Harley Davidson," Sasha said.

"He told you about it," I said.

"He always wanted one."

"He's still a long way from getting over you."

She looked up at me. She was biting her lower lip, though there was a smile trying to break through. "He'll be snapped up."

"He asked us to the May Ball," I said,

"Has he?" she said and we look at each other and there was such a wealth of unspoken thoughts that passed between us.

"But maybe not," I said. "Do you ever see him these days?"

"No. Not in ages."

"I like him," I said - and I wonder if, as I said it, I was casting a lure over Sasha's nose, seeing if she would rise to the bait.

"I would never, ever want to date Paris again," she said, and she tugged at my fly-buttons, watching me all the while as her magic fingers went about their work. "Last night I dreamt of making love with you."

"I dream about it all the time."

"And I think that we shouldn't over-think it; plan it too much."

"I won't be planning on anything," I said, and, now, I often think back to that short conversation; it was a small cog which would set many wheels into motion.

★

A few days later, I was up at Cirencester Park at the weekend watching Jokers Wild. Penny was up there too; I always remember her as being very loud. She had a shrill laugh and noisy chatter and wide expansive mannerisms and these all helped to attract attention. I wonder if she'd always been loud; I don't think she was. A beautiful young woman does not have to do anything much at all to have the men flocking; all she has to do is look serene, and men will come to her like wasps to jam. But, later on perhaps, once the bloom of her youth has started to fade, a beauty is no longer going to garner the same attention; and if she is shallow, and has no other strings to her bow, then she will do other things to get that attention. She will laugh louder and dance harder, and she will be tactile with her hands, and the clothes that she wears will scream "Look at me!"

Penny was wearing skin-tight yellow jeans and a fluorescent blue top and zany red glasses. Her blonde hair was in this scatty coil which was held together by two black pencils. She seized on me the moment that I walked into the Jokers Wild marquee. It was just set off from the main polo field, two sides open to the elements, with a table full of drinks, and a table groaning with food; and cracked cuboid tables that were made of solid oak; and chairs too, I remember those, not deckchairs, or light canvas chairs, but sumptuous sofas and comfortable armchairs. The marquee was empty apart from a young waiter behind the bar.

"Kim!" she said, slipping her arm through mine and kissing me on the cheek. "Just the man I've been looking for."

"How are you Penny?" I said.

She snuggled in closer, holding tight to my arm; she wasn't letting me go.

"And so you're seeing Sasha," she said.

"As I think you know," I said, for of course Penny had spied us naked and making out on that first night in the treehouse.

"My virginal daughter tells me nothing."

It was an odd way to describe Sasha. I let it ride.

"You ever much of a polo-player?" I asked.

"I take it she still is a virgin?" Penny searched my face for any tell-tale flicker in my eyes. I gave away nothing. "A virgin - at her age!"

"Do you ever watch any of the polo - or do you just stay in this tent drinking?"

"I don't know if I like your tone, Kim," she said. "I never took you for a prude. It must be infectious." She let out this crazy howl of laughter. "Sasha can be ever so prudish. Let's get something to drink."

She dragged me over to the bar and the waiter poured us two glasses of Champagne. We were about to leave when Penny grabbed the bottle and tucked it under her arm. We sat on a sofa, red leather in stunning contrast to the green grass; it all seemed utterly decadent.

Penny snuggled into me, and I retreated on the sofa, and without a word, she just moved right up next to me. I felt deeply uncomfortable, but I was also aware that she was Sasha's mother. It is usually politick to be polite to your girlfriend's mum.

"What's this whole business of being a virgin about - hey Kim?" Penny swigged from her glass and gave me a nudge. "What's it about?"

"I think it's admirable," I said.

"Admirable!" she said. "Hark at him! His girlfriend's a virgin and he thinks it's admirable. Hah!"

"Why shouldn't it be?"

"She's wasting the best years of her life."

"I think she's loving them."

Penny leaned forward, thigh pressing against my leg, and filled up her glass. The fizz dripped onto her legs and onto the sofa. "There will be plenty of time for not having sex when she's married - don't you know that Kim?"

"If you say so."

"I'm sure you find other things to do with each other, but nothing's ever really going to top a good fuck - is it?"

"Can we change the subject?"

"She must be tempted though, mustn't she?" She grabbed my leg, digging her bony fingers deep in above my knee. She wore a thick thumb-ring, silver and gaudy. "I'll bet you're a devil in bed - aren't you Kim?"

"I'm going to watch the polo." I stood up, her hand still pawing at my leg.

For a while she just looked at me, and then without a word she got up and went off to chat up the young barman.

I found a seat in the stands and watched the polo. Since I'd started dating Sasha, I had come to understand a little more of the intricacies of the game. For most of the time, it looks like this long string of polo-players who are for ever threading the length of the pitch. The first rule of polo is that no rider can cut across the path of the ball. Instead, a rider can only come onto the ball via its line of travel – so it makes for this strange spectacle of these polo-players all charging after the ball, one after the other. But the truth is that I've never much been into horses, and I certainly had no comprehension of the tactics or the players' skills, so I was not paying much attention; I was just relieved to have got away from Penny.

I only had half an eye on the game, but I suddenly realised that an accident was about to happen. The star player from Jokers Wild, Angelo, was bearing down on the ball, and close in behind him one of the opponents was trying to hook his stick. It was all part of the tactics of the game. Angelo had looked over his shoulder, and for a fraction of a second had missed the rogue player who was careering directly in front of him. It was over in the blink of an eye. Angelo hit the other horse at full gallop and then the horse behind clattered into the pile-up. Horses and riders were lying in this bloody heap on the ground, polo-ponies neighing and one man shrieking and shrieking with the dead weight of a polo-pony on top of him. It was horrific. The other polo-players were leaping off their ponies; medics sprinting, spectators pouring onto the field. I could see Sasha working away on the periphery. She was with the grooms and was leading the polo-ponies off the field.

There was nothing I could do – so I settled down to do what I had been trained to do. I had a little pocket camera, an Olympus Twin, which I kept with me at all times. Just in case. I took it out, and started snapping away. I only had the one roll of film, so I had to be much more judicious than today's snap-happy digital photographers.

I did not go onto the field, because instinctively I knew that it would have been inappropriate. I got a few pictures of the general carnage, and then later on, when the green screens went up so that one of the ponies could be put down, I took more pictures until the film ran out.

Of course it was all awful, but there was a side of me - there is a side of every journalist - that thrills to a disaster, and the bigger the disaster, the bigger the story. Many people outside Fleet Street find it repellent that we can hear tale of the most brutal murder imaginable, and then at the end of it all just say, "Good story". But we do not judge stories like other people; we're not weighing up the morals of the murderer or the wasted life of the victim. We're weighing up whether it's newsworthy - and murders are, unfortunately, big news.

Later on, I would remember the shrieks of the men and of the polo-ponies, and that flat retort of the gun as the animal was put down, and I drank glass after glass of wine, to help dull the memory; and I talked over it at some length with Rudi.

But at the time, as I dispassionately watched this accident unfold, I was fully aware that - at least for my little local paper - it was going to be quite big news. And I had witnessed it; and I had the pictures to boot.

The story made a good show in the Wilts and Glos. They had even used one of my pictures on the front page, a little grainy, but it gave a flavour of the accident. Inside there were more pictures, as well as my eye-witness account of what had happened. The hospital had given me the players' details, and just before we'd gone to press I'd got a condition check; the players were all going to be fine, but two of them, including the Jokers Wild star player, were going to be out for the rest of the season.

I remember feeling quite pleased with myself. It was the first time I'd ever written an eye-witness account before; they'd even given me a picture by-line.

It was that flat time on a Wednesday afternoon after the papers had just come in. The reporters were quietly devouring the papers, basking in the glory of their by-lines, and seeing how the subs had spit-polished their copy.

My phone went. It was Sasha. I had only seen her once at the pool over the previous three days, as she had been weighed down with work. She had been off to London and Sussex searching for a replacement for Angelo and it is no easy thing to hire a high-goal player in the middle of a season.

"Hi Sasha," I said. "How are you?"

"Not very good," she said. "I'm quite unhappy with you." Her voice was so brusque that I hardly even recognised her.

"I'm sorry?"

"Why did you put that story in the paper?" she said. "You even took pictures!"

"Ahh…" I tailed off. It had never even occurred to me that Sasha might react like this.

"Why did you do it?" she said.

"Sasha - dear," I said.

"And you called up the hospital. How could you be so intrusive?"

"I… I didn't…" I paused again, trying to regroup. "Sasha, this awful accident happened in front of over a hundred people; it's a legitimate news story. It was in the Telegraph two days ago. You're not trying to say I shouldn't have written it."

She was icy cold. "What I *am* saying is that you came up to Cirencester Park as my guest and that you were in the Jokers Wild marquee drinking Champagne with my mother, and then you go and repay us by slapping these pictures all over your paper."

"I…" I couldn't think what to say. "I'm so sorry."

"I am so angry," she said, banging down the phone, and I was left holding the dead receiver and feeling like a naughty schoolboy who's been reamed out by the headmistress.

I felt scalded by her words. I left the office and went for a walk. Just who did Sasha think she was, talking to me like that? She was a bloody control freak! Trying to control the news agenda of a local paper - tush! Didn't she realise that this accident had happened in a public domain - hundreds of people had seen it, were talking about it, and there'd been a short write-up in the Daily Telegraph not two days ago. Did she seriously expect my paper to ignore the only interesting polo story that had happened in years? And, really, what did she expect me to do? I was a reporter, for God's sake! That's what I did for a living – and if a story was handed me on a plate, then I'd damn well take it. Did she think I was just some patsy who would jump to her every beck and call?

And on… And on went this whirl of outraged hurt. I'd only been doing my job! It was a story, a legitimate story! And all the thanks I'd received had been a damn good kicking over the phone – certainly not a word of praise from the editor. I seethed and I seethed, though later, after I had calmed down, I did also come to see it from Sasha's point of view; I should have run the story by her. Definitely. The *Patron* could have been alerted.

Perhaps, as a guest of Jokers Wild, it hadn't been a great move.

CHAPTER 15

It was night-time and I was in bed. I was still simmering about what had happened that afternoon and even though I'd drunk nearly a full bottle of whisky, I could not sleep. It was raining hard, the lightning lighting up the sky, and my tree was creaking in the wind, the branches grinding like an old ship at sea. I was thinking about getting up and reading. If you can't sleep, and your brain is whirling like a flywheel, then there's nothing worse than just lying in bed.

But I lay there and I fumed and my cedar tree groaned its sympathy. There was a gap beneath the doors and a cool breeze was coming into the room. I could feel it on my face.

Then, over and above the sound of the tree, I heard the stair creak. It was that seventh step, with its distinctive screech. I heard it and I knew immediately that someone was coming up to see me - and really, at that time of night, there could only be one person who was coming to see me.

It was Sasha.

I was wide awake now, but I did not move. There was no knock on the front door. I heard a sudden roar of the rain as the door was opened and then quickly closed. I could hear soft footsteps in the other half of the treehouse. I couldn't quite make out what I was hearing, but then it all became clear; Sasha was getting undressed by the stove. The thrilling sound of a woman's knickers being pulled down her legs.

I had not moved in my bed. My eyes were tiny little slits; I was watching, waiting, for Sasha to come to bed. It is the best, the very best way, to deal with a bitter and bloody row. No need for apologies. No need for forgiveness. No need to allude to the argument in any way whatsoever. You kiss, you make love, you move on and the matter is forgotten.

Though it was quite dark on my side of the room, I caught a glimpse of breasts and shoulders in silhouette. Though she did not get into bed beside me. She went to the bottom of the bed, put her head under the duvet and, ever so slowly, started to work her way up the bed.

She licked my toes. I giggled. Some men get less ticklish with age, but I am not like that. Toes and armpits, when they are stroked, they both make me laugh. She put my big toe clean into her mouth, and I twitched vigorously, almost kicking her. She licked my other foot. She had my leg in her hands and her tongue trailed over the arch of my sole; it was very erotic. I could see nothing, see nothing at all, but my imagination was flying and with every lick and dink of her tongue, I could picture what it was that Sasha was doing to me.

She had moved up the bed now, and was lying between my legs. Her tongue was trailing, hot and wet, by my knees; her hair was wet from the rain and I could feel it on my legs. Her hair was cold. The contrast with the heat from her mouth and from her tongue was intoxicating.

I stroked Sasha's face, entwining my fingers in her wet hair. How sweet of her - how kind of her! - to offer up this olive branch.

Her head, her hot mouth moved up that just little further, so that she was… she was so close to giving me that kiss that I craved, and yet she did not give it. Her mouth moved about my hips and the tops of my thighs - and on the one hand I was loving it and wanting it to go on for ever, and yet I was also yearning for that one thing she was so wilfully refusing to give me. I laughed and I grabbed her head, her hair, with both hands and I moved those questing lips to where I wanted them to go, but, really, she was more than ready for me - her lips moved up to my belly button and to my stomach, and it was all so close to what it was that I wanted.

Very gently, she turned me onto my stomach. I could feel the callouses on her hands; I'd never really noticed them before. I wondered why she didn't wear gloves when she went riding. She had disappeared again, was kissing the backs of my feet, and the backs of my knees, and then my thighs, and inside my thighs, and, of course, my buttocks, such a mass of hair-trigger nerve-endings, and now I couldn't believe it, but I was actually shivering with desire as I wondered to myself how much longer Sasha could string it out for. Could she really spin it out till dawn? Was that possible? And I wondered, also, whether I ought to be taking a hand, because although it is lovely to receive these bountiful gifts, I prefer it best when it is I who I am doing the giving.

Something was being placed over my eyes. It felt silky; perhaps it was her stockings. I realised that I was being blindfolded - and that was different, but it was new and it was interesting. I trusted her implicitly.

Sasha turned me over again, that tongue, flickering and licking as her mouth worked its way up from my knees to my thighs, and then quite suddenly, she gave me the one thing which I had not expected.

Though not for long. Perhaps she could tell from my general writhing that I was in the heat. Sasha broke off, and though I couldn't see what it was that she was doing, I could feel her working with my hands. She was tying my wrists with another stocking - and again, like with the blindfold, I didn't really know where this was going, but if Sasha wanted to go there, then I would happily follow.

When you are blindfolded and when your hands are bound, then it is like that feeling you have after an accident as you wake up in hospital. You have no option but to submit, and in the right hands, it is wonderful to cede control.

I could not see Sasha, but I could certainly picture what she was doing to me. Her tongue flicked over my chest, my nipples, and now she was working her way up my neck. Every fibre of my skin was screaming for her touch.

She was on top of me now, legs astride me, bearing down on me, and quite suddenly, we were making love. I was utterly shocked. Of all the many things that might have happened that night, this one had never occurred to me. But then, in my whisky-fuelled fantasies, I recalled a conversation that we'd once had. What had she said?

"Let's not over think it; plan it too much." And this, obviously, was the result. The timing was right. Though we had not planned it at all, it was just the right thing to do.

I was quite consumed with desire. This was my Sasha, my virginal Sasha, and how I wished that I could have got my hands on her now, but all in due course. That could all wait for another time. I wanted her more than anything, and after a moment, I was rising to meet her; we were galloping together, sprinting to that final furlong, and I wished that she would kiss me, but she did not, and we fused together and I could feel this shrill shriek of ecstasy that was almost choked in her throat, and I realised that something was very badly wrong.

I wrenched at my wrists, levering them this way and that until I'd pulled my hands apart. I tore off the blind-fold. And there, still sitting astride me, was this foul thing, beyond repellent. I could see just the smallest glint of her blonde hair and the slight glint of her long teeth; she was smiling. It was Penny.

I have never experienced quite such a feeling of physical disgust. I heaved her off me and leapt out of the bed. I grabbed my dressing-gown and put it on. From the lightning outside, I could see her lying on the bed, mock sultry.

"You…" I could barely put my revulsion into words. I had… I had had sex with this witch? "Get out!"

She laughed and stretched up. "You're not even going to offer me a drink?"

In that moment I was so angry that I was capable of almost anything. Without a word, I went through to the other half of the treehouse. I pulled on my clothes, put on my boots. I poured a whisky, the bottle shaking in my hands. I drank it in one. I had been planning to leave the treehouse immediately, but I returned to the bed.

Penny was lying under the duvet now, arms and shoulders artfully exposed. She was grinning at me. "Come back for more?" she said.

I stood there grinding my teeth; I had to restrain myself from physically pitching her out of the bed. Had I… had I really just had sex with this foul fiend?

"You should not have done that," I said. "You should not have come."

"But I did come – it was fantastic." She laughed and stretched up, blowing me a kiss. "Come back to bed."

"Please go," I said.

"Didn't you like it?" she asked. She was propping up her head on her elbow. She licked her top lip.

"I'm going now." All I wanted at the moment was to have this woman out of my sight – and to clean myself. I wanted to swim and swim until I was spent, and then I wanted to spend an hour washing myself in the showers. "Get out of here."

"That's not a very nice way to talk to your lover."

"You're not my lover," I spat. "I loathe you."

"Well it's all money in the bank," she said, and tapped the side of her head with her fingers, as if to say that she had the memories all locked safe under key.

"Get the hell out." As the memories seeped back, I was getting more and more incensed.

"Calm down, Kim," she said. "Take a chill pill."

If there's one single phrase in this world that I detest more than any other, it is that: take a chill pill. I thought of all manner of vile insults which I wanted to hurl at her. I did not. I went round to the stove and picked up Penny's clothes which were littered over the floor.

She was lying back on the pillow now, arms behind her head; she looked quite at home.

I tossed her clothes onto the bed. "I want you gone by the time I get back."

She sleeked back her hair with one hand, doing that weird thing where she tugged it at the roots. "I haven't had sex like that in a long time."

"I wouldn't sleep with you if you were the last woman on earth," I said.

"But you have."

I turned on my heel and I left the treehouse.

The memory still revolts me. I do not dwell on it, but every so often there is a trigger, and the memory comes gushing back, and to me, it has become one of those car crash moments which makes me want to put my head into my hands and weep.

I don't know what I should have done that night. I guess that, after the event, whatever I did was going to be wrong. I was outraged at what she'd done. I found the thought of it utterly nauseous. So I was not polite, and I spurned her, and with a woman like Penny, that was always going to be dangerous.

★

It was a very pensive Kim who was at work the next day. My mind was only a half, a quarter, on the job; I would write a single sentence and then I would drift to thinking about Sasha; and her mother; and then back to Sasha.

I wanted to talk to Sasha. I missed her. Even though I didn't really feel the need, I'd apologise, handsomely, for the story that I'd written about Jokers Wild. I shouldn't have done it. Or at least… No, I shouldn't have done it.

But I was well aware that, compared to what had happened the previous night, the Jokers Wild story was the most piffling irrelevance.

And that was the nub: Did I tell Sasha? Did I not tell Sasha? Tell - or not tell?

If I told her, then… well it was going to be a very tough one to get over. Any way that I dressed it up, it was still going to look absolutely horrendous - because, basically, I'd had sex with her mother. I had had sex with her mother! It was going to be difficult to make a comeback after something like that. True, Penny had sneaked into my house, crept into my bed, all but seduced me. And I could plead my innocence till I was blue in the face. But still there was no getting round that one killer fact: I, Kim, had had sex with her mother!

I remember sitting in the office, elbows on my desk, running my fingers again and again through my hair as I blankly stared at the keyboard. I'd slept with Penny! Only the previous night, not twelve hours earlier, we had been having sex. I could still hear her throaty scream of ecstasy; was that my memory or was that just the relic of some vicious dream?

But maybe… Maybe Sasha would forgive me? She knew her mother, knew what the woman was capable of. Perhaps she'd experienced it before - and so perhaps, just possibly, we'd be able to move on. But… who was I kidding? It would be one hell of a pill to swallow.

Sasha was the Virgin princess - it was part of what defined her. And for her to suddenly learn that her so-called boyfriend had had sex with Penny…

Could there ever be any coming back from it?

I thought about it.

But if I didn't tell Sasha, then… would she find out? Would Penny really be stupid enough, dumb enough - or perhaps malicious enough - to tell her? Perhaps Penny would tell Sasha for no other reason but to spite her - and so it might well be the end of her relationship with her daughter, but she would certainly have put paid to this fledgling romance that I had with Sasha.

I looked over at Rudi. He was reading *The Sun*. Like me, he was already dreaming of Fleet Street and working on the Red Tops.

I thought about telling him - and then I remembered what had happened the last time I'd confided a little secret to him. The story of my night out on the streets with the homeless had gone round the entire office in under three hours flat.

No, I couldn't tell Rudi. I couldn't tell anyone.

But should I tell Sasha? Not to unburden myself of my shame - but rather to head Penny off. Better for Sasha to hear the bad news from me than to learn it from her mother. But what difference would it make - whoever she heard it from, we'd be finished and that would be the end of it. Because - again and again I kept coming back to it: I had had sex with her mother!

The reporters were heading off to the Slug and Lettuce for a Friday night drink when Sasha called. Her voice was much softer.

"How are you?" she asked.

"I've been better," I said. I was standing up, ready to go. I gestured to Rudi and Siobhan that I'd see them in the pub. "How's it cooking?"

"I was very silly yesterday," she said. "I'm so sorry."

This was a most unexpected - and pleasant - surprise. "No - it's me who should be apologising," I said. "I shouldn't have run the story."

"It was just the *Patron* - he went mad when he saw the story, and so I… I lost it with you. I'm sorry."

"Forget it. It's nothing. I should never have run it."

"I love you," she said.

"And I, you," I said.

"I'm in Sussex signing up our new star. Are you around on Saturday?"

"For you - anything."

"I'll be over in the morning," she said.

You can be quite assured that by the time Sasha came round on Saturday, my treehouse had been practically steam-cleaned. Fresh sheets and pillow cases, of course, on the bed and afterwards I went through my home with all the zeal of a forensic scientist. Underneath the bed, I found Penny's rumpled stockings - those same stockings that she'd used to blindfold me. Just the touch of them disgusted me.

I'd bought some flowers and I'd even dusted the treehouse. I drank tea on the balcony as I waited for my Sasha.

She came up the stairs and without a word threw herself into my arms, and in moments we were kissing and pawing at each other, and all was as it once was; it was as good as it had ever been - no, it was better than that, for now we had added another layer to our narrative.

We'd gone back into the treehouse and Sasha was just in the act of pulling off her top, when she looked about her for the first time.

"It looks very clean in here," she said. "Have you had somebody round?"

I had not expected to be put on the spot so quickly. But this, surely, was the moment to tell her about what had happened with Penny.

But there had also been a subtle change in the dynamics. Before this question, I would not necessarily have been lying; I would have not been telling Sasha the whole truth. But now, and immediately, I was going to have to commit myself either one way or the other; and I was going to have to do it with good confidence.

But women, and lovers in particular, have the most sensitive nose for these sort of things.

"Chance'd be a fine thing," I said and I laughed. I must have hit a slightly wrong note, because Sasha was staring at me.

"Guy like you, Kim…"

"Exactly," I said and I kissed her. Her eyes stayed wide open.

"So nobody's been here – nobody at all?"

"How little you know me," I said.

"There's something you're not telling me."

"I haven't told you I love you yet."

I don't know whether she believed it or whether she did not, but after I said that, she kissed me again, lustily, and again we were back in each other's arms.

At that moment it seemed inconceivable that I would tell her about what had happened with Penny. Why would I wilfully wreck this great thing that we had going with each other? Was I really so much to blame?

We'd fallen onto the bed and were kissing and rolling around on top of each other when this shocking image came into my head. I remembered what had happened three days previously with Penny – right there on that very bed; how she'd sat astride me, rode me. It was a vile picture and I could not get it out of my head.

"Let's go to the folly," I said. "We haven't been to the maze for ages."

"If you like."

"Let's have a picnic."

We took bread, butter and Fallot French Dijon mustard in a stone jar crock, and oozing Brie and a haunch of Iberian ham that I'd bought from the delicatessen. I put it all into a canvas bag with some ice and a couple of bottles of Muscadet.

I had the bag slung over my shoulder and we held hands as we walked to the maze.

"Is it right-left, right-left into the middle," Sasha asked. "Or is it left-right?"

"It's left-right," I said. "Just like in the army."

We entered the maze, holding hands and swinging our arms high, like a couple of kids playing at soldiers. Thoughts of Penny already fast fading.

"Do you remember when we first went into the maze," Sasha said.

"I won't ever forget it," I said. We took a left turn. "You ran into my arms and I wanted to kiss you."

She turned and kissed me on the cheek. "Why didn't you kiss me?"

"Timing, Sasha darling. In matters of the heart, timing is everything."

"Maybe you're right," she said, slipping her hand underneath my shirt.

"What?" I asked. "Right in the middle of the maze?"

"Why not?" she said, and when she put it like that, there could only be one answer, and so then and there we went at each other in the middle of the maze, lying between those high holly hedges, ripping at each other's clothes, until we were all but naked and writhing on the wet bedewed grass. Wet grass is quite different from dry; of course it's cold and wet on your skin, but it is also a much earthier experience, as the ground fills you with its energy. You become one with the earth and you are suffused with each other's tastes and textures as well as the rich smell of the earth and the feel of the slick grass as it flicks beneath feet. Try it: you may learn something about your lover. You may learn something about yourself.

When we were spent, we carried on into the maze – and of course, we had entirely forgotten whether on the next turn we were supposed to be going left or right.

How I remember us standing there, naked and clutching onto our clothes as we wondered which way to go. She looked like some glorious forest-sprite, wet skin glistening and with grass in her hair and all over her legs and her back.

"It's just like that story that you once made up for me," Sasha said. "Naked in the maze together."

"And where's the snake?" I said.

"Ah yes - the snake," she said, looking down. "I remember what happened to that snake -"

"Yes, you ate him."

She laughed, ribaldly, earthily, with huge enjoyment.

"I'll leave my knickers - to mark where we were."

Her knickers were of creamy silk and she hung them high on the hedge, the silk in beautiful contrast to the spiky green holly, and at the end of the day, we left the knickers hanging on the hedge. I like to think that they might still be there, a little memento of our tryst in the wet grass.

"So where do we go now?" I said.

"I think it's left."

"Let's go."

It was the wrong way, but eventually we returned to Sasha's creamy silk knickers, and from there we made it to the folly. It was musty inside and we threw open all the doors and all the windows, and I lit a fire downstairs and, like a pair of Stone Age savages, we squatted naked in front of the flames and warmed our hands and our thighs, the grass slowly crisping on our skin, and we stared into the fire and dreamed our dreams, and then smiled complicitly at each other for sheer joy of being in love.

We had lunch on the swing on the roof, at first wrapped in blankets, but when the sun came out we did without, and sat naked in the breeze. I poured the wine and cut off slices of the ham, dipping them into the mustard before feeding them to my love. The mustard dripped down her chin, just as I had meant it to. She was sitting cross-legged on the swing, deliciously debauched.

"I'm sorry we don't make love," she said. "I know you'd like to."

I thought a moment for the correct thing to say - because of course I *did* want to make love with Sasha. But I certainly did not want to pressure her into it.

I wondered if that was it - if that was my new grand strategy: to make love, finally, with Sasha. But it was not; could not be. Grand strategy is all-encompassing; grand strategy should be big enough to last you till the end of your days.

"Sasha, my love, I am in no hurry whatsoever to make love with you."

"But I think that one day I will make love with you," she said. "What's it going to be like?"

I cut off a long thin slice of brie and held it over her mouth and, lasciviously, she turned her head up; I teased and she bit.

"You asked me that same question a year ago, when we were on this exact same swing," I said.

"I asked you what sex was like -"

"And it was very forward of you too."

"You'd got me drunk - but now I'm asking what it's going to be like making love -"

"Sweet love."

"With you."

"A wholly different question," I said. "But easily answered. Imagine a drinking vessel. Picture your favourite drinking vessel. What would you be drinking out of?"

She pursed her lips. She was holding one of Sir Anthony's cut crystal glasses, thick at the stem and at the base, and very thin at the top and etched all around with the most intricate patterns of grapes and vine leaves. "I'll have this glass." She tilted it to me. "This will be my drinking vessel."

"That's what you'll be like as a lover then - refined, elegant, classical, classy -"

"And I'll ping when you flick me with your fingernail." She sipped the Muscadet. "And what will be your drinking vessel, dearest Kim?"

"Me?" I stroked my chin, mock pensive. "That's easy. No question of a doubt about it. It's obvious when you think about it -"

"Get on with it."

"I'd have a beer mug, robust, unbreakable -"

"A tankard?"

"Yes, with fat dimples in the side -"

"Tell me more about this tankard. Is it really going to be compatible with my wine glass?"

"It's got a very thick handle which you can curl your fingers around -"

"As opposed to my very thin stem -"

"And nice thick cloudy glass at the rim -

"Something to really get your lips round -"

"And it holds a pint, obviously, as opposed to your thimble-full of wine -"

"Meaning?"

"Well my drink's going to last a lot longer, isn't it? And then my tankard - well you can just put him straight in the dish-washer -"

"It just doesn't seem very refined though." She carefully put her glass down onto the ground. "I'm getting quite turned on by all this talk of sex -"

"Sex?" I said. "I thought we were talking about me and my beer-mug."

"You and your beer-mug." She purred towards me, kissing my shoulder. "Any chance you could attend to my cut-crystal wine glass?"

"They're very fragile, you know." I stroked her breasts as she lay across my lap. "They can only take the most delicate hand-washing -"

"Of which you are now going to give me a demonstration -"

"Yes - please."

And when I look back on it now, I wonder what on earth has happened with my life that these things that I used to love are no longer a part of it: is al fresco sex really only for the young and the reckless? Well - up to a point. These acts of impromptu sex are not just for the young; they are the preserve of the young at heart.

With Sasha, we used to spend a lot of time teasing each other - both verbally and physically; to both of us, there seemed no finer sport than to bring the other to the brink and then to break off and chat about something entirely inconsequential.

So, later on, as Sasha busied herself with her hands and her lips, I knew that the moment that my fingers started to needily twist in her hair then there would be a brief intermission.

"I'm quite close," I said.

"I thought these beer-mugs were supposed to last much longer than mere cut-crystal wine glasses -"

"They don't last for ever, you know."

She stretched down for her wine-glass and took a sip, rolling the stem of the glass between her fingers. "So you've booked your day off for next week?"

"Yes," I said. "What do they call it these days?"

"A mini-break."

"Three whole days with you."

"You sure about the tide times of this whirlpool?"

"I have checked them," I said. Yes indeed, I had checked and double-checked the tide times, because to get the times wrong - as the writer George Orwell once did - would probably prove fatal. The Corryvreckan is a whirlpool just close by to the Inner Hebrides island of Jura. At the bottom of the Corryvreckan is a stalk of rock that rises up from the sea-bed, and at the right time of day, opposing currents start to pulse around the rock until they synchronise and spin and within minutes they have formed into a vast whirlpool, the biggest in Britain. It's said that when the Corryvreckan is at full spate it lets out a rumbling roar that can be heard from many miles away, like a ravenous mountain-giant that is hungering for food.

"You've really checked the times?" Sasha said.

"Really. But if I was going to drown in the Corryvreckan, there's no-one else on earth I'd rather die with -"

"You're ever so romantic - for a beer mug."

"And what about that beer mug -"

"Please? Did you say please?"

"Yes please -"

"I don't normally like stout." She slipped towards me again, sleek as a cat. "But for you, Kim, I might make an exception."

CHAPTER 16

We had arranged to meet up at the treehouse on the Thursday afternoon after work, so that we could make a dent in the long drive up to Scotland. But long drives, short drives, any sort of drive - they will all be fantastic if you're with a companionable lover. They all add up to frequency and narrative, which turns to propinquity, and which in turn makes for a love that can weather any storm.

I'd packed my bag in the morning and I was back at the treehouse all ready to go. We'd booked a little Bed and Breakfast on Jura for the Saturday, but for the other two nights, we were taking pot luck.

I'd made a pot of tea, and was sitting by the fire dreaming about Sasha: as girlfriends go, things did not get much better.

And my eyes strayed to the rug, and I remembered how - only a week ago - I'd been frantically cleaning the treehouse, trying to wipe away every last trace of Penny. I'd found one of her long hairs on the rug and thrown it on the fire. I shuddered; if only it had been as easy to have erased the memories of that night with Penny.

But there was no helping for it now. For better or worse, I was going to have to live with it. There are some people, I know, who become burdened down by guilt, and who feel this awful urge to confess. But I am not like that. It was a pretty ghastly thing that had happened with Penny, but I didn't think I was too much to blame; it was a memory that I could live with. As far as I could see, there was absolutely nothing to be gained from telling Sasha about it - and one hell of a lot to lose. It would probably finish us, though it was possible that it might not, but any which way that I looked at it, what was the point of telling Sasha? All I'd be doing was plunging a knife into her heart, and then giving it a twist for good measure; to tell

Sasha about that night with Penny would make her just wretched, and it wasn't going to be great for me either. I realised that this was one horrible secret that I had to keep to myself.

I poured more tea, and stared into the fire; in the flames of a wood-fire, there are always patterns of both love and hate, and heaven and hell and of our dreams and our most desolate nightmares.

There was one – and only one – reason why I ought to tell Sasha about that night. It was Penny herself, that dreadful, imponderable woman who up until then had remained quiet, but who might explode at any minute. On one level, I was quite sure that Penny would be keeping as quiet as me about our night together: she had as much to lose as I did – if not more. But on another level, I also understood that Penny was a category of woman that I had never come across before. I did not understand her, could not understand her. I had no clue as to what made her tick – and so although, rationally, logically, I could console myself that Penny would never tell, a part of me feared she might do just that. I didn't know why, and I didn't know how, but with someone like Penny, then anything – no matter how insane – was possible.

Should I talk to Penny about it? That was a possibility. But what would that achieve? We'd not spoken since I'd left her lying in my bed in the treehouse a week before. I weighed it up. Speaking to Penny, trying to head her off, would either just fan the flames or make her even more vexed than she already was with me. Best just to leave it, forget about it; and to hope and pray that Penny forgot about it too.

There was nothing to be done, and that being the case, I should have put the matter right out of my mind. But although I could be objective and dispassionate, I was not quite that dispassionate; I was a yachtsman, sailing my ship across a balmy ocean, and yet always with this dull sense of foreboding and the knowledge that somewhere out there was this rogue sea-mine that might yet sink me.

Sasha came into the treehouse and caught me staring into the fire. "You look contemplative," she said. "Penny for your thoughts?"

I got up and kissed her. "Time for a cup of tea?"

"Let's get going," she said.

I picked up my holdall and we were about to leave when she noticed the new lock that I had put on the door.

"New lock?" she said. "Why have you put a lock on the door?"

"What gilded world do you live in, Sasha, where no-one wants to steal your stuff?"

"But you don't have anything to steal!" she said. "You've got one cassette tape and a boom-box that you nicked from the office."

We were outside now and I was locking the door. "A tramp might come along -"

"I doubt it," she said, and then she cocked her head and looked at me, and perhaps I had just been a little bit too breezy as I'd parried her questions. "It's to stop someone from coming in here isn't it?"

"That's what I said."

Unwittingly - or perhaps wittingly - she went straight for the jugular. "Did someone come and visit while I was away?"

I turned from her and went down the stairs. She followed me and I was glad that she could not see my face.

"No-one comes to visit me - apart from you," I said. "Paris used to visit, but not anymore."

I was striding out across the garden when she caught me by the elbow. She stopped me in my tracks and turned me; she was looking into my eyes. What is this antennae that women have that enables them to spot a lie at fifty paces? I would give my eye-teeth to possess even an ounce of that acuity.

"Nobody visited you while I was away?"

"N-no," I said. I was looking her in the eye, but it sounded limp. I'd actually stuttered.

"Nobody spent the night?"

"Nobody," I said, trying to sound hurt, but I've never been much of a liar, and least of all with someone as needle-sharp as Sasha.

"Okay," she said, and there was this look that passed between us that said that she just knew I wasn't telling the truth. We walked to the Merc and I slung the bags into the boot. We drove off, though not in a companionable silence, but with this prickling frigidness in the air, so palpable that you could touch it.

I put the radio on and we listened to Radio Three for a while, and I meandered along the byroads of Gloucestershire as we headed north, and then quite by chance, an excerpt from The Magic Flute came onto the radio. Not that we really had one, but this was our song. We looked at each other, slyly, shyly, and smiled, and Sasha kissed her finger and placed the kiss upon my cheek.

"I'm sorry," she said.

"I love you," I replied and, as easy as that, we were back on track, and chatting about any piece of ridiculousness that came into our heads.

For a long time now, we had been following a Volvo with a horse box attached to the back; it seemed as if he was also heading north up to the M5.

"Can't you overtake this thing?" Sasha said. Her legs were in my favourite position, outstretched on the dashboard, feet up against the windscreen.

"While you're at it, why don't you tell me to clean this car up?"

"You can take him on that straight stretch in a mile or two."

"You know about the acceleration in this heap?"

"I do."

I knew the road well, and I also knew the long stretch that she was referring to; it was a favourite with the local boy-racers. They used it for playing Chicken.

It was a sultry airless evening, actually quite muggy. We had the windows down and the windscreen was flecked with dead midges.

We came to the straight stretch of road and the Volvo was still pottering along at its modest 45mph. The road was quite clear. I immediately pulled out to overtake. The Merc was an automatic, not as fast as a stick-shift car, but underneath the accelerator was a button. When you floored the accelerator, the car dropped down a gear. Gradually, imperceptibly, we started to accelerate, and the nose of the Merc edged past the back of the horse-box; and then two things happened, the first of which was absolutely inevitable.

Like the tosser that he was, the Volvo driver also started to accelerate - but not by much. The second thing that happened was that right far off in the distance I saw a tiny blob of red, a shimmering vehicle that was coming straight towards us.

I was in two minds whether to hit the brakes and tuck in again behind the Volvo -

"You can do it," Sasha said, and so I continued to overtake, pedal still hard to the floor. Little by little we were gaining on the Volvo driver. We had eased past the horse-box and now we were abreast with the car itself. The car was a Volvo estate, burgundy red. I briefly looked at the driver and at the same moment he looked at me. He was middle-aged and there was something that passed between us, because I realised that he did not much care if we lived or died: he was determined not to let us through. And I had a glimpse of Sasha too, eyes wide, clutching onto the edge of her seat.

But it was too late for us to pull out now, and it would do no good to start hammering at the brakes, because the little red blob on the horizon had now turned into a large red lorry, and the driver was flashing his lights, but there was no way I could stop and there was no way I could get past the bloody horse-box, and the engine was screaming, knuckles white on the wheel, and I could hear the Volvo racing alongside us, and this deep klaxon booming out from the juggernaut, and though now we were just about nosing ahead of the Volvo, it was all way too late, I could even see the screaming driver in his cab and in that briefest of nano-seconds, I realised that we were pretty much toast -

I've had a number of close shaves in my life: that swim across the Thames when Sasha and I were nearly hit by the dredger. That was one of them. And that time in the food-hall on the kibbutz, when the terrorists were checking all the bodies to see that no-one was shamming; that was another. And a time, also, when I was caught in an avalanche and was all but swept to my death to the valley below.

But of all the many places where I have lost some of my nine lives, that straight stretch of Gloucestershire road was by far the most hair-raising; and by far the most memorable. For when we came out of it - as we did both come out of it - we felt so charged and so alive that it was as if we had been reborn.

It was the noise that I remember most. My brakes squealing as, way too late, I pummelled the brake-pedal; and that damn klaxon wailing away from the cab of the lorry; and then the shrill whine of the burgundy Volvo and, over and above all else, this shriek of absolute animal terror from Sasha.

The lorry was all but upon us, the Volvo and the horse-box still blocking us, and it looked like I was going to have hedge it at close on to 90mph when I spotted this layby, this beautiful, beckoning layby on the right-hand side of the road. I pulled the wheel hard over, and we bumped the kerb and skidded on the tarmac and a very split second later the red lorry had thundered past, and the burgundy Volvo was streaking off into the distance, and I was standing on the brakes and we skidded and we bounced through the pot-holes, and then just like that we had come to an absolute dead stop, the car slewed slightly across the layby, but otherwise not a dent on the fender, and I turned the key and switched off the ignition and gradually the dust and the haze started to settle and the engine stopped to tick and Sasha's panting breath softened and we were enveloped by this most total of silences.

I was staring through the windscreen, hands in my lap, and I was thinking about quite a number of things, not least that by rights we should both be dead. I glanced over at Sasha who had gone quite white and who was just staring dead ahead; she was not aware of me, hardly even aware that she was in the car. Over and over again, I was reliving those last moments as we'd tried to overtake the horse box; and the thought that we could have been mashed by the lorry and that the crazy Volvo driver would just have blithely continued on his way. And I thought about the sound of Sasha's screaming, and that occupied me for a little while, and then I thought about that sweet, sacred layby that happened to be in the exact right place at the exact right time, and how perhaps I should erect a little shrine there in memory of the two lives that were so nearly lost.

There were some sheep in the field next to us, Jacob's, with black faces and creamy white coats; and, not far from the hedge, there were two rabbits grazing at the grass, and a crow cartwheeling through the sky, and a car skimmed past, and life continued exactly the same as it had been earlier that afternoon and as it would be the next morning.

And after a while I'd started to feel quite good about the whole thing – it was close, *so* close, but didn't we just pull through? We had made it! We had stared death in the face and we had lived to tell the tale!

I stretched behind and grabbed a couple of cans of beer from all the debris on the back seat. I opened the cans and passed one to Sasha, and she took it in silence and I drank the beer and it was tepid, but that first sip was the most delicious thing that I had ever tasted. I was alive – alive and I could eat and I could drink and I could still taste beer and see the sky and the hedgerows and smell the sheep through the open window! I was alive!

Sasha still hadn't said anything but she had started to drink the beer. She took a long, long pull from the can, and then she did something which I'd never heard her do before – she burped, quite loud, and did not even bother to mask it.

I was looking at her, quite close.

"Charming," I said.

And now, for the first time, she looked at me, those beautiful black eyes, and she brought the can to her lips and she drank, and she drank, and all the while she continued to stare at me. It was quite a large can of beer, but she continued to drink until she had drained it to the last drop. She crunched the can in her hand and let out another burp, this time full in my face.

"I could smell that one," I said.

She tossed the can into the back, and I might have been wrong but I thought I could detect the beginnings of a smile on her face.

"Let's make love," she said.

I looked at her, very calm, very measured, and I took my time before I replied. "We don't have to do this," I said. "You're still in shock."

"I may be in shock, but I want to make love –" and she smiled and corrected herself "– sweet love with you."

"Right here, right now?" I said.

"Who knows when the next lorry's going to hit us?"

"Shall we go to the field?"

"Though I do love this car," she said, opening the car door. "I love everything. I love you."

I got out of the car. In the boot was my satchel with my emergency provisions - a leg of cured ham, a bottle of Barolo wine, and a book of love poetry; I still have that satchel and that emergency pack to this day. There were a couple of old rugs in the back, a little moth-eaten, and I slung them over my shoulder.

We climbed over the fence and hand in hand we walked a while to a great chestnut in the middle of the field. Sasha watched as, with great care, I placed the rugs on the grass in the lee of the tree and opened the wine, and we sat, side by side, with our backs to the tree, and in the manner of lovers the world over, we drank the wine and revelled in the sheer beauty of what it was to be alive that day.

We chinked our cups. They were silver stirrup cups, elegant, given to me by my father. "Here's to virgins," I said.

"Who'd want to die a virgin?" she said, and she leaned to me and I kissed her wine-dark lips.

"I didn't think it right to mention it before, but this virginity thing is much over-rated."

"Now you tell me!"

"Since you'd clung to it like a comfort blanket, I was hardly going to tell you otherwise -"

She shut me up with another kiss. "And what, Kim, have you got for contraception?"

"Oh I wonder." I stretched over to my emergency satchel and from the front-pocket produced a packet of three condoms.

"For me?" she laughed.

"Maybe -"

"How long have you had this special little satchel of yours?"

"I'm not sure -"

"How long?" She pinched my stomach and kissed me.

"Two - maybe three years."

"You cheeky bastard!" She pushed me over so that she was lying on top of me; my cup dropped to the grass. "You'd have used them on the first wench who would have had you."

I laughed - "But only in an emergency!"

She was raining light punches down onto my chest; that hair, how I remember it, surrounding her face like a beautiful black halo. "With the first wench that would have had you!"

I was still laughing as I fended off her blows. "They were always for you," I said. "They were for the love of my life."

"The love of your life!" she jeered, and stretched upwards and pulled off her top. It was a white cotton shirt, like a smock, with a loose draw-string at the neck.

"Admittedly I didn't know it was going to be you -"

"Don't think you're going to talk your way out of this, Sailor." She stretched behind her and unhitched her bra, throwing it onto the ground. "Because it's too late now -"

"But, definitely, when I bought those condoms five - six - years ago, I'd always hoped to be sharing them with the love of my life."

"They're probably past their sell-by date."

"It's quite possible."

She kissed me soundly and then rolled onto her side. She pulled off her trainers and unbuckled her belt and pulled off her jeans; the knickers followed.

"Get on with it, slow-coach," she said, and within the twinkling of an eye, she had stripped me and we were naked and grappling with each other.

"About those condoms?"

"Yes," I said, "I'll put one on in a moment - but first there is something very important I have to do."

"What now?" she said, lying beneath me now, arms about my hips. "Are you hungry - got a sudden urge for some ham?"

"I'm famished," I said, and we kissed and for a while we just lay there, me on top of Sasha, and she smiling with absolute delight as she looked into my face.

"What about a cherry?"

And still we did not move, tip-toeing on the brink. "I think -" I said, and I gasped as she drew me towards her, "I - I think a cherry would just be perfect."

And for a while we did not move, as we revelled in this new experience and these fresh sensations.

"So this is it?" she said, hands lightly skimming at my back.

"This is it."

"I am making love -"

"Sweet love -"

"I am making sweet love," she said, and she hugged me tight, ankles looping about my legs. And we looked, and we stared and there was a cold wind on my back as the shades of our ghosts skimmed over our heads. And the ghosts moved on, and the mood softened, and all felt lighter as I searched into Sasha's face and chastely kissed her lips.

"So do we do anything else or do we just lie like this?" she said.

"Haven't you seen any of those David Attenborough nature programmes?"

"I'm not sure I have -"

"What a cosseted childhood you must have led." I stretched for her cup of Barolo and sipped and let the red wine trickle into her open mouth, and then watched as it dribbled down her cheek. "If you like, I can repeat that initial manoeuvre again - though it is optional."

"Initial manoeuvre? Is that a technical term?" She cupped my face and kissed me. "It sounds ever so romantic -"

I leant over her with arms outstretched and for a moment I looked up, and the world was still the same, and the sheep were still grazing, and the sun was slipping beneath the trees - and yet now, emerging from far off was this new horizon that I had never seen before, for even as we were making love, the glimmerings of my grand strategy were beginning to emerge.

"I shall now proceed to repeat the initial manoeuvre -"

"Is it normal to speak like a policeman?"

"And I shall then repeat that initial manoeuvre -"

"Does it always feel this good?"

"And again -"

And she laughed and she writhed beneath me, "What have I been missing!"

"It probably helps that half-an-hour ago we nearly managed to kill ourselves -"

"Do we have to do that every time we make love?"

"It is not wholly necessary, no. But you should always be aware that there is going to be another little red dot on the horizon -"

"That lorry!" she said. "So we can just make sweet love -"

"Whenever you like."

"Are there any other positions that we should try - or is this it?"

"Other positions?" I said, leaning on my elbow as I scratched at my ear. "I've heard of one. I think we just roll over and then, as if by magic, you're on top."

"Like this?" and she wrapped her leg about my ankle, and we rolled over, and then it was Sasha who was lying on top of me.

"Like that." I cupped a breast in each of my hands and with my tongue, I licked. "I think you will be a most apt student -"

"Are you a teacher or something like that?"

"A Professor, actually -"

"A professor of sweet love," she murmured with a delicious wriggle. "And will there be homework?"

"Without doubt."

"And at what stage do we break out the emergency condom?"

"Perhaps about now?"

Sasha watched with interest as I tore the wrapper with my teeth and put the condom on.

"You didn't even have to look," she said. "You must be very experienced. I'm so lucky."

"You'll be doing it blindfold soon, Sasha darling - do not worry."

She slipped back on top of me, as easy as slipping onto the saddle of one of her polo-ponies.

"Are you sure you were a virgin?" I said. "You seem very accomplished."

"Maybe I'm a natural," she says, and I gaze up at this beauty above me. "I like it up here. I'm in control."

"You have control."

"How long do we keep repeating the initial manoeuvre for?" she asked.

"For as long as you like," I said. "Though you may eventually experience something that is known as an orgasm -"

"Is that another technical term?"

"It is. It's a sort of muscle spasm that stretches the length of the body - and it can be quite powerful; powerful enough to even shut up your endless chatter -"

"An orgasm?" she says in this tone of blank amazement. "Is it possible that I'm about to experience it?"

"It's possible, I suppose." I lifted up to kiss her lip, her cheek. "Let's see if you keep talking -"

And, suddenly much faster now, she moved on me, urgent and strong. "I think… I think this might be the orgasm thingy you mentioned - to give it its technical -" and at that her words were cut off, and I could see the tendons on her neck as her nails bit deep into my arms, and she was looking into my eyes, full lock-on, this expression of quite astonished wonderment flickering across her face, almost as if she'd been shot and she couldn't quite believe it, and the amazement grew and it grew until at length she giggled and subsided, folding forward to hold me about the neck. She kissed me.

"No regrets?" I asked.

"Only not making love with you months ago," she said. "But what about you. I don't even know if you've had this orgasm thing? Have you?"

"No, I have not had this orgasm thing," I said.

"Ohh? So what do we do now?"

"You stay right where you are, you have a little wine, and then, if you have the inclination, you continue to repeat the initial manoeuvre -"

"I love that initial manoeuvre -"

"And if you repeat it often enough you may find that you experience - here's another technical term for you - a multiple-orgasm -"

"A multiple orgasm?" She drank from the stirrup cup and then placed it on the rug next to my head. "I do like the sound of that. Very much."

"Though I should warn you -"

"Yes, *Il Professore* -"

"That though this love-making may become strangely addictive, it should not in any way be seen as a replacement for your oral activities -"

"What?" She stretched up, fingers running through her hair. She glowed. "I've still got to give you blowjobs?"

"And the rest of it -" She'd turned now so that she had her back to me. Her hair trailed down her back.

"I think I've found another position! It's my third!" she said, turning her head to look at me. She smiled and blew me a kiss. "It feels a little different from the other two that we've tried. Are there many more?"

"One - or two," I said.

"And may we try them?"

"Never in my life have I known such an eager pupil."

She giggled and stood up, taking me by the hand. We kissed, hungrily. "Have I the makings of a good lover?" she said, eyes wide.

"You were born for it," I said, as she pressed me up against the tree, the gnarly bark pressing into my back. She clung to me, arms about my neck, her long legs snaking around mine. "You've taken to it rather well."

"It's that propinquity thing -"

"Or that car crash thing -"

She shivered next to me. "That multiple orgasm you mentioned? Is it possible"

"It's possible - how do you feel?"

"Will you join me?"

"That must be the synchronicity thing."

And we kissed, our eyes not inches apart, buckling and straining against each other, now quite locked in love, and as we stared, mouths agape, muscles constricting, our bodies locked, it seemed that our souls had also fused into one.

It felt as if we'd been standing locked together there for some time, Sasha with her arms around my neck, while I had her tight by the waist, and ever so gradually we began to reconnect with the world; I could feel a nodule of the chestnut tree digging into my back, and Sasha started to uncoil herself from my legs until her feet were firmly back on the ground, and we sat side by side in the fast-fading sunlight, our arms slung about each other as we drank the Barolo and dreamt such dreams of what we might yet do with each other, and of the peaks we might climb, and the countries we might visit, and the beds and the briers that we might yet make love in; I would that I had buried a case of ruby red Barolo underneath that chestnut, so that when the black dog was upon me, I could go back to that field, and drink that wine, and recapture a little of what it was to be with my Sasha.

CHAPTER 17

It was quite dusk when we left that field with the sheep and with the chestnut tree and with the hedge that led to the little layby. We held hands and Sasha had a blanket slung over her shoulders to keep her warm, and then when we were back in the car, we did not need to say a word but hugged each other and held each other close.

I pulled out and, in silence, we set off again along that long straight stretch of road which had changed our lives so irrevocably, each with our own thoughts. Occasionally I would turn to her, and she'd be just looking at me, this smile playing on her face, happy as can be.

I was thinking lots of things; all of them revolved around Sasha. Her scream in the car when we'd nearly crashed; and another scream, a very different kind of scream, an hour later when we had been up against the tree; and I realised that, really, what more did I want? How much better was it going to get? Earlier, out under the chestnut, I had begun to discern the outlines of something that had the makings of grand strategy - and now, as we chugged very sedately in the dark, the shards of my great grand plan swirled and rippled until they coalesced into one single central image, and that could be summed up in four simple words. And that is the true delight of grand strategy: it may be broad and all-encompassing, but it is in fact so beautifully simple. It is the essence, the pure essence, of what you are about.

We'd been bumbling along for about thirty minutes when we went through a town, and there was a small hotel in the middle of the town. Without a word, I pulled over. They had vacancies, plenty of vacancies, and I asked for the best room in the house. "How long will you be staying?" asked the landlady. "I'm not sure," I said. I carried the bags up the stairs, and she showed us to our room. The room was large and warm, with a bay window that looked out over the garden, and another window that had a view of the church; and there might have been a television also as well as a sofa, but the only thing of import was that the room had a bed, a large double bed, with a padded headboard and crisp grey linen. The woman was about to embark on an explanation of all the fixtures and fittings when I cut in - "We'll be fine, thank you so much" - and she left, and I dropped the bags on the floor, and the door shut behind her and a moment later we'd both dived onto the bed and were rolling and grappling with each other and kissing such kisses as if they were our last.

Eventually, after our shoes had been hurled across the room, Sasha was lying on top of me, head propped on an elbow as she dreamily played with a kiss-curl of my hair.

"The Corryvreckan?" she said.

I, also, had been thinking about our whirlpool. "The Corryvreckan."

"What do you think?"

"Well..." I slipped my hand beneath her belt and underneath her knickers. "You can have a plan, and it can be quite a good plan, but sometimes events happen..." I kissed her chin "...and after these events, it's sometimes wiser to change the plan."

"And if you were going to change the plan, how would you change it?"

"Not much - not much at all. Only in the smallest, most trifling detail -"

"Such as?"

"I wouldn't bother driving another mile to Scotland and I would spend the entire weekend locked up in this hotel-room making love... sweet love... with you."

She grinned at me. "I like a guy who's flexible."

"Besides - how many times do you want to try and kill yourself this weekend?"

"And I'll bet you'd have messed up the tide times too -"

"Messed them up?" I said. "I never even bothered to check them!"

"Really? I can never tell when you're joking -"

"Maybe, maybe not," I said, tongue firmly in my cheek, so Sasha never did find out if I was bluffing or not, and we never did make it to the Corryvreckan, and nor have I yet, and so I still have not seen it, nor listened to the giant's fabled roar.

We went down for some supper, beer at the bar, and then a bottle of white wine in the lounge, surrounded by the middle-aged mums and dads, and we ate scampi and chips, though I was not much in the mood for food, as I had already set my heart on what had to be done.

I topped up her wine, and I remember how she drank the wine, looking at me over the rim of her glass, as if we both had shared the most wonderful secret. My raging dreams swirled for the last time and settled into this single cut-crystal object; and I inspected it from all sides, and there was not a trace of a flaw, and it was then, for a certainty, that I realised my Grand Strategy and I knew that it was not just good but water-tight.

I'd barely touched the scampi and the chips and the peas. I put my knife and fork to the side and then, like a diver on the high-board, I paused just a moment longer, peeping over the edge, realising that for better or for worse, the next few seconds would be definitive.

I slipped from my chair, down onto one knee, and took Sasha's hands in mine. She looked puzzled, not quite sure what I was about.

"Sasha," I said. "Will you marry me?"

She looked at me and her gaze drifted across the room and then back to me. "You mean that don't you?"

"I do," I said. "I want to marry you and be with you for the rest of my days."

She smiled, but a tight smile, and danced her hands with mine. "You're so sweet," she said. "But I know you're just doing this because of what happened... today..."

"You think I've proposed to you just because we've made love, and because I don't want you to feel guilty?"

"Well –"

"How little you know me," I said. I stared down at the carpet. It was that swirly red and black carpet that you often see in pub lounges. "It is true that our love-making did crystallise my feelings. But only in so far as it made me realise my grand strategy - and that grand strategy is you. I want to be with you. That's it."

"Thank you –"

"Do I still have to stay on the floor like this with all these people watching me?"

"Please get up off the floor."

"And what do you think?" I got back to my seat, now holding Sasha's hands across the table. "I realise you'd be trading down – quite a bit – but for me, things are not going to get much better."

"I am very flattered."

"And?"

"And I want to think –"

And after something like that, it's difficult to move onto general chit-chat, and a few minutes later, we pushed back our chairs, and took the wine and the glasses up to our room. Sasha sat with her glass by the window, looking out to the church, and I ran a bath, hot and deep, and I filled it with every gel and every scent in the bathroom.

I got into the bath, wine by my side; what luxury after my year of showering in the Cirencester pool. I wondered if I'd blown it. What a fantastic irony to have at long last made love with Sasha and then have her dump me because I'd pushed too hard. In basketball terms, they call it "the full court press"; you hustle and you hustle, trying to close the other team down, and if it goes well, they'll start to make mistakes. But the full court press is a risky strategy and it can also backfire spectacularly. But… risky strategies were probably the only ones there were ever likely to succeed with Sasha in the first place. Never in her life was she going to be attracted to the safe, the tame, or the pedestrian… so a guy who'd nearly killed her in the afternoon and who then had the nerve to propose in the evening… well, with luck, and a following wind, he might have a chance. I remembered our swim over the Thames in London, and how that disastrous start had also turned out rather well in the end.

Leastways there was nothing more that I could do that night; there was nothing more to be said. I had made my move and I could do no more – and if I said another thing, then I knew that it would only weaken my case.

I wondered what she was thinking. Well she was going to be thinking, of course, about whether she wanted to hitch her ship to mine, so that we might sail life's storms together - and I knew for a fact that there were many men out there who were richer and had better prospects, whereas I... I was just a fledgling journalist with just these idle hopes that one day I might work on Fleet Street.

But we got on. We got on well; and we stretched each other, and dared each other, and enjoyed each other's company and made each other laugh - and, frankly, what more do you need when you're deciding your life partner? And there was plenty yet that might sink us, because there will always be sea-mines out there no matter who you marry, but we were both big enough to allow the other to grow. Who knew how it would all turn out, hopefully for the best and quite possibly not, but the one thing that I was quite sure about was that for the rest of my days, I would much rather that Sasha was a part of my life than that she was out of it.

The water was getting cold, and my glass was empty, and I wondered at first whether to get out and go to bed, or whether to chivvy Sasha out of her funk, and chafe her for being such a ditherer, but in the end I pulled the plug and turned on the hot tap and ran myself another bath. I could wait. I could wait a little longer. When pressing your case with a woman, it is important to know when to press forward, and when to ease off.

I heard the sound of the door, and I thought at first that Sasha might have gone out to get some fresh air, but there was the sound of rustling by the bed and a moment later there was the double thump of her trainers hitting the wall and I smiled to myself; she had picked up my habit of hurling her shoes across the room. It is very satisfying, just that little bit of rebellion in these dry straightened days when we are expected to line up our shoes at the bottom of the bed.

Sasha came into the bathroom. She had two candles and she was naked. I watched without speaking as she dripped a little wax and then stuck the candles onto the edge of the bath-tub. She turned off the lights, left the bathroom, and reappeared a moment later with a bottle of Champagne, an ice-bucket and two glasses. That picture of her, standing there naked as she ripped off the foil and to blazes with easing the cork off gently, the bottle went with a bang and the cork ricocheted off the ceiling as a head of white foam spurted into the bath. She filled up the two glasses and then, for the first time, she spoke.

"May I?"

"You may."

She passed me a glass and, very elegantly, stepped into the bath. At first she squatted, then slowly immersed herself, legs intertwining with legs until the water stippled at the edges.

She raised her glass and I raised mine too, and although I half knew what to expect - because after all, why else would she have brought Champagne? - I was still both excited and nervy. But I didn't say anything. I couldn't say anything. She was taking things at her own pace now.

So I drank the Champagne and I looked at her, black curls curling into the bath foam, and her arm lying along the edge of the bathtub, and my knee squeezed tight behind her legs.

"Yes," she said. "My answer is yes. Most definitely - yes."

And though I had expected it, I was still momentarily gobsmacked when I heard her say the words out loud. "You will? You will marry me?"

"I would love to."

We clinked our glasses and we drank, and "Here's tae us", and I was babbling about how happy I was, and how happy I hoped to make her, and we kissed and we drank more Champagne, and she laughed out loud as, for the first time, she called me her fiancé, and then, before the bath water got cold, we got out, and we towelled each other down, and, in the correct manner in which these things are done, we fell onto the bed and we started to make love, and, also in the correct manner of things, we were talking, chatting, even as we were loving each other.

"I'll get you a ring tomorrow," I said. I was lying on top of her.

"I thought we were spending the day in bed," she pouted.

"I thought the jewellers might be a bit cheaper here."

"If there are any. I don't care about a ring," she said, like only a woman can when she's in her twenties and in love. "All I want is you."

"And you've got me," I said, and at that, I cupped her face in my hands and kissed her; her eyes strayed to my fingers.

"Though there is one thing –"

"Ask of me what you will –"

"Not that I want a ring. But I've always liked that ring –"

"It's yours." I pulled the Claddagh ring off and she stretched out her ring-finger. "I think heart facing in, don't you?"

I placed the ring on her finger, and though there have been many finer engagement rings, with diamonds and rubies and all the rest of those sparkling baubles with which we aim to please, it looked well on her.

"I'm spoken for." She held up her hand and admired the ring. It was only silver, but it had a solid earthiness about it. "I am your fiancée."

"I love that – say it again."

"I am Kim's fiancée. Would you like me to say it when I have another of your orgasms?"

"And I like that phrase too," I said. "Have another of my orgasms."

"I am Kim's fiancée," she said.

"And with feeling –"

And she had my neck in the crook of her arm, drawing me in close, and with my ear all but next to her lips, she sang out: "I am Kim's –"

Three days we spent in that hotel, what an idyll; we did not step outdoors even once, just the occasional brief foray downstairs for breakfast and lunch, and then long lazy love-making in the morning, and in the afternoon, and in the evening also.

I was just paying the bill with the landlady when her husband the cook came out to the reception, perhaps to take a peek at this couple who had performed such a magnificent feat of endurance over the weekend. "We've just got engaged," I said.

"That explains it," she said. "Come back when you're married."

I slung the bags in the car and drove back to Cirencester. I slowed down as we went past our layby on the long straight stretch. "That's where it all began," I said. "Fancy having another whirl under the chestnut?"

"You tempter." Her hand stroked my knee. "Let's get back to your treehouse. See if it's been burgled since you put that lock on –"

I was driving quite slowly, but Sasha didn't seem to mind. She had been permanently cured of telling me to speed up.

We listened to Radio Four and just caught the tail-end of Desert Island Discs. "I'll be on this programme one day," she said.

"And do you know your eight choices?"

"Some of them. The Magic Flute will have to be there at the top."

"It's our song isn't it?"

"It will always remind me of you." And she stroked my leg again. "Maybe we should have stopped at that layby?"

"It's not too late."

"Why do you only have one tape anyway?"

"If you've got a good tape – and I mean a really good tape – then one's enough. Just like with women."

She laughed and she looked at her feet which, as ever, were on the dashboard. "Have you ever made love on a car bonnet?"

"No," I said. "Surprisingly not – especially considering the enormous variety of my sex-life before you came along –"

"Should we… make amends?"

I looked at her – those legs, that face, that hair. I did not need telling twice. "Immediately," I said. "Without delay. The first farm-track we come across, it's got your name on it."

★

Back in the office on Monday, my colleagues were duly stunned when they heard the news. Katie, the pretty sub, actually started crying, patting away the tears as she kept repeating, "It's so romantic". Rudi clapped me over the shoulder, Siobhan and Phoebe gave me a hug, and George afforded me a hearty handshake as he called up Phil the photographer so that our engagement could be formally announced in the Wilts and Glos. The picture even made the front page, as so it should: editors the world over, even editors on little local papers like the Standard, like nothing more than a picture of a beautiful woman on their front pages. Ideally, Hugh would have liked to have cropped me altogether out of the picture, but seeing as it was our engagement photo, I was fairly central to the story.

I called my parents to tell them the good news. I called from Sasha's home, as she stood nervously beside me. My father seemed genuinely delighted. My step-mother Edie started squawking; they had a brief word with Sasha. It all sounded very amicable.

Lady Claire was also pleased. "I thought there was something in the air that night of your dinner party," she said.

But there were others in Cirencester, particularly Sasha's huge following of love-struck admirers, who were quite put out, who, perhaps, had been putting their love on the back burner in the hope that one day they might be able to sneak in under the radar - and now here was Sasha, only plighting her troth to this jobbing hack; and where the hell had he sprung from anyway?

And then there was one other person who had to be told about our engagement: Sasha's mother. Sasha made the call shortly after I'd spoken to my parents. She told Penny that we'd got engaged and all I heard was this rich peal of laughter. "I mean it," Sasha said. "We're engaged."

"I suppose you know your own mind," Penny said. "You certainly always used to."

"Kim is the person I want to marry."

"We must have an engagement party," Penny said. "I'll throw you an engagement party. Would you like that?"

Sasha accepted.

I've never been much of a fan of engagement parties. They are all very stiff and starchy, a sort of coming together of the clans as these two families warily sniff each other up and down. It may be called a party, but for the hosts, at least, it is anything but.

When I've had to deal with people like Penny in the past - people, that is, who are not my friends - then I have one very simple tactic. If I'm with them, I like to have witnesses in the room; I am never alone with them. When I initially greet them, I give them a hug and a kiss and a most fulsome "How are you?" and then I quickly move on. I do not engage. I do not want to spend any longer talking to these people than is absolutely necessary.

So when it came to the night of our engagement party, a Saturday night in Sasha's grandfather's house, then I was very careful in all my dealings with Penny.

Sasha and I arrived an hour before the start of the party, and we were welcomed into the house by Sasha's grandfather John; he was tall, distinguished looking, with a clipped moustache that he'd had ever since the War. It was an old thatched house, with black smoked beams and an inordinate amount of clutter, cups and photos on every available surface from tables to mantelpieces. John kissed Sasha on the cheek and shook me warmly by the hand and then we were ushered through to the kitchen, ducking as we went through the low doorways.

The kitchen had an air of grime about it, dusty dried flowers hanging from the beams, and an old Aga. Penny was cutting up brown bread for the smoked salmon. Like Sasha, Penny was wearing a short Little Black Dress; very high heels and a white apron. She'd had a blow-dry and she looked well. I could see the beauty that she had once had. She came tottering over to say hello, wiping her hands on the front of her apron. I kissed her on the cheek. Sasha was jittery, her smile just a little too forced, so I did my best to help things along. I was given a bottle of Champagne and opened it. John hovered in the background; getting engaged suddenly seemed all very grown up. All the fun and love was leaking out of the air.

"So when are you getting a proper engagement ring?" Penny asked.

"I like this one." Sasha looked at her Claddagh ring.

"But don't you understand the point of engagement rings - it's to make other women jealous."

"They can think what they like," Sasha said. "This ring's got character."

"Wouldn't want people thinking your fiancé is a cheapskate though - would we now Kim?" Penny turned an arch eye on me.

"Does it really matter?" I said. "If she wanted a rock, I'd get her one."

I passed around the Champagne and Sasha and I held hands as we made awkward small talk about when we wanted to get married, and where we wanted to live - and did I really want to work on Fleet Street or did I wish to spend the rest of my days on the Wilts and Glos? The conversation was skating blithely over the surface, but I was aware - Sasha was aware - of these rippling undercurrents beneath us; perhaps it was my own awkwardness. It is difficult to be light and sunny when there are all these great unspoken tensions in the air. As I was looking at Penny, I was not seeing Sasha's mother, I was seeing this woman who, just a few weeks before, had seduced me. Had I really had sex with her? It just didn't bear thinking about.

We were relieved when the guests started to arrive. There were a few of the polo set, like Greek Gods as they strode amongst my colleagues on The Standard; and a few of Sasha's friends from Gloucestershire; and my parents came too, both of them very safe hands, and my father kissed me on the cheek and kissed Sasha as well, and then started to apply his considerable charm. I stood at the door, nursing my glass as I watched my father and Edie chattering to Sasha; she was laughing. She seemed very happy.

The doorbell went again, and I went to get it. I was quite shocked when I saw who was on the doorstep. It was Paris and Dangerous, both wearing jeans and jackets, the RAC's version of smart casual. Paris was looking good - very slick, very well groomed, clipped hair that was slicked with Brylcream. He had a bit of a tan and he'd been working out.

I welcomed them in. I wondered who on earth had invited them; certainly not me, and I didn't think Sasha would have asked them either. I was about to get them some drinks, when Penny came out of the kitchen. "My two beautiful boys," she said, and she embraced them both. Dangerous lifted her off her feet and she had her arms around his neck. "You make me feel so young!" She giggled as he held her, legs kicked back, just as women are supposed to do when they're in love.

She stroked them both on the shoulders as they joined the party, and then she turned to me. "I couldn't borrow you a moment, Kim?"

"Of course." Alarm bells instantly clamoured.

I followed her down the passage, past all the musty coats and the umbrellas and the polo-sticks and into the kitchen. We were the only two people in the room.

"I'm being run off my feet," Penny said. "The sausages need taking out of the oven and we've still got so much salmon."

I finished off my glass of Champagne and then started work on the salmon, briskly slicing the bread and then slathering on the butter. As we worked, this tangible silence of unspoken words spread between us.

"So you're engaged to my Sasha."

"Yes I am." If I'd had any sense I'd have dropped the knife and fled the room. "She's great."

"And it looks like you've deflowered her. Unless I'm very much mistaken."

I changed the subject, blurting out the first thing that came into my head. "I love smoked salmon."

"She couldn't hope for a more accomplished lover." Penny stooped to take the sausages out of the Aga. "As I should know."

She pulled out the tray with a wet dish-cloth. "Shit!" she said. "Burnt myself."

Briefly, I looked up. "Very nasty."

Penny went over to the sink and ran cold water over her hand. I wasn't really aware of what she was doing, but the next thing I knew she had come up behind me and had spanked me on the bottom with a fish-slice. "Very nasty yourself," she said.

I turned to look at her and as I did so, I saw Sasha standing in the doorway, arms crossed.

For a while she watched us, sizing us up, and then Penny also became aware that Sasha was watching us.

"Hi there!" I said, enforced jollity. "Got some smoked salmon to take round."

Sasha sauntered into the kitchen. "Who invited Paris and Dangerous?" she said.

"I did," Penny said.

"Of course you did," said Sasha.

"I am hosting this party, you know."

"I knew you'd do something."

"I'll invite whoever I please to my own parties."

I broke off from cutting the salmon and put the knife down. I watched the two women squaring off to each other, wondered if there was any way I could defuse the situation.

"Is that why you wanted to throw this engagement party?" Sasha said.

"Don't get in a pet, Sasha - it's all right." Penny looked at me, and then Sasha looked at me.

"I'm going out for some fresh air," I said. I looked at Sasha. "Coming?"

She followed me out of the French windows. I could feel her still bristling next to me as I put my arm round her waist. She did not respond. We stood in the middle of the lawn and she turned to me.

"So what was that all about?" she said.

I said the only thing that could be said. "What was all what about?"

"Why did my mother spank you like that?"

I shrugged. "You know what she's like. I've got even less control over her than you have."

Sasha was about two feet away from me, looking deep into my eyes, plumbing my very thoughts.

"Has my mother ever to come to see you at the treehouse?"

And there it was - the question now baldly out in the open, and I was having to steel myself to tell the most bare-faced lie. I don't know what I do when I'm about to tell a lie, but it sometimes feels as if this red warning flag goes up above my head, and a great klaxon starts booming, "Lie Alert! Lie Alert!"

I continued to look Sasha in the eye. I tried to keep my lie smooth and simple. "Just the once - I told you about it."

And Sasha just looked at me, and I was finding it all so thoroughly unnerving - how the hell did she know that I was lying? How had she so unerringly zeroed in on the only falsehood that I had ever told her?

"So she never came back again? She never came back to the tree-house?"

"No - no -"

"And she's not the reason why you decided to put a lock on the door?"

I looked away from her, turning my face to the moon as I let out a laugh; it sounded strained. "What is this, Sasha - the Grand Inquisition?"

"What's happened between you and my mother?" she said.

"Sasha - this is our engagement party. We're going to be married!" I said. "Shouldn't we be joining our guests?"

But Sasha could not be turned. "If something's happened, then I want to know."

I made to give her a hug, but she stepped back. "Honestly Sasha -"

There was a coo from the kitchen. It was Penny. She'd taken off her apron and was beckoning to us. "It's time for the speeches!"

With absolutely nothing resolved we followed her through to the main room, where John made a few words, and Sasha and I raised our glasses though we were feeling miserable inside. Engagement parties - is it any wonder I hate them?

Sasha drifted off, though there had been no rapprochement between us. There had been a toast to the unhappy couple and then she was away, throwing herself into the party, where she soon became the centre of attention; perhaps I should have been with her. At engagement parties, and at weddings also, it is normal for the happy couple to perform as a double act - but we did not. I chatted to my friends and Sasha to hers, and I remember looking over at her, and seeing that she was talking to Paris. She was showing off her engagement ring; he made a face and she started laughing. I looked at them and then I looked around the room to see how the rest of the party-goers were enjoying themselves; and I saw Penny. She had also been watching Sasha with Paris, and now she turned and she looked at me; and at that moment, I realised for a certainty that Penny was not a woman who wished me well. And - more unusually - she did not wish her daughter well either.

CHAPTER 18

It is difficult to make up after a row if there has been no actual row.

Rows are rarely to do with the subject at hand; they tend to be the spark that lights the powder-keg.

But if there isn't that spark, there is no explosion - so the resentment continues to simmer until eventually it rots and festers.

So with Sasha and her witchy-little ways, she knew that something had occurred between her mother and me; and she also knew that I'd been lying through my teeth in the cover-up.

And now Paris was back in the picture.

With a woman like Sasha, a very beautiful woman, you have to play ex-boyfriends very, very carefully. You have to go through this act that your fiancée's history doesn't matter a damn; and perhaps it does, and perhaps it doesn't, but the one thing you're sure of is that no good will ever come of venting your jealousy. Beautiful women will always have their camp of admirers, those guys who are playing the long game for the day, the inevitable day, when the beauty needs a shoulder to cry on. And if you're lucky enough to have the love of a beautiful woman, then you must accept that these hangers-on are all part of the package.

So, yes, Paris and Sasha were back to being good buddies, and of course he was my buddy also, and they never once alluded to their brief relationship; or at least certainly not in my presence. I remember wondering if Paris was taking a leaf out of my own book: was he playing the same game that I had once played with Sasha, never flirting, never once touching her, never being anything other than the rock-solid friend who was utterly untouched by her beauty?

Sasha and I had been in the Slug and Lettuce having a drink after work and Paris had come to join us; just the three of us sat at a round table, me in my staid jacket and tie while Paris was in his beautiful black biker leathers, his helmet-hair sleeked down like a skull-cap. He'd parked his bike outside; like Sasha, he was quite a head-turner.

We'd been talking about the details of our days. I'd been writing up court cases and Sasha had been handling her volatile charges, and as for Paris, he'd got up at lunchtime and had spent the day charging round Gloucestershire on his Harley.

A barman came over to the table with a glass of Champagne.

"Sasha?" he asked.

"Yes?"

"This is for you." He put the glass on the table and passed her a note; even though we were engaged, this sort of occurrence was still fairly common.

We looked over at the bar. Her admirer was wearing a blazer and he looked familiar. He waved.

Sasha, bless her, did not even bother to look at the note - and nor did she accept the Champagne. "Thank you." She smiled at the barman. "I only accept drinks if my friends are included."

A few minutes later, the man in the blazer turned up at the table with a bottle of Champagne and four glasses. "Can I join you?"

Sasha and I shrugged but Paris pulled up a chair; perhaps he was aware that it would cause friction.

The admirer was called Freddie. "You guys, I see you here so often it feels like I ought to know you." He poured the Champagne. "Even if I don't know you, I want to know you."

He was doing his best to be chatty, charming. Paris and I were included in his conversation, but it was obvious to all that he was only interested in Sasha. It's an interesting dilemma: what do you do when a stranger is hitting on your girlfriend? It's nothing too overt; it's not quite enemy action; but nevertheless you know that if you weren't there, then the suave stranger would be doing his best to lure her into the bedroom. It's a difficult one. Maybe it's the nature of relationships; maybe it's the direct corollary of dating a beautiful woman. If you are with a beautiful woman then other men will desire her - and, obviously, they will do what they can to make her their own.

Freddie was a property developer, a lady's man, with a cow-lick of black hair and gleaming white teeth; I was watching him as he did his best to entertain us. I had said hardly a word, but Paris was engaged, as if he had found another ally in the court of Queen Sasha.

And as for my Sasha, she was not engaged but not disengaged either; although she was always cool with these suitors, I think she was not averse to the attention. It was all part of her due.

I went off to the toilets and a few seconds later Paris had joined me. He was a couple of feet away from me.

"Nice guy," he said.

"Freddie?" I said. "He's a tosser!"

"Now, now, Kim! You can't be like that over every one who's got a crush on your Sasha."

"Freddie would be a tosser whether or not he had a crush on Sasha." I went to wash my hands.

"I've never really offered my proper congratulations to you both. You make a great couple."

I stared at him in the mirror. I was not sure if he was being ironic. It was one of those conversations where by far the most important things were being left unsaid.

"And you've bedded her to boot!" He came over to the basins. "Lucky devil."

"Who says that?" For my part, I had not mentioned a word of my love life to anyone.

"Says Penny."

"How staggeringly indiscreet of her."

"Penny's not all bad, you know." He wiped his hands on the front of his leather jacket. "Do you have a downer on everyone who wants a slice of Sasha?"

"Not at all." My hands were already dry. I continued to dry them on the towels.

"You've already got the cake," he said, standing at the door. He held the door open for me. "There's no need to get jealous when other people want a taste. Penny's her mother, for God's sake!"

I looked at him as I walked out of the toilets, wondering about all the different planets that revolved around this single blazing sun that was Sasha. Was I being unreasonable? Perhaps there was no cause for concern - because, as Paris had said, I'd won the prize. Sasha loved me, wanted to marry me, and would soon be saying to me those glib little words which meant so much: "Forsaking all others, so long as we both shall live."

★

Your memories of old loves are like icebergs - all that you can remember of them is the very tip that peeks out of the water. You remember the moments of high drama, high tension, perhaps a few of the spats, and some of the more outstanding love-making; but for the most part, the everyday goings-on are forgotten. They have become that lump of ice that is submerged beneath the water. But though you may not remember them, they are still there, hidden so deep that they have become a part of your very fabric.

So for those three months after our engagement, I can recall a few of the highlights, but mainly I have a memory of immense joy tinged with this distinct uneasiness: how ever would I, a mere trainee hack, be able to hold onto this woman? When I was in the black dog, I would dwell on how I could ever compare to these smooth bastard thirty-somethings who lived in Cheltenham and Gloucester; and the rich dogs like Paris and Dangerous whose wallets were never empty; and the beautiful people, the polo-players, with their studied manners and their easy charm.

I never breathed a word of these doubts to Sasha. To her, I was this cheerful, irrepressible force - for I, of course, was the guy who was in the driving seat. While many other men may have longed to be there, it was actually me who was taking Sasha back home at night.

But I was also aware that there was still many a slip twixt the gold-band and her ring-finger. So, just as with my fastidious courtship, I was playing to my strengths. These may have been limited, but they were most definitely different. I may not have had looks or money or a car, or even a particularly impressive job - but I was quirky; I preferred the tangential route to the straight path; and I had an impish sense of humour which for some beautiful and quite inexplicable reason, Sasha adored. Sometimes it all came together and sometimes it did not, but my darling Sasha did at least give me full points for trying.

The polo season was in full swing, the evenings long and balmy, and there was me, loved-up to the hilt, and my beautiful fiancée matching me in almost every respect. It was a Friday night, middle of July, and, as ever, I was due to see my Sasha.

"What have you got lined up for me tonight?" she said. "Something exciting?"

Phone cradled at my ear, I surveyed the newsroom. I'd been at the Wilts and Glos for over a year-and-a-half and I loved the place; I had become a veritable news-hound, thirsting for the next story, even if it was nothing more than a page lead. "Something exciting?" I said. "When have I ever laid on something that wasn't exciting?"

"You, Kim, manage to make an adventure out of even the most mundane activities –"

"Who would have thought that a simple drive to the Corryvreckan would lead to a proposal of marriage –"

"Quite," she said, crisply. "What have you got planned?"

"Something rather special. Tonight, Sasha my love, is the anniversary of Lord George Byron's swim across the Hellespont –"

"Are you fibbing again?"

"Be that as it may, we are celebrating Lord George's greatest swim."

"His greatest swim? I thought you told me he swam the Grand Canal after a party in Venice –"

"Detail, darling –"

"So what are we doing?"

"Something special!"

"And you'll want me to dress up too?"

"Though we're not going to the bingo –"

"Where are you taking me then?"

"Bring some boots and a warm coat –"

"A trip up the Sapperton Tunnel? That would be lovely."

"You're going to think you've died –"

"And gone to heaven? I've already been there." With that, she blew me a kiss.

Rudi came with me back to the treehouse. We had some wine and then he drove off in the Merc for our *rendez-vous*.

I had high hopes for the evening. I had picked up the idea for our date from, of all people, Prince Charles. He'd mentioned it in some magazine article about the Highlands and I had immediately seized on the idea. I'd never realised that the Prince of Wales was such a romantic softie.

Sasha came round to the treehouse at about eight and, absolutely smitten, we sat there caressing each other; how often do you do that now with the one you love?

"Where's your table gone?" she asked.

"Needed mending," I said. "Taken it to the workshop." My fingers teased at her breasts. "Do we make love before – or do we make love after?"

"Can we do both?" she said.

"That is the correct answer." I slipped my hand up her skirt and immediately she was tugging at my belt; what it is to be young and in love, though take it from me, it's even better if you've got a treehouse.

"How long have we got?" She dragged me onto the bed. "Trains to catch, anything like that?"

"Fifteen minutes – maybe twenty."

"Twice, then?"

"Absolutely."

And just like that, there we were making love, 0-60mph in approximately thirty seconds flat. Sasha had not even taken her boots off, and that was all as it should be, for as with everything else in life, we only thrive on variety, and so the five-minute quickie can be as magical and as memorable as the two-hour marathons. Even as we were making love at the edge of the bed, Sasha was unbuttoning my shirt and I was pulling at her jumper. It was quite thoroughly debauched, and by the end of it all, half-naked and with our clothes cast hither and thither, we must have looked like this perfect picture of depravity - and to those who would tut and sneer, I would only say that though our love-making may have been driven by lust, it had also come to be the most perfect expression of our love.

As quickly as we had stripped, our shirts and jumpers were returned, and belts were re-buckled and her pleated skirt was smoothed and re-adjusted, and just like that, we were back to being just another young couple enjoying their Friday night.

"Shall we go?" I said. Though it was warm outside, I pulled on my coat.

Sasha looked at me, dreamy with love. "One minute ago, we were making sweet love -"

"You'd never guess would you?"

"I can still feel your kisses on my lips -"

"And anywhere else?"

She slipped her arm companionably through mine and we walked down the stairs and into the garden. "Yes - I can feel your echo."

I unlocked the garden-gate and with one step we were out into the wilds of Cirencester Park. We walked up one of the broad grassy avenues that had been carved out of the forest, with Cirencester Church at our backs. It was all but dusk, as the woodland reverted to the thick forest, darker and seamier than it was in the day as the sprites came to life.

"I have no idea where we're going," Sasha said. "We're not going to Coates?"

"No."

"Are we walking all the way to Sapperton Wood?"

"No."

"Not many other places to eat in Cirencester Park. We're going nowhere."

"I know." I turned. She looked so impossibly beautiful. I kissed her on the cheek. "There's nothing for miles. Miles and miles. Nothing but us and the fire-flies in this deep, dark forest."

"Like Hansel and Gretel."

"Do you trust me?"

"In certain matters," she said elliptically.

We continued to walk until it was quite dark, and after a while we became aware that ahead of us, right in the middle of the avenue, there was a small light. Occasionally, carried over the wind, we could also hear little snatches of what seemed like music, though it was difficult to tell.

Sasha took my hand. "A light," she said. "I think I even recognise the music. Is this anything to do with you?"

I smiled but said nothing.

"What have you got there?"

The music was quite clear now. It was The Marriage of Figaro. And the source of the light was also becoming more apparent. It was right dead centre in the middle of the park, The Seven Rides, it is called, the hub at the heart of seven broad avenues. It is an incredible spot, for as I remember it, each avenue leads to a view of either a church or a monument, and in the day-time, as you stand in the middle, you are surrounded by these great vistas of glorious Gloucestershire. Just over to the side was Pope's Seat, a rustic Rococo folly which looked like a small but very ornate entrance arch. It was named after not a Pope but the poet, Alexander Pope, who'd had a hand in designing the park. Of an afternoon, Pope would sit writing in his folly as he took his muse from the distant spire of Kemble Church.

Sasha walked up to my Pembroke table that had been set up in the dead centre of the hub. It was this brilliant oasis in the middle of the park, a fairy-tale mirage. Rudi had excelled himself. The table had been laid with a white linen tablecloth and on it were six jars with a candle in each. The crockery and the cutlery was of the very finest, sparkling silver knives and Sir Anthony's cut-crystal glasses; and two pristine white napkins; and a small vase with a posy of flowers. The placings had been set at the corner of the table, and at the far end, there was the food – a loaf of white bread and a selection of cold meats, and some pickles and a bottle of white in an ice-bucket, and a bottle of claret, already opened. At the foot of the table, Mozart was booming out from my old boom-box.

Sasha stalked the table, her hand trailing on the linen. "And this is for us?" she said. "I feel like Goldilocks."

"This is for us."

"But… but who did it? How did it…"

"Maybe it was the forest fairies," I said.

"Some fairies –"

"And they'll clean it up too, if they're not too drunk."

She hugged me so hard. "I love you so much."

I pulled out her chair and she sat down in silence, gazing at the table and at the food. I poured the wine and sat next to her, knee to knee, and while the gloom settled all around us, I twirled my wine-glass and revelled in being at the centre of this universe.

Sasha drank and I helped her to some of the food. She ate a little and then put down her knife and fork and just stared about her. With the candles so close, all we could see was the table and each other. Overhead, you could just make out a few of the very brightest stars.

She took my hand and kissed my fingertips. "Will you still be doing this when we're married?"

"And when we've had children. And grandchildren too. Not a day will go by when I will not be trying to dazzle and entertain you."

"Whose idea was it?"

"A very dear friend of mine – you might know him. Prince Charles." Sasha moued at me. "It's true! He takes his guests trekking in the Highland Hills, and then at sunset they arrive at this beautiful location, where a table has been set for dinner –"

"Just like this one!"

"Not quite as lavish as this."

We talked a little about weddings and such befuddling stuff as is used to force eager fiancés into a quick surrender. We had already decided that we were going to get married the next June, exactly a year after we'd got engaged, so that our every wedding anniversary would remind us of the little red dots on the horizon, always there, always waiting to wipe us out without a moment's notice.

"What sort of wedding do you want?" Sasha said.

"I don't care about the wedding." I helped Sasha to some more of the cold beef. "I just want to be married to you. I want to have you in my life for the rest of my life. We can have any sort of wedding you like -"

"A wedding to fill up the whole of St John the Baptist's Church?"

"If you want."

"Or just the two of us and a couple of witnesses in the registry office?"

"Even better - though I would love to see you in a wedding dress. You'd be something else -"

Sasha threw her head back and laughed. The thought of it still seemed so outrageous: the pair of us, so grown up and so married. "And where are we going to live? And what about our treehouse?"

"We'll always have the treehouse."

"And when you're a fully qualified journalist?"

"Fleet Street?"

"Do you know anyone there?"

"I do know one guy, actually. Mike Hamill. He's the chief reporter on *The Sun*; I gave him a story once. I like him."

"On *The Sun*?" she said. "I'm surprised you even read that paper. Is it a paper?"

"You'd be surprised. It's a slick outfit. The reporters aren't anything like what you'd imagine -"

"Meet my husband Kim - he's a reporter on *The Sun*."

"Or maybe I could try the Mail if you like -"

"Even worse!"

"I'm not so sure you approve of my intended career."

"I'll -" she finished her wine and stroked my cheek. "I hadn't really thought. I suppose I thought you were going onto one of the broadsheets -"

"Great papers of record. Ever so respectable."

"But if you want to work on *The Sun*, then go for it!"

I said that airy thing that could only ever come from a young man who is quite blinded by love. "We'll sort it out." I moved onto Sasha. I always prefer asking questions to answering them. "And you? What is the grand strategy? Is it polo?"

"I don't know," she said. "I hope that horses will be in my life, but this polo crowd…"

"Are a little too much?"

"Spending my days clucking around after these charming boys like some mother-hen, and then being pawed over by the *Patron*. I'm not sure it's really for me."

"Your delightful *Patron*," I said. "How is he? Did you have a good season?"

"A very good season. Two trophies, pictures in the magazines -"

"Not to mention all the Polo lovelies who are hanging on his every word -"

"Not that he's got anything much to say -" She broke off and started laughing. "He did the funniest thing two months ago. I never told you about it, because I knew you'd want to put it in the paper, but anyway it's all old news now."

"Oh yes?" My ears pricked up.

"It happened just over there," she said, pointing. "By the polo ground."

"Right there?"

She laughed and picked up a gherkin between thumb and forefinger and popped it into her mouth. "Right there. They'd put up a marquee. It was some charity dinner. Prince Charles was there too."

I was aware that I was suddenly very still. If a Royal is involved in a story, particularly a senior royal like Prince Charles, then a story has much more heft.

"We'd had the dinner and then there was a charity auction - signed shirts and polo-sticks, everyone throwing their money around. The final lot was a piece of porcelain of two polo-players. It wasn't very nice, but they'd all had a lot to drink and Prince Charles was there, and there were a lot of bids. The *Patron* was plunging. He wanted it and, like most things in his life, he eventually got it -"

"He never got you though -"

She kissed me. "That's because I wasn't for sale. He paid about £40,000 for this piece of china, and everyone was clapping and cheering as he went to the rostrum to pick up his prize. He accepts the statue from the wife of the chairman, kisses her on the cheek. But he was holding the statue quite awkwardly and the next thing he's dropped it on the ground. Smashed to bits."

"What happened then?"

"The place erupted. Prince Charles was in hysterics. He loves it when things go wrong at these formal dinners -"

"That is one hell of a story!" I said. "Why didn't you tell me?"

"I told you - I didn't want to put temptation your way. I knew you'd want to run it!"

"But it's still a story!" I said.

"Nonsense!" she said. "It happened two or three months ago. You were only just telling me stories go stale after a week."

"Stories like this are news even if they're six months old."

"You don't know what you're talking about, my love."

"I think I do, my sweet. Have I told you I love you?"

"Not for at least ten minutes."

"I love you - and I'm telling you it's news."

"And I love you too, my darling little trainee reporter who still doesn't know -"

I shut her up with a kiss.

It is an easy mistake to make. News will ideally be as up to date as possible - the fresher the better. But if you have a good exclusive, then it does not much matter how old the story is. Only just recently, a story broke about Hitler's secret love-child. The actual events may have happened well over ninety years ago, but because the story had never come out, it was still a world exclusive; people were talking about it. Therefore it was news.

"Is there pudding?" Sasha asked.

"Of course there's pudding," I said. "What do you take me for?"

"My little rookie."

I dipped into my coat pocket. "One Twix," I said. "And one apple. Happy?"

"Inordinately happy."

Our arms entwined and we fed each other a finger of the Twix. I gave the apple a polish and presented it to Sasha. "This is our challenge," I said. "We must eat the apple between us - but we can only touch it with our mouths."

"And if we succeed?"

"You will get to make sweet love under the stars, and you will look up to the sky and all those billions of galaxies, and you will know that there is not a single being in existence who has been loved as much as I love you -"

"A small exaggeration - surely?"

"Not a bit of it," I said. "Since the first recorded syllable of history, no-one has ever loved as much as I love you -"

"Such hyperbole!" she said. "I'm surprised you don't burst into flames for shame."

"More than Anthony and Cleopatra, Romeo and Juliet..."

"Othello and Desdemona -"

"Certainly more than Othello -"

"Shut up and let's eat the apple."

We sat there knee to knee at the corner of the table with the apple between our lips and our eyes not three inches from each other, and it was a good thing that I took a quick first bite because Sasha had the giggles. She brought her lips again to the apple and, little by little, like two Soldier Ants devouring a palm-leaf, we nibbled into the apple, working away at the edges, and at the top, lips brushing against lips, and fingers now pulling at buttons, and it is all so erotically charged that we have not even finished the apple before Sasha is bracing herself against the edge of the table and, as ever, as always, and as it for ever will be in my memories, we are making love as we still champ at this apple that is between our teeth, bite by mesmerising bite, until at last there's nothing but the core left and I take it now, and chew, and swallow it whole, and when it has gone we are kissing crazily, all tongues and teeth and lips and this glorious taste of apple. We are almost at the brink, wild with desire, and I hold it just there, because it is in my nature to delay the moment just that little bit longer - because, not always, but generally, the longer you can postpone it, the greater the gratification; I don't know if those prim Presbyterians ever meant the term "delayed gratification" to be applied to love-making, but it is nevertheless apposite.

"Just imagine -" I said.

"Do we always have to stop for one of your little chats?"

"If I don't say it immediately, I might forget what I wanted to -"

"What did you want to say?" Sasha was starting to tremble. I could feel the tremors from her arms to her ankles.

"What would have happened if we'd been eating a pineapple?"

"Peeled, I hope."

"Not easy with the skin on - bit rough on your lips."

"Maybe next time a ripe plum?" she said.

"Or we could try a Big Mac -"

"So messy -"

"That's why I thought you'd like it."

"Please?" she said.

"For you? Of course."

Sasha had been looking into my eyes, but a moment later she was looking behind me.

"I think there's a car coming."

I looked around. There was a car - and it was coming at some speed. The headlights were arcing high and low as the car bounced up the avenue.

"Jesus!" I laughed and as I hauled at my trousers, Sasha snatched at her coat. We ran hard into the darkness and hid behind Pope's Seat, peeping round the corner of the stonework to see who had come to disturb us. Sasha had her hands on Pope's Seat and I was snug behind looking over her shoulder, my hands tight about her waist.

We watched as the car tooled up to our table and then stopped. I recognised the car immediately. It was Dangerous' red pick-up.

Sasha writhed and pressed against me. We watched Dangerous get out of the car and I lifted her skirt.

I was looking over Sasha's shoulder. Dangerous and a few of his cronies had got out of the pick-up. They looked around and then started helping themselves to the last of the food on the table.

Sasha's breath was coming in quick pants and she was holding hard onto my fingers.

"Beauties in vain their pretty eyes may roll," I said. "Charms strike the sight, but merit wins the soul."

"Are you…" Sasha said. "Is that Pope you're quoting?"

"Fools rush in where angels fear to tread."

"It is Pope!"

"The difference is too nice - where ends the virtue or begins the vice."

"Poetry!" she squealed. "As we're making love! Did you learn all this for me this afternoon?"

"Blessed is the man who expects nothing, for he shall never be disappointed!"

"In the hope that you might have at me up against Pope's Seat?" She gasped. "Well it was worth it!"

She pressed and she writhed, and for a while I was distracted from reciting any more of the poetry that I had indeed learned just that afternoon. The Hoorays were now throwing the remains of our supper into each other's open mouths.

"Tell me, Kim," she said. She had one trembling arm about my waist now, and one arm braced against the stone. "This sort of thing happens a lot with you - doesn't it?"

"I'm a magnet for it."

"But is it normal? Is this what lovers do?"

"Make love up against age-old follies as they watch a flock of gannets polish off their supper?"

"Yes - yes -"

"I can't really speak for anyone else - but yeah, Sasha, darling, this is all perfectly normal."

"And with your girlfriend on the kibbutz - Karen -"

"Did I ever tell you about the time the terrorists attacked the dining hall -"

I could hear Sasha chuckling. "Before I knew you, I used to dream what love-making would be like. I used to imagine it in a bedroom, with a bed and a door -"

"Never fantasized about the great outdoors?"

"I am getting strangely addicted to it…"

"The bastards are finishing off the wine." Two of the Hoorays were sat in the chairs, our chairs, sipping from our glasses, while Dangerous was swigging the wine straight from the bottle.

"I'm going to scream -"

"Well kiss me -" and she twisted her head and her mouth opened under mine, and her shriek was transformed into a drawn-out mewl that rippled through my lips to the back of my brain. I happened to have my eyes open, still keeping an eye on the students. Dangerous cocked his ear and looked in our direction. A rabbit, perhaps, snapped up by a fox. I looked at Sasha. She was quite rigid beside me, eyes wide open as she watched me.

Dangerous tossed the bottle over his shoulder and it smashed on a rock, and then with nothing left to eat or drink, the Hoorays roared off in the pick-up, two red lights receding into the night, and soon there was just us in the darkness and Mozart's Queen of the Night matching the rhythm of our heartbeats.

So many things I remember about that night - and so many things that would come of it, both in the short-term; and in the long-term; and in the very long-term. That supper in the park was tactics, strategy and grand strategy all rolled into one. And, if I had my chance, would I alter it? Well these are the things that we ponder upon as we contemplate the trajectory of our lives: what would we change? What would we do differently?

Well, as I look back on my life and on my loves, I realise that I have been blessed. But when it comes to Sasha… There is one thing, definitely, that if I could, I would change - only who knows how it might have all turned out. It is one of those things that I dwell upon now as I stare into the fire. The wood burns, the smoke eddies ever upwards, and then there in the flames is my Sasha, lithe in my arms, urging me on to teach her all that I know.

CHAPTER 19

The first and initial consequence of our night in the park was that Sasha had a blistering fit of temper.

Though I might have drunk a lot on our night in the park, the next day I could still remember exactly what we had talked about. Two days later, on the Monday morning, I acted on it.

The call was too risky to make from the newsroom, so at lunchtime, I mooched off to one of the public phones by the church; I didn't even need any money. I had the Freephone number.

I got through on the second ring. In the background I could hear that newsroom hum that I would come to know so well.

"Kim, my boy!" he said. "How are you?"

"I'm good thanks, Mike - how are you?"

"Never better!" he said. He was Mike Hamill, *The Sun*'s ebullient chief reporter - though to have met him, you would never have dreamed that he was a journalist, let alone a Sun reporter. He looked more like an entrepreneur or an advertising magnate. Two years previously, when I'd been working at a hotel in Dorset, I'd given him a story. He'd paid me handsomely, treated me to lunch at his club, and had told me to feed him any more titbits that came my way. Now I was going to do just that.

Mike and I went through the preliminary strokes before we moved onto business. "Something tells me that you might have a story for me," he said.

"Just thought I'd run it by you. Might make a filler."

"Fire away -"

I told him about the charity night at Cirencester Park, and the *Patron*; and then I told him that Prince Charles was there too.

"This is more like it," he said.

I told him how Charles had been doubled up with laughter when the piece of porcelain had been smashed. I did not embroider the story. You should never embroider stories that you sell to *The Sun*; they do enough embroidery of their own.

"When did this happen?" Mike said.

"Two months ago – maybe three."

"Do we know the charity?"

"No."

"What's the name of the Jokers Wild *Patron*?"

I gave it to him.

"*Excellente!*" said Mike. "Any little details that you may have missed?"

"That's everything I know –"

"And you haven't told anyone else?"

"Of course not."

"Good – give me a call when you're next in London. I'll have some money for you."

I bought a sandwich at Waitrose and, well pleased with myself, went back to the office. As a trainee reporter on the Wilts and Glos, I should of course have given up the story to my own paper – but I'd received damn all thanks for the exclusives that I'd given them in the past, and so I had come to that realisation that eventually comes to most local reporters: why not make a bit of money on the side by selling my exclusives direct to the nationals?

It goes without saying that this was a sackable offence – and as for Sasha... Well I didn't know what she'd make of it. But if you throw down a challenge to your lover, then you can hardly start bleating when that challenge is accepted; how little I know women.

The story appeared four days later in *The Sun*, a page three lead, complete with pictures of the *Patron* and the smashed statue. My quotes were also there in full, now attributed to a "gobsmacked dinner guest".

I hadn't bought *The Sun* that morning, so the first I knew of it was when Hugh tore into the newsroom. The reporters had only just got in. We were contentedly sipping coffee, and because it was the end of the week, I'd brought in a box of cream-cakes.

Hugh was brandishing a copy of that day's Sun. "Does anyone know about this story? Why did we miss it?" He looked at me. "Why did we miss it?"

I wiped my mouth and, like the rest of the reporters, looked at the editor, interested and curious. George came out of his office and leaned against the wall.

"It's a bloody story about the polo-set," he said. "Guy buys a china statue for forty grand and then drops it into a hundred pieces. Well why didn't we have it? Why didn't we have it? You - Kim. I thought you were supposed to be engaged to one of the polo managers. How did you miss it?"

"I'm sorry," I said. "I didn't know anything about it."

Hugh looked round the newsroom, bristling with rage, before his eyes again returned to me.

"Do you know this guy?" Hugh said. "This guy who smashed the statue?"

"He's an acquaintance, yes - but I don't really know him." And then I went further. It was a classic mistake - just like in the witness box, you should keep your answers succinct and to the point. "The *Patron* is not in the habit of telling me how he's humiliated himself in front of Prince Charles -"

I bit back the words as soon as I'd said them.

Hugh was on to it in an instant. "How did you know Prince Charles was there? I never mentioned Prince Charles."

I could feel the newsroom watching me. "I..." I momentarily stuttered. "I heard it on the radio. Before I came to work."

"You heard it on the radio? On the radio? Which station?"

"Radio Gloucestershire. I think."

"Radio Gloucestershire? You think?"

"Probably," I said. "Might have been one on Radio Bristol."

"And why didn't you mention it to George?"

"What was the hurry?" I said. "We're not out for another five days."

Hugh stood looking at me, very deliberately nodding his head. He tossed his copy of *The Sun* into the bin and stalked out of the room. I was a picture of studied indifference as the other reporters stared at me. I picked up my coffee and continued to read the paper.

There was, naturally, one other person who was not at all happy with the story; that phone-call was not long in coming.

By now it was just before lunch. I was wondering whether to head out to Fairford to have a wander round my news patch when the call came through.

"You sold it to *The Sun*!" she said.

Rudi was at the desk next to me, bat-like ears flapping.

I pressed the phone tight to my ear. "Hi there," I said.

"I thought you were a reporter on the Standard!" Sasha said, louder now. "I never thought you'd be selling it to the tabloids!"

"Hi," I said, very sweetly. "Just a bit tied up at the moment. Can I call you back later?"

"You're the bloody limit!"

She slammed the phone down - though I continued to talk as if Sasha was still on the line. "Yeah sure," I said. "See you later. Love you."

I replaced the handset and flipped open my notebook, as if reviewing some old notes.

Rudi rolled his chair over to me, bumping into my desk. "You rogue," he whispered. "You flogged it to *The Sun*!"

"Ridiculous," I snapped. "Of course I didn't."

"And now you're girlfriend's not happy either." He gave me a dig in the ribs.

"Don't know what you're talking about."

"You can't kid me," Rudi said. "The prat who dropped the statue is Sasha's boss."

I had not realised just how quickly this story would start to unravel. There may not have been a smoking gun but, by default, the trail of breadcrumbs inevitably led right to my door.

"You are out of your mind!" I hissed. "I'd never sell a story to *The Sun*!"

Rudi crowed with laughter; the other reporters started to look up. "She gave you the bloody story!"

"Poppycock!" I said. "And do you mind keeping your voice down - you're a human fog-horn!"

He punched me on the arm and rolled back to his desk. "Buy me a pint and I won't say a word."

Sasha, being a darling, and being my fiancée, did not hold it against me. I was reading by the fire when she came into the treehouse that night. Immediately she slipped behind and got me in a headlock, her elbow tight under my chin.

"You are a low-down greasy scum-ball," she said.

"Thanks," I said. It was difficult to speak. "But at least I know what a story is - even if it's three months old."

"And what are you going to spend all your blood money on?" Her head was down beside me now, lips close to my ear.

"Is this how you speak to all your fiancés?"

"I said…" She gave my neck another squeeze. "What are you going to spend your blood money on?"

"Booze and fags and women."

She lifted my chin right up with her forearm. "What did you say?"

I pawed at her arm, trying to prise her off me, but she had me in a full lock. I couldn't shift her. "I was going to spend half of it on you -"

"How much? You greasy scum-ball?" Another squeeze to the neck.

"All of it," I rasped, my voice thick in my throat. "All of it!"

"And what are you?"

"A greasy scum-ball?"

"Yes, you are a greasy scum-ball." She suddenly moved to the front of the chair, where she seated herself on my lap. "But you're my greasy scum-ball."

And we kissed, and we grappled, and we did those things which have to be done to show that all is forgiven, forgotten. How easy it all was. How good-natured, how very simple - and, now that I am married, how I wish that moving on were so simple. But the longer a relationship lasts, the more baggage that seems to come with it, and each fresh row brings up these age-old bones that once more have to be chewed upon.

And that was that – was that, except stupidly the next week I did buy Rudi that pint of beer, and that was an error; not necessarily a strategic error, but definitely a tactical one.

★

I had to take some exams. After my degree, a few years earlier, I'd never expected to take another exam again. And now, there I was, mingling with all the other trainee reporters from Gloucestershire as we went through mock interviews to find out about the latest accident to have occurred in that mythical journalistic town of Oxdown. Our stories had to be written up in our best weekly paper prose, and we had to answer a few questions to test the fertility of our brains: "The Oxdown Gazette will have its 50th anniversary on Valentine's Day – come up with some suggestions as to how you will celebrate with the readers". Answer: do a deal with the local bingo hall to give your readers a cheap night out courtesy of their local rag. There were also questions to test our resourcefulness, our tenacity and our diligence, as well as all those other lofty principles to which a newspaper reporter should aspire. Rudi had told me beforehand to play everything with a very straight bat, which was never my style, but for the period of one day, I managed to keep my natural irreverence in check, playing both modestly and with respect. At the end of it all, I was given a certificate which stated that I was now a fully-fledged reporter with – no vain boast – shorthand skills that stretched to a hundred words per minute. Though I was now qualified, I still had a few months of my apprenticeship left to serve.

I had also been learning about that other big perk of the journalists' trade that I have already touched on: the freebie holiday. My first freebie, of course, had been that week in Turkey with Mousie, but I had now graduated to the next level of freebie holiday. First you decided where it was that you wanted to go, and then you fixed up the holiday with the relevant tourist board.

There was only one place I wanted to go that year and that was the Hellespont. A few months earlier, I had even bothered to do a little research on swimming the Hellespont - and had discovered that there was an official swim, a race even, that was held every year on August 30. The race had been going for a couple of years, and the Turkish tourist board was keen to promote it. I promised them a feature in the Wilts and Glos and in return they paid for my holiday with Sasha. A few other journalists would be making the trip.

We flew from Heathrow to Istanbul and then it was a six-hour bus ride down to the Hellespont. We travelled through Gallipoli, with its cypresses and its olive groves and its arid fields of bleached sunflowers. Undulating countryside that was dry and parched. First World War bunkers dotted about the landscape, all that was left of the Gallipoli battlefields. And the Turkish music coming loud over the coach's speakers, as if the same song was being repeated over and over again.

We drove onto the ferry at Eceabat, and made the crossing from Europe to Asia, and from Gallipoli to Troy, and from the new world to the old. The Hellespont was like glass and Canakkale was nothing but a blur in the distance; it looked miles away. Vast container ships ploughing up and down the Hellespont and on to the Sea of Marmara and up to the Black Sea; and white jelly-fish the size of dustbin lids; and a sky that was pastel blue at the edges, on the horizon, and which turned to the most brilliant blue imaginable when you looked high overhead.

At Canakkale, children were jumping into the sea off the jetty and the town was awash with red Turkish flags; I'd never been to a country with such nationalistic pride.

The journey had been row-free and stress-free, and most of the trip Sasha had slept next to me with her head warm on my shoulder. We got to the hotel and then, obviously, we made love - how glib that sounds now! - and went down for dinner. Most of the other swimmers were men and they were drawn to us; no, that is not quite right. They were not so much drawn to me. They were drawn to Sasha. There was one man, Angus, who we liked. He was a tough Glaswegian, with craggy, weathered features; the face of a sailor who's come in from a gale. He was about my age and was also a journalist – though much more experienced than me. He'd been in the trade since he'd left school. He worked on the local paper in Cambridge. It was an evening paper, which was a step up from a weekly like the Wilts and Glos. We had an affinity and we bonded as hacks have always bonded: in stories and in drink. But Angus had covered stories that I could only have dreamed of covering. He'd done murders and robberies and when he'd been working in Scotland had been one of the first reporters on the scene in Lockerbie; he'd seen the plane and all the scattered wreckage.

I turned to Sasha, who was sitting next to me. "That's the sort of stuff I want to be covering," I said.

"You go for it then," she said.

"And what it's like being a reporter in Cambridge?" I said to Angus.

"I'm not a reporter," he said.

"Are you on the news desk?"

"No – I'm the deputy editor."

"Wow." I looked at Angus afresh. Of course he was still just the same guy that we'd been drinking with, eating with, for the past two hours, but that was when I'd thought he was on a par with me. When you find out that a person is much higher up the pecking order, then the dynamic is subtly altered. Let us say that when I am in the company of editors, then I mind my Ps and Qs.

The next day we had a warm-up swim and the Hellespont was as warm as the Caribbean and so flat that there was not a ripple of a wave to be seen. In the evening we had pasta and a pep-talk to go through all the safety rigmarole. They told us about the weather the next day. It was going to be windy, at least a Force Five gale blowing in hard from the North-West; those of us who had not swum in these conditions before were advised not to make the trip.

The Hellespont the next day was one of the most inhospitable stretches of water that I had ever seen. That morning we'd had an early breakfast and dropped our kit-bags at the Canakkale Fort. Then we'd tramped through the town in nothing but our Speedo's and our goggles and these dinky little white spa slippers that they'd given us. I held hands with Sasha, though we didn't say anything. She'd coiled her long hair up into a bun and in her red swim-cap, she looked rather pixie-like; the cap wasn't smooth against her head, but poked up into this perky elfin point.

"You look like one of Santa's little helpers," I said as we walked onto the ferry.

There were several hundred of us. It was cloudy and the water was choppy and wild, and then with a blast of the horn we were underway and the ship was rolling and some of the swimmers were throwing up over the side. We strolled off the ferry at Eceabat and walked the half-mile down to the beach, the locals eyeing us up as if we were madder than mad - and as we tried to spy Canakkale in the distance, hidden in a haze of mist, and with the waves crashing into the shore, this swim looked like an act of the utmost folly. We could just make out the hump-backed hills on the horizon and the telecommunications mast which was to be our initial aiming point.

The Hellespont, we'd been told, funnels into a 1400-metre bottleneck at Canakkale, and consequently the current is much, much stronger at the finish-line. So if you are ever to swim this waterway, you need to have crossed it much higher up. While you're still two miles out from Canakkale, you must be at least halfway over - otherwise you'll be bobbing out in the middle of the Hellespont, and the current will have you in its grasp, whisking you past Canakkale and straight on out into the Aegean Sea.

We knew all this, had been told all this the previous night - but now, on the European shore, it all seemed fantastically arbitrary: "Head for the Telecoms tower until you're halfway over, and then gradually head for home."

We didn't have wet-suits and so we huddled out of the wind like Antarctic penguins. I was smoothing Vaseline onto Sasha's back to stop her swimsuit from chafing. Her arms and thighs were stippled with goosebumps. She was swinging her arms wide to try and keep warm.

Angus was next to us, his pasty white skin tufted with black hair. "You ought tae try the Firth of Forth on New Year's Day. That would make your hair curl," he said.

"I don't know about the Firth of Forth," I said. "This looks quite tough enough for me."

Though she was shivering, Sasha was smiling. "Though it is what you wanted."

"This is what we put in all the training for."

"No, we didn't," she said. "We did that so that we could be with each other - and so that you could have your hot showers. The Hellespont is just the cherry on top of the cake."

"But this is the end of the journey."

"And journeys end with lovers meeting."

And it may have just been the wind licking at my chest, but I had this shiver of a premonition, my intuition screaming at me to savour the moment. The Hellespont had always been the goal; for over a year now, we had dreamed of swimming it together. But beyond that, there was nothing else to aim at. I couldn't imagine what happened after the Hellespont; I couldn't picture anything at all. Would we still continue our incessant wild-water swimming or would we find some new windmill to tilt at?

Sasha worked some Vaseline into my armpits and into the seams of my Speedo's. "We'll have many more journeys," she said. "Don't worry about that."

She stood back to admire her handiwork. "It's a nice look," she said.

"Sexy, even."

We hugged each other, and the Vaseline from my arms stuck to the side of her black costume, delineating her breasts. Angus eyed her critically as he passed round a bottle of salt tablets; the salt stops you from cramping up. We swallowed the tablets without chewing, and then gingerly walked to the water-line. We shook hands and the gun went off and then this horde of red-capped maniacs plunged into the Hellespont.

The hills disappeared and my world had contracted to nothing more than this milk-grey horizon. I started off directly behind Sasha, but in a matter of moments she was lost to me and my world had been reduced to nothing more than pounding waves and kicking feet and mouthfuls of surf and seawater. I tried to get into a rhythm, but it was difficult with the waves and the current for ever pushing us back towards the beach. Every time I rolled to catch my breath, I would wait a beat to see if it was safe to open my mouth. And every four or five breaths I would look ahead of me to try and catch a glimpse of the telecom mast; I rarely succeeded.

I couldn't even think about my stroke and keeping it smooth and fluid. It all felt jerky and snatchy, and rather than being slippery in the water, I felt like a log. A wave caught me as I opened my mouth and instead of air I was sucking down sea-water.

Don't even think for a moment about getting out of the water at the fort at Canakkale, just concentrate on pulling smoothly and kicking easily; and roll and breathe; and roll and breathe; and count to twenty; and when you've reached twenty, take another peek at the horizon and start off counting all over again.

A fist smacked me full in the face, catching me on the nose, and for a moment the pain even distracted me from the pounding waves. I thrilled with vicious rage. I trod water and felt my nose with my fingers. There was blood on my fingers and I could taste it now. I wondered what sort of fish would be attracted to the blood in the water; were there sharks in the Hellespont?

I continued to swim. I was in the middle of this pod of thrashing swimmers and little by little, I was starting to get into a rhythm: concentrate on my arms, stretching myself as if drawn by a string; make sure that I was getting a proper pull as my hands finned through the water; and count the kick - "One, two", roll and breathe, "one, two", roll and breathe.

There came over me this grand dawning realisation of what it was that I was doing. This was no mere swim in the Thames at Lechlade;

I was swimming the Hellespont. This was it! I, Kim, was swimming the Hellespont - and my Sasha was swimming it with me. It seemed utterly other-worldly, just the weirdest thing - why on earth was I doing this? And pull and roll and breathe, and my mind drifted to Sasha and I wondered how far ahead of me she was now, and this pain lanced down my arm, a different kind of pain which I couldn't place, and then I saw it, and realised that I'd swum into a jellyfish, not the white ones which do not sting, but one of the bucket-sized blue ones. It felt like my arms had been raked with a stinging nettle, but there was nothing to be done about that, nothing to be done about my nose, or about the sting, or even this inexorable current that was sweeping into the Aegean, because nothing mattered at all now but the next stroke and the next stroke, and although I could pull out if it got really bad, I couldn't pull out because that would mean that I wouldn't be able to make the next stroke.

A cry went up - "Sewage ahead!" - and suddenly I was swimming through shit that some ship has voided straight into the path of the swimmers; it was beyond disgusting, my arms streaked brown. A piece of soiled lavatory paper was stuck to my hand. I took very great care with my breathing, rolling my head till my mouth was well clear of the water and I thought I was through the sewage, but then I was swimming through a second lot of it; it was revolting - just who were these inconsiderate bastards who'd emptied their toilets direct in our path?

And I roll and I breathe and I see that I am swimming past a swimmer who is actually being sick; perhaps she'd swallowed sea-water or some of the sewage. She was really floundering. I didn't recognise her at first, she was so very different from how she normally was in the water, but then I saw her hat, that little elfin hat with its pixie peak and I realised it was Sasha.

I swam over. "Sasha, it's me!" I called, but if she heard me, she did not show any sign of recognition, and her breakfast was coming up, and now that I looked about me, I could see the sewage and the toilet paper floating on the surface. It wasn't that she was sinking, but she was not doing well; she couldn't catch her breath properly. I think she was swallowing more sea-water.

I slipped in beside her, and tried to support her, arms about her chest. I kicked with my legs, and her mouth opened wide and there was more sick, and as I looked about me, I saw that for the first time we were alone. Way off I could see a few arms cutting through the water, but we were clear from the rest of the pack, just the two of us alone in the Hellespont. Sasha was sick again, but this time it was a dry-heave and there was nothing left to come up. She was quite limp now, like a wrung-out rag,

I slipped in underneath her. She was floating on the surface now and I had my hand underneath her chin; I was towing her along in the classic lifesaving style, letting my legs do the work. I was looking straight up at the sky. One of the rescue boats came over. "You want to get out?"

"No," I said. "She swallowed some sewage."

The boat stayed close by to us as we continued to drift down the middle of the Hellespont, Sasha still limply letting me hold her up. I looked back at the low, rolling hills of Europe; they were being whisked away from us by the fast surging tide.

I felt Sasha kick.

"That was awful," she said.

"You okay?"

"I've been worse," she said.

"Want to pull out?"

She wriggled away from me. Her face was quite white and there was vomit on her chin. She wiped her mouth with the back of her hand. "Have we suddenly turned into a couple of quitters?"

"No, I don't think we have. At least, not the last time I looked."

"And it all adds to the narrative."

I laughed. "It's propinquity, baby!"

"You saved me. I owe you."

"You were always going to be fine."

Together now, side by side, we started to swim again, and now that we are out of Eceabat and in the middle of the stream, we had got more of a handle on the rhythmic swell of the waves. As I breathed I turned to Sasha, and as she breathed, she would turn to me, and after a while we had so synchronised our strokes that we were breathing at the exact same moment, our heads not four feet from each other, as we roll and breathe and I looked and I stared, and I fancied that I could even see a smile on her face; she was living the dream; we were living the dream - and we were living it together.

I was quite suffused with love for this woman. I might have been swimming, and I might have been swimming the Hellespont, but all I could think of was that it was Sasha who was next to me, and that we were swimming it together, and that I loved her.

I experienced that glorious transcendental state that occasionally comes to swimmers and runners, and people who are fully engaged in the moment. I was in flow - not really aware of my arms or my kicking legs, but bubbling with this incredible joy, and I roll and I breathe, and there was my Sasha, still beside me, her slick wet mouth all but pointing to the heavens as she breathed her next breath.

It was the best swim of my life - and the raging waves, and the cuffed nose, and the jellyfish stings and the patch of raw sewage... that would all just add to the narrative. We never remember those plain-sailing trips. The only things that lodge in the mind are the times when it's been tough and, yes, when you've swallowed some shit and you've heaved your guts up. And of course it's hellish at the time, but afterwards, these are the moments that we linger on, and finger over, and we smile to ourselves because we know that it might have been tough, but we damn well did it.

And there was Sasha, that impossibly graceful stroke of hers still holding up in the choppy water, and though I might not have appreciated it a year back, I could now more than identify with those demons that drove Lysander to swim the Hellespont twice daily so that he could be with his love. Seriously? If Sasha had been on the other side of the Hellespont from me, locked up in her temple of Aphrodite, then I wouldn't have blinked twice at the prospect of making that swim to be with her; and of course the water might have been wild, and it might have all ended in disaster - as is the way that all love affairs must end - but given the choice between being with Sasha or meekly sitting at home by the fire, then I'd have been with Lysander every stroke of the way.

But if ever there was a stretch of water in the world that was steeped in gloom, it is the Hellespont - why, it even gets its very name from Helle, the girl who was flying on the ram with the Golden Fleece, and who lost her grip and fell from a height to her grey watery grave. And I could picture all those Anzac soldiers, slaughtered in their thousands in the Gallipoli hills.

By now we were shooting past Canakkale itself, and though we were swimming hard for the Asian coastline, we were still 300 yards off by the time we were swept past the finish line at the Canakkale Fort. What did we care? We might have missed Canakkale, but we were still going to make Asia. We had swum the Hellespont!

We finally made landfall about a mile down from Canakkale. We lay on the shore amidst the pebbles and hugged and kissed for sheer joy at having done it all, and for the delight of having done it with each other. The sun was peeking out and started to warm us and everything was glorious.

We walked, hand in hand, back along the shoreline, but after a while we came to one of the many Turkish military bases, and we had no option but to head inland. We walked barefoot for over a mile along the back roads of Canakkale. I'd tucked away some money into the rear pocket of my Speedo's and we stopped at a little café for some Coke and some apple tea, pouring in the sugar until the elmer chai was near saturated. We sat in the sun on the pavement, drinking tea, and suffused with such love and such a feeling of well-being that to have said a single word would have been to have broken the spell. We sipped, we looked at each other, and we grinned at each other like chattering monkeys as we realised our overwhelming good fortune: we had each other, so what else did we need?

I paid for the drinks and Sasha leant over, kissed me on the lips. She squinted at my nose.

"Ouch!" she said. "You took a hit there." And then she saw my arm which from wrist to bicep was flushed red from the blue jellyfish, and she tutted and we trotted back to the fort.

271

We had missed the cut off and we'd missed the medals – but what did that matter when we had swum the Hellespont together? We picked up our kit-bags and then home to the hotel and a hot bath, and now that I was out of the Hellespont, the pain was really kicking in – and Sasha was saying, "let me see if I can distract you…" and if only I could be distracted like that every time I had a hurt, then I would daily put up with being swiped in the face; and the jellyfish could do their worst with me; and I would swim through steaming piles of ordure. Yes, for my darling Sasha, I would put up with any number of indignities.

She was in contemplative mood when we had dinner in a town-centre café that night. We were with Angus and were washing down calamari with the local Raki, cold and cloudy and tasting of aniseed.

Angus had been looking at Sasha and had noticed the friendship ring on her ring-finger. "Is that an engagement ring?" he asked.

"We got engaged in May," Sasha said.

"I'll bet there's a story behind that," Angus said. He had wrapped the calamari between two slices of bread and was eating it like a chip-buttie.

"There is."

"Will you tell me?"

"We were nearly killed in a car crash," she said.

"The near-miss," Angus said. "Helps focus your mind on what's important."

Sasha stretched over the table, took my hand in her own, and kissed my fingers. When I think back to that moment, and the look of devotion in Sasha's eyes, it all but makes we weep.

"You look very happy together," Angus said.

"I've got my guy. I've just swum the Hellespont," she said. "I am absurdly happy."

And I remember that phrase too – for once it's out, the spell is broken. It's like when you're in flow – you are so joyously engaged with what you're doing that you're not aware of it. But once you do become aware of it, then you are no longer in that moment. And that goes, also, for happiness. Once you've stated that you're happy, then you have all but marked the high-water mark of your happiness, and nothing that comes after will be a match for that high-spot. And there is hubris too - how aware of it I was, particularly at the Hellespont, that one-time land of the Greeks, where there was always a feeling that the Gods enjoyed nothing more than bringing people crashing back to earth with a bump.

Sasha turned to me, knees stroking against my thigh. "What is our next journey?" she said. "What is the grand strategy?"

"My grand strategy has always been you - and always will be you," I said, and the wind blew, and the door of the restaurant banged, and I knew, then, that it wasn't just Sasha who was riding for a fall. Our happiness was by now so intertwined, that if one of us was hurt, then the other would be equally devastated; if not more.

CHAPTER 20

For some months now, I have been dwelling on how I will write this next chapter - and now here it is, the Hellespont swim is over, and the chapter is upon me and there is nothing else for it but to dive straight in.

To celebrate our Hellespont swim, we'd decided to have a party. We'd thought about having it in the treehouse, but it had seemed risky to have a lot of drunk people perched up high in my cedar, so instead we'd gone for having the party in Sasha's house. It was one of Cirencester's mews houses, two up, two down, with a little bathroom upstairs, which she shared with Susanna; we invited a lot of people, friends and colleagues as well as a good smattering from the polo-set and the RAC. They were all going to be there.

The house would be packed, but there was plenty of room in the back garden, and upstairs in the two bedrooms, and, if necessary, out on the cobbled mews.

I had been off to the local off-licence and had filled the car up with beer and cheap wine. It was going to be a late party, starting at 10pm and continuing till the last person had left. There was no need for nibbles or food.

We'd had a bath together, and then I'd shaved in front of the bathroom mirror, Sasha jostling me for room as she'd tried to do her make-up. She was wearing bra and knickers, black, inordinately sexy. We'd brushed against each other, nudged each other, and that was all we needed, and in a moment I'd tossed my razor aside and she was in my arms, and I was easing her back towards the door.

We were not saved by the bell; it ruined us. "That'll be the ice," she said.

"Call out the window." I nuzzled her ear, hungry fingers already tugging at her bra. "Tell them to leave it on the doorstep."

"They need paying."

"I'll get it," I said, and I slipped on her dressing-gown and bolted down the stairs. I gave the man a tenner and took the ice through to the kitchen, hacking at the plastic bags and tipping the ice over the white wine and the beer.

By the time I'd got back upstairs, Sasha was already dressed. She was in her bedroom, with its double-bed and its pink duvet, and its creamy carpet and pine shutters. She wore dark stockings and that green dress that had always been one of my favourites.

I stalked into the bedroom behind her, arm encircling her waist as I kissed her neck. She laughed and pulled away. "Aren't you always telling me about delayed gratification?" she said.

"I wrote the bloody book on it," I said. "Don't you know about jam today?"

"What about jam tomorrow?"

"What about jam now - *and* jam tomorrow?"

"I hope you'll still be like this when we're married -"

"Eager - husky with desire."

"That is exactly how I like you." And she was kissing me now, ardent as ever, only this time it was Susanna who was distracting us, and the front door banged, and a moment later Susanna was calling up the stairs saying, "Can one of you two give me a hand?" and so with a rueful kiss, Sasha left the bedroom and dutifully went downstairs to help her housemate.

I continued with my shave, and put on jeans and a plain white shirt, and I joined the girls outside for a drink; and I remember that too, sitting next to Sasha, thighs touching, and holding hands as we looked at the night sky.

The doorbell rang and Susanna sprang up to get to the door, and I gave Sasha a kiss. "It's showtime," she said.

"Let's do it." And the first guests arrived, and they came out into the garden, and the drinks were poured, and in very short order the party was in full-swing, and the front room was packed and the kitchen was packed and the garden was so hugger-mugger that it was like the old football terraces, this swaying, heaving animal that was moving to the beat of my boom-box.

Now, these days, today, I am married and I have three daughters, and I have started re-reading the classic fairy-tales. There is one tale that never fails to strike a chord. You will know it well. It is Sleeping Beauty. But, until recently, I had forgotten the detail.

I wonder what would have happened if, in Cirencester, I had recalled that tiny little detail from Sleeping Beauty. It is more than possible that my life and my loves might have turned out so very differently. Who knows.

So this is how the story goes: at long last, and after a lot of prayers and a lot of wishes, the King and the Queen have had their baby daughter. The Princess is everything they could ever have wanted, and they hold a Christening for their daughter, and the twelve fairies who live in their Kingdom are invited. The King and Queen invite twelve fairies because they have only twelve sets of golden crockery. The fairies arrive: they are all beautiful and lissom and have long blonde hair. They dine off this wonderful golden crockery, and then each fairy in her turn gives some boon to the baby girl. She will be a wonderful dancer, says one; she will sing like a lark, says another; she'll never go hungry says the next; and so these boons are conferred, but as it is, they're not going to count for anything much at all, because, by chance or perhaps by design, the King and the Queen have forgotten to invite the thirteenth fairy in the kingdom, and so into the Christening storms this witch, and she is incandescent with rage - furious at the snub, and livid with life, and quite determined to make somebody pay. She curses the baby girl to die on her sixteenth birthday, and the last fairy is able only to modify that curse just a little, and so the beauty is doomed to sleep for a hundred years...

If only I had realised that, somewhere in that story, there lurked a moral: if you specifically snub people from your parties, then you do so at your own peril.

And there were two people who had not been invited to our party - and this was not by accident. We neither of us wanted them there.

The first was Paris' idiot-oaf friend Dangerous who, time and again, had proved himself to be the most complete liability.

And the second person who had not been invited to our Hellespont party was Penny. Of course we knew it was a snub. But, for our own very different reasons, we did not want her there. And since it was our party, then - or so we naively believed - we could invite who we pleased. Hadn't Penny just told us exactly that at our engagement party?

The first I knew that there was a problem was at close after midnight when Lady Claire came through to the garden. She touched me on the elbow. "If I were you, I'd sort out what's going on upstairs," she said. Her mouth was a thin grim line.

"Really?" I said. "What's happening up there?"

"Just get up there - and quickly."

I started shouldering my way through the crowds, and I would have gone directly upstairs, but just as I was in the kitchen, I came across Angus who'd driven all the way from Cambridge to be with us. He'd only just got in and he didn't know a soul. I was pleased to see him. I joined him in a beer. We clinked bottles and after a while I forgot all about Lady Claire's warning - what was she fussing about? I decided that whatever was going on upstairs, it would sort itself out soon enough.

I'd just brought over a couple more beers and had clipped off the tops. Angus and I were standing by the kitchen door when there was this scream from the top of the stairs and it was just ear-splitting. One shriek and then another shriek, and now there was shouting and the sound of feet drumming on the floorboards overhead.

I slipped my beer to Angus and I ran up the stairs. I didn't know what it was, but if Sasha was screaming, then it was going to be bad. There were a few people milling in the passageway upstairs. I shouldered past them and through to Sasha's room. The door was half open and Sasha was standing in the doorway. I could see her in silhouette and she was in tears, both hands to her mouth.

I opened the door, slipped in beside her, and…

Penny was lying on top of all the coats that had been left on Sasha's bed, and on top of her, with his work-boots still on and his trousers round his ankles, was Dangerous. His huge hands were around Penny's hips.

Penny was looking at Sasha and then her gaze turned to me. I could see that her pink skirt was rucked up around her waist. She certainly didn't seem embarrassed. Dangerous reeked of booze and he was barely even aware of our presence.

"Get out!" Sasha screamed. "Get out, get out! Get out of here now!"

"Okay - we're getting out," said Penny, very languid. "Take a chill pill, Sasha."

Sasha started screaming again, "Get out!" but I had my arm around her shoulder now and was hustling her away from the door. I could not get her out of that room quick enough. I took her down the stairs - and I then made my second big error of the night. I should have taken her back to the treehouse. I should have got her well away from that hellish party. But I did not. I took her out to the garden, and sat her down on the bench where we'd been sitting earlier. She was crying, face in her hands, these choking sobs that were shaking her whole body.

This went on for a few minutes. I was stroking Sasha's back, and I remember how the other guests were giving us a wide berth. I dully registered that Paris was there too, skittering in the background.

Well there was nothing to say after what we'd just seen, so I said nothing at all. It was just unbelievably squalid - Penny and Dangerous coupling together on the coats? On Sasha's bed? I couldn't get the picture out of my head. It made me feel queasy. And that look of drunken bravado on Penny's face, not even remotely nettled that she'd been caught having sex by her own daughter.

I didn't want to see Penny again, and there was no way that we'd be sleeping in Sasha's bed that night, so, too late, I decided to make a move.

"Let's go back to the treehouse," I said. I took Sasha by the hand, and she followed me through to the kitchen. Her mascara had run down her cheeks, and she was still shaking.

The timing was excruciating.

We were just by the front door when Dangerous and Penny happened to be coming down the stairs. I wasn't going to hang around. I opened the front-door and, without a backward glance, tugged Sasha out onto the mews. I was bustling Sasha down the street when I heard a shout from behind.

"Oi - you two!" she shouted. "No need to be so bloody hoity-toity!"

I had my arm round Sasha now. We were walking briskly down the mews. I saw Dangerous's Harley-Davidson parked in the street.

"Kim!" she shouted. "Mr Butter-Won't-Melt-In-Your-Mouth! Don't you remember what happened in the treehouse?"

And I wasn't sure if Sasha has heard what her mother had said, but I was hustling her along the cobbles as quick as I could now.

And Sasha's pace faltered.

And stopped.

"What did she say?"

Sasha turned to me, looked at me, face on the verge of crumpling, and I had this feeling of the most imminent and terrible disaster.

I was clutching at Sasha's hands, but I could hear Penny laughing now as she strolled up to us. Dangerous was a few steps behind her.

"Oh, Kim," she said. "You didn't tell? I thought that you lovers had no secrets from each other."

Penny stood beside us, hands on hips, head flung back. She was wearing white stilettos and a white top and that lurid pink skirt.

"Let's go, Sasha," I said, and I took her hand, but she would not move. I could see these various thoughts flickering through her eyes, but eventually they fused together into one single solid fact.

She almost shook herself. "You had sex?" she said. "You had sex in the treehouse?"

I turned my head and swept my hand across my hair, because now the cataclysm was upon me - and I knew it was going to be worse by far than anything that could have occurred on that long straight stretch of road where we nearly met our deaths. At least that would have been quick, instantaneous - and this horror show was going to run for some time yet, and though it was over twenty years ago now, I can still feel it; I am still there in that mews with Sasha and her mother.

I could not deny it any more. I said the only thing that could be said. "She forced her way into the treehouse," I said. "She blindfolded me - practically raped me."

Penny spoke up. She was smiling, well pleased with her handiwork. Her hand strayed to the back of her hair and she gave it a tug, physically jerking her head backwards. "I remember it well," she said.

"Penny - please leave us," I said. I tried to lead Sasha away, but she was just standing there, head shaking in shock.

"But you lied," Sasha said. "You lied and lied again. I asked you… I asked you if someone had been round -"

"She forced herself on me," I said. "She came into the treehouse in the middle of the night, and she got into the bed - and I thought it was you -"

Again, Penny spoke up. "Well he would say that wouldn't he?"

I rounded on her. "You are vile."

Sasha's shoulders slumped. "It's over," she said. She turned from me and she started walking off down the mews.

I followed her, clutching at her arm. "Sasha - I did lie to you, but… I thought it was for the best. Really -"

She shrugged off my hand, walking more briskly now. "Get away from me - please," she said. "I just want to be alone." And she broke into a jog, and for a while I ran with her. "Sasha," I said, "Please." But she batted me away with her hand and as I stuttered to a halt, she ran to the end of the Mews, and she turned and then she was gone.

I stood there looking after her. Penny ambled up beside me.

"I hope you're happy," I said. I burst into tears and I walked away.

I trudged back to the treehouse and poured myself a whisky. The fire was dead and I stared into the grey ash and the charred wood, but there was nothing for me there now but disaster. And so there I sat in the armchair, head in my hands, as I pondered my own folly and wondered what the hell to do next. Should I have told Sasha about that night with Penny? Of course I should. With someone as mad as Penny, it was absolutely inevitable that, someday, one day, it was all going to come out. And it would have meant that I wouldn't have had to have lied. For a little while, it might have made for troubled times, but better by far to have seized the nettle all those months ago, than to have left it to fester and rot. That, though, was all in the past. What was I going to do now? When would I go round to Sasha and grovel for forgiveness? The next day – or the day afterwards? Or should I give her a few days to cool off? The sky was turning from black to grey to gold, and all the colour came back to my treehouse, the red of the armchairs and the black of the Jøtul, and the dark ochre of the rude bark on the tree; and the leaves on the tree were coming to life too, brilliant green against the red sky as the sun filtered through the branches. Would Sasha ever see this again? Would she ever set foot in here again; would we ever make love again? Was it really over – or, once she'd heard me out, would she be able to find it in her heart to forgive me? And perhaps she might have, and perhaps she might not, but very soon it had all become a matter of the most trivial irrelevance as Penny went and did the one thing which, truly, there could be no getting over: she killed herself.

★

Of all the ghastly places to learn about Penny's death, I heard about it at the local police station. It was the Monday morning after the party and I had not seen or heard a thing from Sasha. I had not tried to contact her either, but I'd thought that I might pop round to her house that evening after work.

I'd been sent off to Cirencester police station, just by the court house. There were a few other reporters from the evening papers and the radio stations. One of the inspectors took us through to his office and gave us a round-up of all the weekend's news. I wasn't saying anything much; I was barely even in a fit state to be there. The man had been talking about some burglary in Cirencester, though I hadn't written a word of it in my notebook – and then suddenly he said something that made my ears prickle. This tide of the most complete horror swept over me.

WILLIAM COLES

"Oh and this is an odd one," he said, reading from a print-out. "Got a motorcyclist who's gone off the Clifton Gorge, local woman. Cirencester. She's dead. She was riding..." He licked his finger and turned the page. "Seems she was riding her boyfriend's bike. Harley Davidson."

I felt like I was going to faint.

"What was her name?" I whispered.

"She was wearing no helmet. Unusual. Sounds like suicide to me. Let me see now - Cirencester woman, age 49. Her name was Penny -"

I didn't hear the rest. I thought I was going to be sick.

I stumbled out of the room, out onto the street, and blindly started to walk around Cirencester. I don't know where I went, or anything at all much about what I did over the next three hours. All I could think was that Penny had killed herself in the Clifton Gorge. Penny had killed herself? It sounded just extraordinary - fantastical. I remembered that conversation we'd had over a year ago, when she'd stumbled into the treehouse. She'd talked of suicide - had even talked of going off the Clifton Gorge. How she had described it? Six wonderful seconds of freedom. I'd told her to call the Samaritans. Had that been a cop-out? Should I have done more?

But... much more to the point: what on earth could Sasha be going through?

Eventually I found myself in her mews. I knocked on the door, and when nobody came to the door, I knocked again. I heard footsteps coming down the stairs. Paris opened the door.

"Hi," I said, and made to walk into the house.

"Kim," he said. "She doesn't want to see you."

"I'm going to see her," I said, and though he tried to block me, I shouldered my way past. I went up the stairs and found her lying curled up on the floor in the bathroom. She looked like she hadn't stopped crying for two days. I knelt down next to her on the lino, touched her lightly on the shoulder.

"Sasha," I said. "It's me."

She looked at me, eyes quite misty red from crying. Her lips quivered and she tried to speak, but nothing came out.

"I am so sorry," I said. "I am so sorry."

I sat next to her, back to the wall, feet up against the bath-tub. I didn't say anything. I touched her shoulder. I stroked her and she started to cry again, tears falling straight onto the lino floor.

I stroked her shoulder again, and bent over to kiss her on the cheek, and at that she flinched. "Please go," she said.

"I'm so sorry."

"Please go," she said again.

"Can we talk?"

"I don't want to talk," she said, sitting up now, and rubbing her eyes with her fingers. "Please go."

"Please don't do this."

"Just go - I don't want you here."

"Please -"

"Please leave."

I didn't know what to do. Stay or go? Take her at her word, or tough it out? And in the end... I did what she asked.

I quit the bathroom and I stumbled down the stairs. Without a word Paris opened the door and I wandered out into the mews, and after that... I didn't know what to do next so I fell back onto my old failsafe. I wrote Sasha letters, letter after letter which I dropped off by hand. I begged for forgiveness and tried to explain what had happened and offered her what sympathy I could for what had happened to her mother.

I think now that it was a mistake. Letters are all very well if they are written with love, but if you are apologising, asking for forgiveness, then it would better be done face to face so that they can see the contrition in your eyes.

I did go round to the mews a couple more times over the next week, but no-one ever came to the door. I should have just done what any half-decent reporter would have done and camped out on her doorstep. But I did not. I would knock and knock and when there was no reply I'd trudge back to my dismal treehouse.

A week later, I saw her on the street. She was walking towards me and we had both seen each other from thirty yards away. I was so pleased to see her. I had this ridiculous smile on my face.

"Sasha," I said. "I'm so sorry. How are you?"

"I'm all right," she said, and for a moment she looked at me, and then she just carried on walking. "I don't really want to speak to you at the moment." Struck dumb, I stood and watched her as she walked away.

The same thing happened a few days later when I saw her in the newsagents. She'd not seen me, but I had seen her. I went up behind her as she paid for her newspaper. "Sasha," I said. She turned and looked at me with dead eyes and then just lowered her gaze. The spark had gone out of her. "No," she said, and she left the shop.

I don't know how it might have all panned out, but a week after that I heard that she'd gone back to Argentina to stay with her uncle and I suppose, when she eventually came back to Cirencester, that we might have had a chance of starting afresh, but we were never given that opportunity.

CHAPTER 21

It felt not so much like a break-up as a bereavement - this woman who had been so much a part of my life, and who now so suddenly was no longer a part of it. I was like the most craven drug addict, trying for a fresh start, and who is put through the most awful cold turkey. Every hour, every minute, I was thinking of Sasha, remembering my memories. Wondering what she was doing with herself. And wondering what I might have done differently. It was hellish and everywhere I went in Cirencester, whether the pubs or the supermarket, was a reminder that she was no longer in my life. Worst by far was my treehouse and my maze, which had now become nothing but a hollow mocking echo of those glorious days and nights that we had spent with each other.

But it only lasted a month, because soon enough Hugh had put me out of my misery.

I'd been like a zombie for the previous weeks, listless and shiftless, and with a complete lack of interest in anything at all to do with local journalism.

Hugh had called me through to his office, and I presumed that he was going to berate for my slapdash attitude.

"Close the door," he said. I shut the door behind me.

He sat behind his desk, gestured for me to take a seat, and for a while stroked his moustache as he sat there appraising me.

"Your story in *The Sun* a few weeks ago," he said. "The charity statue being smashed in front of Prince Charles."

"My story?"

"How much did you make when you sold it?"

"I don't know what you're talking about."

"You're a very accomplished liar, Kim." For the first time, he smiled at me. "Let's see if this will refresh your memory."

He placed a small tape-recorder on the desk, looked at me to check that I was paying attention, and then pressed the play button.

I could hear the sound of a phone ringing, and then somebody picking up. "Accounts," she says.

Then I hear Hugh's voice. "Oh, I'm so sorry to bother you." His voice is smooth and unctuous. "It's one of your Gloucestershire freelancers. I sold a royal exclusive to *The Sun* some weeks ago. Just wondered when the cheque was due."

The woman sounded bored. "What did you say your name was?"

"Lascar," Hugh replies. "Kim Lascar."

"Let me have a look," she says, and I can now hear the sound of a keyboard being tapped. Hugh's eyes have never left my face.

"Royal exclusive?" she says. "Charles in fits at smashed charity statue?"

"That'd be the one," Hugh says.

"Payment's due at the end of the month," she says.

"Thank you so much," says Hugh - and the phone is replaced, and now there is nothing but the hiss of the tape.

Hugh stretches to the tape-recorder and turns it off. He taps the tape-recorder in the palm of his hand and for a while we say nothing.

"Did they pay you well?" he said.

"Eight hundred quid."

"Why did you sell it?"

I shrugged, entirely indifferent as to how the interview would turn out. "I got sod all thanks for any of the exclusives that I did bring in. I thought I might as well sell them on to somebody who appreciated them."

"Do you realise what we've done for you - trained you up, turned you into a professional reporter. And how do you repay us - by selling your stories to *The Sun*?"

"I've enjoyed my time here," I said.

"Is that it?" he said. "Is that all you've got to say?"

"Thank you for taking me on."

"Get out," he said. "You're out of here. And if you think that I am going to give you even a sniff of a reference, then you are very much mistaken."

I left Hugh's office and went to the newsroom. It took a couple of minutes to sling my oddments into a Waitrose shopping bag, and then I informed my colleagues that my farewell drinks would be held in the Slug and Lettuce that evening. I walked out of the Standard offices for the last time, rudderless, shiftless, loveless, and a few days later, I was to leave Cirencester itself, and, with it, all those mental jogs that ever used to remind me of Sasha.

★

And the years pass, and I would find fresh love, but always at the back of my mind I was aware of this dull throb that was Sasha. I tried writing to her a few times, but she never replied.

I saw her twice in *Tatler* magazine - still doing her stuff, still with her polo team, still being cuddled by the fat *Patron*.

But as new loves came into my life, I got over her.

Or at least I thought that I'd got over her.

After a year or so, I had begun to believe that, finally, my feelings for her were dying; were even dead. And then I would see a picture of her in the papers, and back it would all come, washing over me, and the love would still sting like salt on a knife-cut and I would be reminded of all that I had lost.

I would never have seen it coming, but Sasha was to become a celebrity. Her picture regularly featured in the likes of the Telegraph or the Daily Mail.

There was another thing that I never saw coming. She married Paris. When I first heard the news I felt this mixture of jealousy and the most bilious rage. I wondered how he had contrived to woo her. Probably with patience and with guile and in much the same time-honoured fashion that I had wooed her myself.

They had children and Paris' fortune and his contacts were more than enough to send Sasha into orbit. She started up a company making expensive perfumes and creams, and in very short order, both Sasha and her firm were household names.

When she became famous, the highlights of Sasha's life started to get played out in all the British newspapers. I would idly flick through the latest goings-on of London's most beautiful couple, Paris and Sasha, and every time would sense this surge of love and loss.

One thing I always noticed about the pictures though. She still wore that ring - that Claddagh friendship that I had given her that first day we'd made love. She wore it now on her right hand, a mirror to the wedding ring on her left hand. Later on, after she and Paris had divorced, I saw from the photos that the friendship ring had moved back onto the ring finger of her left hand. And I thought... I thought a lot of things. I thought about getting in touch; and then I thought better of it. Best, sometimes, to let those sleeping loves lie.

Her voice though was a different matter. I could just about withstand the photos in the papers, and the sight of that silver ring on her ring finger - heart out, I saw. But when I heard her talking on the radio, and sounding exactly - just exactly - like how she'd sounded all those years ago, it took me right back to our treehouse.

I am off to a lunch meeting on a Friday. I've got into the car and immediately the radio comes on. Elise, my wife, has been listening to Radio Four, though I do not listen to Radio Four any more. I am about to change stations when I hear a voice that I know so, so well, and instead of driving on, I listen to Sasha. I smile and with a wry shake of my head, I turn up the volume. She's finally got her wish. She's on Desert Island Discs.

She is about quarter way through her eight records. I listen as she goes through the rest of her picks. They were a mix of modern and classical, each a little signpost that marked another chapter in her life.

"And your eighth and final record?" asks Kirsty Young.

"The Magic Flute." Sasha replies.

"Why have you picked that?"

Sasha's about to speak when there is a slight hiccup. "It's just... It reminds me of a place and a time and a guy I once knew. It's called propinquity. It's about frequency; and it's about narrative. I was very happy."

"Would you like to tell us anything more?"

"He only had one tape." Sasha laughs at the thought of it, and I… I am also chuckling at the memory. "We used to play it over and over again - on one side was The Marriage of Figaro and on the other was The Magic Flute." And then, though there's no need to say any more, Sasha continues. "We used to go swimming together. We would swim in the rivers."

"You were wild swimmers?"

"Yes - it was a dare that we shared."

Mozart's Papagena comes on. It is a beautiful love song, two little birds plighting their troth to each other - and now that I'm hearing the music, I really am right back in Cirencester. The music creates a far more powerful connection than any mere memory: it arrows straight to my central cortex. As I hear Papagena, I can see Sasha standing there on the balcony, about to step into my arms.

When Sasha next speaks, she names the book that she will take to her desert island. She wants to take a book of knots so that she can learn to handle ropes. Then she is asked about her luxury item.

"Just a tool-box," Sasha says.

"And what will you do with your tool-box?"

"I'll build a treehouse in a Cedar of Lebanon. If I had a treehouse, I would be…" There is a slight catch that comes to her voice. "I would be more than… content." And it may just be my fancy, but at the end, her voice breaks and for the rest: the rest is silence.